YOSEMITE RISING

This is a work of fiction. The events described are imaginary. Real places are used fictitiously. Any resemblance of characters and events to real life is coincidental.

In memory of my brother, Jimmy.

YOSEMITE RISING

JULIE EMBERS

MEADOWLARK BOOK ONE

THE GREAT GREY OWL

SOME FAMILY SECRETS ARE NEVER SPOKEN OF. MOST DO not contain legends that could free an entire world, but Elizabeth's mother knows something is different about her daughter. Margaret sits on the bed, clutching its comforter. "We should've told her a long time ago."

"Margaret! We have to go," says her husband Jack. He grabs hold of the travel bags and heads out of the bedroom, for the car. There isn't time for wallowing. He stops halfway down the hallway, lets go of the bags, and returns to the room.

Margaret sits on the bed, hanging her head.

He joins her, wraps his arm around her waist, and pulls her in tight. "She wasn't ready until now," he says. "Let's go. We don't want this to turn into more regret."

She takes his hand, sweeps Elizabeth's present from the bed, and heads for the car, toward the moment she's been running from her entire life.

Jack takes the driver's seat moments after Margaret has settled into the passenger seat. He closes the door and silence captures them. In that awkward moment just before the car starts —that quiet moment—where everything that should be said finds its chance—Jack speaks. "You were a good mother." He rests his hand on her knee. "You *are* a good mother."

He knows when to let go—that holding on any longer will make her crumble with the decision they've made—but he can't seem to unclench his fingers from hers to grip the steering wheel and pull out of the driveway.

She stares at the modest house they had hidden their daughters in for almost a decade.

Jack watches their life disappear in the rearview mirror— watches all their memories fade behind them.

A black Hummer pulls away from the curb two blocks back.

Margaret takes a breath, trying to avoid her reflection in the sideview mirror. Jack is being so sweet, so patient. She looks at him. His eyes are glued to the rearview mirror more often than the road. She turns to look out the back.

"No. Don't," he says.

She sits back, sinking a little in the seat.

"They've been following us for a while," he says.

She laughs. "You're not thinking—"

"They pulled out when we left the house."

"They're probably going into town," she lowers her voice, "just like us."

He glances down at the gift in her hand. "Do you believe that?"

She doesn't know what to believe anymore.

The edge of Corvallis, Oregon emerges in the distance. Jack speeds up. They need more time. Margaret needs more time. At the first intersection, Jack cuts the car left like a maniac, just in case they are being followed. Momentum throws Margaret up against the door. As the car straightens, she turns around. The road behind them is clear. Jack slows a little. He smiles at her and she smiles back. It's only paranoia. Since Elizabeth was born, it felt like someone was watching them—following them. There never was anyone that they knew of, just a feeling she had. But Jack feels it, too. The past few days that feeling has grown stronger.

Jack's driving returns to normal. He stops at the next traffic light, lets out a sigh, and smiles at her. "You know I love you."

She grabs his hand and leans to kiss him.

The traffic light turns green. He takes his foot off the brake and sits back up, abandoning the opportunity of affection. Something moves out of the corner of her eyes.

A black Hummer is speeding down the side street toward them. It crashes into the passenger door. The car's momentum shifts. All at once the world spins into darkness.

"He's dead," says a man.

It is not Jack's voice that Margaret hears. She opens her eyes to a grey sky. Raindrops drip down, stinging her eyes. *Where's the car?* She turns her head to the direction of the voice. Asphalt scrapes against her cheek like sandpaper.

Two men are standing beside her car, looking at their feet, blocking whatever draws their attention down. Their uniforms are identical: solid black, like those of a police SWAT team.

"You go deal with the public. Use the terrorist bit. That should smooth over any questions. I'll take care of her." The man turns around. He looks military—clean cut, but younger, too young to die for his country. His eyes are a dark blue, reminding her of the sky that's hidden nine months out of the year. She doesn't recognize him.

His partner heads off to handle crowd control.

"Margaret, something tells me you've been expecting us," he says, stepping closer, exposing the body behind him.

Jack.

Her husband hangs limp in the driver's seat. His warm eyes have gone hollow. She tries to move—to run to him—but can't. Pain floods her right side. She reaches to soothe the pain, but only her left hand moves. When she touches her right side, her fingers slide into blood.

"Who are you?" she asks.

He leans down beside her, placing his hands against her ears.

"What do you want?"

Raindrops pelt the cement around her.

"Your daughter," he says.

She looks away, up at the sky. High in the clouds, something flies—something moves. She squints at a Great Grey Owl.

OMEN

ELIZABETH SHOULDN'T HAVE LOST HERSELF TO LOVE, but she did. Sixteen and completely, maddeningly in love. That is the only reason she woke up so damn early on a Thursday.

She's supposed to meet Dominic at La Café, right across the street from their high school. She tries to focus on the coffee shop's bright yellow bricks, sticking out bold against the grey sky. Amber light radiates through the cafe's large front window. An etched Eiffel Tower design sparkles within its glass.

A car gusts by. The wind pulls at Elizabeth's umbrella and the rain drenches her before she can regain control of it.

Maple leaves tear from the branches of a sidewalk tree and follow her across the road, smacking the side of the building.

Elizabeth can see a man through the glass, sitting in the back of the café. *How the hell did Dominic beat me here?* He is never on time. She spins the new promise ring he gave her with her thumb. Dad forbids Hazel and Elizabeth from getting married until they graduate high school. Hazel graduated last year, so this new rule is really only made for Elizabeth. Dominic knows this rule. He has promised to ask for her hand when the time is right. The ring isn't much—a gold band with a cubic zirconium —but he promises to buy a real diamond right after graduation in eight months. Mom will be so excited. It kills Elizabeth to have to keep it a secret, especially from her mom. She nudges the cafe door open and shakes off the umbrella.

A small bell hanging above the door jingles.

The man at the far end of the cafe isn't Dominic. It is an old man with skin as wrinkled as autumn leaves. He is dressed in jeans and a blue plaid shirt, but he looks uncomfortable in them. His grey hair is pulled into a ponytail, except for a piece below his right ear, which is twisted into three turquoise beads that secure an eagle's feather.

Out of the entire empty café he has chosen the seat Hazel and Elizabeth always sit in. Except now, it's just Elizabeth. It is only October, but it still feels weird going to school and her big sister not being there. Their lucky booth sits at the back of the cafe, close to the cash register. A mosaic dragonfly hangs where there should be a window. It glistens in the light. Elizabeth had only missed sitting in that seat one time before a school test and flunked. Out of all the tables, he had picked that one.

The scent of fresh-baked cookies carries from the back kitchen and fills the room. Every other booth is empty. If he leaves soon, she will still have time to take his seat before school starts. He has ordered tea. If he is ordering breakfast, there won't be enough time to switch seats.

Crap.

He looks at Elizabeth—stares at her.

The busy sidewalk outside could provide a distraction for ignoring that guy, so she swings her backpack into the closest booth. It sits to the right of the door, squeezed up against the large front window.

Something hard whacks the side of the wall.

Shit, my phone! Elizabeth can't afford to fix another screen on that damn thing. It had taken two weeks to pay for the last one. She reaches for the backpack.

The cafe door opens behind her. The little bell jingles with a cold rush of wind.

Thank God for another customer. Before she can turn to see who it is, warm lips press against the side of her neck. She closes her eyes, trying to not wish her virginity away.

"Hey. Sorry I'm late, babe," says Dominic. He sprints across the room before Elizabeth has a chance to turn her head. By that time, he's already placed both their orders.

A pencil-thin girl stands behind the counter, smiling at him and of course he is eating it up.

He glances back to Elizabeth. "Do you want whipped cream on yours?"

"If you can fit it in." She bites her bottom lip as the words escape. *There are so many things I could do with that whipped cream.* She glances over at the old man.

His eyes are wide, like he's reading her thoughts.

Did he hear that?

For the first time since Elizabeth arrived, his eyes lower to his cup.

That's crazy. He can't read my thoughts. Clearly Elizabeth had gotten up way too early. She looks away, through the etched window.

Maple leaves flap as they cling to their branches. As soon as they let go, they'll be dead. Wind pushes the incoming rain against the windowpane.

A metal napkin holder reflects the light above the table. Its placement is no less than perfect to capture the old man approaching from behind her, already two steps away.

He stops beside the table and she has no choice but to face him. His voice is strong, "A-wah—"

Elizabeth's heart chokes. Sweat builds in her palms. Her ears feel like they are on fire, burning as she tucks a few curls behind them. It's uncomfortable that she doesn't speak his language.

"Do not become the moth," he says, resting a hand on her shoulder.

A moment of peace—pure contentment—floods over her. She closes her eyes and lets a sigh of relief escape.

The tips of his fingers slide through her curls as he pulls away. The warmth of the room swirls as he whispers, "Do not become the moth."

Then there is silence.

"One white chocolate mocha," Dominic says, sliding in beside her.

She opens her eyes. The old man is gone.

"So you all packed for this weekend?" Dominic slides a little closer. "Don't forget a sleeping bag."

She stares at him—past him—to where the old Native American had been.

"Are you okay?" he asks.

"Where did the Native man go?" She sits up, searching the room and the sidewalks outside for him.

Pieces of half-stuck leaves wave from the cement.

"I didn't see anyone." Dominic sips his coffee. His finger half-covers the name *ANNA* scribbled in black marker and a phone number.

"I bet you didn't." She gives him that one raised eyebrow look, waiting for an explanation. It will be fun watching him squirm out of this one. His smile always gets him into trouble. He always has some girl trying to pick him up. Elizabeth spins the ring on her finger, hoping it will reassure her self-esteem.

A grin sweeps over his face. His fingertips brush her cheek, pulling her lips to his. The smell of his aftershave draws her deeper into his kiss. He leans away and whispers, "You have nothing to worry about."

She glances past him, at the counter, but the little slut who tried picking up her boyfriend is now hiding in the back room.

Dominic sits back, switches their coffee cup sleeves, and rests a hand on Elizabeth's knee. His fingers slide up her leg, warming the wool of her stockings, pushing the lace edge of her dress up. He leans into her, pressing the weight of his lust against her lips, pinning her head against the window.

Her cellphone beep-beep-beeps.

Crap. Class starts in ten minutes. She pushes Dominic back and fumbles for the backpack behind her. As she sits up, he kisses her neck. His hand inches up her thigh. The blood in her body flows, trying to reach his touch.

"I can't be late again." She smiles, nudging him off. "Besides, I might have a date with"—she spins the coffee sleeve —"Anna tonight."

"Oh, would you let it go?" He scoots out of the booth, moving for the cafe door.

The bell jingles above the door as he opens it.

Elizabeth gets ready to leave. *The dragonfly.* She almost botched the whole damn test. Rubbing her fingers across the sparkling mosaic dragonfly won't be enough for an A in microbiology, but it sure as hell is worth a shot. She sprints back for the lucky booth.

Dominic lets go of the door, returning with her.

The seat is still warm. She slides her fingers over the pieces of square mirror, following the metal lines. It is the first time Elizabeth can see why her sister loves this dragonfly so much.

"Oh, I almost forgot." Dominic pulls a glass jar from his backpack. "I know it's getting hard to find insects now."

"What is it?" Elizabeth scoops up the jar. This ridiculous 50-insect project for entomology is due tomorrow and she was one short. *It doesn't matter. I have fifty now.* She leans over the table, restraining the pressure of her lips, and kisses him.

Her phone rings.

Her heartbeat skips. This time it isn't an alarm she has set.

One missed call. 7:57. Three minutes until school starts.

It's probably just Jan reprimanding me for being late. Elizabeth stuffs the phone back into her backpack without bothering to see who it was and grabs the glass jar from the table. A gypsy moth flutters within. She stands to leave.

Her phone rings again.

She slides the backpack off her shoulder and digs back into its front pocket.

Two missed calls. 7:58. She is officially late. *Crap.* She shoves the phone back into the bag. *I really need to buy a cell phone case.*

The phone rings a third time.

She fumbles to look at the screen. It's her sister Hazel. *Why is she calling me this early in the morning?* Elizabeth answers.

"Lizzy, where are you?" Hazel's voice is louder than usual, but she sounds distant. She hasn't called Elizabeth by her childhood nickname since the day their dog Haju died. "Where are you, Lizzy?"

"At the café." Elizabeth sinks back down, clenching the glass jar in her hand, staring at the mosaic dragonfly sparkling from the wall.

"Is Dominic with you?"

"Yes," barely escapes her lips. *Why is she asking?*

Hazel sighs. "I'm five minutes away ...."

The call ends.

Elizabeth looks up at Dominic. His eyes are filled with the same concern now engulfing her. The specimen jar slips from her fingers onto the table. The moth inside loses flight, spinning with the rolling glass. Elizabeth's stomach tightens as she exhales all the air from her lungs. Sadness creeps into her every thought. The next five minutes are spent in a haze, trying to make sense of the conversation, dissecting each word to the other half of her—to Dominic.

The cafe door opens.

Hazel's high heels beat through the threshold, stomping out the bell's jingle. Her synthetic tan looks almost natural against a tight chestnut ponytail. Her dark eyes drip with mascara. They hold an emptiness—a piece lost from everything that makes her whole. She doesn't have to say a word.

Elizabeth feels it. Her father will never walk her down the aisle. Their mother will never kiss her children goodnight.

Embrace

IT WAS A CAR ACCIDENT. THE FACT THAT THEY DIED instantly was supposed to be a comfort. *Why would it be?* There is no comfort, not in death. A piece of Elizabeth's heart fades dark. Her stomach hurts from crying. Every breath burns. Each step from the café blurs into the sidewalk. Rain pours from the sky. The leaves have stopped waving from the ground.

Dominic drives Hazel and Elizabeth home. Puddles fill the space outside the Hutchings' residence. Inside, empty air fills the house. The climb to Elizabeth's second floor bedroom is too much. *It's just too much.*

Dominic scoops Elizabeth into his arms, giving her his shoulder to cry on. Warm tears drain down her cheeks. He squeezes her as if it is okay to cry.

Hazel's high heels echo through the stairwell from behind. There are no words; they both know that.

Dominic clenches Elizabeth tighter as he opens her bedroom door, carrying her through its threshold. He kisses her forehead, setting her feet softly land on the floor. He cups her wet cheeks and kisses her, smearing the snot from her upper lip onto his.

He lets go and she climbs into the bottom bunk bed.

Hazel kicks off her high heels and slides into bed beside Elizabeth. It has been a long, hard day. Elizabeth snuggles closer beside Hazel, trying not to think. She tries so hard not to think about how many moments are gone, how in a matter of minutes her life has changed. She lets the tears drain out of her, soaking into the pillow. She doesn't care anymore.

Hazel, her co-partner in crime growing up, wraps her arm over Elizabeth.

That is enough. Just her presence is enough. It is the moment Elizabeth clings to—the only moment that keeps her alive.

THE MOTH

THEY SLEEP, WRAPPED IN EACH OTHER'S LOVE, FOR THE rest of Thursday. By nightfall, Hazel has woken up, kissed Elizabeth goodbye, and snuck off to bury herself in work. When their dog, Haju, died, Hazel cleaned the whole house like a maniac. Elizabeth was only eight at the time. It was half a lifetime ago. If she could just go back to that moment, change something, anything ... things would be different.

Dominic places the glass jar with the moth on the end table beside the bed. His warm body replaces Hazel's. His arms wrap around Elizabeth, securing her beside him, pulling her in tight.

Soon, the red digits of the alarm clock turn past midnight and he is snoring. The clock's glow flutters with the caged gypsy moth's dance. Its white wings swirl with red as it tries to escape. Its struggle for freedom is so beautiful, so painful. It keeps Elizabeth company in the hollow darkness.

Dominic tosses, reminding her that she is still alive. Moonlight ripples through the trees, caressing the bedroom windowpane. The red digits of the alarm clock fight with the moon's glow for Elizabeth's entertainment. The corners of her lips pucker, holding back her sorrow, holding back her tears. The world melts into darkness as she closes her eyes, but sleep will not come. A shadow creeps over her.

Something moves outside the window.

She sits up, whacking her head on the top bunk.

"What the hell are you doing?" Dominic mumbles, rolling over. He is of no use after his head hits the pillow.

Elizabeth's head throbs and pounds beneath her palm. Minutes are lost rubbing the pain in her forehead. When it eases, she glances out the second-story window.

A two-foot Great Grey Owl sits across from her in an elm tree. The darkness of the night dissipates into the shadows, leaving only the bird's feathers stained with darkness. Rain sprinkles down, ripping the orange and brown leaves to the ground. Sunlight warms the horizon.

I've made it through the worst night of my life. Elizabeth slides from the bed to press her nose to the windowpane. The warmth of her breath fogs the glass.

"Come back to bed," says Dominic.

Her heart jumps. *Shit.* He scared her.

He pulls back the covers and smiles, unsure how to handle her. He still has both of his parents. He'll never understand this.

The windowpane squeaks beneath Elizabeth's fingers as she turns from it. Dominic is already half naked and more than willing to fill her emptiness.

She climbs into bed and buries her face into the pillow. His hand slides up her thigh and tugs her stockings down. The tips of his fingers slide beneath the elastic of her underwear. The tightness of his boxers press against her leg.

Music blares into the room as the alarm clock goes off.

Elizabeth hits the snooze button. 6:45.

The large owl still sits in the tree outside the window, looking as if it is staring at her.

Dominic pulls her back into bed. Sex could clear her mind, if she let it. He gently kisses her. Saltwater streams down her cheeks. She wants to feel something—anything. He hushes her as he inches her dress up. His body presses against the thin cotton of her underwear. She inhales, forcing her breasts to press harder against his chest.

Someone knocks at the front door down stairs.

Elizabeth pulls away from him, allowing the world to take back her warmth. She tugs the dress down below her waist and hurries downstairs.

The owl screeches.

She trips, catching herself before falling. Her fingers rest on the brass doorknob. *Okay, I can do this.* She takes a deep breath.

One comment—one "how are you doing"—and she'll have her face pressed right back into that pillow again. *Don't do it, don't cry* ... She opens the door.

Zach stands outside, ready for entomology, as he has done every Friday for the past eight weeks. His California tan is still deep for autumn. The brown of his eyes holds no sympathy, no pity. Elizabeth is in the clear. He doesn't know she's crumbling on the inside.

His sandy blonde hair had been darker when they were children. Until last year, Elizabeth hadn't seen him since they were eight years old—the last time the Hutchings' were at their summer house in California—the day he kissed her.

If I stand here any longer, I'll lose it.

"Hey," Elizabeth says, walking away from the door, "give me a second." She heads upstairs to her room, fumbles into a pair of jeans and pulls a hooded sweatshirt over the lace dress from yesterday.

"Where do you think you're going?" Dominic leans out from the bed, pulling her onto him. His hand slides up under the sweatshirt, rubbing the delicate fabric of her dress.

"My project is due." She pushes away from him and sits on the edge of the bed. She can stay in bed wasting months on grief, or stumble through until winter break. She slides into a pair of flip-flops and ties her long blond curls into a loose ponytail. "If I don't go, I'll flunk my classes and won't get into college. I'll lose myself completely."

"Isn't there a rule that if ..." He silences himself.

She stands up. She knows what he is going to say. *Elizabeth could be excused for bereavement. Maybe losing herself in school work will help.* Hazel always does her best when shoving her emotions to the floor.

Sun warms the gypsy moth on the bedside table. It flutters until Elizabeth cups the jar.

"I'll catch up with you," says Dominic as he rolls over, cocooning himself in her bed. He has study hall first period and always skips it on Fridays.

Elizabeth nods. Tears rush down her cheeks. One deep inhale stops the rest. She holds it, clenches the jar, and heads downstairs to join Zach.

His smile fades as she joins him. "Are you okay?"

"No." She hurries past him for his Mercedes outside, trying to keep one step ahead. *He will ask what's wrong—they all will. How could they not? Elizabeth wears it all over her face.* She flings open the front door. Cold air digs down into her bones.

There, perched alongside the house, is the owl. It stares at her, watching the wind destroy what warmth she has left.

Zach bumps into her back, pushing her off balance, then saving her fall. She looks back up at the owl, but it is gone. The branch is left vibrating.

"Did you see that owl?" Zach's saving grip on her arm pulls her closer.

"Yeah," she says, tugging the sleeve of her hoodie down to wipe her wet cheeks.

Zach lets go of her arm as they walk to his car. It is quiet, even for a Friday morning. He is quiet. He is so much in his head he doesn't bother to put on the radio and heads for school. Elizabeth can't stand the silence.

"So are you and Melissa going to Alex's tonight?"

He slows at a red light, glancing at the empty tree line.

"Zach?" *Don't do this to me. Don't ask me questions. Please fill my head with idle conversation.*

"Do you know that Native folklore suggests owls are the messengers of death?" Zach stops the car and brushes a curl from Elizabeth's cheek. "They believe if an owl speaks to you, it is a bad omen."

She glances down at the jar in her hand. The moth flutters helpless within. "I'm sorry," She looks away from him and at the car's window. "I can't. I just can't."

He reaches for her.

She scrunches herself to the door. Unable to clear her head of the idea that any more bad omens could enter her life right now. She opens the passenger door and runs for home.

Zach's voice fades behind her, "Elizabeth!"

It is hard to breathe. Elizabeth's heart pounds with each step. Mud splashes between her toes. She throws open the door to her parents' house. *Dominic was right. I should've stayed in bed.* She climbs the stairs to her room, wanting—needing—to crawl into bed, to sink beneath the covers.

Sunlight trickles across the floor. An empty tree fills the window, now framing the silhouettes entangled on her bed. A girl's legs are wrapped around Dominic's bare ass. His triceps flex as he grips the edge of the mattress, pushing himself into her. Her hair saturates Elizabeth's pillow still wet with tears. The purple thong wrapped around the slut's ankle falls to the floor.

The doorknob slips from Elizabeth's grip and the bedroom door closes behind her.

"Oh shit." Dominic climbs off of his whore and Elizabeth's bed. "Elizabeth. Wait!"

Everyone in school knows Megan Garret is a slut. Dominic said last weekend that this guy in his fifth period algebra class got herpes from her. And here she is, laying fully exposed, making no attempt to cover herself up, smirking from ear to ear on Elizabeth's bed.

The world swirls. *How could he? I would never ...* Elizabeth can't move. Her stomach tightens. She can taste the acid creeping up her esophagus. Just the other night he promised her everything. She had given him everything—two fucking years of her life. She had done his homework, washed his car, and given him countless blow jobs. What had he given her? Empty promises and a cheap-ass ring. She pulls it off of her finger and throws it at his ugly, pathetic face.

I need to get out of here, away from here. The bathroom is one step to her left. She goes for it, but trips and falls to the floor. Her cheekbone whacks the tile. She clenches the glass jar in her hand that encases the moth.

"Babe," Dominic bends over, reaching for her, his erection pointing straight at her face.

"Get away from me!" She closes her eyes, but tears leak out.

He's supposed to be there for her.

Leave me alone. She feels him back away, but it doesn't ease the crushing pain in her heart. On exhale, she cries. She can't hold it back any longer. *Why? Why me? Why now? Why the fuck is everything falling apart?* Her cries turn silent. Life won't even grant her the release she needs. She has nothing left. The clarity of the bathroom blurs, doused in a sheet of tears. She heaves a breath, hoping the floor will swallow her whole. Any life would be better than this. Nausea pushes through her as her cheek smears against the tile. Numbness takes hold like an old friend.

"Elizabeth," he whispers.

Blood rushes through her veins, pouring into her fingertips. Her fingers tighten around the glass jar and she hurls it at Dominic's fucking head. She hurls it so hard and fast, she falls backward to the floor.

It misses his head and hits the edge of the doorway, shattering. Shards of glass ricochet off the wall, raining down on Elizabeth.

"I didn't cheat on you. It was nothing. I didn't even finish so it doesn't count."

Blood rushes back to her heart, pounding like bricks. His subsequent words are deafened against its beat. A piece of glass fogs beneath her breath. Her cheek throbs against the floor. The lifeless moth lays at the tip of her right hand.

"This is your fault. You shouldn't be such a prude."

Why is he still talking? She pulls the white wings of the moth closer and draws its limp body between her fingers. White powder smears onto her skin. *Why won't he leave me alone?*

"I love you," he whispers, sitting in the doorway, naked, on his knees.

He has done enough.

It doesn't matter anymore. Warm tears drain from her eyes, whether she wants them to or not. Light reflects off their droplets. The broken glass shimmers. She can't move. There is no place to go. She closes her eyes and releases the fragile body from her fingers.

A piece of glass cuts into the side of her hand. She grabs it. Its edge slices into her thumb. The flood of pain forces her eyes wide open. Blood flows from the cut in her thumb. She shoves her left sleeve up. The blue veins are like the branches of a tree on white canvas. They blur with tears. She forces the water from her eyes and clenches the shard of glass. More blood drips from her thumb, but the pain has numbed. The edge of it cuts deeper as she forces its jagged edge through her left wrist. Blood pours from the vein and the weight of her hands fall against the floor. The tile isn't as cold as it had been. The pounding in her head eases. The piece of glass slides from her fingers. The moth's broken body disappears in a puddle of blood.

Then Elizabeth feels the pressure of *his* hands pressed against her wrist. *His* fingers crush what's left of the moth's broken wings.

"Do not become the moth," the old man's voice trails through Elizabeth's thoughts into the darkness.

MEADOWLARK

ELIZABETH'S SISTER KNEW SHE SHOULDN'T HAVE LEFT
her, but she has to close the McAlester deal. Hazel had spent too
many damn hours on the acquisition. The commission alone
would be a quarter of a million dollars.

She hurries through the office on two hours of goddamn
sleep. If she loses this, she will be with the bottom feeders again.
That is not an option. Elizabeth will understand—she always
does.

The conference room is already packed. Her boss, Mr. Pierson, stares through the glass wall as she transitions from the hallway into the room. Flirting won't help this time.

She throws her large zebra-print purse beside the door and joins the group. "Good morning, gentlemen. Shall we get started?"

"Yes, let's." Mr. Pierson's wry eyes attempt to crush her.

"So on page two-forty-three you have ...."—*the same old boring crap*. She can recite the lecture in her sleep. *Sleep would be grand*. Eleven white men stare at her boobs. They aren't even paying attention to the speech. Once her circus act finishes, she takes a seat beside the only young guy—Parker Philip. He is in his thirties, a bit of a tight ass, but he loosens up after a few drinks. Not that Hazel drinks.

"Thank you, Ms. Hutchings." Mr. Pierson heaves his fat ass up. He loves being the center of attention. Hazel's short spiel lasts five minutes; any longer and he gets attention hungry.

A phone rings.

Mr. Pierson stops mid-sentence. His beady eyes flick over the crowd. "Whose phone is that?"

Someone's in deep shit now.

It rings again. The noise comes from the door, echoing throughout the still room—from the zebra-print handbag on the floor.

Crap. Hazel forgot to silence her phone. Her cheeks burn. Apologizing will only make it worse. She stumbles from the conference chair toward the door.

The phone stops.

Oh, thank God. She grabs the purse, slides back into her seat, and fumbles for the phone within.

It rings again.

The burn of her cheeks spreads as she pulls it out with a frustrated, "Sorry."

It's Dominic.

No, no, no. He never calls Hazel. The room, the deal, even Mr. Pierson's beet-red face fades to the background. Her hand shakes as she answers the call. "Hello?"

"What do you think you're doing?" Mr. Pierson says.

Dominic breathes heavily, "They took her to the hospital. She tried to kill herself. I'm sorry. I'm so sorry …"

Hazel hangs up. She droops into the chair. Nothing seems real. *How could I be so selfish? What the hell am I doing at work?*

All those grumpy old faces are staring at her.

The phone slides from her fingers onto the table. She wipes her lips, smearing red lipstick across her cheek.

"Gentlemen, please excuse me," she says, more from habit than from forming the words on purpose. She gathers her things, walks to the door, and looks back at Mr. Pierson. His face looks like a cherry about to explode. It doesn't matter now, *nothing matters now.*

She sprints through the office toward the elevator. *What if I don't get there in time?*

The door opens.

I'll never get to say goodbye.

The elevator eases down into the basement.

She's all I have. At the car, the keys slip from her fingers. She bends to pick them up and bangs her head on the side of the car. It's like the universe is punishing her. *Elizabeth, you hold on. You fight.* She fumbles with the keys and finally gets in. *Lizzy, you stay with me, goddamn it.*

She peels out of the parking garage, speeding for the hospital. All the moments she regrets pop into her head. One, is of the time she chased Elizabeth through a field of buttercups. Laughter filled the warm air. Her sister had stolen a pink ribbon from her and tied it into her blonde curls. Hazel grabbed for Elizabeth and they both fell. Instead of crying, her little sister laughed. They lay among the yellow flowers, staring up at a blue sky. And the thought leaves her.

The hospital emerges in the distance and the past fades. The clouds grow darker. It feels like a whole other lifetime now. Hazel parks in front of the Emergency Room entrance. An autumn breeze sweeps her toward the sliding ER doors.

They slowly creep open, taunting her patience.

"You can't park there," bellows the receptionist.

"I'm looking for my sister, Elizabeth Hutchings."

The woman's anger fades as she clears her throat. Her nails click against a computer keyboard. "She's still in surgery. Dr. Stein will be out as soon as they finish. You can have a seat. I can have someone move your car, if you'd like."

Hazel's hands shake as she slides her keys across the counter.

She turns to take a seat, but a dizzy spell sweeps over her. It is another minute before she can let go of the counter and make her way over to the semicircle of chairs in the waiting area. She plops down, facing the entrance. She never sits with her back to a door.

The ER doors slide open.

A cold draft brings two young men in. Their uniforms are jet black, military or special ops style. The first has dark blue eyes and deep brown hair. He is much more fit than his partner, who is a foot shorter. The short one licks his lips in a provocative manner, staring at Hazel.

Her phone vibrates. It's a text message from Dominic.

How is she?

Hazel types back, *IDK, she's still in surgery.*

Dominic types, *I'm sorry. Tell me what I can do to fix this. Tell her Megan doesn't mean anything. I love her.*

Hazel holds in the button of her phone, waiting for it to shut down. *He cheated on her? Son of a bitch! She was supposed to be safe with him. He was supposed to* ... She shoves her purse to the floor and looks up to find both uniformed men staring at her from across the room.

Mr. Blue-eyes redirects his attention to the receptionist who is now intently listening to the phone.

His partner, however, does not. He licks the bottom of his lip again, biting it in a provocative manner until the receptionist hangs up. She nods at them and they simultaneously look back over at Hazel.

The hairs on the back of Hazel's neck stand up. She crosses her legs and arms, not knowing what to do with herself.

Blue-eyes leads the way, taking the seat to her left. His partner, now chewing on his lip, sits across from her. His freshly pressed black uniform accentuates an orange biohazard symbol embroidered on its right sleeve. The word MEADOWLARK is embroidered in white overlaying the orange symbol. The O aligns perfectly with the biohazard symbol.

The agent across from Hazel sets a black briefcase on his lap. A chain attached to it rattles. It's other end is handcuffed to his wrist.

An old man approaches from the hallway to Hazel's right. He is a fossil dressed in a white lab coat, pale green scrubs, and a hairnet. The ID badge chipped to his coat pocket indicates that he is Dr. Stein. He offers a delicate hand. "Miss Hutchings, I presume."

"Yes." Hazel fumbles to a stand, shaking his hand.

"Please, sit." He takes the seat to her right.

She sits back down.

The medical words drag on as he explains the procedures he's done to her sister. "The surgery went well. Elizabeth is in stable condition. We have to wait for the sedative to wear off before you can see her." He glances back at a woman behind him. "This is Miss Grady. She will be handling your sister's case."

Case?

The woman takes Dr. Stein's place and sets a manila file on

her lap. "We need a statement from you about the events, or what you suspect might have occurred."

"Um ... our parents died yesterday—I had to go to work—and she was supposed to be okay with Dominic. She was supposed to be okay—she wasn't supposed to ...." Hazel looks into the woman's eyes. Tears drip down her cheek. It's so unreal.

"Has your sister ever suffered from depression?"

"No."

"Has she ever tried to harm herself before?"

Hazel's heart sinks and with the next breath, she speaks softly, "How dare you? I don't know what you're implying, but my sister wouldn't do such a thing—she wouldn't do that to me."

Ms. Grady may have said other things, asked other questions, but Hazel stops listening. The whole room fades into the exterior of her shell. If she builds the walls thick enough, nothing else can hurt her.

The woman ditches any effort to get information from Hazel and walks away. Hazel's head collapses into her hands. The emotional wall she carefully built crashes down, bringing her sadness into the open. The lobby fills with the cry she has so desperately tried to keep contained. She holds her breath, restraining the next cry. It pulsates to get out. She can't burrow deeply enough into the musty chair of the waiting room. There has to be a tissue somewhere in that huge purse of hers.

"Go ahead. I'll be there in a minute," Blue-eyes says to his partner.

The handcuffs rattle as the man across from Hazel stands.

She wipes her eyes, soaking the side of her hand.

The briefcase swings to the shorter man's side as he follows the doctor's fading footsteps. The handcuffs are a black metal, not silver, nor painted. A sword hangs at his side.

Hazel wonders, *Is that a samurai sword?*

"Are you okay?" Blue-eyes says to her.

There isn't enough air in the world to fill the words she needs to respond. A light nod is all she can give. Her fingertips slide to her lips, restraining any cry from escape. *I'll be okay.*

He holds out an orange handkerchief.

She forces a weak smile, takes the cloth, and buries her face in its fabric. The cotton soaks and smears with mascara. *Okay, Elizabeth will be okay. I can do this. It will be okay ...* She lifts her face from the handkerchief. It is a mess. "I'm so sorry. I didn't mean to—"

She looks up to an empty lobby.

FLATLINE

BLUE-EYED AGENT BENJAMIN SWINGS THE OPERATING room doors open. A chubby nurse stands beside a young woman still unconscious on the operating table. *It's her.* It has to be.

His partner, Jay, stands at the patient's feet, glancing up from the girl's chart.

"Is it her?" Agent Benjamin's blue eyes deepen as he walks over to the patient. His heart pounds.

"It appears to be." Agent Jay exchanges the chart for a key from around Benjamin's neck. He uses it to pop open the briefcase handcuffed to him. Inside is a case file. He pulls it from the interior pocket.

Everything has to be done by the book. Benjamin yanks the file from Jay's hand. The hospital chart and case file are identical. It is a match.

"You better not fuck this up," Jay says.

"Find me a syringe." Benjamin throws the folder and chart into the briefcase, then snaps on a pair of surgical gloves.

The nurse flinches. She stands like a turkey blinded by headlights, unwilling to move out of the way.

Just ignore her. Benjamin inhales slow and deep, holds his breath, and picks up a small glass vial from the briefcase. A black liquid sloshes inside.

Jay slowly hands him a syringe, relaxing at the transfer of responsibility.

Benjamin embraces it. He fully exhales before sticking the needle's tip into the black liquid. Air bubbles gather in the syringe. He steps toward the patient and gently flicks the needle's side. "Nurse, please roll the patient toward you."

The nurse's lips quiver. She stands there, unmoving.

Freakin' turkey. Benjamin glances back at Jay. He closes his eyes and shakes his head, trying to keep his cool. Even with all the power the United States government has given them, some still resist. He rolls back his shoulders and moves around to the opposite side of the operating table. If he gets too close, he'll end up punching turkey-nurse in the face. It's his weakness. The trait his commanding officer said would get him killed. So he takes another long breath and grits his teeth through the words, asking yet again, "Is the patient's name Elizabeth Hutchings?"

"Si," the nurse's voice lowers.

Jay steps around Benjamin and pins his chest up against the nurse's back. He grabs her right arm, digging his nails in, squeezing harder and harder.

The nurse's posture cripples slightly and she moans out, "Si."

Jay releases her.

She obediently rolls Elizabeth's hip toward herself, exposing the girl's back to Benjamin.

Perspiration oozes from his pores as he slowly slides the needle into Elizabeth's spine. The rhythm of the heart monitor slows. A golden curl drifts from her left shoulder, dragging the hospital gown with it to reveal the edge of a tattoo. *A tattoo?* He has gone over her case file several times and never came across any reference of any tattoos.

He empties the black liquid from the needle into her. Then carefully slides the needle out. His fingers brush the hospital gown on her shoulder and the fabric falls away. Black ink curves into tribal lines forming a turtle. *How can it be?* He has studied every inch of her photographs and social profiles. He looks up at the nurse. "Are you sure this is Elizabeth Hutchings?"

Sweat beads on the nurse's forehead. Her arms struggle to hold Elizabeth in place. A bruise has begun to form beneath Jay's grip. She squeaks out another, "Si."

Agent Benjamin looks back down at Elizabeth's frail, limp body. Two years tracking her and he has never been this close. Her pale cheeks are smeared with day-old mascara. Her back is covered in goosebumps.

"Let's go," Jay whispers. He releases the nurse, grabs the briefcase, and heads for the door.

"Okay, let her down easy," Benjamin says to the nurse.

She does as she is told.

He nods, indicating that she is free and no longer needed.

She unwillingly returns his nod.

Working for Meadowlark has its perks. People are forced to listen to you. Agent Benjamin glances down at Elizabeth. Her slashed skin is mended with stitches stretching up her wrist. The job also has a downside. He walks away, stopping at the operating room door. Elizabeth could almost pass for Sleeping Beauty, except her path is no fairytale. It is much darker.

The heart monitor flatlines.

Benjamin exhales with relief and allows the door to swing shut behind him. Both corners of his mouth form a grin.

Dr. Stein and three nurses sprint down the hallway past him, toward the operating room.

Benjamin steps into view of the lobby, ignoring the weight of Hazel's eyes on him as he passes.

The emergency room doors slide open to a black Hummer. A large Meadowlark symbol takes up the entire side doors. Music pounds inside and spews from the car when he opens the passenger side door, sliding in. He rests his forehead against the window after closing the door, watching the hospital disappear in the sideview mirror.

"Dude, what's wrong with you?" Jay yells above the music, nudging Benjamin's shoulder. He speeds the Hummer downtown. "Whoo! Let's go celebrate."

Benjamin hoped Elizabeth would have been awake. He has always wanted to see the color of her eyes up close. He had seen them in photographs and on social media sites, but on stakeouts he had always been too far away. The Chief of Meadowlark described them as an ice blue, but who the hell knows if that is accurate? The Chief is the boss's boss and no one gets to meet him.

October's rain fights with the windshield wipers.

Benjamin's reflection in the side view mirror is dark, drained by the clouds. He reaches for the briefcase. Maybe he missed the tattoo.

Jay pulls up to one of those side-entrance bars with chipped paint, harmless enough to eat at in their uniforms.

Benjamin focuses on every mole and scar listed in Elizabeth's file, but nothing—there is nothing about her tattoo. He tucks the folder back into the briefcase.

Jay gets out and disappears into the bar.

Benjamin examines the empty vial, rolling it in his hand. By the time he stows it and secures the vehicle, Jay is already inside, sitting at the bar with two beers in front of him. How he convinced the bartenders to serve him is beyond Benjamin. Each agent was pulled from a military high school two years ago.

Each one seemed to be handpicked and came equipped with their own survival skill. Benjamin takes the stool next to Jay. The sword at his side clanks against its wood, hinting at Jay's persuasion over the bartender.

The bartender shuffles out from the backroom with two clean mugs. He is in his late forties and pale, like his skin hasn't seen the sun in years.

"Would you relax?" Jay nudges a beer toward Benjamin and gulps his down.

Benjamin's fingers drum against the counter as he glances up at the clock.

"We'll go get her in a few hours, and then … case closed," says Jay.

"I suppose you're right." Benjamin chugs the beer, letting it calm his nerves. It's not like he has never had a beer before, or a few at that.

"What a waste of a fine piece of ass." Jay swallows a second beer the moment it hits the counter in front of him. He points his finger up at the bartender and another refill soon follows. "You knew taking this case that she would have to die—at all costs."

Benjamin nods. He knew.

Escape

"I DON'T KNOW WHY ELIZABETH'S HEART STOPPED, *but we got it pumping again and she appears to be in stable condition now.*" Dr. Stein's words repeat in Hazel's head.

"*... Appears to be in stable condition.*" *Goddamn it. Lizzy, you fight for me. Don't give up. I need you.*

Hazel's heels pound down the corridor, easing as she approaches room 205. She stops outside the door, wipes the tears from her eyes, takes a deep breath, and steps into the recovery room. Her heels click against the tiled floor. She pauses, then slips off her shoes.

A nurse stands beside Elizabeth's bed, injecting something into the IV of her sister's good arm.

Elizabeth greets Hazel with a warm smile. She doesn't tell her how horrible she is for not being there, for skipping out on her in the middle of the night, and not holding her hand through all of it. She just smiles—that's it.

The heaviness of Elizabeth's ice-blue eyes meet hers. Residual tears glisten on her cheeks. Beneath the pain meds, Elizabeth searches for Hazel's empathy.

It is there.

What happened? How did we end up like this? Hazel exhales as she sits down on the hospital bed. She wraps her arms around her little sister—embracing warmth, such pure life. Not even the stench of medical disinfectants can move her. Nothing could move her. Elizabeth's gown soaks with Hazel's tears. Snot drips from Hazel's nose as she pulls away, looking for a tissue.

Elizabeth's left wrist rests limp at her side, secured in two inches of gauze.

A frown melts across Hazel's face. She has no choice but to take a deep breath and suck it up. There is no one to hold her up and keep her from falling into despair. She forces a smile and reaches for her purse. *To hell with a tissue.* She wipes her nose with her sleeve and heaves the purse onto her lap. "The hospital threw out your clothes."

Elizabeth lowers her head in shame.

Hazel looks into the bag. A smile takes hold of her. *There it is.* What every woman needs when her life goes to shit is a big change. She holds up a box of chestnut hair dye.

"You want me to dye my hair?" Elizabeth pulls at her blonde curls and the intravenous needle wiggles.

"No, I want you to do whatever *you* want. But I know for a fact that you have dyed your hair every single time you've gone through a breakup. Nothing is preventing you from starting completely over right now." Hazel has to look away and tell herself not to cry. She looks out the window and closes her eyes, repeating in her head, *It will be okay.* She opens her eyes.

A Great Grey Owl sits on a tree branch outside. The night's wind picks at the leaves clinging to its branch.

She looks back at Elizabeth. "Are you really going to make me go through the list and hair colors?"

Elizabeth's eyes glaze with sedative.

Hazel smiles. "Let's see, there was little Johnny and that rustic-red color ...."

"Okay, okay give me that." Elizabeth grabs the box with a smile. "Just shut up already."

Hazel helps her out of bed and to the bathroom. Elizabeth rests on the toilet seat. It has been years since Hazel dyed her sister's hair. They used to take up a whole weekend gabbing about boys and painting their nails. On Monday mornings, Mom would get them up early to curl their hair. *Mom.*

41

"Are you okay?" Elizabeth rests her hand on Hazel's arm.

"Yeah," says Hazel. Tears escape her. She clears her throat, slides on plastic gloves, and applies the chemicals.

Elizabeth releases who she used to be as the mixture stains her blonde hair brown.

The door creaks open and a nurse pops her plump cheeks into the bathroom. "Are you girls dyeing your hair in a hospital?"

Hazel freezes, mid squirt.

The woman pushes the door open, stepping into the small area. A bruise on her arm, just below her right sleeve, is noticeable.

"No, ma'am," says Hazel. She attempts to cover her mouth, but smears brown dye all over her top lip. *Oh my God, this better not stain.*

Elizabeth bursts with laughter.

The nurse looks down at Elizabeth. Her eyes widen with recognition. She glances at the girl's bandaged wrist, forces a smile, and pulls the door closed. "Keep this door shut."

Any more time contemplating the moment will take away from the time Hazel is gifted to have with her sister. She squirts the Hershey-colored chemical onto Elizabeth's hair and lathers it in, concentrating on every touch, exhale, and moment spent dyeing and washing her sister's hair. She wraps Elizabeth's curls in a towel and steps back.

"So, what do you think?" Elizabeth tugs on the towel. It falls to the floor. Wet chestnut curls cling to her clean cheeks. The pale blue of her eyes pops.

"You look like Mom," says Hazel.

Her phone rings out in the main room.

"You better get that," Elizabeth says, looking past Hazel to the mirror.

Hazel's heart pounds in reluctance.

"Go get it." Elizabeth looks at her and smiles. "I'm not going anywhere."

Hazel's feet slide across the tile as she sprints to the bed, wearing stockings. She only graduated high school last year. Who knows if their parents had life insurance? Who knows how far in debt Elizabeth's surgery has put them? It was probably the hospital calling to collect, and she hasn't even been discharged yet. She grabs the cell phone from her purse.

There is a knock at the door and the nurse enters.

The phone stops ringing.

One missed call: Mr. Pierson.

Crap.

The nurse approaches.

Hazel begins, "I apologize if we conducted ourselves inappropriate—"

"Your sister is going to need clean dressings for the first few days." The nurse glances at the bathroom door. She withdraws a piece of paper from her pocket. "And this is a prescription for the pain meds she'll need. Make sure she schedules a follow-up appointment with a counselor."

Hazel takes the paper. *A counselor? I suppose she'll ... Wait. Patients are never discharged in the middle of the night.*

She lowers her voice and her accent thickens. "I can't officially discharge her, but there were these two men ..."

The bathroom doork nob turns.

"... The hospital has signed your sister into their custody."

"What do you mean ...?" Hazel's voice raises.

"I don't have the answers, and I don't think you should stick around to find out." The nurse glances back at the door and rubs the bruise on her arm.

Elizabeth steps from the bathroom, leaning against the wall for support. The collar of her hospital gown is saturated in chestnut dye.

The nurse hands Hazel a set of pale green scrubs and hurries to Elizabeth's side. Brenda Martinez always keeps a spare outfit in her locker.

"Do you like it?" Hazel says, sliding over on the bed, allowing Elizabeth to lie down.

Her little sister's drained body appears pasty beneath the fluorescent lights.

"You must have had a shitty day," Elizabeth says, wiping a wet curl from her forehead, sinking down into the sheets.

"Yep, those pain meds should be working now." Nurse Martinez glances at her watch and writes on the medical chart.

She takes Elizabeth's blood pressure, pats the gauze around her wrist and unravels it. Her eyes meet Elizabeth's. "I like it. I think it makes those eyes of yours pop. Now make sure you dry that hair and stay out of the cold. You don't need your immune system working any harder than it already is." The nurse's hands shake with anxiety as she loops clean gauze around Elizabeth's wrist. Her eyes repetitively return to the door.

"All done." Nurse Martinez pats Elizabeth's knee, stands up, and hands Hazel a stack of gauze. "You might want to help her get dressed." The nurse taps on her watch and exits the room.

"Hazel, what's going on?" Elizabeth slowly pushes herself up to a sitting position.

"Apparently we're leaving." Hazel slides the shirt over Elizabeth's head, slowly working her arms through. She should have never left for work. She should have never trusted anyone else to look after her sister, never left her alone.

Water drips from Elizabeth's chemical-fumed hair, saturating Hazel's blouse.

Closing her eyes doesn't stop the warm tears from spilling down her cheeks. She pulls away and grabs Elizabeth's hands. "We'll get through this. Okay?"

The door creaks open.

Hazel's heart skips a beat.

Nurse Martinez pushes in a wheelchair. The faint sound of the elevator pings from down the hallway. She freezes, halfway across the room. Five seconds, four, three, two. She glances back at the door and then continues toward the girls.

"You better go now." She pulls the intravenous needle from Elizabeth's vein. Her stubby fingers fasten a cotton ball with a band-aid over the puncture. She heads for the hallway, looking back. "I wish you the best of luck."

She leaves the door open as she disappears down the hall.

"Okay, let's hurry up." Hazel's heart pounds. She grabs the nurse-pants off the bed. Once Elizabeth slips into the loose scrubs, Hazel holds out her $300 wool coat. Elizabeth's body sways as she steps away from the bed's edge. Hazel wraps Elizabeth in the coat, eases her into the wheelchair, and grabs hold of its handlebars. Her blood pressure races.

They make it to the room's edge, just as the elevator pings from the hallway.

Unwanted Guest

Hazel drives until the cement walls of the city fade quickly into rich forest. Now the sound of the Pacific Ocean rumbles in the distance. Elizabeth is unconscious for most of the car ride.

A blanket of fog has drifted across the small beach town of Otter Rock by dusk. Hazel clenches the steering wheel, weaving her SUV along the Oregon Coast.

Fishing boats twinkle in a pitch black ocean. The dark highway hides Elizabeth's reflection in the passenger side view mirror. Hazel leads them directly where she wants Elizabeth to be. The vehicle's headlights push through the fog as Hazel turns down a long gravel driveway. Conifer trees scrape at the vehicle's metal doors until releasing into a cleared homesite, occupied by a Victorian beach house. Windows wrap around every inch of it. Even the front door is a sheet of glass.

Warm lights dance within its interior, across the porch, over the pebbled driveway, and stop short of the car. The car headlights illuminate the difference between. Their glow eases the water vapor's denseness. Inside, a man and woman sprint toward the front door. It is Elizabeth's best friend Jan, and her boyfriend Alex.

"We're here," says Hazel. It is the first thing she has said since leaving the hospital. She pulls the key from the ignition and rests her hand on Elizabeth's sleeve. She clears her throat, keeping her from saying anything, and pulls away to exit the car. "Are you coming?"

Rain begins to splash against the windshield. Alex stands at the front door, holding it open for Hazel. Jan sprints for the SUV. Her rain boots slosh across the river of pebbles. She rips open the door. Cold air rushes in. Elizabeth slides out, tottering with the sedative still working deep in her veins. Jan steadies her. The pebbles sting like ice beneath her bare feet. Her knees buckle, refusing to hold her. Jan grabs her, stabilizing Elizabeth's body against hers. Jan reeks of beer. Her hug, on the other hand, is refreshingly short. "Come on, it's freezing out."

They hurry to the house as the sky pours. Elizabeth's heart beats heavy as they approach the porch. The rain won't be able to wash away what Elizabeth has done, or the guilt she feels. If she stays long enough in it, the bitterness of the dark will freeze her—forever.

Jan enters first, stepping past Alex. His tender smile washes away any dread Elizabeth had conjured up in her mind. Jan started dating Alex sophomore year and he easily became the brother Elizabeth never had.

He greets her with a light hug, revealing his wetsuit to be dry. An ocean breeze coaxes Elizabeth away from him, into the house.

The foyer is a small hallway that opens up to a large living room wrapped in windows. A kitchen sits to the right, consisting of a counter and a few barstools that sections the space into two rooms. Friday night's party had been canceled. Elizabeth had spent so much time planning this Halloween weekend. She had wasted so much time with *him*. A sigh escapes her. The sedative won't allow her to shed the tears that have been building.

In the living room, a wood stove crackles beside a fabric couch that faces the wall. It is an interior wall with a plasma television hung above a decorative bookshelf. A hallway separates the living room from the barstools at the kitchen counter. The hallway that leads to a bathroom at its end with two bedrooms sitting opposite each other.

Hazel's voice seeps down the corridor from the bathroom, indecipherable.

Elizabeth sits down beside Jan, who mutes a commercial selling pills for depression.

Hazel's voice grows into argument.

Elizabeth sits up. *Is Dominic here?*

"Relax, he's not here. Alex uninvited him." Jan looks at her with no judgment. She is the only person Elizabeth knows who accepts everyone's faults—takes everything she receives and turns it into something positive.

Hazel approaches from the bedroom hallway. Her face is red and turned to the ground. She tries to speak and at first chokes on the words. "I have to go to Albuquerque." She sits down beside her sister, grabbing her hand. "I'll be back by the end of the weekend. Promise me you'll pick me up from the airport."

"I promise," Elizabeth says.

Hazel squeezes her hand.

"Hazel ..." Elizabeth looks down at their entwined fingers. The gauze wrapped around her wrist hides the evidence of her torn heart. She has no words. There aren't any words to express the guilt she feels.

"You can tell me when I get back." Hazel leans over, kissing Elizabeth's cheek. "I did have a shitty day." She pulls her hand away and places it against Elizabeth's cheek. "But that just means"—a tear falls, rippling down the curves of her fingers—"you owe me."

A laugh slips out. Elizabeth's teeth dig into her lower lip, attempting to force back her tears.

Hazel leans her forehead against Elizabeth's. Her thumb smears a rogue tear running down her sister's cheek. She gives Elizabeth one last kiss before standing to leave. Then she is off, answering her phone before making it two steps toward the door. "Yes, I will be on that flight," she says. Her purse falls out of her hand. She bends to retrieve it, turning back one last time. *I love you* moves through her wordless lips. Then the moment is gone. She continues on, arguing over the phone, and walks out.

Jan elbows Elizabeth, then tosses a cell phone into her lap— Elizabeth's phone. "I hope you don't mind that I cleared out all of dickhead's stuff and blocked his ass."

The doorbell rings.

She clears her throat. "Why don't you go get cleaned up? We're leaving soon. You can sleep in the car since it's a long drive."

The last thing Elizabeth wants to do is go camping.

Jan pats Elizabeth's knee and hurries to answer the front door.

Elizabeth schleps herself to the bathroom. Seeing one more person will be unbearable. Let alone a 12-hour car ride. The shower becomes her sanctuary, its warm water her solace. Water saturates the gauze on her wrist, weighting her arm down like a broken tree limb. She unravels the material. Droplets of water fall like elephants, pounding down against the line of stitches. It hurts, despite the pharmaceuticals pulsing through Elizabeth's veins. Hot water streams down her back. A sharp pain cuts through her spine. She ends the shower and pulls back the curtain. Cold air rushes over her, forcing goosebumps from her skin. Steam gathers on the mirror, then drips onto the sink. Humidity weighs against the sedative in her veins. She manages to secure a towel around her chest and enter into the hallway. No one is in sight, but voices carry from the porch.

There is a small, dark blue bedroom to the right. Alex's surfboard is propped in its corner. Elizabeth takes the bedroom to the left. It is twice the size. A king bed takes up the left side of the room, leaving just enough space to walk around its frame. It overlooks a huge bay window that carries the sound of the ocean's crashing waves. Across from the door is a long dresser. The large mirror attached to it could warn off any intruders. Pictures of Alex's grey-haired dad, smiling beside his young trophy wife, surround the room. The closet door beside the dresser is cracked open an inch. Elizabeth sits on the edge of the bed, wrapped only in a towel, leaving a trail of wet footprints behind her.

"Hey you ..." a male voice comes from the doorway.

Not him. Howard Gomez is an asshole whose mouth has no filter and whose brain is always leaking some new male chauvinistic bullshit. But he is Alex's surfing buddy and is only around when they party at the beach house. So she endures. He slithers into the room and stands over Elizabeth, bending down so his face is directly level with hers. She doesn't look up. His hand falls between her knees. Her thighs tighten.

"I heard about you and Dominic. You're pathetic." He grabs her jaw and pulls her whole face toward his. "Bitches like you are crazy."

Elizabeth's jerks her face from his grip. There is no need to remind her of her vulnerability.

He glances back at the door and leans closer. "Or maybe you just need a real man to fuck the crazy out of you—"

"Hey, we're ordering pizza." Alex stops as he enters the bedroom. "Is everything okay?"

Howard stands up and heads out of the room, grinning as he squeezes past Alex. "It's all good."

Alex rolls a travel suitcase in behind him. He heaves it onto the bed and sits down. "If Howard is being a douchebag, let me know."

"When is he not being a douchebag?" Elizabeth smiles, nudging him. She would rather Alex have a surfing buddy than see him surf alone. And there is no way Elizabeth is going in the ocean. Vertigo rushes through her. "What's in the suitcase?"

Alex's face goes blank. "This isn't yours?"

The smile drains from her. He had grabbed the wrong bag from Dominic's car. The travel tag is pink and glittery, but it isn't Elizabeth's. She can't believe he was planning on taking that slut camping with the group. Elizabeth had planned everything.

Alex stands, reaching for it, realizing that it isn't hers.

"Leave it." She rests her hand on his. *It doesn't matter anymore.*

"I'm sorry, Elizabeth. My stepmom leaves clothes in every vacation house. Pick out anything that fits." Blush fills his cheeks. "She's about your size."

"And age," Elizabeth adds with a weak smile.

Alex chuckles, more from relief that Elizabeth smiled than

from the poor joke. "Anyway, don't feel obligated to hang out tonight. We'll have time to nag you this whole weekend. Get some sleep. I'll let you know when the food gets here ..." He makes it to the door before stopping. "You know it wouldn't be the same without you."

I know. Warmth gathers beneath Elizabeth as she sinks into the mattress. A break in the clouds allows moonlight to trickle through the window. Dust particles dance in the lunar rays. The tips of her fingers brush the suitcase lying beside her. She rolls onto her back. A wave of pain floods her spinal cord. Cold air attempts to penetrate the wet stitches in her arm. The darkest hour is being too numb to feel the coldness.

RESEARCH

IN THE LIVING ROOM, JAN BRAIDS HER HAIR WHILE watching the movie *Poltergeist*.

Alex returns from Elizabeth's room, blindly walking down the hallway browsing his phone, over to the couch. "This article says the hantavirus was confirmed in eight deaths and twenty thousand people were estimated to have contracted the virus." He flops down beside her. "Are you sure you still want to go?"

"Alex, would you stop reading your phone and go pick up the pizza?" Jan grabs a bag of potato chips from the coffee table and stuffs her face.

He isn't listening.

She kisses his cheek and shoves him off the couch. "I want to leave in an hour."

He balances without taking his eyes off the cell phone and heads back down the hallway.

Howard plops down on the couch next to her and yanks the bag of chips from her hands.

"You're such a dick!" She slides off the couch, throws a pillow at him, and storms down the hallway after Alex, stopping just outside his bedroom. He is sitting on the bed, still glued to his phone. The master bedroom across the hallway is open. Elizabeth is lying on her side, shivering beneath a towel on the bed. It has loosened and her whole back is exposed.

What the fuck is that? Jan creeps into the room. Black spider veins spread out from the center of Elizabeth's spine. Jan slides her fingers along the cold gooseflesh of her back. In the center is a tiny biohazard symbol branded between her vertebrae. Chills ripple through Jan. She retrieves a throw blanket from a nearby dresser. Rain pours against the window as the Pacific winds pound to get in.

The doorbell dings.

She covers Elizabeth, tiptoes from the room, and sprints toward the front door. Howard is still sitting on the couch with his feet propped on the coffee table as she sprints by. She yells at him, "Don't hurt yourself."

At the door, Zach stands on the porch, flooded by motion lights and pelted by rain.

She unlocks the door, opens it an inch, and a gust of wind rips it open the rest of the way.

Zach's arm muscles flex as he catches it and hurries inside, forcing it shut behind him.

Jan smirks, looking past him into the night. "So you decided not to bring Melissa, huh?" Her smile puckers behind clenched lips. She nods toward the back of the house, and nudges him. "Go."

THE BOX

THE WARMTH BLANKETING ELIZABETH SEEPS THROUGH the blanket, dissipating into the room. Pain engulfs every inch of her body as she rolls onto her back.

A gentle knock amplifies from the blurred bedroom door. A masculine silhouette makes its way toward her.

"Hey?" Zach's voice carries into the room.

She slowly blinks, forcing her eyes to focus, concealing her bandaged wrist beneath the blanket as he steps closer.

"Are you ready to go?" he asks.

She turns away, to the window.

Moonlight fades with the incoming fog.

"This is new," he says, sitting down on the bed beside her, grabbing a chestnut curl, twirling it through his fingers until reaching the curve of Elizabeth's turtle tattoo.

She pulls the blanket to her chin and sits up. Goosebumps ripple across her body. She looks back over her shoulder. It has been a while since she admired the turtle etched into her skin. Mom finally caved one day. Elizabeth didn't know why and she never asked. She made her mom drive her to the tattoo parlor the instant she agreed. Now Elizabeth is left with only the wish that she could ask her mother. Elizabeth gives up trying to see the tattoo, and gives up on her thoughts. It is no use. She turns back to Zach.

His lips press against hers. The blanket slides from her fingertips as she embraces it. His shirt firms against her, warming her.

"Wow!" Jan flicks on the bedroom light. Her eyebrows raise to her hairline as she heads back down the hall. Her voice trails, "Pizza's here."

Zach's lips leave Elizabeth's only for a second. They linger an inch away. He leans back in for another kiss, but she pulls away.

"I can't." She scrunches the blanket up to her neck with a slight shrug. "I just can't right now."

"I know." His thumb brushes a tear falling from her cheek. He kisses her forehead and slides off the bed. "You look beautiful, by the way."

He leaves her, easing the door closed behind him.

She runs her fingers through her damp curls. Her head is heavy, like the weight of the fog hanging in the trees has seeped inside blurring every emotion and thought.

The dresser mirror captures the reflection of a broken woman. That damn suitcase is still beside her. *Freakin' slut.* Dominic and Elizabeth had been together for two years. Little slut-Megan knew that. The whole school knew that.

Elizabeth turns her focus to the closet and slides off the bed. The blanket tumbles to the floor. Tonight, she could find a million things wrong in her reflection. She closes her eyes, walking past its judgment and into the darkness of the closet.

One flick of a switch and the five foot, jam-packed closet space illuminates. Designer clothes bulge from hangers. High heels line the floor.

"So?" Jan comes in behind Elizabeth. She tries so hard to hide the smirk plastered to her face. It is the same look Jan had after she lost her virginity to Alex last month.

Elizabeth shrugs and thumbs through the wall of pink outfits. *It was only a kiss. Wasn't it?*

"I'm sorry about the suitcase. I thought it was yours." Jan wraps her arms around Elizabeth—sharing her warmth. With a deep sigh she lets go. "I've always wanted to rummage through Lucy's clothes."

The house creaks with the ocean winds.

Vertigo sways Elizabeth. There is no way she is wearing pink. A pair of denim jeans catches her eye and slides on easily. Next, she finds a grey tee-shirt tight enough to act as a bra.

Jan pulls a large shoebox off the top shelf.

Something falls to the floor.

"You have to wear these." She holds up an expensive looking pair of knee-high combat boots. Her grin expands.

"So, did you find everything?" Alex steps in behind Jan. His eyes shoot straight for Elizabeth's tight tank top. "Oh, I guess she doesn't have a bra that would fit you."

Jan elbows him in the stomach and clears her throat. Lucy had a boob job done the day after her first date with Alex's dad —the day after his first blow job, no doubt.

"She talked you into the boots, huh?" He wraps his arms around Jan's waist, resting his chin on her shoulder.

Elizabeth's foot hits the object that had fallen to the floor. It is a hand-carved redwood box. She picks it up. The detail is worn, but the faint depiction of a waterfall flows into the word AWANATA.

"Oh, that's my dad's pride and joy." Alex takes the box from Elizabeth's hands and pushes it back onto the top shelf. "He's a huge collector of Native American artifacts."

"So anyway," Jan continues. "We went shopping with *them*, I said I loved these boots, but of course I couldn't afford them. So Lucy bought them. That was five months ago." Jan tears off the price tag. "Lace up, let's go."

Elizabeth slides on the boots. They are so heavy. The whole world is heavy. She follows the couple down the hallway for the car outdoors.

Jan has already braced the front door open by the time Elizabeth enters the living room. "Grab my purse, behind you!"

The tie-dyed bag is tucked beneath the coffee table. Elizabeth reaches for it with her left hand, not thinking. The swollen tendons and stitched edges of her skin burn from its weight as she lifts it. The bag falls to the floor.

"I'll get that." Alex rushes back to help. "Are you okay?"

Any answer will be as blurred as the day has been. Elizabeth stands up with no words—completely speechless.

"Oh, I had this filled for you." He digs around in the bulky purse. A prescription bottle rattles in his hand. His eyes scan Elizabeth's as he hands over the bottle, trusting her not to kill herself with a bunch of pills. "Let's hit the road."

Elizabeth could get lost for days, swimming in pills. Numbness would be divine. She would need them if Dominic showed up. The small thought of him makes her uneasy about keeping the bottle.

Alex holds open the front door. The Pacific storms have died to an intermission. Cold air slaps Elizabeth in the face, jolting her exhaustion.

Outside, Jan has taken the driver's seat of Alex's white Prius, drumming on the steering wheel. Elizabeth can't believe they are all still going. Howard sits in the backseat, wolfing down potato chips. She can't believe it is going to be a 12 hour car ride with him. Zach loads the last items into the trunk. Elizabeth reaches for the back door, opposite Howard.

Zach's hand slides on top of hers. He whispers in her ear, "How about I sit in the middle?" His warm breath leaves her skin as his fingers spread between hers, softly pulling them from the door. He takes the middle seat.

Elizabeth tucks her hair behind her ear and sinks in beside him. Remnants of sedatives drown the swaying of the narrow highway as they head south, to Yosemite National Park. Returning here will never be the same.

The Missing Girl

Back at the hospital, Agent Benjamin waits for the elevator doors to slide open. The stench of medical disinfectants is overwhelming after a few beers. The evening sun has set and the corridor blares with fluorescent light. His heart races as he walks toward Room 205. Jay staggers behind. As soon as they gain custody of Elizabeth, their shift will be done. Their entire mission will be over.

A nurse steps from a room down the hallway. Her arms are filled with a crumpled ball of bed sheets. She sees the men, freezes, and then hurries off in the opposite direction.

Benjamin feels an instinct to follow her, but what for? *Get the girl and get out. Forget the nurse. She's no one.* It has taken him eighteen months to be in the same room with Elizabeth. Every day he has watched her—every day. *Get the girl and get out,* he reaffirms to himself.

He enters Room 205. It is empty. His heart drops. Jay bumps into his back, knocking himself backward. She is gone. They will never find her if Benjamin doesn't stay calm. He says to Jay, "Check the other rooms."

The momentum of Jay's turn sweeps the smell of hair dye from the bathroom. The fresh linens on the bed and the clean wastebaskets contain vacant clues.

Shit. Benjamin pivots back into the hallway and shouts down the empty corridor at his partner, "That nurse!"

The stairwell door slams.

Jay sprints down the hall for it.

Benjamin runs for the elevator and begins pounding on the button. *Come on.* The doors inch open. He steps inside. The walls feel like they are shrinking in on him. Everything he has worked so hard for is dissipating. The elevator descends back downstairs. Just before he suffocates, it pings, and the doors open. He squeezes out and charges the night receptionist's desk.

"Can I help you?" The woman places a half-eaten donut down and sucks on her fingers.

Benjamin rests his elbows on the counter. He has to stay calm. They have to find her. He will find her. "Where is the suicide patient?"

The receptionist stares at him, sucking the sugar off her thumb.

"Elizabeth Hutchings," he says, restraining the urge to smack those sticky fingers out of her mouth. They have to find her—he has to find her. He glances around the lobby. *Where the hell is Jay?* He glances back at the woman.

She stares at the emblem on his sleeve. Her lips tighten. She wipes her hands off on her pants, then searches the computer. "Room 205," she says, looking back up at him. "Is there anything else I can help you with?"

"So she has not been discharged?" He grits his teeth and leans on the counter, trying to read the screen.

The receptionist's smile fades. She sits up straight, pulls in her chair, and drums on the keyboard, searching for the answer. "No."

His hands ball into fists. His teeth clench together. One more look at her and he will pop. "The nurse that just cleaned the room, get her down here. Right now."

The receptionist stares at him, frozen like a damn turkey. What is it with people in this hospital? It is like there is something in the air that makes them unable to answer simple questions.

The door to the stairwell flies open. The receptionist jumps. Jay exits with one hand already on the hilt of his sword. He joins his partner and draws the weapon, forcing its blade inches from the receptionist's neck.

The color drains from her face and her lips sag into a frown.

"Miss," Benjamin says, easing Jay's sword down with his hand, "where is your security room?"

She points at a closed door off to the left.

"Crap." Jay grabs the phone behind the counter, dialing 1-1-1 which instantly connects him to headquarters. He speaks two words, "Code Black."

It is going to be a long night. Benjamin makes his way to the security room. It contains one chair jammed beneath a computer desk. Musty air fills his lungs. Black and white monitors mirror the stagnant night. *Let's see where you went.* He stops the record button and rewinds the day.

Video of him disappearing from the hallway into Room 205 is the first to be displayed. Prior to their arrival, the corridor was empty.

Jay steps in, leaning against the wall. "So where did she go?"

Time on the screen freezes. *No!* Static fills the monitor. *No.* Benjamin fast-forwards back to the elevator scene. *The nurse.* The video catches the nurse hurrying away from the agents. The stack of bedsheets covers her face. She turns from the camera and descends into the stairwell.

"Hey. That's the operating room nurse," Jay says.

He is right. Another monitor captures her getting into a late-1990s Dodge Intrepid. It speeds out of the employee parking lot.

Benjamin storms out of the room, to the receptionist. "I need the names of the nurses who assisted Miss Hutchings's surgery this morning."

She stuffs the last piece of donut in her mouth and clicks through a few screens. "Betty Young and Brenda Martinez."

"Their addresses." He pulls out a notepad.

"I can't release that information," she says, letting go of the computer mouse and rubbing her eyebrow, trying to stave off a headache.

"If you don't give me the information, I can't find the patient your incompetent facility lost track of. And if I can't find her, you'll be dead within the week. So let's cut the bullshit. You know we'll get clearance and you'll just be defending the stupid decision you made to waste our time."

"Or we can kill you now," Jay says, exiting the security room, withdrawing the samurai sword from his waist.

The woman reaches for the mouse so quickly it almost falls to the floor. In two clicks, the printer kicks on.

Benjamin says to Jay, "Update headquarters. We need to find her before the next outbreak."

Jay picks up the phone.

Benjamin smiles at the receptionist. She has no idea what shitstorm is coming.

ANCIENT CLIFFS

OVER 700 MILES AWAY, IT IS A CRISP FALL MORNING AT Yosemite National Park. Faded brown, red, and yellow leaves shiver against a breeze. Dust-flakes from the ancient cliffs blow through the trees lining the mountain's edge. Whispers of Native lore curve with the wind against the land, and part at the surface of a windowpane. Cold mountain air drifts over the smooth glass, whispering one last time before continuing on. The sleeping morning rattles with a soft beep. The rustic park ranger residence fills with the smell of hazelnut coffee, that brews in the kitchen downstairs.

Ian Jones pushes a pile of park history books from his bed mattress as he sits on its edge. Just a few more minutes of sleep, that is all he needs. But if he is late today, Billy will surely have his ass. He rests his head in his hands and looks up at the uniform lying out on the dresser. It had taken Ian six years to get into the park system. There is no way exhaustion will plague him now. He drags himself out of bed and begins ironing his uniform. Once the forest green pants are done, he starts on the light grey shirt. The national park badge is the most difficult to iron. It puckers as he creases the left sleeve. The badge is made of thick embroidery, weaved to create the curve of a mountain, a sequoia tree, and a buffalo within the shape of an arrowhead. A smile fills Ian's face. It is Halloween. He went trick-or-treating as a park ranger every year of his childhood, and now he has finally manifested it.

He makes his way downstairs to the kitchen. Park housing typically comes with the tranquility of a campground morning, but today fallen leaves rustle outside the cabin's front porch.

Ian places a coffee mug on the counter before heading to the front door to investigate. It creaks as he pulls it open. The rickety screen door behind it taps against the threshold with a passing wind. He presses his hand against the screen, ceasing its noise.

The rustling noise grows louder. A raccoon and her two kits run out from beneath the porch, scampering off into the woods behind Ian's work vehicle.

He glances down at his wristwatch. *Crap.* It has taken too long to finish the morning's routine. He is late. There is no time for coffee. He locks the front door, jumps into the white cruiser, and speeds down the dirt driveway. The cabin disappears behind him in the rearview mirror. The same route to work never gets old. Beauty rips to the sky from the ground, forming mountains around the valley.

The campground awakens as he drives by. The closest residence is that of Park Manager Billy Hanes. Billy and Ian's cabins are identical, except Billy's had been well-maintained over the years. The windows are dark, indicating that he is already at work. *Crap.*

Ian restrains from speeding to the Valley Visitor Center. When he gets there, the parking lot is crawling with people whose clothing is torn, hair tattered, and faces sickly. He parks in the middle of the road. A woman walks by with half of her fucking cheek missing. *No...* He presses his face against the window. A man limps by. *He looks like a—*

The passenger side door flings open. Ian's heart jerks.

"What's wrong with you?" Billy asks, sliding into the passenger seat as if the outside world is only an illusion. "Oh, there's some zombie bullshit event going on tonight. It's Halloween. Let's go."

Ian stares past him, at two young women. They stand on the curb taking pictures with their phones, laughing, dressed as the walking dead. He whispers, "Where to?"

"Bridalveil Fall," says Billy. "There's a wounded eagle up there."

Ian takes his eyes off the costume party filling the road and eases the car out of the parking lot, through the sea of visitors. Today won't be a typical day, even for Halloween.

Along the ride, the number of zombie costumes increases. Billy grunts and mumbles under his breath the whole ride. He is close to retirement and despises unofficial events the most. The majority of which are usually extreme hikers and climbers, not zombies.

The early hours of the day leave plenty of empty parking spaces in the Bridalveil Fall parking lot. A paved trail quickly takes the park rangers to the base of the waterfall. It is beautiful. *Breathtaking.*

Several visitors have gathered at the top of the trail.

Waterfall mist chills Ian's face as he approaches them. "If I can have everyone's attention ..."

The crowd turns to him. He freezes. They all look so disgusting. The lifeless bird at their feet looks more alive than their painted zombie faces.

Billy puts on a pair of latex gloves and throws a pair at Ian, making his way to the small crowd. "Would everyone please take five steps back from the animal? I would also like to remind each of you that it is a federal crime to take an eagle feather. So if you have one, please hand it over to Ranger Jones at this time."

The crowd chuckles.

Billy lets out a grunt and bends down, reaching for the dead bird carcass.

Ian's stomach tightens. There is something tugging at the back of his brain, something he had read. *What is it?* He searches the faces in the crowd like they would know. *The park book. The Native warning.* He yells at Billy, "No!"

The crowd's necks almost snap at the sudden outburst.

Ian lunges forward, attempting to restrain Billy, but it is too late. Billy scoops the eagle carcass up, shaking his head at Ian in disapproval. Ian's cheeks burn with embarrassment as the crowd's eyes focus on him.

"I would like to thank each of you for visiting this beautiful park," says Billy, redirecting the focus back onto him. "Have a great weekend. Yosemite welcomes you." He bites his tongue the whole way back to the car, then holds out the bird to Ian.

Ian shoves his rubber gloves into his pocket and shakes his head in decline. "I'm sorry, sir, but Native mythology warns against handling an eagle until four days postmortem. They believed that something living on the birds, would crawl from its feathers onto the skin and—"

"And what? Turn me into a zombie?" Billy's eyebrows narrow, squeezing lines into his forehead. "Those are mere stories. They don't apply to us. Open the trunk."

Ian unlocks the back, rests his hand on the back of the vehicle, and looks back at his superior's old, withered face.

"With all due respect, we are standing on Native land."

"Would you like to explain that to all these people? See if modern society cares about what should be done. So, we not only tell the public that the number of confirmed hantavirus cases has increased again at the park, but we're also going to leave this dead, rotting bird along the trail for four days?" Billy glances up at the cheesy zombie costumes still crowding the hiking trail. "Do you think these people would give two shits? Get your head out of your ass."

Ian takes the driver's seat, starting the car. The hum of the engine calms the tension as Billy gets in. Silence guides them back to the Visitor Center. The moment Ian's foot hits the brake, Billy opens the car door to get out.

"You know," says Ian, looking around the parking lot, "I think these are probably the only people who would care."

Billy looks at him, gets out, and throws the door shut.

A breeze rips the leaves from the trees. Autumn winds begin to sweep into the valley.

Ian hopes they are just stories.

VISTOR CENTER

HOURS LATER, IAN WALKS INTO THE VISITOR CENTER, uneasy. The stories of lost history swirl in his head until he sees a young woman standing beside the front desk. Her skin glows like the moon shining against the dark winter night. She twirls a chestnut curl between her fingers as she gawks at a group of zombies passing by. The blue of her eyes is the color of a clear sky. Ian steps closer, finding himself standing right beside her. He clears his throat. "You know the park history program is amazing."

She looks at him.

A man standing nearby inches closer to their conversation.

"Or if you happen to be staying up at Curry Village, there's a campfire program tonight," Ian says.

"That sounds like fun." The nearby man inches all the way over, wrapping his arm around her waist, asking, "Will you be there?"

"Where are my manners?" Ian extends a hand out to greet the pair. "I'm Ranger Ian Jones, and you are?"

"Elizabeth." The girl crosses her arms, giving a light nod.

"I'm Zach." The man offers out his hand.

Ian doesn't care who this guy is, but he forces a, "Nice to meet you," and shakes his hand, steadying his grip. He can't take his eyes off Elizabeth. *There's something about her.* "Hopefully I'll see you later," he says to her.

CAMP CURRY

ELIZABETH AND THE GROUP LEAVE THE VISITOR CENTER, heading deeper into Yosemite National Park. Her eyes stay glued to the window and the mountainous rock framing the valley. It is as if the Gods themselves pulled the earth up toward them.

The perfectly sliced mountain of Half Dome appears through the windshield. Its deep grey color molds into the setting horizon. The famous white face stained into its flat side looks like a middle-aged man with a severed nose. Chills trickle down Elizabeth's spine at its sight.

Jan pulls the car into an overflowing parking lot. Conversations and laughter fill the night's air despite the chill. Everyone else gets out, except Zach, who has to scoot out of the middle seat.

An unsettling feeling that Elizabeth will never return to her parents' house hits. She looks for a way to escape the thought. The only path left, is for her to follow the group. She could easily allow sleep to take her from the world, if only for a few hours. In her dreams she would still have a family. She would still be able to tell her dad that she loves him with all her heart. That every second he is not here, tears her apart. She would tell her mom she misses their conversations. That there will never be another person who completes Elizabeth's sentences more than her. Only in her dreams can she see their smiles one last time, hear their voices, feel their arms embrace her. If Elizabeth could just sleep, life would be bearable.

"You coming?" Zach slides out of the middle into Howard's empty seat, extending his hand out to Elizabeth. The open door allows the autumn air in, drying her tear-stained cheeks. Zach takes her hand, sharing his warmth.

They slide out of the car and he tucks her beside him. The first step reminds Elizabeth of the pain pills she had taken again an hour ago. Her equilibrium levels out and Zach lets her lean on him. With each stumble, his grip tightens. He is everything Elizabeth needs at this moment.

The entrance to the campground is framed by a wooden sign. Its white lights spell out the name *Camp Curry*. Zombies of all shapes, sizes, and artistic detail fill the site. This year Halloween was supposed to be perfect. They had planned it for months. Elizabeth wasted all that time—so much time—on Dominic.

Zach's hand tightens as they step over a tree root, making sure Elizabeth clears it. His grip is as real as it had been when they were eight years old. They had been playing around the lake. Elizabeth leaned too far over the water's edge and Zach grabbed her just in time, saving her from falling and drowning. Shortly after that Elizabeth started swimming lessons.

Now, Zach holds on as they approach a sea of glowing-white tents with green doors lining the pathway. A stream of light drifts up along the mountain's cliff. The stars above rest on a black blanketed sky.

Alex stops in front of tent 667. "I think this is—"

The door flings open.

Victoria Pulaski bursts out, pushing her way straight to Howard. His hands slide into her back pockets and they slurp each others' faces. She is exactly what you would expect, to be with a guy like him.

Alex and Jan take tent 668.

"What happened to you?" Victoria's voice carries from behind Elizabeth.

Elizabeth's sedated heart races back to normal with the words. There is no doubt Victoria is talking to her. The crisp air fails to soothe the burning tips of her ears. She is grateful for the blanket of darkness that night provides. Her cheeks burn with embarrassment as a distant tent breaks with laughter.

"She changed her hair," says Zach, pulling Elizabeth closer, opening tent 668's door. She had forgotten he was there, yet he never let go.

"Yeah," is the only word Elizabeth can muster without breaking.

"I can see that," says Victoria, crossing her arms.

"Come on, let's warm up." Zach holds open the door, nudging Elizabeth past him, inside. The flimsy wooden door slams shut behind him.

Inside, the tent's A-frame is identical to a Monopoly game piece, only covered with canvas. A double bed is pushed up against the rear wall. Jan unravels a neatly folded pile of linens to make the bed. Alex spreads out across the mattress, hindering the process. There are two single beds beside the door, one on each side. Elizabeth takes the one on the right, flopping down upon its bare mattress. Zach sits beside her, pulling out a thinly rolled joint.

"Dude, you're going to get us in trouble," Jan says to Zach, playfully kicking Alex off the bed to tuck in the sheet's corner. Alex plops back down almost on her hand. She joins him, pulls a makeup kit from her purse, and begins to smear Alex's cheeks with a thick white foundation. The original plan was for everyone to dress like zombies. It is the whole reason they drove twelve hours.

Elizabeth snatches the joint from Zach.

The tent falls silent.

"You wanted to try new things." Zach holds out an open hand, revealing a Zippo lighter. He had carved a turtle by hand on its front, identical to her tattoo.

She stares at him with her mouth hanging open, expecting an explanation.

"I carved it in the car while you slept." He smiles. "You can have it."

She takes it and lights the joint with ease. A tiny flame dances until it ignites the paper, burning a thin line along it. Elizabeth takes a drag. *Inhale and hold*. Soon enough she will be able to rest her head and make it into the morning. *Exhale*. White smoke swirls toward the ceiling lamp. *Inhale and hold*. Minutes creep by and soon they all share in intoxication. A little wall heater kicks on. The sides of the tent inch inward. Hazel's wool coat becomes too warm for Elizabeth. Sweat beads on her forehead. She speaks first, "You remember the time we ran from the cops in the woods?"

Jan laughs. "And you lost your shoe."

Elizabeth bursts with laughter. White streams of smoke dissipate into the tent's atmosphere. It's okay to laugh. Right? And besides, Jan and Alex look ridiculous with their faces painted to look like zombies.

"This tent's freaking me out. Can we get out of here?" Alex slides off the bed and hurries for the door—for the cold, dark night.

"You up for it?" Jan has crossed the room and waits beside Elizabeth with her hand held out.

Elizabeth nods, then slides her fingers between Jan's. They have been friends since third grade. It has been years since they passed novel-length notes between classes and spent endless nights talking about boys. But Jan is still here. They plan to grow old together, sitting on a porch in their 90s, ogling young men as they walk by.

"You okay?" Jan stops outside, not far from the tent, blocking Elizabeth's path. "You're squeezing my hand."

Elizabeth nods, loosening her grip a little. Jan knows a hug would cripple her in front of all these people. Instead she gives a light smile and continues down the path for the Pavilion of food. By the time they arrive, a few people have gathered around a large campfire. The flicker of light invites them. Elizabeth looks for an open spot to sit. There is one against a fallen tree on the opposite side of the fire. Elizabeth releases Jan's hand and heads for it.

"Aren't you gonna get something to eat?" Jan's face fills with worry.

"No. I'll meet you guys out here." Elizabeth hurries to the open spot. The tree's hard, ridged bark gives her something to lean back on, something to rest the weight of the world against. The earth is so cold. The pitch black sky slowly turns into a sea of twinkling lights. Clusters of stars continue to appear. Among the forest of invaders, Elizabeth is the only one looking up.

Jan sits beside her, offering a water bottle. Just the sight of it makes Elizabeth thirsty. She takes a large gulp to quench her dry mouth. The liquid burns down her throat. "Vodka?"

Jan hushes Elizabeth, taking the bottle back. More people gather around the campfire. The fire's glow dances over a sea of zombies, while drunken conversations drift into the air.

"So what's one thing on your bucket list?" Zach climbs over the log and squeezes in behind Elizabeth. He throws a handful of crispy leaves into the flames.

Nearby conversations fade to the background. Ghosts of the past cast shadows upon nearby trees; within them is Elizabeth's family history. She tugs at her hair. "Dreadlocks."

"Your parents will kill y—" Jan tries to choke back the words.

"I'll be right back." Zach wiggles out from behind her and sprints back toward the tents.

Alex follows.

"Are you sure you should be making decisions tonight?" Jan takes another swig of vodka, then offers it out again.

Elizabeth declines, pulling her knees into her chest. "You know what else I've always wanted to do?"

The dancing flames are captivating, the fire's crackle so peaceful.

"Stand naked in a waterfall."

Jan bursts with laughter. It is good to hear her laugh.

Alex returns, stuffing his face with cheese puffs. The white makeup on his lips smears with orange residue.

Elizabeth can feel Zach's eyes on her, even through the darkness. His whole face lights up as he enters the fire's ring of light. He is carrying a large block of beeswax.

"Dude, with surfboard wax?" Cheese balls spew from Alex's mouth.

"Let's do it." Elizabeth grabs the water bottle from Jan and swigs it. Zach scoots in behind Elizabeth. His fingertips clasp a curl. A sharp tingle ripples from her scalp to the tips of her fingers, warming her.

The campfire fades in and out as he twists each strand. The colors of autumn dance within the flames while the alcohol concentrates in Elizabeth's veins. The pile of kindled wood at the campfire's center looks as if it is the only thing keeping a dragon from hell from entering our world.

A female park ranger approaches. Her young, bronze skin looks so beautiful against the campfire light. Her features and long brown hair hint that her people belonged among this land. She looks straight at Elizabeth. Her eyes widen.

Crap, she can smell the pot. Paranoia sets in. *She knows*.

A chill trickles down Elizabeth's spine. The weight of eight tiny legs brush her fingers as an orb spider climbs up her hand. She screams and flicks it— into the flames. The chill lingers as she leans back into place.

Her entomology teacher once told of a wasp that lays its egg in an orb spider's web. It infects the spider, turning it into a zombie of sorts. The spider abandons its web design and begins weaving a web wholly to support the wasp's larva. Then the spider sits there and waits. When the baby wasp hatches, it devours the spider.

PERMISSION

Park Ranger Ian hurries through the Visitor Center. He stops outside Billy's office, pacing back and forth, biting his thumbnail.

"Get in here and stop doing that. I've taken care of the eagle, and the United States Wildlife Service will be out this evening to retrieve the carcass." Billy coughs.

"I'd like to apologize for earlier today." Ian rips a piece of his nail off and spits it to the floor. Billy's office looks like a closet furnished with a desk and two empty chairs for visitors. Ian sits down, noticing the pile of bloody tissues overflowing from the trashcan in the corner. "Can I do the campfire program tonight?"

"Sure, I don't feel too good. I suppose the last thing I need is to be around a campfire filled with monsters." Billy forces a smile.

"Zombies," Ian says, glancing back at the trashcan. "Sir, maybe you should go to the hospital."

Billy shoots him a stern look.

"So have you decided what we're going to do about the hantavirus situation?" Ian asks.

"Tomorrow we'll redistribute the pamphlets left over from before. Mentioning the outbreak on Halloween, with all those zombie-freaks out there, could cost me my job." Billy rubs his eyes. "Would you drop me off on your way there?" Billy stands, bracing his weight against the wall.

Ian rushes to his side, guiding him through the Visitor Center and into his cruiser. A cloudy night sky pushes against the cliff of Half Dome in the distance. It is a short drive to Billy's cabin. The bright headlights capture Billy's empty house. He doesn't say a word as he climbs out of Ian's cruiser.

"Hey," Ian yells out the window. "I'll drop off dinner after I'm done."

Billy gives a weak wave before going inside.

Ian races the car down the main road. The campfire's glow intensifies as he approaches Curry Village. An old, beat-up park ranger truck is parked not far from the fire. Only one ranger drives that thing. It is the only truck with a crew cab, but it looks like a heap of junk.

"Where's Bill?" Nevaeh bangs against the passenger

window. Her long brown hair hangs loose over her shoulders. The tan of her skin accentuates her soft, Native American features.

"He's not feeling well," Ian says. "So I'll be helping out tonight."

"Oh my god, this is about that girl everyone is talking about. The one you embarrassed yourself over." Nevaeh laughs, looking over at the crowd huddled around the fire's ring of light.

"You know, I thought you'd understand more than anyone." Ian climbs out of his cruiser, grabs a bundle of wood from the trunk, and storms past her.

"Oh, Ian, don't get your panties in a bunch. Why do you think I would believe all that folklore stuff?" Nevaeh asks.

Ian steps through the crowd of people into the campfire's glow. Its flame dances across the ring of faces surrounding its edge. *Where is she?*

Nevaeh clears her throat, passing him to take a seat in front of the fire.

Conversations fade.

There she is, sitting across the fire from him. A smile fills his face. He throws a few pieces of wood into the flames. Burning ashes spray to the sky and dwindle in the cold air. Each drunken, sober, naked, and zombie-painted face stares at him. The stillness carries his voice, "I would like to start out by welcoming all of you"—*he glances over the painted faces*—"alive or dead."

The crowd laughs and factitious moans fill the night air.

"I'm Ranger Jones. And this"—he extends his arms to the sky—"this is Yosemite." The program typically goes into the colonel history of the park. Tonight will be different. Ian stands there speechless.

Panic washes over Nevaeh's face.

He stares at her. Her bloodline has been thinned out by two generations, but she still holds the beauty of their genes. Still, modern culture has captivated her youthfulness and she has already begun to deny her family's roots.

Elizabeth's full attention is on Ian.

The kindling wood pops.

Tonight the valley will hear its forgotten tale.

"All of you can clearly see the beauty of Yosemite National Park. Before the arrival of the Europeans, the Ahwahnee Indians were a pure culture immersed in the very land you stand and sit on. It became vulnerable as its protectors were pushed from its soil. These mountains still bear the scars from white men raping its ground, looking for gold. But you didn't come here for a history lesson." He sits down beside Nevaeh. *They are the only group that could ever possibly care about this.* "Ranger Nevaeh has an ancient story she would like to share. A story once told within these valley walls."

The fire flickers against the frozen silhouettes surrounding its flames. Their hungry eyes turn to the last of Yosemite's bloodline. The roots of the land can only be spread by her. Otherwise its history will die, being completely engulfed by colonized commercialism.

THE LOST LEGEND

THE AHWAHNEE PEOPLE BELIEVE THAT COYOTE-MAN created the world and led them to this valley a long time ago, when the sky still had no moon. He lived amongst them for several generations, but immortality came with a price. Death claimed those he fell in love with and sorrow pushed him from the land.

The Ahwahnee Chief walked alone every night, waiting for his friend Coyote-man to return. One evening, he drew close to the waterfall's edge.

Something was in the water.

As he approached, the stars' faint glow revealed a pale baby. He grabbed the umbilical cord that was still attached and pulled her from the water.

They say death himself tore the color from her skin and hair, and pulled the color from her eyes, leaving them dark as water's depth.

The Chief wrapped her in his arms and took her back to the village, warming her by the fire. The dark sky faded into dawn. He had spent all night feeding the flames of the fire, keeping death from taking what was left of the girl. Only when dawn broke did the Chief pull back the bearskin blanketing her. Pale turquoise eyes blinked back at him.

Sixteen years he raised her, preparing her for marriage to his son. That night did come. The Chief would finally be able to welcome her into the tribe and call her his daughter.

The ring of fire burned in celebration of her wedding. She kissed her groom throughout the day, lusting for night's end. As dusk approached, the beat of the drum lured the young man from her side to the circle. As he danced, she felt a presence beside her. When she turned, Coyote-man was there. He had returned.

"Give yourself to me and I will give you everything you've ever wanted," he says.

She looks back at the crackling fire, the Chief's warm smile, and the trees swaying in the wind, listening to the sound of the waterfall. "I already have everything."

"I've waited several lifetimes for you, and you've been here all along—dancing—dancing to the beat of *their* drums for sixteen years."

"Excuse me ..." she says, getting up to leave.

Coyote-man grabs her arm. "I've followed mere clusters of stars against a pitch black canvas to return here—to this campfire—to you, Awanata."

She yanks her arm free from him, bothered that a stranger knows her name. He lets go and she retires for the night with her groom. The day had been perfect until he showed up.

That night Coyote-man split the thunder from the sky and its rain saturated the land.

Awanata awoke to a pale, sick husband. The rest of the tribe grew ill and the old began to die. There had always been a cost for her life. Was it time to pay up?

By night's return, the dead rose, killing the living. Death was coming for Awanata. She stayed beside her groom until his moans became too much to bear. Before he could rise-up from the dead, killing her, she sprinted from the village, up to the waterfall's path. The wet, cold earth seeped between her toes. She stepped into the freezing cold water, ready to return her soul to its depths.

"Stop!" Coyote-man said, standing behind her on the river bank, his left hand already offered out to her.

Darkness rises from the depths.

"I will stop all this," he said. "Just give yourself to me."

"How do I know you will keep your promise?" Awanata has heard many stories of Coyote's tricks.

He covered his left hand with his right.

"What are you doing?" she asked.

He removed the top hand, revealing a ball of light sitting in the palm of his left. He offered it to her.

The flow of ice water around her feet was so familiar. Its pain felt like home, but the light was too beautiful to resist. She reached for it. Its warmth filled her fingertips at moment's touch, spreading throughout her entire body. She asked, "What am I supposed to do with this?"

He looked up at the stars and smiled. "Put it anywhere you want. It's a mess up there anyway."

She cupped the light in her hand and threw it into the sky. Lunar rays spread over the valley for the very first time. Laughter spilled from the village below.

When morning broke and the moon faded from the sky, Awanata's groom awoke to an empty bed. He rushed outside to find his bride.

She was not there. But a white face—her face—is stained into the dark grey granite of Half Dome. Even during a new moon, the people would never forget her sacrifice.

But as you can see, these valley walls have lost their people, and her legend, too—near forgotten.

REFLECTION

THE FIRE CRACKLES. NOT ONE WHISPER FOLLOWS. IAN lets the crowd laze in the moment. He has never felt so out of place in his uniform before now. "Feel free to hang out," he says. "We'll be putting the fire out in an hour. Thank you for coming, and enjoy your stay at this beautiful park."

He has done a poor job at keeping his eyes off Elizabeth. Zach sits tightly behind her, twisting sections of curls. Ian wonders, *Why would she ruin her hair?*

All the ancient stories lying on Ian's bedroom floor swirl through his mind. He can't breathe. He shoots to a standing position and storms toward the Pavilion. The Pizza Patio restaurant is closed, but the deck is jam-packed with laughing zombies. *This isn't happening.* Ian has crammed far too many stories in his head over the years.

They're just stories.

The Pavilion dining hall entrance is dim. A cobblestone fireplace in the lobby forces a choice of pizza parlor to the left, coffee counter to the right, or the grand dining hall straight ahead. Ian walks past the fireplace's stone wall, entering the main dining room. A vaulted ceiling opens up overhead.

Ian promised Billy dinner, and since he is a vegan, Ian starts at the salad bar. He fills one Styrofoam container with lettuce and another with macaroni and cheese. His own is loaded with a cheeseburger and fries. He balances the containers and nudges the backdoor open, lingering in its threshold to admire the architecture. Ceiling lights warm the brown paneled walls. The outside air whistles. Ian has never longed to stay inside so badly before. He steps back a little, hesitating.

"Hey," Nevaeh grabs the door from the outside, holding it open for him, "where are you going?"

"Home, you got this." Ian smiles at her. "You did a great job." He steps out of the doorway and passes her. "See you in a few hours."

"So you're not going to talk to her?"

He stops. "No, she's busy. And I promised Billy I'd drop off some food."

"I noticed when she checked in … her name—"

"I know, it's Elizabeth."

"Yeah, Elizabeth Hutchings," she says, raising her eyebrows.

Ian shoves the containers into Nevaeh's arms and sprints for the campfire. He stops at the edge of visitors still crowding its glow. The tip of his boot slides into the ring of light, attracting a few odd glances from those around him.

Elizabeth is standing, talking to another young woman in her group. The men are nowhere in sight.

Sweat covers Ian's palms. He tugs at the bottom of his coat and walks over to her, catching his breath. "Elizabeth, can I talk to you for a moment?"

The young woman beside Elizabeth freezes like a deer in headlights.

What am I doing? This is so stupid. "Is your last name really Hutchings?" he says.

"Yes. Why?" Elizabeth steps back away from him.

"So your great-grandmother was Florence Hutchings?"

She stares at him.

"Her parents were the first white settlers of Yosemite. She was the first white child to be born on this land." He takes a step closer to her, glancing around the campfire. "Why don't you come back to my place?"

"She's not going anywhere with you." Jan steps between them. The alcohol on her breath fills his nostrils. She grabs Elizabeth's hand and leads her back toward the tents.

He stands there, watching the two disappear into the dark.

Nevaeh approaches behind him. She had watched the whole thing. There was no way she didn't. "Why don't you take this to Billy? Like you said, I'll wrap up here on my own." She hands him the food. "Don't lose your job over some fairytale bullshit."

She's right. He heads to his vehicle and climbs in, inching the cruiser through the crowd. The tires crunch over gravel until fading into smooth asphalt. Work never gets old, but the day has become worn. Endorphins fade by the time Ian reaches Billy's cabin. He is drained and exhausted.

Ian grabs the food and makes his way up to the dark residence. There is no doorbell. A screen door barricades a solid front door from contact. The rusted hinges creak as Ian pulls open the screen door, lightly knocking against the front door. "Billy, you in there?"

No reply.

A breeze gusts by, pushing against the styrofoam containers in Ian's hands, tottering them off balance. He searches the surrounding darkness and fumbles for his keys—the master key for the park. The wind pushes against him as he forces the door open. Inside, the cabin's layout is identical to his own. A modest living room opens up to a small kitchen at its rear. To the right is a set of stairs that lead to the second-story bedrooms. Billy's house is still decorated the way it had been when his wife moved out. Not many people can bear the real isolation of living in the middle of a national park. Outdated pictures of Billy's kids line the walls.

Ian slides his finger across a picture frame, pushing the dust into a ball until falling to the floor. He moves into the kitchen, turning on a dim light above the stove. He places the food in the refrigerator.

Bright streams of light fall on the counter. Something about the bills and papers spread out in a mess catches his eye just as the rubber seal of the refrigerator door closes. He cracks the door back open, allowing the light to illuminate the counter. The pile of bills and envelopes are all scribbled with small, erratic pen marks. Ian thumbs through the mess for a blank piece of paper. At the very bottom is a post-it, scribbled with weak ink lines. The back of it is still blank. It will do. He writes: *BILL, FOOD IN FRIDGE,* and sticks it to the refrigerator. The stove's light illuminates the room enough to guide him back to the door.

A rustling sound comes from upstairs.

Ian stops. He takes a step back and pauses. A dizzy spell sweeps through his head. He shakes it. *I think I've intruded enough. I'm sure he's okay. The last thing you want is someone bothering you when you're sick, or dead asleep.*

Ian tiptoes to the door and pulls it shut as he exits. The porch door taps against his back as he locks the front door.

A rustling noise comes from the right side of the cabin.

He eases the screen door shut. The rustle of leaves becomes louder, closer. Ian holds his breath and approaches the corner of the house where the porch ends. He flings his body around the side, bracing for confrontation with one of those zombie-costumed kids. His heartbeat tightens, but his shoulders relax. "Oh, It's only you."

Three pairs of raccoon eyes stare at his awkward stance. It is the mom and her two kits.

A breeze drifts down from the mountains, lifting the porch door from its hinges, causing it to slightly tap against its frame.

IT BEGINS

WHILE RANGER IAN SETTLES DOWN FOR THE NIGHT, JAN and Elizabeth return to their tent in Camp Curry. Jan releases Elizabeth's hand as they plop down on the double bed in tent 668. The lantern hanging in the middle of the tent spins with the walls. They have had too much to drink. Jan braces her head against her hand, leans over Elizabeth, and kisses her. Her tears run into the freshly twisted dreadlocks of Elizabeth's hair as she pulls away. She nuzzles her forehead against Elizabeth's. "I love you."

Alex and Zach stumble into the tent like dumb frat guys.

Jan sits up, wiping her tears. White makeup has smeared onto Elizabeth's forehead. Jan wipes it off, smudging it between her fingers. In some parallel world, Jan sits alone, mourning her best friend. She can't shake that feeling. She wipes the makeup from her face with a towel from her bag, and blows her nose. "Oh my God, I have to pee!"

"Just pee behind the tent. Maybe it will keep the bears away." Alex laughs as he falls onto one of the single beds by the door.

"That's disgusting." Jan sprints out the door before Alex can stop her. "I'll be right back."

I'm not pissing in the woods.

The glowing tents form a maze through Curry Village. The distant campfire dwindles into smoke. Zombie costumes fill the campground, thinning out the farther Jan walks. The trail to the bathroom grows dark. Drunken conversations weaken in the distance. She sways between the trees lining the path.

A dim light ahead illuminates a community bathroom building. Jan leans against a tree. The bark is so thick, so uneven. She pushes off, propelling herself forward. An orange glow reaches into the night from the women's propped-open bathroom door. A spider dangles in the doorframe, swinging with a breeze.

Jan drops to her knees and crawls under the spider. *It could still drop on my head, crawl up under my dress.* Her knees bang against the tile as she rushes through.

The large wings of a moth flicker against the ceiling light, casting a shadow on the floor.

Jan clears the bathroom entrance and the spider still sways in the doorway. Her heart eases. She straightens her dress, finding the bottom trim soiled. Good thing it was from a secondhand shop. She stumbles to the second stall from the entrance, pulls down her black panties, hovering over the toilet seat. Who knows what you can actually catch from sitting on a public toilet? Some women are as disgusting as men, if not more. Even if the stall seems cleaner than usual.

Cold air blows under the stall, pushing Jan off balance. The skin of her thighs lands against the cold porcelain. *Gross*. Now she will have to take a shower. What if she just got AIDS? No, that is stupid. You can't get that from a toilet seat. Probably the clap or something that would make her coochie drip.

She hoists her underwear up, flushes, and leans against the stall, fidgeting with its latch. She gets it, and the door swings inward. Those kinds are the worst.

A male park ranger stands in the lavatory doorway.

"Oh my God, you scared me." Jan steps out of the stall. "So you work here?"

He says nothing. The spider hanging in front of him swings with each breath.

She steadies herself to the sinks. The man totters just outside the door, watching her. She reaches for the faucet. He steps into the bathroom. The spider clings to his cheek and crawls up his scalp. He doesn't try to shake it. His pale face accentuates the dark circles under his bloodshot eyes. Sweat saturates his grey park ranger shirt.

Jan doesn't move. *What the heck is wrong with this guy? The spider has to be in his hair.* She leans against the sink. That last shot of vodka had been too much.

The man scuttles closer.

She laughs. "Oh, you're good. That's funny. Great costume! You got me. Wow!" *Best zombie costume ever.*

He steps closer. His body lurches out of focus while she laughs. Intoxication weights her eyelids shut. She grips the lip of the sink, restraining from falling backward.

His body leans in behind her. His breath presses against the back of her neck.

"You know, I like a man in uniform," she says, spinning to face him, grabbing the front of his shirt to draw him closer. He is much older than her, but drunk fantasies always overpower that minor detail. She presses her lips against his, but he doesn't return her passion. She withdraws her lips and squints at his name badge. "Billy Hanes," she says, "this is an awesome costume. So Billy, you always take advantage of young, intoxicated campers?"

Before he can answer, she grabs the front of his uniform and forces another kiss. His lips feel like sandpaper—dry and coarse —unmoving. The smooth edge of his front teeth chomp into her bottom lip.

"What the hell, man?" She pushes back from him, wiping her mouth. *I'm bleeding?* She looks at her hand and the blood covering her fingers. *He bit me!* She makes for the door. "What kind of a *freak* are you?"

He grabs her right arm and twists it behind her back, forcing her to look at herself in the mirror. She wiggles. He nudges her wrist higher up the curve of her back. Agony shoots through her body. She clutches the sink, but the pain doesn't ease. She thrusts her head backward, cracking the cartilage of his nose. Blood drains from his nostrils. He doesn't flinch or let go. His nails dig into her wrist. She screams and it echoes off the concrete walls. He slams her cheek into the curve of the porcelain sink. She grips its edge with her free hand. Her head throbs. The sink drain swirls with blood pulsating from her lip.

His weight pushes her hip against the sink's edge. His fingernails split as they dig deeper into her wrist. His knees press into the backs of hers. She wiggles again, trying to free herself, to take back control.

This isn't happening.

He forces her wrist higher up the small of her back.

She cries with pain, begging for him to "Stop!" The only way to ease the pain is to bend over more. She tries by shoving her cheek harder against the porcelain—anything to ease the pain in her arm. There is nowhere to go. *This is not going to happen to me.* She forces all her weight to stand, but he shoves her head back down and her cheekbone smashes against the sink. Streaks of black mascara drip from her eyes into the drain. Drool leaks from the ranger's mouth, pushing the black liquid down the sink. Her cheek throbs. Adrenaline mixes with the alcohol in her veins and the pain of her arm begins to disappear.

He inches her arm up more, paralyzing her with pain. Any

higher and her arm will break. His weight slowly lifts from her.

Now! She stands up. *Run!*

The reflection of Billy's bloodshot eyes in the mirror widen with the sudden movement. His mouth opens and he lunges for the back of her neck. She runs for the door. He grabs her arm, yanking her backwards onto the tile floor. She crawls to the third stall that hugs the far wall and slides the latch. He pounds against the door, drops to the floor, and crawls underneath.

Jan screams, stumbling backwards, bumping into the toilet. She has got to get out of there and the only way out is up. She jumps onto the toilet seat. *Shoot.* There is no toilet water holding tank to hoist higher up on.

He reaches for her, shimmying almost all the way into the stall. She pulls herself up on top of the partition wall, tottering on the edge of the lavatory stall. Her biceps burn and her muscles shake. His fingernails snag her stocking and catch hold of her shoe, ripping it from her foot. She flings her leg over the top of the stall and loses balance, falling into the next stall, crashing to the floor.

Billy has gotten to a stand on the toilet seat and peers down over the top at her.

She yanks the stall door open and sprints for the exit.

Night's air chills the tears falling down her cheeks. She is free. That is all that matters. The dark outline of the trees undulate in front of her as she sprints down the path. The trail grows darker as the bathhouse light fades behind her. Her foot snags on an exposed tree root and she trips to the earth.

Deep moans creep up the trail from behind her.

She shakes her head, trying to ease the fear rising like a tsunami. She pushes off the ground and runs. The line of trees framing the trail scrape at her with their branches. Then they end. The sole of her remaining shoe hits asphalt. A dimly lit cabin window penetrates the darkness. She is lost. The clouds have faded and the stars' twinkle provides enough light to follow the main road back to camp.

Night Sky

Inside that cabin, Ian pours a cup of hazelnut coffee. A wood stove warms his living room. A short nap always recharges him for midnight rounds, but tonight refreshment eludes him. His immune system is failing.

A car speeds past his driveway and a dizzy spell washes over him. The hazelnut smell grows bitter in the air. He sits down, sliding his work boots on. The laces dangle, barely touching the floor. He grabs a set of keys from the counter and dumps the repulsive coffee down the sink. As the brown liquid swirls into the drain, nausea floods him. His stomach violently forces its contents up. He stays still, hovering over the sink's edge.

Leaves rustle outside the front porch. The screen door taps with each passing breeze. The light of the living room brightens with each blink, blinding Ian's view. Pressure fills his chest cavity as his fingertips search for the light switch to dim the room. His muscles feel like potato bags hanging from his arms. He turns off the lights, allowing darkness to cover the cabin. His pupils widen and relax. Only a dim light above the stove is still on. *Much better.* His system calms down.

Leaves rustle again outside.

Those raccoons will be the death of me. He pulls open the front door and pushes the screen door out, preparing to yell at the raccoons to go away.

It stops, hitting a dark silhouette.

Ian's heart pounds. He forces his eyes to focus on the figure. "Shit, man."

Billy stands outside on the porch, staring at him through the flimsy screen door.

Ian pushes the door open more so Billy can grab it, then walks away, heading for the couch, expecting Billy to follow.

The screen door bangs shut behind him.

"I'm almost ready," says Ian. "You feeling better?"

There is no answer.

Ian sits on the couch and ties his shoelaces. Cold air seeps across the floor, touching his hands. He glances up at Billy, who still stands outside. "So are you coming in?" says Ian. "I want to ask you some questions about the park's history."

Silence carries between them.

Ian leaves the couch to return to the door.

Billy stands still, watching Ian's every move. The weight of his breath is heavy and deep.

"Billy, are you okay?" Ian momentarily loses his balance as another dizzy spell sweeps over him. He has to refocus. The dim stove light illuminates only the blurred edges of his friend's image. Ian grabs onto the doorframe and steadies himself.

Billy's stare is empty, unfocused, and blank. His clothing is soiled and torn, matted with leaves and twigs.

"Maybe you should go back to bed. I'll get Nevaeh to cover rounds tonight." Adrenaline courses through Ian's veins, waking him up a little.

A spider crawls down Billy's forehead, dropping onto his shoulder.

A passing breeze pulls warm air out of the house. The storm door screen brushes the tip of Billy's nose. He slaps his hand against it, sliding his fingers down the mesh barrier. His pinky catches on the door's wooden trim. He doesn't yell, scream, or stop as it cuts into his flesh. His fingers ball into fists and he punches through the screen door.

Ian slams the front door shut and backs away. His heartbeat deafens any clue of Billy's next movement. The window beside the door tempts his curiosity, but his eyes stop on the front door's unlocked door knob. He turns the lock, then leans to peek out the window.

Billy punches through the glass.

Shards shoot toward Ian's face. He shuts his eyes. Billy's

broken fingernails scrape into his cheek. The raw layer of exposed cells burns. He backs up, falling to the floor.

Billy's old, flabby body crashes through the window.

More glass sprays down on Ian. He shelters his face with his forearm, closing his eyes for only a second. Billy's teeth slice into his arm. A warm liquid drains onto Ian's chest. He opens his eyes.

Billy's teeth sank into Ian's forearm flexor like a lion tearing at a gazelle. Billy jerks his head back and tears a chunk of skin from the wound.

A dry heave hurls Ian forward and forces Billy off of him. He kicks Billy further away and stumbles to his feet, cupping the wound of his arm. Blood seeps through his fingers. He staggers up the stairs.

All the doors are closed.

Shit. He will have to let go of his arm to turn the doorknob. He goes for the bedroom on the right. Blood smears across the doorknob and the brass slips beneath his fingers. He wipes his palm on his pants. *Shit.* Then he tries again. It turns just enough and he falls into the bedroom, slamming the door shut behind him. He climbs to his feet, locks the door, and withdraws the belt from his waist. His head grows heavy. His heartbeat weakens. His eyes shoot around the room for something that can stop the bleeding. *A pillowcase.* He dumps the pillow from it, dresses his wound, then tightens the belt around it. The cotton soaks with blood.

He searches the room for something, anything he can defend himself with. His eyes stop on a book lying open on the floor. The open page is an image of a coyote howling beneath a moon drawn in ink.

Billy pounds against the bedroom door. The wood splits. The door brakes. Pieces of wood spray into the room.

A patrol car's spotlight drifts through the tree branches lining the driveway. It is Ian's only chance. He forces his way to the window, trying to open it. It is stuck—painted shut. He pounds around the window frame, chipping the paint away from its seam. It takes three more attempts before pitching open. He yells out the window, "Help!"

There is a noise behind him. He glances back at the door. Billy slams into him, knocking the air from his lungs. His body crashes through the window.

Cold air shoots up all around him. The black sky is so beautiful, so clear, the stars of a new moon never created so much ecstasy. His body hits the ground and goes numb.

Billy lands on top of him, tearing his teeth into Ian's neck.

All Ian can feel is a mauling pressure. He stares up into the endless abyss of the universe. A passing breeze drains all the warmth from his body.

A muffled gunshot carries through the air.

Droplets of Billy's blood spray across Ian's view, tainting the twinkling stars red. The perfect image of the night sky floods with the pieces of Billy's brain.

Within Ian's last gasp of air, Billy's distorted and motionless face pierces his view, etching itself into his last thought: *Coyote-man has returned.*

ESCAPE

A SECOND GUNSHOT ECHOES IN THE DISTANCE. ALEX sprints from the tent, anxiously awaiting Jan's return.

Elizabeth's eyes are still on the green door when Zach presses his warm lips to hers. His hand rests on her cheek. She inhales until her lungs can hold no more. The weight of his kiss never leaves her as he unbuttons the front of her thick wool jacket.

Cool air chills the thin grey tee-shirt that hugs Elizabeth's body. Zach pulls Elizabeth close, gently biting her bottom lip. She grabs the bottom of his shirt—he leans back and she pulls it off him. His fingers brush the gauze wrapping Elizabeth's wrist.

113

He holds his breath and leans against her, brushing a waxy dreadlock from her cheek.

Elizabeth turns away. *What the hell am I doing?*

His warm chest presses harder against hers.

She looks back at him, bracing her palms against his chest, nudging him back from her. She lets the jacket fall from her shoulders and pulls off her top, pressing her body up against his.

There is a void, a broken piece in her heart she needs him to fill. He kisses her, pushing her body deeper into the mattress. All his weight presses against her as she cups his butt, encouraging it.

"Are you sure?" He kisses her neck. "Sure you want to give yourself to me?"

Every tendon in Elizabeth's body tightens with the words. She pulls away from his lips and he lifts some weight off her. She searches his eyes. They are already searching hers for an answer. He stares back at her, not daring to say another word. His muscles flex in the lamplight as his hand drifts up her jeans. She pulls him closer, forcing his lips against hers, wanting to feel desirable.

He exhales. She kisses his neck and grabs the top of his pants. He pulls back for a second at the touch of her cold hands. The button releases and he forces himself closer, barely leaving room for Elizabeth to grab his zipper. He stands up and kicks off his pants.

The tent door is thrown open. All the warmth is ripped out of the tent.

Jan stumbles in with one shoe on. She looks like shit. Her bottom lip is bleeding and her makeup is smeared down a swollen cheekbone.

What the hell happened? Different possible scenarios play out in Elizabeth's head.

Jan hurries over to the bed Elizabeth and Zach are making out on and bends down beside it, throwing Elizabeth's shirt to Zach, then stuffing her backpack. Once filled, she heads for the door, kicks off the one shoe, and grabs a beer.

Elizabeth sits up, fumbling to put the shirt back on, thanking God that she hadn't taken off her laced-up boots.

Zach already has the wool jacket held out for her as she leaves the bed. "I've waited this long," he says.

Elizabeth grabs it and hurries after Jan into the dark, cold landscape. At first Elizabeth can't see anything—it is too dark and the tent was too bright.

"Are you ready?" Jan asks, standing to the right of the tent. A cigarette flops between her lips. She presses the cold beer bottle against her cheekbone.

Elizabeth steps toward her, but she moves away and heads for the parking lot.

"Hey," Elizabeth says, cutting in front of her. "What happened?"

"What? What do you think happened?" She snaps, then glances over Elizabeth's shoulder, taking a deep breath. "I thought I saw a bear and fell in the woods."

Elizabeth follows her stare through the parking lot to Alex, who is leaning against the car, smoking, waiting for her. Tears drip down Jan's bruised cheek.

The gauze. Elizabeth unravels it from her wrist, folding the fabric, and gently wipes the mascara and foundation from Jan's face. Jan refastens her tattered ponytail and grabs Elizabeth's hand, leading her toward the car. Elizabeth digs into her pocket and pulls out the pill bottle. Jan turns at the sound and Elizabeth hands over the prescription.

"Hey. Did you get lost?" Alex smiles as he sees Jan, hurrying to wrap his arms around her.

"Yeah, I did," she says. "Can we head home?"

Alex looks to Elizabeth for an explanation of the sudden mood change. Elizabeth shrugs off his curiosity. Jan turns to get into the car, but Alex stops her. The darkness of the night has failed to hide the contusion forming over Jan's cheekbone. His fingers shake as he reaches to touch it. "What happened to you?"

"Oh, I tripped on a root along the path…" Jan stumbles over the words.

"Bear," Elizabeth says. "She thought she saw a bear … and tripped. So how 'bout she tells us the story on the way home? In the car, where there are *no* bears." Elizabeth holds her hand toward him.

"What?" he says.

"Keys," Elizabeth says.

He crosses his arms in protest.

"It will just be for a little bit. I'd say I am the most sober to drive." Elizabeth extends her fingers more.

Alex reaches into his pocket, handing over the keys. Jan slides into the back seat of the car, pops a pain pill, and cracks open the beer. Alex goes to get in beside her, but she pulls the door shut, pointing at the front passenger seat, telling him, "You need to help her drive."

Elizabeth takes the wheel, concentrating on the road. Alex sits beside her, and Jan pulls a sleeping bag over her head, passing out in the backseat. Elizabeth should have asked Zach to join them, but there wasn't time. And she doesn't know what she is doing with him yet. She wants to feel loved and appreciated, and he does all those things. But if they go any further right now, it won't last.

Childhood memories of him sitting beside the lake rush through her thoughts, blurring the drunken pedestrians walking through the parking lot. The farther they get from camp, the more nocturnal animals scamper through fallen leaves. Elizabeth stops the car at the main road intersection.

A cabin tucked between the trees across the street is lit up by a circle of park vehicles. It looks like a crime scene with yellow tape and possibly every Park Ranger in the valley on duty.

A black Hummer speeds by, heading for the cabin. A reflective biohazard sign ornaments its side with the word Meadowlark. The man driving looks over at Elizabeth as they pass, then slams on the breaks.

I should've gone by now. She grips the steering wheel and pulls out, getting as far away from there, as fast as possible.

YOSEMITE RISING

THREE MINUTES AFTER THE GROUP LEFT, Howard was
screwing Victoria's brains out.

Whispers of Ranger Ian's death floated through the park by
the time the sun peeked into the valley, brightening half the tent.
The night had been wasted on sex and cheap alcohol. Howard's
back is pressed up against Victoria's shoulder. She nudges him,
finding that his shirt is soaked with sweat. *What the hell?*

Howard shivers.

Someone knocks at the door.

"Are you guys coming to breakfast?" says Zach.

Victoria slips out of bed and slides into a pair of sneakers.

She opens the door. Zach's intoxicating hazel irises meet hers. *It's freezing out.* She grabs her jacket. "Howard, I'm running to the bathroom. Get up and meet us in the dining hall."

Zach's face is covered with a shitty-ass grin.

Victoria slams the door shut behind them. "So did you finally get a piece of ass? You know you could do so much better. Sloppy seconds, Zach, really?"

Dominic instantly became Zach's best friend two months ago. Zach had moved up from California, stumbling into the same town as his long-lost friend Elizabeth. She was miles away by now and Victoria had Zach all to herself. They continue to a small bathroom near the food pavilion.

"Vicky, why can't we just be friends?" Zach opens the bathroom door for her, standing beside it, waiting.

We can't be friends because I want you so hard. She grabs onto the doorknob and squeezes it as she pulls it closed, wishing he wanted her.

"I promise you I'm better to look at than put up with anyway," he says through the door.

Howard's a freak in bed, but he doesn't have a six-pack to run her fingers down. Just the image of Zach's sweaty chest brushing up against her is enough to deepen her desire for him. She splashes her face over the sink with cold water. The mirror captures the reflection of a young woman who needs to work out more and who always gets what she wants—damn it. She punches the reflection staring back at her. Pieces of broken mirror spider web over her image. Her knuckles throb. That is better. She watches the cold water run over her hands, easing their pain. She splashes her face and gazes back at the mirror—it can't judge her now.

She heads for the food Pavilion. Inside the main lobby, a cobblestone fireplace splits the entrance to the dining hall. She glances at the coffee stand. *Damn, I need a coffee.* But if she lingers, Zach will surely be done eating without her. Besides, she can easily get one on the way out.

The main dining room is much brighter than the room preceding it. The ceiling stretches up another story.

She bumps into someone. Her heart jerks. "Fuck."

It's Howard. He moans.

"You scared me!" Blood rushes to her cheeks.

His breath smells like shit, filling her nostrils. He is still in his soaked tee-shirt and boxers. They cling to him. A sweet-sour smell wafts from him as a person walks by. He is wearing socks, but no shoes. Mud cakes the bottom of his feet and seeps up between his toes.

"You should probably go get back in bed, get changed, something," says Victoria, glancing around the room at the eyes gathering on her. She walks away from him, scanning the bustling dining room for Zach. He is sitting at a back table beside a set of exit doors. She loads a tray with pancakes, a Danish pastry, chocolate milk, and an orange juice. She skips the cheap coffee, pays for the food, and sways through the people and chairs, sucking down her orange juice, then joins Zach, sitting down opposite him. She picks up the Danish, asking,

"Where is the slut, anyway?"

The dining room falls silent—the scraping of silverware, clinking of cups, and muffled conversation ceases instantly.

Zach's face goes blank, staring past Victoria at something behind her. It sounds like someone is pouring a jug of water onto the floor, right behind her. She drops the Danish. Zach clenches the fork in his hand. The smell of urine taints the air. A chill trickles down Victoria's spine. She looks back over her shoulder.

Howard stands hunched like a gorilla behind her. His skin glistens with sweat. Urine drips from his boxers. Zach jolts up from his seat. The chair screeches against the tile floor. Howard's hands tighten into fists. He charges, knocks Victoria to the floor, and throws the table from his path.

Zach pivots, shifting all his weight to run in the opposite direction, for an exit. He makes it to a set of doors and grabs hold of the doorknob. Sweat gathers in his palms, lubricating his grip, and his fingers slip.

The room erupts with panic.

He squeezes harder and forces the knob to turn. The door gives, swinging open. A sigh of relief is greeted with a breeze from the mountains. One deep inhale will be enough to push him forward—escaping. He steps onto the porch outside and takes in a breath, about to step off.

Something grabs his ankle, yanking it out from under him.

He falls. His head hits the floor and everything goes black. The veins in his head throb against the floorboards. He squints through the pain, then closes his eyes.

Howard bites into Zach's heel.

Zach screams with the vomit-inducing pain. Breakfast pushes up his esophagus.

Victoria heaves the table off her legs and scrambles to her feet. Pieces of pancake smear into the bottom of her sneakers. She slips on the hard floor and falls. Her nose smashes against the carpet. Blood leaks from her nostrils as she regains focus on Zach.

His screams fill the entire campground. Howard is crouched over him, tearing into his ankle with his teeth. Blood drains into a puddle on the floor.

Victoria pushes herself up to all fours, lunging for Howard. Her stomach smacks the floor as she falls, but her hand has reached around his ankle. She pulls, yanking him, attempting to free Zach from his torment. Her fake nails crack and rip the real ones beneath. Howard stops resisting her and turns, facing her. His cheeks are smeared with blood, drool drips from the corner of his mouth, and snot pools on his upper lip. He comes at her. She only has enough time to close her eyes. A flood of pain pushes against her sinuses. His weight pins her to the floor. Her eyes shoot open, meeting his.

They are dry, red, and glazed over. There is nothing there, nothing behind them—no awareness, no light. They are right there in her face, staring at her. His cold nose presses against her cheek as his teeth dig into the cartilage of her nose. The smell of shit fills her lungs with each of his breaths.

Warm blood streams from her nose toward her eyes. Howard's teeth dig harder and deeper into her nasal cavity. She kicks her legs to budge him, but inferior strength keeps her in place. She bucks her legs with everything she has got.

Howard doesn't budge. His jaws chomp at her nose and a crack-pop noise precedes excruciating pain. His sweaty forehead lifts off hers. Sweat beaded on his skin, trickles down his temples. He chomps back down on her face.

Her head throbs. Blood drips into her eyes. A jolting stream of pressure and pulsating pain thrust down on her eyes. She tries to open them, but can't. She tries again and again. She can't see anything but an abyss of darkness. She feels the rapid breathing of Howard's chest pinned against hers.

Her body craves the tears that she can no longer shed. Numbness penetrates her neurons as she lay still and quiet in the darkness.

Spilled Blood

Zach opens his eyes. He is laying on the wooden deck outside of the dining room. The sound of an animal snarling, takes his attention towards his feet. He rolls onto his back, pushing to sit up. A sharp pain shoots through his head. He rubs his jaw. Adrenaline dulls the throat-clenching pain coming from his ankle. He bears the agony and sits all the way up. His foot is soaked in a puddle of blood. The flesh of his ankle is torn and ragged.

A blurred silhouette moves in the background. It crisps into Howard, whose sweat-stained clothes are also covered in blood. He had turned all his attention from his mangled foot below him to Zach. His mouth opens and chunks of flesh and blood drain out into the puddle.

Jesus. Zach scoots backwards.

Howard crawls after him.

A gunshot rips through the air.

Blood splatters across Zach's face as Howard's head falls facedown against the side of Zach's shoe. Howard's blood spills out, seeping into Zach's wound.

THE SUITCASE

ELIZABETH COULDN'T STOP THINKING ABOUT ZACH. SHE left him with Howard and Victoria, out of all people. But it was definitely nice not having Howard in the car. She drove half the night as Jan and Alex slept. Orange lights draped across distant houses, framing the landscape. Not every house was lit with decorations, but she appreciated each one that was. Halloween was finished in an autumn breeze.

By the time they make it back to Ian's dad's beach house, it is late the next morning. The orange lights have dwindled into grey skies.

Elizabeth parks, practically falling out of the car, lugging her feet up the porch stairs. Her fingers drift over a strand of lights wrapping the porch stair rail. She hadn't noticed them the other night. Exhaustion has engulfed her and she only makes it to the living room before crashing onto the sofa.

Jan hurls her purse to the floor and heads for the bathroom. The rat-tat-tat of the shower fills the house by the time Alex locks the front door.

"So are you going to the party with us?" He shouts from the kitchen as the microwave radiates popcorn.

Elizabeth is too tired, too drained to do anything. She settles farther into the couch and flicks on the television.

"In other news, Yosemite National Park Rangers are still searching for the bear that fatally wounded several park visitors and staff this weekend ...."

Alex flicks off the news from the kitchen with the remote. Video 01's blue screen replaces the newscaster's face.

Wounded visitors?

"What's wrong with you?" Alex says, nudging Elizabeth as he sits down. The microwave beeps. He jumps up, hurrying back into the kitchen.

Jan enters the living room wearing red fishnet stockings and a slutty nurse's costume. The bruise on her cheek is covered with an inch of foundation. Red lipstick does a perfect job of hiding her swollen lip.

A movie kicks on and instrumental music begins with a trombone or something. I know that music anywhere. It is the iconic horror flick: *The Shining*. The film starts with a yellow Volkswagen Beetle winding through the forest, way out in the middle of nowhere Colorado—even though it was really filmed in Glacier National Park, Montana. The movie was released in 1980, but it is a classic. Elizabeth never rewatches it. It is too freakin' scary. The exterior film clips for the Overlook Hotel were filmed at Timberline Lodge up on Mount Hood in Oregon. That movie has ruined every ski trip since Elizabeth can remember.

The woodstove crackles. The beach house windows warn of an approaching storm. Jan sits down beside Elizabeth, taking Alex's spot. She hands her the prescription bottle of Percocet. The hem of Jan's dress drifts up her thighs, exposing the red tulle lining beneath.

"Do you want to talk about it now?" Elizabeth asks, rolling the bottle in her hand.

"Talk about what? There's nothing to talk about." She forces a smile as Alex walks over, joining them. He places a bowl of popcorn and a six-pack of energy drinks on the coffee table. Jan cracks open two bottles and offers one to Elizabeth.

Alex sits down beside Jan. His fingers brush her cheek and gently turn her face toward him.

"The news just said people died at Yosemite. You guys don't find that strange?" Elizabeth says.

Alex gently kisses Jan. His cotton shirt presses against the white vinyl buttons of her nurse outfit.

Elizabeth fumbles for her phone, slides from the couch, sets the beer on the table, and heads for the bathroom, scanning her contact list for Zach's number. She doesn't have it. She never needed it. Dominic always called him. Alex has to have it. She opens the bathroom door.

Alex's lips press against Jan so deeply that the passion almost touches Elizabeth's own. She pulls back from him for a breath. He kisses her neck. His fingers follow the curve of her collar to the top button of her nurse outfit, tearing it open to a red lace bra.

Elizabeth closes the door to the bathroom. Her heart pounds. She puts the toilet seat down and rests her head in her hands. She is so tired. She just wants to sleep. That's all—just sleep. She slides her fingers down the edge of the light switch, flicking it off. Darkness engulfs the room. Flashes of Zach's naked, tight chest push through her thoughts. Then they fade into Dominic's bare ass pushing himself onto that slut. And she has never wanted sleep more.

Ill Intentions

THE WIND HOWLS AGAINST THE WINDOWS. THERE IS NO telling what time it is when Elizabeth snuck out of the bathroom for bed. Clouds have blocked out the sky, concealing the time, but it is no longer night. The ocean waves pound against the coastline, overpowering the sound of a car pulling down the pebbled driveway out front.

Elizabeth slides from the king bed. Pictures of Alex's stepmom stare at her from the dresser. It is her jogging outfit and clean underwear Elizabeth has borrowed to sleep in. Elizabeth's reflection judges her from across the room. She tugs at one of her dreadlocks. Jan finished twisting them in the car. They look nice, Elizabeth supposes. It will take some getting used to. She still doesn't recognize the reflection in the mirror. *What happened to you?* She has lost her parents. She has lost so much of what her future was supposed to be.

Keys rattle in the front door.

She heads down the hallway for the front door, passing several photographs—all staged, not one genuine. People with money don't have to capture memories like the rest of us.

Alex stumbles into the house with a bag full of Dungeness crabs.

Elizabeth turns on the television, hoping to catch something more of the bear attack at Yosemite, before offering any help. She glances down at the fresh gauze wrapped around her wrist. *It's not like I'll actually be of any help.*

Jan doesn't come in behind him.

Where is she? Elizabeth peeks out the door. Just as "where" leaves her lips, the passenger door opens.

Jan steps out.

Elizabeth yells back into the house at Ian, "So how was the party?"

"Dude it was awesome ..." Alex continues talking, but Elizabeth is not listening.

"Is she feeling all right?" she asks him.

"Not really," Jan says, entering with her arms wrapped around her stomach, hurrying by. "I'm going to bed."

"Hangover?" Alex shrugs his shoulders and offers no other explanation.

Television commercials switch back to the local news.

Alex grunts in detest and storms toward the news-box, turning it off. "Turn this crap off. I swear it's playing more than commercials. I can't even get on the internet. And when I do, it's nothing but end-of-the-world bullshit everywhere."

Elizabeth is not really listening. Alex will eventually tell her all about what he is bitching about later, there is no doubt about that.

Jan heads down the hallway, turning into Alex's room. If it is a hangover, she won't want company or noise.

Alex flicks the television off. "You know, my Dad's getting a divorce ..."

A violent cough bellows from the bedroom.

"So feel free to keep any of the clothes." His eyes freely follow Elizabeth's curves, as they have always done since the day they met. Somehow, Elizabeth had never noticed it before. "Maybe now that you're single, my Dad's almost single ..."

Elizabeth laughs. *Ewww. Gross.* She grabs a throw pillow and whacks Alex in the face with it.

He laughs in a way that could get them both in trouble.

"I'm going for a jog," Elizabeth says, grabbing her cellphone and a pair of headphones off the coffee table. Any jacket would only feel like a wet comforter ten minutes into it, so she braves the cold wind in borrowed clothes.

Evergreen treetops line a deep grey sky. A 90s song deafens any natural noise from getting in. The pebbled driveway pounds beneath her sneakers as she walks into a jog. Fog rolls through the mountains, over wind-broken branches lining the distant rolling cliffs. She stops to watch the clouds overtake the mountain. It is so easy to lose yourself. Drops of rain sprinkle in. Elizabeth has lost so much of herself. She heads back to the beach house, because there is nothing else she can do.

A storm quickly sweeps in.

The orange Halloween lights are off when she returns. The smokestack reveals a kindling wood stove. The windows are dark. The pulsating beam of the lighthouse in the distance, grows slightly brighter. Elizabeth tugs the headphones from her ears and stands at the driveway's edge. Alex's car is gone. The pebbles crunch beneath her feet. She reaches the porch and slowly opens the door. Through the glass door, the interior is still. The door is unlocked.

The wind takes the first chance it gets to crack open the front door, shoving Elizabeth into the house. The kitchen is as dead as the buckets of crabs sitting in the sink. The woodstove crackles next to an empty couch. The hallway has darkened with the sun's descent and Alex's bedroom is pitch black. Elizabeth grabs a pair of jeans and a tee-shirt from the master bedroom. On the way to the bathroom she stops across from Alex's room, takes a deep breath, and steps inside.

"Hey, Jan, how are you feel—" She bumps into something and falls backwards into the hallway, losing the clothing in her hand.

Enough light flows through the bedroom door to reveal a female outline standing a foot before her.

Elizabeth gathers the clothes that have fallen from her hands. "What the hell? You scared the crap out of me!"

Jan stands in the dark, unmoving. Something drips from her navy-blue nightgown. A thin layer of cold air funnels the smell of vomit out of the room.

Elizabeth stands, taking a step back from Jan. "Why don't you get back in bed? I'm going to go hop in the shower."

Jan steps closer.

"Where's Alex?" Elizabeth steps backward, into the bathroom, shutting the door and turning the lock. She presses her back up against it. Adrenaline pulses through her veins. *Stop being stupid.* She eases away from the door, and turns on the shower, letting it run hot. The small room fills with steam, fogging her reflection over the sink. The smell of vomit intensifies. Elizabeth's shirt is wet, soaked with bile or whatever Jan has all over her. *Gross.* She undresses then wipes the condensation from the mirror. The reflection of her mother stares back at her. She doesn't scold Elizabeth for the disobedience of hairstyle, because she isn't really there. She will never be there.

The light beneath the door flickers and then darkens.

A faint scratching sound comes from the door, like an animal is clawing at it.

The mirror returns to a clouded picture. *This is crazy.* Elizabeth puts off any more thoughts and climbs into the shower. Warm water sprays out of the shower head, hissing off the tiled walls. It pulls the sadness and tears from her. They wash away into the drain, leaving her numb. She pulls the soap bar from the edge of the tub, foaming it in her palms. She closes her eyes. *It isn't fair.* She buries her face in the suds. *It isn't—*

Something crashes to the floor and shatters in Alex's room.

She pulls the shower curtain back, opening her eyes in flex. The soap burns. She swings her face back into the shower so fast, the shower curtain rips down. She fumbles to get out and opens the door, yelling, "Are you okay?"

Jan's face is right outside the door.

Elizabeth steps back, slipping in the puddle that has formed beneath her feet, tottering to regain balance.

The white of Jan's eyes has turned yellow with red, cracked veins. Her hollow pupils stare through Elizabeth as if she isn't really there. Her cheeks are flushed, accentuating the bruise on her cheekbone. The skin of her lips is dry and peeling. Her scalp bleeds in patchy sections, where small clumps of hair are missing.

Everything goes silent. Elizabeth's heart pounds.

Jan has a gash across the top of her foot. Chunks of pulled-out hair stick to the fresh blood oozing out onto the floor.

Elizabeth slams the bathroom door shut, forcing all her weight against it. She focuses on the doorknob lock. If Elizabeth eases off the door, she can lock it, but that will also leave her vulnerable to Jan pounding her way in there. *Screw it.* Elizabeth drops her shoulders and bolsters one against the door, locking it. She slides down the door, sitting with her back against it. Steam from the continual hot shower begins to suffocate the room, while cold air rushes from under the door, chilling Elizabeth's wet, naked body. She forces herself to get up, to dry off quickly, fighting with her damp skin to pull on a shirt. Her dreadlocks drip, soaking into the shirt collar. Then she stuffs her damp legs into a pair of jeans.

The light beneath the door brightens as Jan's silhouette moves away.

What am I doing? This is crazy. She's my best friend. I bet it's just a joke. Elizabeth chuckles at how ridiculous it is to be cowering in the bathroom. She stands up, looking at the light seeping in through the bottom of the door.

Darkness returns. Jan has returned.

Elizabeth doesn't want to believe what her heart is already telling her. She turns off the shower to hear what's going on outside better. The shower tapers to a drip. Elizabeth sits on the closed toilet seat, watching the light dance beneath the door until it stops. The shadows disappear and the light returns again, revealing a puddle of water at Elizabeth's feet.

There is no way, no way I am going out there. What had been on the news that Alex changed so suddenly? Damn it. What am I doing locked in a bathroom? I must be going crazy. Poor Jan is sick as hell, bleeding, and I'm cowering in here. But what if I'm not going crazy and—

Elizabeth forces herself to lose concentration.

Please, let me be crazy.

She grabs the toilet bowl brush and flings open the door. Her toes slide through the puddle on the floor. If she is fast enough, she can make it down the hallway, to the living room, and then around the corner to the front door. It feels miles away. She pushes all her momentum out of the bathroom. Her wet feet slip in the hallway and she falls, skidding to the edge of the living room.

Something moves on the right, in the corner of her eye.

She clenches her jaw, bearing down on the new bruises she is sure to have. She fights the delusions of fear, and reminds herself that *it's only Jan*. She rolls onto her back, trying to calm her nerves.

Jan stands up from the couch like a choked chicken, somehow walking toward Elizabeth. Her skin droops. Blood streaks behind her foot. Her diaphragm expands like a balloon with each breath.

Elizabeth scrambles to her feet. Jan charges from the right and crashes into Elizabeth's shoulder, knocking her to the floor. Elizabeth rolls onto her stomach and into a pushup position. *If I don't make it to the door, my life will be over.*

Jan grabs Elizabeth's ankle. Her nails dig into Elizabeth's skin. Elizabeth's arms buckle and she falls flat to the floor, stunned by the pain. The only way out is to roll, twisting Jan's grip from her ankle. With a rush of adrenaline, Elizabeth kicks Jan in the face and sprints toward the front door. She grabs its doorknob, but it is locked. She glances back at her friend.

Jan has pulled herself off the floor.

Elizabeth unlocks the doorknob and shoves her shoulder against the glass. It doesn't budge. She forgot the deadbolt.

Jan is coming.

Elizabeth unlocks the deadbolt and shoves the door open. A cold wind blows against her face. It tugs the warmth of the house out into the frigid air, enticing Elizabeth to stay. It would be so easy to give up. She springs from the porch. Her bare feet dig into the ice cold pebbles of the driveway. The trees blur into a tunnel as she sprints from the house. Every step she takes mirrors the pounding of her heart. Her feet touch asphalt, pushing her farther—faster—away from the house. Her leg muscles burn. Her heart aches, pounding out the distant roar of the ocean.

She eases into a walk and the cold of the road stabs through her feet. She pauses, resting her hands against bent knees, contemplating the thick fog rolling in around her. Fear and a suffocating sense of blindness engulfs her.

Two soft beeps break the rhythm of her heartbeat. She scrambles for the phone in her pocket. *Another sound will give away my location.*

It is a message from Hazel.

Elizabeth searches the dense vapor looking for a sign of Jan, but the constant roar of the ocean deafens all possibilities of a warning. The ocean wind attempts to tear the phone from Elizabeth's fingers.

The text reads: *Heading to the airport now. Pick me up at 11pm—Newport.*

Something is coming.

Visibility has faded to a three-foot radius and that is not far enough to see anything. Elizabeth's heart pounds, forcing her to jog into a sprint. The noise comes closer. Dim headlights appear in the distance, growing brighter with approach. She moves to the shoulder of the road. The vehicle screeches to a halt.

New Mexico

DESSERT STRETCHES AS FAR AS HAZEL CAN SEE. SHE has left Elizabeth with friends so she can close this huge career-changing deal, but now hurries to catch an earlier flight home.

The light brown landscape of New Mexico is gorgeous. It makes the blue Native American bird logo stand out at the airport in Albuquerque. The sky rumbles with jets as Hazel's limousine speeds towards *Departures*. Once there, the driver slams the vehicle into park and jumps out, retrieving Hazel's one small carry-on suitcase.

Hazel scoots from the backseat, catching her reflection in the rearview mirror. Her northwestern skin is sun-beaten from the foreign climate of New Mexico, despite hours of synthetic tanning. A tired and forced smile is the only tip she gives the driver when retrieving her luggage from him. The kiosk attendant receives a similar smile. Hazel could have taken a later flight, but that meant another night away from home—from her sister.

The only problem that occurs is between airport security and Hazel's mascara, which is now at the bottom of a trash can. The terminal is calm for a Sunday afternoon. As Hazel is rounding the bend to the terminal checkpoint, one of the suitcase wheels brakes off. She stops in front of a small gift shop located in Concourse A to stow the broken wheel.

There is still time to pick up snacks, so she fills her arms with chocolate and magazines, then spills them out onto the checkout counter. She watches the people marching through the terminal as an old woman rings up the items. A line of people grows behind Hazel. Boarding time approaches. The diversity of culture and age is something she loves about traveling.

A newspaper at the back of the line grabs her attention. It reads: YOSEMITE OUTBREAK, ALL QUARANTINED.

Hazel practically yells back at the cashier, "Can you add that paper?"

"I need to scan it," says the woman.

Hazel glances back at the line and the man standing beside the paper. His pudgy face is red with impatience, ripening against a bright yellow sweater vest.

"Hey. You, dude, in the back." She musters her biggest smile. His beady little eyes meet hers. "Yeah, you, can you pass me one of those?"

"I don't see why people buy this crap." The man grabs the paper and tosses it forward.

Hazel continues to smile with a, "Thank you."

The cashier takes her time scanning the paper. Why wouldn't she? She has no place to go.

Hazel bends over, stuffing the chocolate and media in her purse. The aroma of coffee lures her farther down the terminal, away from her gate. She finds a coffee shop and is second in line when a male attendant announces the boarding of her flight. She will make it—she has to—but there is no way she is going to get on that plane without a decent cup of coffee.

The same man returns to the intercom as she grabs the cardboard cup radiating with heat. "This is the final boarding call for Hazel Hutchings, flight 1801 to Portland, Oregon …."

Hot coffee spills as Hazel sprints to Gate B8.

The intercom attendant walks away from the gate's podium, heading for the passenger boarding bridge.

"Wait!" Hazel yells.

The man, likely a distant cousin of her limousine driver, turns around. He looks annoyed until noticing her $100 blouse dripping with coffee. Amused, he takes her boarding pass, glancing back at the computer podium and then at the tunnel, contemplating scanning her into the system.

There is nothing she can say that will win him over. There isn't enough time to play games.

"Hurry," he says, waving for her to follow him into the passenger loading bridge, speed-walking to the aircraft door.

A flight attendant paces there. Her hair is a deep, Irish red. Her skin is covered in faint freckles.

The man leans in, whispering to the flight attendant, "You guys better push off—fast—before they ground you too."

"Attention!" The intercom announces over the terminal speakers, faintly echoing down the corridor. "All flights within the United States have been canceled. Please see the closest kiosk for further …."

The flight attendant grabs Hazel's arm, forcing her into the aircraft. More coffee spills on Hazel's blouse. The door slides shut behind them. Every seat in first class is taken. *Mr. Pierson's such a dick. The least he could have done was spring for first class.* The plane begins to roll out onto the runway. The motion jerks Hazel back and forth. She grabs onto the last First Class seat before the main cabin. The man with the yellow vest smirks in his smugness as she walks by.

"Please stow all electronic devices and fasten your seatbelts."

Hazel finds her seat. The half-empty plane gives her the choice of any seat she wants, so she takes a whole row to herself toward the back. The airplane rattles down the runway and the flight attendants complete their safety spiel in record time.

Hazel fumbles to withdraw a small present wrapped in silver paper from her suitcase before stowing it above. Exhaustion blurs Hazel's focus as she exchanges the box for the cellphone in her purse. There is still no reply from Elizabeth.

The cabin lights dim and the jet engines propel the aircraft into an evening sky. Hazel sinks into the cushions until her body is parallel to the earth again. The "fasten seatbelt" sign turns off.

"You are now allowed to move about the cabin," the captain announces.

In an instant, the man in the yellow vest enters the main cabin and sprints to the back bathroom, slamming the door shut behind him. Apparently designated bathrooms only apply to the less wealthy.

A chill seeps in from the constant rush of air outside the airplane and trickles up Hazel's spine. The horizon darkens. Clear skies cloud. The cabin's light reflects against the window, hiding the beauty of the earth below.

The windowpane captures the reflection of the redheaded flight attendant in the aisle behind Hazel. "Would you like a pair of headphones for the movie?" she says.

"No thank you." Hazel doesn't bother turning around to face her. The woman had manhandled, her for crying out loud.

"Well, how about I leave a pair here? If you don't use them by the time the movie starts, I'll pick them back up."

Hazel waits for her to leave. She tilts her head back just enough for a sip of coffee, and the damn plane hits an air pocket.

Lukewarm liquid splashes up her nostrils.

A hand grabs the edge of the aisle seat. The chubby-faced man, stuffed in his yellow vest, gazes at the floor as he ascends back to first class.

Light pollution reaches for the airplane windows from a large city below. The cabin dims as the movie starts.

The flight attendant returns, taking the headphones from the cushion. "I would like to apologize to you."

About damn time. Hazel faces her.

The woman restrains further conversation by chewing on her bottom lip, and sits down in the aisle seat where the headphones had been. Her hands nuzzle between her chattering knees.

Hazel crosses her arms. There is no excuse for her mistreatment.

The attendant slides into the middle seat. Her name tag identifies her as *Shirley*.

Hazel leans back against the cold wall of the airplane.

"I live in Seattle ... I have a family and kids and ... there is something going on they're not telling us," says Shirley. Her eyes are swollen with tears.

Hazel's shoulders droop, filling with empathy.

"I'm sorry. I would never, ever treat someone like that. I would never grab a person by the arm. Really, I'm a patient person. I'm so sorry. But I have to get home to my kids."

"You're freaking me out," says Hazel.

"I know. I'm sorry. I am really sorry." Shirley sniffles while excusing herself.

"Wait," says Hazel, grabbing her arm. The yellow-vested man sprints by for the rear restroom again. "Can you tell me what's going on?"

"I can't." Shirley keeps her eyes on the man passing.

"What if I forget the whole incident?" Hazel says.

Shirley takes a deep breath and wipes her nose with her sleeve before sitting back down. "I haven't heard anything official, but over the past few hours a lot of rumors have been spreading. There have been several flu outbreaks and some violent attacks in Yosemite. A few Internet videos were posted an hour ago." Her entire face changes and she searches the cabin for eavesdroppers. "Once they ground a flight, no one knows when they'll lift air restrictions. When I heard that announcement, I panicked."

"So what happens when we get to Portland? I have a connecting flight to Newport."

"It all depends on the FAA's decision. The captain is the only one who has direct contact with the control tower, so we won't know until we get closer to landing... Excuse me." She shoots to a stand in the aisle, following a shirtless man who has stopped only a few rows ahead. She places a hand on his shoulder. "Sir, you need to put your clothes back on."

The man's body sways as he pivots to face her. It is the same asshole from earlier, but now without his yellow vest, or any shirt for that matter. His complexion is drained and his eyes are swollen. The hair on his chest clings to his skin with dripping sweat. His belt hangs loose, unbuckled around his soaked boxers. He leans forward, vomiting all over the floor and Shirley's shoes.

She screams. Chunks of undigested food and bile soak through her stockings.

He slowly lifts his head, unable to concentrate on the redhead now running away from him, for the back bathroom.

Hazel cups her own mouth, restraining the reflex to barf, grateful for the trace smell of spilled coffee that lingers on her blouse cuff.

The flight attendant from First Class rushes down the aisle behind him with several small barf bags and napkins. "Sir, please move to the back of the airplane and find a seat."

He lumbers toward Hazel, bringing the smell of vomit closer. Every effort to hold her breath fails. The smell gets stuck in her throat, gagging her. She wants to cringe away, but she can't take her eyes off of him.

Shirley exits the back bathroom to find the shirtless man standing an inch from her face. She shimmies out of the way as he pushes past her into the restroom. She pulls the door closed behind him.

Hazel slides back down in her seat, forcing her attention on the window. *They should lock him in there*. The minuscule city lights flow into a sea of darkness beneath the airplane. The stir of conversations fade to occasional whispers once again. She rests her cheek against her hand. The wind sailing over the plane's metal wings guide her to sleep.

A Ride Home

As Hazel's airplane heads home, thick fog wraps around Elizabeth's body, dissipating into the warm glow of headlights on the Oregon Coast. Elizabeth moves off the road to the foliage. A white Prius emerges, stopping beside her.

Alex's forehead wrinkles from behind the steering wheel. The passenger window automatically draws down. He yells, "What are you doing jogging in the middle of the road?"

Elizabeth has no words.

"Well, come on, get in. I can't believe you're still jogging out here ...." He chuckles until she opens the door.

She searches the blanket of fog for Jan one last time before sliding into the passenger seat.

"Why in the world are you barefoot?" he says, staring down at her feet.

She gets in, not daring to make eye-contact with him, staring at the dashboard. *What the hell am I going to tell him?*

"Hey, are you okay?" He places a hand on her shoulder.

She jumps, slowly looking at him. His eyes survey the car windows wrapped in clouds before meeting hers. Elizabeth blurts, "There's something wrong with Jan. She's ... not acting right. She attacked me—tried to bite me ...."

His eyes lock on hers, bringing nothing but silence. Then he lets out a hard laugh. "Has Zach been filling your head with stories?" His laugh tapers off and he shifts the car into drive. "I think you need to get more sunshine."

She sinks into the passenger seat even more. It is true. The lack of sun during the winter does have an effect on people. If you can't make the change to dark skies for nine months out of the year, it will drag you down into an abyss of depression.

Warm air glides from the heater vent across Elizabeth's cheek. The cold glass window fogs as she leans her head against its pane. Alex is probably right. *There's a good explanation. Jan's probably just sick. Or I'm sick.*

"So, I think I'll take Jan to the doctor when we get back. Make sure it's not that virus I read about." Alex tightens his grip on the steering wheel.

"What virus?" Elizabeth sits up.

"I don't remember. Some outbreak at the park a while back …." He slows the car.

Law enforcement vehicles are parked on the neighbor's lawn up ahead. The faint sound of an ambulance siren blares in the distance, crescendoing, approaching.

Alex's place is two driveways down on the left. A sheriff blocks the north lane, directing them to the left, farther from the crime scene. But his attention isn't on them or even the road. They are the only car.

Elizabeth slumps in the seat. She doesn't know or remember why Hazel rushed her from the hospital, but she knew it wasn't authorized. Elizabeth pulls her feet back from the floor heater and turns away from the sheriff, concealing any possibility of identifying her. She follows the sheriff's gaze to the neighbor's front lawn, walled off with yellow caution tape. Something lays on the ground. *A body?*

The sheriff pats the roof of the car, coaxing them to continue past.

Is that a kid? Elizabeth turns the thought away.

Alex inches by, pulling into the beach house driveway not far up the road. The front door to the house is ajar.

Elizabeth's heart sinks.

"You didn't close the door when you left?" Alex grips the steering wheel, shifting his weight, and speeds down the driveway. Pebbles clunk beneath the car's frame.

"What do you not understand about—I was running from her?" Elizabeth gestures to her scratched and frozen feet, caked and smeared with mud.

"We need to get her to the hospital. You wait here and I'll go get her." He gets out of the car and walks toward the still house.

Elizabeth locks the car doors behind him.

He glances back at the noise and shakes his head with laughter, like she is being ridiculous. He enters the house, closing the front door behind him. One window after another fills with interior light. Smoke rises from the chimney. The moon takes its place overhead.

Elizabeth takes out her cellphone, slowly pressing 9-1-1. Her thumb hovers over the *SEND* button.

A faint owl's hoot jolts the phone from her hand and it crashes down upon her frozen foot.

Ouch. She searches the visible tree line, but it is empty.

"What's your emergency?" says a female dispatcher, muffled on the car floor.

Elizabeth bends over to retrieve the phone and bangs her head against the glove box. "Ouch!"

Alex appears at the glass door wearing his surfer outfit and waves her in. Apparently they won't be going to the hospital.

"Hello?" says the dispatcher.

What am I going to say? Elizabeth grabs the phone and hangs up in a panic. She hurries for the house. The cold pebbles feel like coals freeze-burning the bottoms of her feet. The pain eases as she climbs the porch steps and hurries inside, locking the door behind her. She yells down the foyer hallway at Alex, "Did you find her?"

Elizabeth's phone rings.

She answers, but before she can say, "Hello," the dispatcher beats her to it.

"Hello," the woman says. "I received an emergency call from this number—"

"Oh, I'm sorry. I hit the wrong number." Elizabeth hangs up. Her heart pounds, thinking of the sheriff down the street—the house—the body.

"No. I haven't found her." Alex moves back to the living room. "But why does my sofa smell like piss? And there's blood on the floor."

"She cut her foot," Elizabeth says.

The cushion where Jan had sat, waiting for Elizabeth to get out of the shower, is soaked. Goosebumps crawl over her skin, as if Jan is standing there, dripping with vomit. The smell of urine pervades the room, burning Elizabeth's nostrils. Her toes are numb. Fatigue washes over her. Sleep beckons. "I think I need to lie down."

Her fingers find the edge of the hallway, guiding her to the master bedroom. The pictures of Alex's stepmom are almost comforting. A grunt escapes her lips as she throws herself onto the bed. She notices the closet door is open a crack. Its contents are completely dark. *She could be in there.* Elizabeth's chest beats against the mattress, blocking out any other noise. *What if she's in there?* No sleep is worth dying for. Elizabeth forces herself off the bed and moves toward the closet, sure her veins will burst from the pounding of her heart. *She wouldn't really kill me, would she?* She shoves the door open. It bangs against the wall and ricochets back toward her. She catches it with her palm.

The closet contains only clothes.

Relief doesn't replace the nausea pitted in Elizabeth's stomach. She slips into a pair of jeans and a long-sleeved shirt that hangs off one shoulder. So much for keeping her warm. It doesn't matter. She sits on the closet floor and pulls the knee-high boots back on. Heat slowly returns between her toes.

She looks up at the closet light—to the polished redwood box sticking out over the top shelf. Then peeks over her shoulder at the bedroom door. There is no noise, no hint of where Alex is hiding. She gets up on tip-toe, stretching to inch the box off the shelf. It falls into her grasp. The tips of her fingers follow the curves of the waterfall running into the word: Awanata. *It's the same girl from Yosemite's story.* She opens it.

Deep brown buffalo fur lay folded inside. Elizabeth's hand quivers as she pulls back the first piece of fur. Inside is an eleven-inch white bone dagger. Four inches make up the hilt which is etched with a red tribal design. The remaining seven inches is the blade. The tribal design flows onto the blade forming a full moon at the tip, a howling coyote beneath it, followed by the word 'Pyhij' that weaves into the hilt's design.

Elizabeth carefully takes the dagger and slides it down the inside of her boot. She is sure the pounding of her heart will give her away. Alex will storm into the closet calling her crazy for anticipating anything out of the ordinary. And maybe she is crazy. But the house stays quiet. She locks the bedroom door, collapses onto the bed, and grabs her cellphone to call Jan.

A faint ring lets out through her phone's speaker. It echoes out from across the hallway.

TURBULENCE

MILES AWAY, COLD AIR BLASTS FROM A TINY VENT ABOVE Hazel. Dreams flow in and out with the airplane turbulence. The seat jolts beneath her, ripping her out of slumber. The seatbelt-sign illuminates with a bing. The only other sound is the faint gush of wind outside the aircraft. She sits up and repositions the vents above. The cold night's air seeps through the plane, filling the cabin.

Redheaded Shirley and the First Class flight attendant stand at the partition between first class and the main cabin. Their whispers stop. They simultaneously glance past Hazel to the rear of the aircraft.

"Hey, folks, this is your captain speaking. We are due to arrive at Portland International Airport in twenty minutes. The approximate local time will be 9:50 pm. The weather is rainy. Temperature is fifty-five degrees. We ask that you stay in your seat, as we expect moderate turbulence as we make our descent." The intercom switches off and the cabin begins to stir with waking passengers. The naked man has disappeared from the back, but the rear restroom is occupied.

Hazel clenches her knees. The coffee from take-off has filtered through her and her bladder is about to explode. She grabs the straps of her handbag and rushes toward the first class restroom.

Shirley greets her with a smile and waves to the other attendant to stand-down. The first class attendant keeps her mouth shut, but flares her nostrils in detest.

Hazel squeezes into the tiny bathroom, pulling down her stockings. The toilet seat drops out from beneath her thighs. Turbulence jerks her between the narrow walls of the room, causing a mess all over her stockings. *Great! Just great!* She supports herself against the walls and slides the leggings off, throwing them away. She reaches for the door's latch, but the plane jerks and she falls backwards.

A female screams outside the door.

Grunts of agony follow.

"Let me in," Shirley yells, pounding against the door.

Hazel turns the light switch off to stop the deafening roar of the bathroom vent. She rubs her temples waiting for another sound—something to indicate that it is safe to unlock the door.

Shirley screams again. Then there is a thud outside. The sounds are all muffled.

The aircraft begins its descent. Hazel falls backwards onto the toilet and braces her hands against the walls. The plane wheels skid to a stop. The landing throws her around like a rag doll. The weight of her body jerks forward and her head whacks the edge of the sink. Something in her nose cracks. A bump forms on her forehead. Pain shoots through her sinuses. Gritting her teeth doesn't ease the ache. Warm blood drips from her nostrils. The dark bathroom sways—or she sways, it is hard to tell. She wipes the blood from her lip, smearing it onto her cheek. The cabin is silent. She searches the floor for her purse. Her hand finds it, knocking the contents all over the place. She tries to blindly scoop them back in. Her fingers brush the soft cotton handkerchief left by the blue-eyed agent at the hospital. She presses it to her face.

"What the ...?" a male voice yells from the other side of the door, as if just exiting the pilot's cockpit.

A pair of feet stampede from the rear of the aircraft toward the voice.

Hazel holds her breath as he passes.

"Help! Ron, help me! Open the goddamn door!" The man says, pounding against the cockpit door. His screams overtake his words.

Hazel hugs her legs into a ball. Whatever it is out there claws at the bathroom door. She is breathing too loud. The scraping intensifies. Her lungs collapse with each breath, as if the air seeping through the doorway has thickened.

The rapid fire of a silencer gun fills the cabin. Two kicks to the bathroom door break its lock. Artificial light floods in. Hazel's fingers tighten around the handkerchief pressed to her nostrils. She struggles to keep her eyes open, but it is too damn bright.

A male figure stands in the doorway. The son-of-a-bitch is wearing a black military uniform bearing the Meadowlark symbol in orange. He is armed and aims straight at her head. His face is shielded by a tactical mask. He says to another, "What should we do with this one?"

A female agent appears beside him. Her dark brown eyes are anything but inviting. Each strand of her hair is perfectly molded to her head and wrapped into a bun at the back. She says, "No loose ends."

The man takes the shot.

The room spins. Hazel becomes nauseous. Her forehead and sinuses throb. The room blurs. The handkerchief falls from her grip. Her head rests on the wall beside her.

The man lowers the weapon. "Agent Jane, you need to see this."

The woman steps back into Hazel's blurred view.

The ringing in Hazel's head echoes. The blurred figures become clear. She can see the body of the shirtless man. Blood pools beneath his cheek outside the bathroom. Empty eyes capture Hazel's reflection in the abyss of his stare. Beads of perspiration bead on his loose skin, which is stained with a blood-red handprint that slides down his neck. His silhouette fades as the background lines flow into red hair, soaked in blood. Shirley's torn and mangled body lays behind him.

The male agent reaches for a second pistol holstered in his duty belt and hands it to Agent Jane. A red laser beam floats across the floor from its scope.

Hazel closes her eyes. The ringing in her ears is replaced by the pounding of her heart. She thinks of her sister, *Elizabeth*. An abyss of darkness draws around her as the light fades into nothing.

Nowhere To Run

A DOG BARKS IN THE DISTANCE, STIRRING THE TRANQUIL night. Moonlight glistens on the withering leaves outside. Elizabeth rubs her eyes and jolts to a sitting position. *Crap, what time is it?* Her head pounds. She grabs the phone lying beside her: 10:13. No messages.

She slouches back into the bed pillows. Maybe it had all been a dream. She looks down at the knee-high boots weighting against her feet and the shirt hanging off one shoulder—clothes she would never choose.

The dog in the distance yelps and the night becomes peaceful.

Two eyes glow in a conifer tree outside the window. The Great Grey Owl stares at Elizabeth. Its feathers blend into the dark sky, rustled by cold air. It sits still.

Blood pounds though Elizabeth's heart. She clenches the phone in her hand and slides from the mattress. The fog has lifted enough to see the treeline. She presses her nose to the cold windowpane and whispers, "What do you want?"

The glass fogs beneath her lips. The stitches running down her wrist throb with each heartbeat. She takes her eyes off the owl, focusing on the moonlight trickling over the line of stitches of her left wrist. She pulls the sleeve of her shirt down and the collar falls farther off her shoulder.

Elizabeth glances back at the tree branch. It is empty. The house is quiet. Her stomach growls and she searches the circle of fog one last time. In the corner of the yard a silhouette stands in a cluster of trees. Elizabeth steps back, bumping into the bed. Whatever it is doesn't move for twenty minutes.

This is ridiculous. Elizabeth keeps an eye on the shadows and steps toward the window. Nothing changes. *So stupid.* She unlocks the bedroom door. The creak of its hinges echoes throughout the house. Alex's room is dark. The smell of vomit is obscured by a thick citrus scent. The bathroom door is closed and no light escapes it. The hallway tunnels to a moonlit living room. The wall of windows captures what lunar rays penetrate the layer of fog outside. The urine-soaked cushion is gone. Elizabeth sits down on the remaining portion of the couch and turns on the television. The screen fills with breaking news: scenes of hospitals, car accidents lining the streets, grocery store shelves empty and looted. She sinks into the cushion.

"While government officials claim there's no connection between the bear attacks this weekend at Yosemite National Park, zombie preppers insist the recent incidents are in fact proof of an outbreak. Fears grew today after an Oregon man attacked and killed his girlfriend at Curry Village this morning. Park officials state that Homeland Security has taken over the investigation.

"Skeptics believe the whole event is due to an unofficial 'Zombiefest' that was being held at the park. Visitors have reported several 'biting' incidents. Anyone who has been bitten should seek medical attention. As I stand here, they are preparing to close down the park. Back to you—"

"Alex!" Elizabeth yells down the hallway. The remote slips from her fingers. She scoots to the edge of the couch. "You're going to think I'm crazy, but you have got to see…"

She notices a thick fluorescent line drawn horizontally across the living room wall. She stands up from the couch. Something is wrong. She runs her fingers along the textured walls and follows the line around the room. The line digs into the plaster of the wall as it nears the first window frame.

A leaf falls to the ground outside.

The line continues over the glass of the window. Elizabeth squats down, level with the mark. Moonlight trickles through the trees and over the faint yellow line as she swipes it with her finger. It is damp—fresh. *Highlighter?* Her heart races. The line continues around the room and back to the edge of the hallway.

The alarm of her phone goes off.

Shit. It is time to pick up Hazel from the airport. She attempts to take the damn thing out of her pocket, but it catches on the seam. The alarm continues on. She frees the phone from her pocket and turns off the alarm. She scans her surroundings to see if she has awoken any monsters, but the bright light from the screen has rendered her temporarily blinded in the dark. She begins to slide the phone back into her jeans just as her vision starts to readjust. The night's details sharpen, but the end of the hallway remains pitch black.

The darkness shifts at its end.

Elizabeth freezes.

It moves closer. The flickering light of the television stretches down the hallway, unable to reach the shadow. It is Alex, inching his way toward the living room. Synthetic light curves over the muscles of his arms. His orange sweatpants make his skin appear drained and loose. His chin hangs down. His eyes should follow his chin, facing toward the ground, but they don't. His empty eyes stare down the hallway at her.

She sprints behind the couch and throws her phone at him. It ricochets off his torso, landing on the floor. It is no use. He rushes her. The cell phone cracks beneath his foot. She hesitates at the sound. His fingers catch a dreadlock, yanking her backwards to the floor, pinning himself on top of her. She pushes against the weight of his chest with her left hand. It trembles with weakness. His nails dig into her scalp as he pulls her head toward his teeth. She fumbles for the dagger with her right hand. *Damn it.* It is in her boot, but tucked beneath her jeans. She tries yanking the pant leg up, but it catches on her boot. She inhales, shoves Alex back with all her might, forces her pant leg up, yanks the dagger out, and jams the blade into his throat.

His hands wrap around her neck. His knuckles tighten, squeezing the walls of her esophagus. She grabs the dagger with both hands and with everything she has, pushes against it, forcing the blade deeper. Alex falls backwards. Elizabeth pushes it deeper, through to the back of his neck. He begins to choke on his blood. Her thumb slides over the etched bone hilt, smearing blood into the lines of its coyote design.

She rips the dagger out and climbs to her feet. Blood drips along the floor as she sprints for the front door. She passes the kitchen counter. *His keys.* Elizabeth stops, turns back and grabs them. Four steps more get her to the glass front door. She shoves it open and stumbles down the porch in a blur. Wet pebbles slide beneath her boots as she skids to a stop beside the Prius. It is locked. Alex has a key for everything on his stupid keychain. Elizabeth's heart aches to mourn Alex, but if she does, she will die. She concentrates on the three key possibilities before her. The first one slides easily into the keyhole. It begins to turn, then the metal jams. Perspiration gathers in Elizabeth's palms as she tries to yank it back out, glancing up at the house.

Alex stands behind the glass door, staring at her.

The ocean's wind seeps into Elizabeth's bones. She yanks harder, jiggling the key. "Come on!"

He disappears deeper into the house.

Sweat oozes through her pores, enticing the cold air. *Come on*. She tugs on the key.

The front door shatters. Alex has jumped through the glass and tumbles out.

Elizabeth wiggles the key and tugs harder. It frees. She falls backwards. The keys go flying. Her hip slams against the wet pebbled ground and her butt soaks. *The keys. Where'd they go?* Her fingers scramble over the pebbles for them, searching the shadow beneath the car. *It's useless, I'm going to die.* All she can think about is Hazel stranded at the airport. Her fingertips bump into the metal key ring. *Yes!*

She climbs to her feet and forces the second key into the door handle. It unlocks. Elizabeth exhales in relief, pulls it out, and gets in behind the steering wheel. The engine purrs. The vehicle's false sense of security fills her. She shifts the car into reverse and glimpses back up at the house. Broken glass covers the patio. *Where is he?* She leans out of the door to pull it closed.

Fingernails scrape across her arm.

Shit. She thrusts all her weight against the gas pedal. The engine revs, still in park. She jams the stick-shift into reverse and cuts the wheel right.

Alex is pitched to the ground.

She straightens the wheel and car, shifting into drive. The pebbled path is covered in darkness and fog until she turns on the headlights.

Alex's lifeless body lays facedown on the driveway in front of her.

Alex. Her heart aches. She grips the steering wheel and rests her forehead against it. Tears drain down her cheeks, expressing the loss she cannot speak. *This must be hell.* She glances up at the stitches lining her wrist. *What have I done? Have I died and this is my punishment? This is my hell.*

The headlights capture movement. Alex's body twitches. He stands. His fingers slick back his hair and dig into his scalp, yanking a clump out. It falls from his fingers to the pebbles below. Blood gushes from his throat.

Elizabeth closes her eyes and stomps on the gas pedal. The car tires spin, flinging stones, catching enough traction that the vehicle shoots forward. The driver's door swings shut. Elizabeth cannot see—cannot bear to unclench her eyelids to watch as the car runs over Alex. She can hear the impact and the sound of bones popping beneath the tires. Her heart dies. The car bumps into the air, thumping over his body. Elizabeth forces her eyes open. The tires hit asphalt. The rearview mirror is dark and empty. *I have killed him. I've killed my friend.*

WEATHERED SIGNS

FOG RUSHES OVER THE PRIUS AS IT WEAVES SOUTH along the dark coastal highway. A pop song blares from the radio. Elizabeth cranks it louder, drowning out any thoughts. They are too painful to listen to.

The dashboard glows a soft blue. Its clock turns 11:11. Music fades into a reverent male voice reporting, "Airport officials have not commented regarding Flight 1801's lockdown at PDX. The traffic surrounding this area is still bumper-to-bumper due to the immediate cancellation of all flights."

This can't be happening. Elizabeth finds herself speeding down the highway. Tree branches draw lines against the canvas of the night. Music on the radio returns. She leans just an inch to scan the radio stations and the steering wheel jerks. The car scrapes into a guardrail. Elizabeth swerves out of it, nearly careening over the opposite edge of the road into the ocean.

Once she regains focus and the car is back on track, she returns to search the radio. Channel after channel is nothing but songs and commercials. Neither of which are helpful at the moment.

Streetlights begin to illuminate the desolate road. A traffic light at the edge of town turns red and Elizabeth is forced to a stop.

A car packed with teenagers, likely her age, pulls up alongside her. A boy in the backseat slides his hand down the half-lowered window. His moan carries out. Elizabeth's heart skips at the sight of their dark, wide eyes. The streetlight fades green. He cranks the window down and reaches out toward her. Laughter fills their vehicle and they pull away, leaving her feeling stupid. *Stupid kids.*

Stoplights slow the traffic through the coastal town of Newport. Each light has its own homeless beggar. A scruffy man on the nearest corner walks up to the Prius' passenger window. His tattered clothes slosh against the glass.

Elizabeth keeps her eyes forward. She doesn't know how she feels about them. Some days she hands them money, others she avoids them like the plague. It is always a constant battle between empathy and disgust. And tonight, it is her least concern.

The beggar's palm hits the window, smearing mud down its glass pane. The writing on his cardboard sign drips with rain.

Elizabeth's empathy pulls at her and she cracks the window. "I don't have any money!"

Warm air seeps out of the gap and disperses into the cold night air. Condensation forms between the homeless man's palm and the sheet of glass. His fingers press against the window, his nostrils lift toward the opening like an animal's. His neck jerks in an uncomfortable way and he stares at Elizabeth with hungry eyes—then immediately shifts his focus to the white pick-up truck behind them.

The driver is drumming his hands on the steering wheel to the beat of music. He is in his fifties, likely the son of the old woman sitting beside him, waving money out the passenger window. The skin hanging from her arm flaps with the gesture.

The wet cardboard falls from the beggar's hand as he gets closer to the truck, reaching for the money. But he doesn't take it. He grabs the old lady's arm and chomps down on it. Blood drains down the flapping skin. She screams. Her son jumps out of the vehicle, running full-steam around the front of the truck. He is halfway when granny's arm snaps.

The red hue cast by the traffic light turns to green.

Elizabeth forces her eyes to the road ahead and speeds off— downtown, toward the bridge—anywhere away from there.

Pacific rain pummels the vehicle as it crosses the green steel bridge arched over Yaquina Bay. Outside air seeps through the cracked passenger window, creeping across her skin, numbing any connection she holds to reality.

A small blue sign designates *Newport Municipal Airport* coming up on the left. It is 11:22 at night. Elizabeth takes a sharp left onto a long driveway that leads to a small building. Windows wrap around the side, facing an empty parking lot. They continue around to the front, where a glass door faces the airport runway. Details crisp as she speeds closer.

Oh no. She is going too fast. She hits the brake. The front tire slides up onto the curb, but the car stops. Fog strangles the light escaping from the wall of windows. The sidewalk is still. She turns off the engine, gets out, slams the door shut, and leaves the keys to rattle in the ignition.

As she enters the small lobby, stale air wafts into her face, grounding her back into reality. A door to an employee lounge is six feet ahead. A counter sits to its right, stretching to the other side of the room. At its far end is a crystal vase stuffed with fresh yellow roses. The windows begin there, follow behind Elizabeth, and end near the lounge door.

A woman in her forties steps into the room from the lounge and smiles.

A man stuffed into a security guard uniform follows. His chubby fingers adjust his belt and tuck in his white shirt.

"I'm sorry, but we're closed," the woman says, with that same warm smile.

"My sister's plane ..." Elizabeth rushes the counter, "she's

supposed to be here by now … I heard this report on the radio."
She tries to breathe. "Please tell me the eleven o'clock flight is
running late." *It has to be running late.*

Her smile fades. "I'm sorry … but all flights have been
grounded and cancelled for the night."

Tears escape Elizabeth. She buries her head into her arms.
This isn't happening.

The faint sound of an aircraft approaches from the North.

"What's that?" Elizabeth asks, lifting her head.

"Those are private owners." She grins, probably happy that
her shift will soon be over. "If you can give me a name, I can
run a search for you."

"Hazel Hutchings, traveling from Albuquerque. I don't know
what flight. She told me to pick her up tonight, at eleven
o'clock." She glances up searching the lobby again. *This can't
be happening.*

"Here it is. Her connecting flight—from Portland to Newport
—has been cancelled. Her flight from ABQ departed on time
and arrived in Portland at …" The woman swallows hard. Her
eyes go frantic reading the screen, and then she looks at
Elizabeth. It is as if someone has dumped a bucket of sadness all
over her. "I think you should see the news."

No. Elizabeth's heart sinks. She follows the woman into the
employee lounge. It is a small room furnished with a dining set,
two lounge chairs, and a half-size refrigerator. Everything hugs
the walls, including a flat screen television at the end of the
room. *No.*

171

"BREAKING NEWS" takes up most of its screen. There is no sound.

No. "What about my sister's flight?"

The woman's eyes turn away from Elizabeth and she unmutes the volume.

"We just received breaking news regarding Flight 1801. Airport officials have just confirmed that there are no survivors ... the CDC arrived on scene ... witnesses ... shots fired ... all are confirmed dead .... Albuquerque Airport officials are also working with Homeland Security ..."

It all fades. The whole room fades to a blur. Elizabeth's heart pounds. She tries to force her eyes to stay open, to watch the television, but she can't. Tears stream down her cheeks. *No....* She turns toward the woman who lightly nods that this is Hazel's plane. *No....* It can't be real. She can't be gone. *I'm all alone? I'm all alone.* Elizabeth looks down at her wrist. *No, not her.* She forces her goddamn eyes open. With fisted hands and clenched teeth, she yells at the woman, "Well, what are you doing here? Why are you still here? You need to go home, you need to pack ... You need to be somewhere safe."

"Ma'am, you're going to have to control yourself." The woman rests her hand on Elizabeth's bare shoulder. Her touch feels so real.

"You have to get out of here." Elizabeth grabs the woman's hand, pulling her toward the lobby. "We need to find a safe place for tonight."

"You need to calm down." The security guard approaches

behind her. He grabs Elizabeth's arms, pulls them behind her back, and twists a pair of handcuffs around her wrists. The metal digs into the fresh stitches.

Elizabeth gags. It is all real. The room blurs beneath a layer of tears. Cries of loss force out with every exhale, but are deafened in her mind. Emptiness stabs her chest. Each breath caves into her breaking heart. It isn't fair.

The security guard mumbles about something, but there is nothing—nothing that matters. Even the pain has numbed. Elizabeth gasps for air. Inaudible cries mold her to the floor.

The security guard scoops her into his arms, carries her into another room, and rolls her onto its couch.

She draws her knees into her chest. Each breath hurts, but she does not care. She can't breathe, doesn't want to breathe. *Not her. Not Hazel! This can't be happening* ... She squeezes the salty water from her eyes. All the light left in the world disappears. The abyss of grief pulls her to sleep.

There, she can see her sister again. *Hazel waits for me in a field of wildflowers. We were only children then, amazed at the beauty around us, watching butterflies and bees drift from one wildflower to the next.*

Hazel presses a bright yellow buttercup beneath my chin saying, "Now let's see if you like butter."

The petals tickle. I giggle and her face lights up.

"Wow. You really like butter," she laughs, handing me the flower ...

New Reality

Monday brings sunshine. Its rays trickle through a large window on the other side of the room. It is warm, the only comfort Elizabeth has. The cushion beneath her cheek is soaked and smells like a musty basement. She turns her head, but the slightest movement digs the handcuffs deeper into her skin—into her stitches. It is still real. She is still alive.

The room is different from the lounge. Not that Elizabeth really remembers what it looked like last night. A desk sits across from the couch. An open door, to the left, leads into the lounge and then another to the lobby. It is quiet. There is another door to the right that is closed. Elizabeth calls out, "Hello?"

There is nothing but silence.

Her cheeks are sticky from dried tears. The handcuffs dig deeper into her wrists. She presses her cracked and dry lips together, restraining the nausea pitted in her stomach. She sits up, feeling the pressure to pee. She yells louder, "Hello?"

The woman from last night rushes in with her finger pressed to her lips, shushing Elizabeth. She glances back over her shoulder at the lobby. "You have to be quiet."

"I really need to use the bathroom." Elizabeth squeezes her knees together.

"That's not my call, but you really need to be quiet." She heads back to the lounge and disappears.

"It's my call," says the security man as he steps from the backroom—a blue tiled bathroom. He is a lot taller than Elizabeth remembers, and his frame blocks the entire doorway.

"Can you let me out of here?"

He doesn't move.

"Did I do something wrong, officer?"

"Yes ... No ..." He takes a key from his pocket and makes his way to her. His hands shake as he unlocks the handcuffs. "I detained you for your own protection."

The metal loosens, bringing a wave of nausea. Elizabeth forces herself not to throw up.

Snot drips from his nose and he wipes it with his sleeve, sitting down at the desk.

Elizabeth rubs her wrist, easing the imprinted line of the handcuffs in her skin.

His pity bears down on her through words. "I'm really sorry for your loss."

"May I use the restroom?" She looks away from him, unable to handle the grief.

He nods toward the rear door and props his head in his hands.

Elizabeth sprints to the bathroom and pushes the door shut behind her, but it stops three inches short of closure. There are two sinks framed by a large mirror across the room. Beside the toilet is a full-length window with its blind drawn.

Muffled conversation carries through the cracked door.

The seat is up, and a thick, deep yellow saturates the toilet bowl. The security guard must be dehydrated. Elizabeth sits, doing what she has to. She restrains from flushing the toilet or washing her hands so she can hear the conversation.

"I have to make sure she is stable enough first," the man whispers.

"John, if you lost someone ... and like that—We can't keep her here. I don't know what's going on, but I'm going home, which is what both of us should've done last night after the—" She catches Elizabeth peeking at them out of the corner of her eyes. "So ... what's your name?"

Elizabeth steps out of the bathroom.

John darts toward her like a lumberjack about to take down a tree. She freezes. The motion is too similar to that of Alex and

Jan. She cannot move. He squeezes past her, into the bathroom, and slams the door shut. A hoarse cough echoes beneath the door. Vomit sprays into the toilet.

Elizabeth sinks back into the couch, silent.

The woman stares at the bathroom door with wide eyes, concerned.

It opens.

John steps out and sits down beside Elizabeth, who slides over—away from him—as far as possible, hugging the armrest. He coughs, wiping the sweat running down his forehead with his sleeve.

Elizabeth looks at the woman. "How long has he been sick?"

"Oh, he's not sick. He just has bad allergies." Her voice shakes. Her hands clasp tightly in her lap. She swallows hard and looks back at her. "So, any ideas?"

"What do you mean?" Elizabeth says.

The man hacks up a violent cough.

Elizabeth's heart jumps.

The woman nods toward the adjacent room, leading Elizabeth into the employee lounge.

Elizabeth paces in front of the television.

The woman takes a couple of hoagies from the small refrigerator, throws one over and heads for the lobby. "Eat. I need some chocolate."

Elizabeth is starving. She devours one whole hoagie sub while turning on the television and waiting for it to actually flick on.

"All flights have been canceled. Anyone with flu-like symptoms is encouraged to stay at home ..." a newscaster reports.

Elizabeth glances at the open door that leads back to the security guard.

"All government offices and public schools will remain closed until next week." The newscaster continues, "Local hospitals recommend that you stay in bed and not seek emergency medical treatment unless clear life-threatening symptoms appear. Again, the best thing is to stay home."

Something bangs behind Elizabeth.

She turns to find the kitchen chair closest to the lobby door, has fallen. The woman stands beside it. Her eyes are wide and she doesn't move. The chocolate bars in her hands are squished in clenched fists. Elizabeth steps back from her. "Are you okay?"

"There's a man walking around outside." She looks at Elizabeth, but her gaze goes right through her. "He's just standing outside, staring through the door at me."

Elizabeth grabs her arm, jerking her out of the doorway, peeking to see if he is still there. The lobby is empty. The wall of windows captures a two person airplane parked on the runway outside. There is no sign of any man. Elizabeth grabs the door that leads into the lobby and eases it shut. "There's no lock?"

She shakes her head no.

Elizabeth presses her back up against the door, looking around the room. "Did you see where the guy went?"

"No. He was just here—at the front entrance—just staring at me," she says. She paces in front of the open office door where her boyfriend sleeps.

He coughs.

We both women freeze, turning their attention to the noise.

He sits hunched on the couch, drooling in his sleep.

"How long has he had that cough?" Elizabeth asks.

"I don't know. It started after our lunch break yesterday …. Well, actually during lunch break … we … he started coughing while he was . . ." She blushes.

John's body begins to convulse and he falls to the floor. His eyes roll to the back of his head. The woman rushes for his side. Elizabeth tackles and restrains her until he stops convulsing. His chest fills with a deep moan. Elizabeth lets go of her. She dives to his side, and shoves her arm under his, attempting to lift him up. She looks at Elizabeth. "Can you help me?"

Hell no. Elizabeth shakes her head in decline. There is no way she is getting near him.

"Please?" the woman pleads.

Fuck. Elizabeth supports the damp pit of his arm and helps heave his body back onto the couch. They sit him back. His perspiration smears around Elizabeth's neck and he lets out a deep moan. She springs off the couch.

"Elizabeth Hutchings is still wanted by police in connection with the murder of Alex Muir," the newscaster's voice carries from the adjacent employee lounge. "Anyone who knows her whereabouts is urged to contact Homeland Security."

Elizabeth's heart jumps. She is frozen.

"What are you not telling me?" says the woman. "Is that your name?"

"I should go." Elizabeth heads for the lounge.

The woman cuts her off. "Please."

"You'll think I'm crazy," Elizabeth says.

"You might be surprised." She glances over at the man she has been screwing around with for months, and nods to the lounge. The women move into it together. She offers out her hand, properly introducing herself. "I'm Tina."

Elizabeth hesitates before reciprocating it.

Tina sits at the kitchen table. "I've been up all night watching the news. You've missed a lot. Aviation has shut down, government offices and schools have been closed. They say it's an attempt to stop some superbug. But before social media crashed, people were saying that ... this is the zombie apocalypse."

"Which social media site?"

"All of them. Well, I think so anyway. Everything is down for routine maintenance." She pauses, her eyes widening. "Excuse me."

Tina's period always comes on out of the middle of nowhere. She hurries to the bathroom, flinging its door closed behind her. It slams shut. She sprints to the toilet and shoves her stockings down, nicking the fabric. The toilet seat is cold beneath her thighs. The window blind taps against the windowpane beside her. Cold air seeps into the room at its bottom. Passing gusts of autumn's air suck the blind closer to the glass, then push it back out again. Tina grabs a clump of toilet paper.

Something outside bangs against the windowpane.

She sits still.

Another breeze sucks the blind back against the glass with a thump. Then another pushes it away.

She pulls at the toilet paper roll slowly, listening for anymore exterior noise. Wondering if its all in her head from a heightened state of anxiety.

The smell of rotting flesh blows through the window blind. Tina leans back against the toilet tank. Another breeze pushes itself into the room. She leans forward, peeking around the side of the blind. The windowpane is a solid glass panel that takes up two-thirds of the top portion. The remaining bottom third is a hopper-style window that has been cranked open, pitching out.

A man—the man from outside earlier—stands hunched on all fours outside the window. His hair drips with rainwater. His hands are sunken into the mud, and his cheek presses against the bottom window screen. His nostrils flare.

Tina pulls her feet back toward the base of the toilet, instinctively away from the window.

He sits up. His yellow-crusted and swollen eyes watch the blind for any movement—sign of prey.

Had he noticed? She keeps still. If she lets go of the blind now, he will notice.

His nose presses against the windowpane, condensation forms beneath his dry and cracked lips.

She waits for the next breeze to suck the blind to the window again, before letting go, and stands. If she can make it to the door before he crouches down again, she might have a chance of escaping before he realizes she is there. She goes full force toward the door, but the drawstring of the blind snags on the hem of her skirt and pulls up. She takes three more steps before realizing it is caught, then freezes with her back to the window. Menses run down her leg. She glances back over her shoulder.

His grotesque eyes follow the blood dripping down her inner thigh. It soaks into her stockings.

A small space heater kicks on behind her, pushing the room's warmth through the open window.

The man becomes an animal—snarling and tearing at the window screen. His fist brakes through the mesh, but the opening's size restrains his grip from her. It doesn't take long for him to abandon the failed attempts to reach her and stand up, releasing a fierce groan.

Her hands shake as she reaches for the string caught on her skirt. It releases, swinging free. The blind rushes to close, stopping five inches short of total concealment, tapping against the glass. A sigh of relief that she is hidden from him is enough to return her attention to getting out of there.

The window shatters behind her. Pieces of glass shower against her back. The man pummels into her like a freight train. Her body goes flying. Her head whacks the floor.

Alone

"ARE YOU OKAY?" ELIZABETH TAPS AGAINST THE bathroom door. *She has been in there forever.* "Tina?"

No answer.

Elizabeth flings open the door. It slams against the bathroom wall. Tina's limp body is laid out on the floor. Her eyes are open, facing the door—facing Elizabeth—but there is no life left in them. A man is bent over her legs and his face is pressed between her thighs, jerking like an animal on prey. He looks up. Pieces of torn flesh and blood slide down his chin.

Elizabeth can't move, but she must. She manages to stretch for the doorknob, grab it, pull it closed behind her, and spins to sprint away. Her nose brushes against cotton—the security guard's shirt. His body walls her off from the rest of the room.

Without thinking, Elizabeth ducks under his love handles and runs for the lounge. The door leading into the lobby is still closed. She tries to stop to open it, but momentum hurls her into the door. *Shit.* She bounces back just enough to regain balance and open it. The exit is only a few steps away. She goes for it, clasping her fingers around the doorknob, and pulls.

It doesn't budge.

She glances behind her. The worn exterior of the security guard blocks the doorway to the employee area. His body is nothing more than a hollow shell that steps closer, groaning.

Elizabeth faces him, pinning her back against the front door. She needs something to break it's glass. *The flowers in the vase.* She sprints for the yellow roses at the end of the counter. The security guard follows. His groan morphs into a growl. Elizabeth can smell his breath behind her as the tips of her fingers slide into the water of the crystal vase. She swings it around, slamming it into the side of his skull. It slips from her hand and shatters against the wall.

He falls to the floor.

She jumps over the counter, kicking a mug of curdled coffee over. She lands on the other side and picks up the mug, running at him.

He stands up, crushing the flowers into loose petals. Blood oozes from his temple, dripping down his cheek. He claws at her from across the counter. His fingernails tear into her bicep. Before he hurtles the countertop, Elizabeth rounds its side and throws the cup at the front door.

Glass rains onto the floor. The mug skids across the sidewalk, breaking into pieces. The remaining glass shards of the door create a barrier to the outside world—like the exit to escape some sick funhouse.

Pain or death.

She charges the opening with her shoulder. At the last second, she stops, but her shoulder continues through the door enough for her sleeve to catch on a piece of glass, ripping the fabric, leaving the bare flesh of both shoulders exposed.

The security guard charges from behind her.

She faces him, bending her knees to brace for his impact.

He comes full steam and lunges.

Elizabeth shifts all her weight to the left.

He crashes through the jagged glass door and falls on top of the shattered mug.

She jumps through the door, landing on his leg, losing her balance, falling to the ground beside him.

He stands up, having never taken his eyes off Elizabeth. Pieces of porcelain protrude from different sections of his cheek. The mug's handle dangles from the torn flesh beneath his eye.

Elizabeth's pulse accelerates. The walls of her vision focus on the Prius. She goes for it. The soles of her boots slip on the rain-beaten pavement. She slides across the hood of the car. Beads of water soak into her jeans. She tears open the driver's side door and forces the ignition, and stomps down on the gas pedal, throws the car into drive.

The car revs, going nowhere.

Goddammit. Elizabeth had not pressed the brake before shifting. She stomps on it. The security guard comes around to her side of the vehicle. She pulls the car door shut and hits the locks. He rips the mug handle from his face and punches through the driver's side window, shattering it.

Pieces of glass spray across Elizabeth's left cheek. His fingernails tear into her shoulder as he grabs ahold of her. She slides into the passenger seat, freed from his grip, and fumbles for the passenger-door handle to get out. She grabs it, pitches it open, and falls out onto the ground. He is already halfway across the seat after her. She scoots back from the car like a crab. Her lower back scrapes into the asphalt. It hurts. A stabbing pain pushes the partially digested hoagie halfway up her throat. Every second counts, but they are wasted, crippled by nausea.

The security guard falls out of the car onto the ground and reaches for her boot. His fingers brazed its sole. One more attempt and he will take full control of the situation.

She forces herself to stand.

Rain begins dripping from the sky.

Don't move. It is all about timing.

He climbs to his feet. Infection has seeped through every cell of his body, leaving a hollow capsule.

Just two more steps. Elizabeth holds her ground.

He takes them.

She sprints around the front of the car.

He moves quicker than she had anticipated. There is no time to safely take the driver's seat. She pushes herself into a sprint—until her lungs hurt—past the driver's side door, round the back of the car, and hops into the passenger seat. Pieces of glass scrape her jeans and the seat fabric as she slides behind the wheel. She grips the steering wheel so tightly that her fingernails dig into the palms of her hands. She throws the car into reverse, spinning it around, and speeds off down the driveway, toward Oregon's coastal Highway 101. Not thinking—by pure instinct—she turns right, going north, never looking back.

Every building in the city of Newport, Oregon looks beaten by the sea. Its copper green bridge stretches higher over Yaquina Bay, taking Elizabeth back into town. Vacant shops line the main stretch off the bridge.

The first light turns red.

Where do I go? There is nowhere to go. *Where do I go?*

The light changes.

Elizabeth forces the gas pedal down, accelerating to thirty miles per hour, blowing through the next two street lights. A small sign on the right points to Corvallis. She heads east—home.

The small beach town quickly fades into rural mountains. Elizabeth passes the smaller town of Toledo. Light rain clouds darken in the distance. It is a long drive through no man's land.

The red "check engine" light turns on. The fuel gauge sags past empty. The car coasts to a stop. Elizabeth forces down on the gas pedal. It is no use. There is nothing left to give.

A cloud bursts overhead. Rain pours into the broken driver's side window. Elizabeth slides over. Mist accompanies the autumn air, rushing across the seat for her. Goosebumps cover Elizabeth's skin. She sits there, staring out into an empty world until sunlight pokes through the clouds, calming the weather. She searches the car. There is nothing. It is pretty much empty, except for a pack of condoms in the glove box. Elizabeth slams its door shut. Walking for miles would be better than sitting there vulnerable and freezing to death. She throws open the door and continues east on foot.

Desolate houses stretch between the miles, until there is a clearing—a rest stop. Elizabeth sprints across the main road, taking the driveway to the building. A wooden sign labels the land as Ellmaker State Wayside. She is halfway home.

The bathroom building sits on the opposite side of an asphalt loop that is used for parking. Cement panels cover the building's exterior, giving it a creamy, refined wood-like look. A storage door segregates the women's restroom to the left and the men's to the right. A privacy fence shields both doors from the road.

Elizabeth is in the middle of nowhere and the sun is setting. Anything can be hiding in the woods. *Anything*.

The dark clouds that have followed her, blow faster across the sky.

She runs into the women's restroom. She is not safe yet. The brown door leads into a two-stall bathroom with one sink. Fluorescent lights flicker, lighting each corner. Rain pours against the roof. The door closes behind her and she pins her back up against it, sinking down until her butt hits the floor. Her heart jumps. *I have to check the stalls*. She leans over, laying her cheek against the floor.

There is no sign of anyone.

All Elizabeth wants to do is sleep, but it isn't safe, not yet. She forces herself up to make sure no one is standing on the seats hiding. She shoves the first door open. Her heart pounds so loudly she hears no other noise. It is empty, except for a plunger beside the toilet. She grabs its sticky handle and moves onto the next stall, thrusting its door open.

It doesn't budge.

Great. She glances back at the front door, hoping that it stays shut, that no other enters, then bends down, sticking her head beneath the stall, making sure it is all clear.

There is no one—nothing.

Exhaustion overtakes her as she staggers to the sink, grabbing its edge, letting it bear her weight. She looks at the woman staring back at her in the mirror. She has lost everything. There is nothing left. Tears fall down her cheeks.

She turns on the faucet, drowning out the growl of hunger in her stomach. Ice cold water trickles through her fingers and flows over her cupped hands. She splashes the saltwater from her cheeks. The mirror's reflection could kill her, but she hits the light switch, refusing to let it.

Three small privacy windows on the side of the building capture every dimming ray of daylight outside. Sun rays dance as they always have.

Elizabeth huddles in the corner closest to the door, beside the sink. The floor sucks out all the remaining heat from her body. She loosens each shoelace of her boots before kicking them off. Steam from her toes disappears into the rising moonlight. The dagger stashed in her boot falls out onto the floor, cast in shadow. Her stomach's growl echoes against the walls. She closes her eyes. For tonight, even death would be too exhausting.

DETAINED

A CAR DOOR SLAMS OUTSIDE, THEN A SECOND ONE. Elizabeth's head throbs against the cold bathroom wall. The damp air has filled her lungs all night and coated her throat. She shoves her boots on and picks up the dagger, sliding it back beside her ankle. She presses her ear up against the door, listening for anything.

The men's bathroom door creaks open.

She holds her breath, straining to hear the slightest evidence of conversation.

There is none.

If there are two men, she is screwed. What woman can stand up to two guys? Especially if they are indecent. She cracks open the door. There is no one, nothing but a black Hummer with tinted windows parked out front. On the door is a logo with the word Meadowlark and a biohazard symbol perfectly centered behind the "o." Unease enfolds Elizabeth. *It's a vehicle. It can get me far away from this place.* She doesn't wait to contemplate choosing between being a good girl and escaping from two men in a world with no laws. She sprints for the Hummer.

The men's bathroom door creaks open.

Elizabeth has reached the Hummer by the time two men, dressed in some sort of black military uniforms, step out.

They see her and their conversation ceases.

Something bangs against the back passenger window behind Elizabeth. She squints through the tinted glass. Someone is in there. A woman whacks her forehead against the windowpane. A piece of duct tape covers her mouth and stretches halfway over her cheeks.

What the fuck?

"Get her!" yells one of the men.

Adrenaline shoots through Elizabeth's veins. She leaves the Hummer, sprinting towards the road. The rest-stop clearing fades back into a wall of forest along the highway. The air is heavy in her lungs. Her stomach cramps. Her muscles burn. She has to get away, but can't—she can't go on any longer. That is it. She stops, resting her hands on her knees. Her muscles tighten as she braces for impact.

One of those men plow into the back of her like a bulldozer.

Elizabeth's cheek slams against the ground. Every particle of stale air escapes from her lungs. She tries to replace the lost breath, but can't, not with his weight pinned against her back.

"You shouldn't have run," he whispers behind her ear, getting up.

Elizabeth gasps for air. Dirt fills her mouth.

He jerks her left wrist back and slaps a hand-cuff on her like she is a criminal. His grip tightens around the cuff and the metal digs into her wrist a little deeper. "That's for running."

She clenches her teeth, restraining tears. She won't be weak.

He nudges her wrist up the small of her back. It hurts. Elizabeth digs her cheek into the mud, trying to alleviate the pain, screaming out. The man yanks her other hand back, cuffs it, and lets it go. He helps her stand, spinning her to face him. He is much more attractive then she thought he would be. His eyes are a deep blue. They study hers, as if searching for something.

The Hummer's horn blares.

The man pushes Elizabeth towards the vehicle. His partner's eyes are locked on her the whole way. The woman in the back seat has her cheek pressed up against the tinted window pane. She doesn't turn her head or move her eyes as they walk around the back of the Hummer. The man's grip tightens around

Elizabeth's arm as he opens the back driver's side door.

Elizabeth hesitates. The woman's hands are handcuffed behind her. Elizabeth steps back, bumping into the man behind her, turning to face him.

The sleeve of his uniform is embroidered with a biohazard symbol and the word Meadowlark, identical to the vehicle's logo. A samurai sword is fostered to his side. He rolls back his shoulders as a form of intimidation.

Elizabeth meets his eyes, but he looks past her, saying nothing. She slides into the back seat.

The driver is stocky compared to the other man and a bit less concerned with appearances. He tilts the rearview mirror down to stare at Elizabeth's breasts.

What a pig. Elizabeth shifts in the seat, and the rear view mirror's focus shifts.

The Hummer pulls out onto the road, making a U-turn, heading in the wrong direction.

Elizabeth leans her head against the window. The grey, rainy day perfectly mirrors the life she deserves. They backtrack all her steps—all the distance and progress from yesterday. She turns to look at the woman beside her, catching Mr. Blue-eyes staring back at her from the front seat. She isn't safe, but at least her mouth isn't duct-taped yet.

Alex's abandoned Prius appears up ahead.

The driver elbows his partner and stops the Hummer in the middle of the road. Both men get out.

Elizabeth faces the woman. There is something familiar about her pale green scrubs. "Hey, are you okay?"

She doesn't answer.

"Hey." Elizabeth nudges her leg.

The nurse's forehead skids against the windowpane as she turns to face Elizabeth. She looks so familiar. No fear fills the nurse's eyes, despite the duct-tape sealing her lips. Her eyes widen and she lunges across the backseat at Elizabeth. Elizabeth screams, trying to scoot away, pressing her back up against the door. The nurse's face lands on Elizabeth's thigh, her teeth gnarl beneath the duct tape, trying to rip open her skin.

Mr. Blue-eyes yanks open the nurse's door, grabs hold of her handcuffs, and throws her to the ground. She rolls, struggling to stand up. He pulls a gun from his holster and slams the car door shut. Elizabeth can't see her, but she hears the gunshot blasts that take the woman's life.

His partner returns to the driver's seat from Alex's car. His eyes go right back to the mirror. A shitty grin covers his face.

Mr. Blue-eyes slides back into the car—calm. He shows no remorse for the life he has taken. They drive away, leaving her lying in the road.

Elizabeth can't help but think of how she left Alex—his crushed and broken body lying in the middle of the pebble driveway. She forces her eyes to the moving pavement outside, trying not to judge these men or herself too hastily.

Rural houses dot the edge of Newport.

They head north on Highway 101, bringing them to the house of yesterday's crime scene, but they drive past it, slowing at the driveway to Alex's beach house.

Elizabeth's stomach knots. *Why are we here?*

They pull down the driveway. Elizabeth does not want to see Alex's body—see what she had done to her friend. She turns her face to the window and closes her eyes. She awaits their reaction to the crime scene. The pebbles crunch beneath the tires. *What are we doing here?* The vehicle stops.

"We're here, get out," the driver says, pushing his door open. The Pacific winds push back. Once he manages to get out, he pulls open Elizabeth's door, forcing her out of the back.

The ocean wind teases the goosebumps of her skin and she takes a step for the house.

He blocks her path, pushing her up against the car. His chest presses against hers. He grabs her breast, tightening his fingers. It hurts. He bites his bottom lip and pushes his other hand up under her shirt. The warmth of his skin is almost inviting against the nauseating cold.

"Hey!" Mr. Blue-eyes shouts from the porch.

The tips of the driver's fingers pull away and he shoves Elizabeth towards the house.

Elizabeth glances back, down the driveway. She has to know, has to see what she did to Alex. But it is empty. He is gone. Rain has washed away all the evidence of her crime.

The surrounding woods creak with the wind. The house is dark. Overhead the autumn clouds swell with rain. Fallen branches crack on the forest floor, like something is coming.

Elizabeth climbs the porch steps, standing outside the front door with bound hands. She had made it out of that house once, but there is no guarantee she will be allowed a second.

She steps through the shattered door. Glass crunches beneath her boots. Cold ocean winds have filled the house. The smell of crab strengthens as she heads toward the kitchen. Crab legs are still sticking up out of the bucket in the sink.

Across the counter is a tattered female body, sitting on a barstool, slouched against the counter. Her hands are cuffed behind her back. She lurches her head up. It is Jan. Her pupils mirror pools of darkness. She stares at Elizabeth. There is no kindness, no warmth. The rose color of her skin has drained and the remaining patches of her hair are drenched in sweat or rain. Elizabeth's best friend is gone. The grotesque creature slouching against the counter barely resembles her. Vomit clings to her navy blue nightgown.

"You see this?" The driver grabs Elizabeth's arm, yanking her closer. He draws a handgun and aims it at Jan. "This is Code Black. This means," he waves the gun between himself and Mr. Blue-eyes, "we're the only law left in your world now."

He presses his dry, cracked lips against Elizabeth's. His saliva smears into the creases of her skin. The smell of shit seeps from his mouth into hers, filling her lungs. He pulls away, admiring the gun's beauty and power.

Elizabeth steps back from him.

"Do you think I won't take what I want?" He shoves Elizabeth to the wall, and presses the tip of the barrel to her jaw, pushing her bruised cheek against the textured paint. His other hand grabs the inside of her thigh. He forces the gun harder, while his fingers slide up her leg.

Son of a bitch. She turns her face toward his — letting the gun's barrel dig deeper into her cheek — and spits in his face.

He pulls the gun away, wiping his cheek. Rage fills his face. He clenches the weapon, swings it back, and with full force punches her in the head with it.

The room flashes into a tunnel of darkness.

She feels nothing.

THE KEEPER

WHERE AM I? ELIZABETH WONDERS.

The ceiling moves as her body bounces, draped in someone's arms as they walk. She tilts her neck an inch to orient herself. Her ears begin to ring with the slightest movement. Her head pounds, her left cheek pulsates. One of the men carries her down the hallway, turning right into the master bedroom, and throws her onto the king-size bed. The slut's suitcase bounces as Elizabeth's jaw skids across the soft blanket, scraping into her throbbing cheekbone.

The mattress behind her sinks with his weight as he sits.

She rolls onto the floor, trapped between the wall and the bed, hidden from his view.

The bedroom door slams shut. Stillness rises.

Then there are footsteps—inside the room—coming around the bed for her.

Deep-blue eyes look down at her as he rounds the end of the bed. She digs her heels into the carpet, kicking herself backwards into the corner. Elizabeth is too weak, too tired, too heartbroken to fight anymore. He kneels. She shuts her eyes and pulls her legs in. The soft skin of his cheek brushes hers as his arms wrap around her.

"Please don't," she whispers.

The warmth of his fingers brush her hand as he grabs the handcuffs.

Elizabeth winces. *Don't.*

"Relax. I'm not going to hurt you." His words kiss her cheek as the cuffs fall free. He backs away, giving her the same look as before, like he knows her from somewhere. "What's your name? I'm Benjamin."

"Carol," she lies.

"You should get changed, quick. We're leaving and you'll be coming with us."

"Why?" she stands up.

"Because you look like shit." He tosses a prescription bottle to Elizabeth—her prescription bottle.

Elizabeth's heart drops and her cheeks burn with the simple lie she has told.

"Perhaps that will help with the pain," he says.

"No. Why do I have to go with you?" Elizabeth asks clenching the bottle as he steps closer. She glances past him, at the closed door—to the animal waiting outside. "Can't you just let me go?"

"No offense, but you don't look like the type of girl who could survive a zombie apocalypse, without a lot of help." He steps past her, rummaging through the dresser.

She searches the room for a piece of reality, something to ground her. *A zombie apocalypse? No. There's no way.*

"Catch." Benjamin tosses a whisky bottle from the drawer.

Elizabeth catches it and smiles. Alex's dad likes to drink on rainy days while trapped inside with his young wife who never shuts the hell up.

Benjamin looks at Elizabeth, narrowing his eyes. He is trying to read her thoughts to find out what is so funny.

She avoids him by taking a swig of the whiskey to force down a pill, then heads for the closet. Inside, the light is dim with incandescent light, but she closes the door—for privacy—for a moment to think. Darkness seeps from the corners as she peels the shirt from her torn shoulder. Its fabric scrapes against Elizabeth's cheek. She throws it to the floor, trading it for a faded Beatles tee-shirt nearby on a hanger, slipping it on. Cold air rushes under the door, taunting her bare feet. She trades the torn jeans for a new pair that can be worn over the knee-high boots, transfers the bone dagger, and pulls the pant leg down over the bootlaces. There is no way they will suspect anything.

She grabs a brown corduroy jacket off the back of the door and rejoins Benjamin in the bedroom.

He has emptied the suitcase out onto the bed—*her* suitcase. Elizabeth's stomach knots. Purple lace underwear lays beside a blue vibrator in the pile of stuff. A red silk nightgown lays atop of Dominic's favorite band tee-shirt.

Blood rushes to Elizabeth's cheeks. She focuses on the pain throbbing within her left cheek, instead of rehashing any moments of him. The side of Elizabeth's head where the other agent had hit her hurts less than to focus on the memories. She slides her fingers beneath the corduroy jacket, rubbing her sore shoulder.

Benjamin's eyes widen. He freezes and nods at her. "Did you come in contact with any bodily fluids?"

The past twenty-four hours are a blur. Elizabeth has lost everyone—everything. She is not going to relive any part of it to recall encounters with bodily fluids. Reliving any moment will cripple her.

"Saliva, blood, sexual excretions?" He rests his hand against his holster. "Were ... you ... bitten?"

Elizabeth shakes her head no. "No, it's just a scratch."

He crosses his arms and returns his focus back to studying the items dumped out on the bed.

The pain medication kicks in, invitingly numbing Elizabeth's mind as she sits down on the mattress. A wave of vertigo rushes over her. She grabs onto the comforter, stabilizing herself. It passes and she focuses on Benjamin's uniform logo. Then it blurs again. "What's Meadowlark?"

"In 1864, President Lincoln established the Yosemite Valley Grant Act. Within it, Meadowlark was established." He lifts a velvet jewelry box from the suitcase. It is identical to the box Elizabeth's promise ring had come in.

Her eyes fill with tears.

"You see, the Natives who lived in Yosemite believed Coyote created the world—this world."

The weight of Elizabeth's body shifts. A chill crawls up her spine with the familiarity of the story.

"The story begins after Coyote had created the world and its creatures. Coyote and his friend, Meadowlark, were taking a walk in the forest when they came across the first creature to have ever died in the world. Coyote's empathy pushed him to resurrect the animal, but Meadowlark told him not to. Meadowlark said its body and energy should return to the earth from which it had been made. So Coyote agreed." Benjamin pops open the box. "It was Meadowlark who ensured the dead would remain dead, and Coyote keeps his promise: that the dead will never rise again."

"So you're zombie hunters? That's why you're here?" Elizabeth asks.

"I suppose that's an accurate statement." He pulls a bracelet of freshwater pearls out of the box.

Elizabeth's heart releases. She exhales in relief that it isn't another ring.

Benjamin slips it into his pocket. "And a Keeper."

"A keeper of what?" she asks.

"Elizabeth Hutchings," he says.

Me? Elizabeth hops off the bed and heads toward the closet. Her face burns. Even with restraint, her voice cracks with the question, "Who is she?"

"A woman we've been searching for, for two days." He takes a step closer. "Look around for anything out of the ordinary."

Elizabeth looks back at him through the dresser mirror.

TEMPTATION

Agent Jay had been Benjamin's partner for eighteen months. They had an agreement that when shit hit the fan, Jay got first dibs. But Benjamin had grabbed that girl and headed for the bedroom so fast. *Son of a bitch*. He kicks the kitchen cabinet and pops open a beer, chugging half of it before sitting at the barstool.

The disgusting, infected young woman sits beside him, slouched and unmoving. He pulls a pack of cigarettes from his front pocket and slides a condom out from between the cardboard and plastic. He taps the box on the counter to compact the tobacco. The zombie's chest rises and falls with each breath. Jay takes out the one cigarette that is upside down—the lucky one of the pack—and lights it. It burns and smoke swirls into the room. *Fucking Benjamin.* Jay glances down the hallway at the closed door. He clenches the cigarette between his lips and stands up, looking for a way to release his frustration. He bends down, grabbing the zombie girl's swollen ankles and forces them together behind the chair's front legs, cuffing them. Her skin has a blue tinge—a corpse tone. He tears the condom wrapper open, sliding the cold, wet rubber down the soft, warm skin of his penis.

The zombie's soaked nightgown hides nothing. Her knees are spread just enough to tempt him. He is taking a chance by going any further. If the condom were to break, he would become infected. He glances back at the bedroom door—at Benjamin having his way with that girl. The zombie squirms. He steps closer and takes her, fulfilling a sick fantasy.

The condom pops.

No. Panic washes over his excitement. He looks into her yellow eyes, now intent on tearing him to shreds.

All the lab tests showed one hundred percent infection from intercourse. He is fucked. It is only a matter of time before the virus infects every living cell in his body. *Fuck it.* He pulls off the prophylactic and finishes to ecstasy.

Satisfied, he disposes of her with one kick of the barstool.

Her head whacks the floor.

He finishes off the cigarette flapping in his mouth, noticing the condom on the floor. *Fucking bitch*. He spits on her, kicking the rubber underneath her back. Her used body convulses and then stops moving. He bends down to un cuff her ankles so nothing seems odd to his partner, and notices a cellular phone beneath the sofa.

The bedroom door opens.

His fingers slide across a cracked screen as he pulls Elizabeth's cellphone out.

Benjamin steps out of the bedroom door ahead of Elizabeth. She wants to clench the dagger in her hands, but it is not possible. She can't defeat them both and as of now, only one of them is a threat.

He stands at the end of the hallway opposite them, tossing something to Benjamin. "Call headquarters for the serial number."

Benjamin catches Elizabeth's cell phone and returns to the bedroom. His one-sided conversation carries into the hallway as Jay approaches Elizabeth. Tension pins her shoulders to her ears. Benjamin returns to her side, allowing her shoulders to ease back down a little.

"It's hers," Benjamin says. "A Code ZA20 has been officially issued. We are to report back to the office and head out with the whole team."

Jay continues his approach, stopping two inches away.

"Dude, let's go," Benjamin says while scooting past, nudging his partner's shoulder.

Jay grabs Elizabeth's wrist and slaps the handcuffs on her, binding her arms in front of her body. His lips lean toward hers. "Let's go."

The handcuffs hang loose enough, but the swollen skin of Elizabeth's stitches rubs against the metal.

Jay pulls out his gun and nods in the direction of the front door. "Go."

She steps from the hallway. There is a puddle of blood beneath Jan's head on the floor. She's lifeless. She gasps, unable to move.

He points the gun at Jan.

"She's dead, for Christ's sake." Elizabeth closes her eyes, trying to wipe the image of her best friend's cracked skull out of her head.

The barstool scratches against the floor.

Elizabeth opens her eyes. Jan wiggles back and forth. Elizabeth cups her mouth, trying to restrain another gasp. The rustling noise stops—Jan stops and looks at her. She rolls the stool onto its side and kicks, pushing herself toward Elizabeth. Her long hair mops through the blood oozing from her cracked scalp. Elizabeth runs for the door.

She's my friend. She's my friend …

She steps out the door, into the splintering cold. A gust of wind sucks away all the warmth that clings to her. She doesn't want to continue on. She wants to give up, fall to her knees, and allow the hard pebbles to dig into her skin—let the rain pour over her. But there is no rain.

Benjamin leans against the Humvee's hood, waiting—so calm and peaceful.

"Aren't you going to do something?" Elizabeth charges him.

He opens the back passenger door for her to get in.

A gunshot rips through the fog from the house.

Elizabeth nearly falls into the backseat. He slams the door closed, jumping up front.

"Do you know what we're supposed to do with people like you?" Benjamin turns to look back at her. "Code ZA20 is what someone like you would call … the beginning of the zombie apocalypse. See, the virus is spreading at such a rate that it is now considered irreversible and uncontained."

Footsteps crunch across the pebbles, headed for the vehicle —Jay is coming. Elizabeth keeps her eyes on Benjamin.

He faces forward. "It's actually lucky for you."

Jay hops in behind the steering wheel and peels out down the driveway.

Elizabeth's body rocks, unconfined by a seatbelt.

The house explodes behind them.

"In any other situation we'd have left you in that house." Benjamin glances back, past her, through the rear window.

Pieces of wood shatter against a smoke-blackening sky. Jay readjusts the rearview mirror. His dark eyes narrow at Elizabeth's reflection.

THE MOON'S GLOW

THE HUMMER FOLLOWS THE WINDING COASTLINE north. Elizabeth sways as the vehicle hugs the mountain's cliff. Moonlight shines over a clear ocean, painting the darkened landscape with stars. The tires weave over the center line and back toward the shoulder. Jay's head bobs with each gust of wind. They have made the descent to the flat beach of Lincoln City. Portland's summer getaway is a ghost town.

They head east, passing paved sidewalks and shopping centers that ultimately flow into forest. There are no streetlights, no shoulder, and no other cars. The headlights capture a mere five feet ahead in an abyss of darkness.

ZA20. Elizabeth asks, "So why the twenty? I get the ZA, but why the number?"

Something steps into the headlights up ahead on the right side of the road. It is a man. Jay doesn't slow or adjust the car. His head hangs to the right, bobbing back and forth with the vehicle's motion. The Hummer clips the man. He falls to the ground and the Hummer flys over the edge of the road. Elizabeth would slouch down in her seat, but there is no time. The car careens into a tree. The impact throws Elizabeth prostrated on the floor. She cannot move. A ringing noise in her ears engulfs every sound of the night. Adrenaline pounds through her veins. Gradually, she pushes herself back up onto the seat.

Benjamin's body hangs limp over an inflated airbag in the passenger seat.

A crack in the windshield over the steering wheel, branches into a large hole. Jay is gone. The headlights glare off the side of the tree trunk they have hit, capturing a bed of leaves on the forest floor.

Elizabeth leans over the front seat, digging her fingers into Benjamin's front pocket, searching for the handcuff's key. The tips of her fingers hit something metal. *Got it!*

The leaves move outside. A shadow emerges in the left headlight. Jay stands in front of the vehicle. His nose is broken and dripping with blood. A large piece of glass protrudes from his forehead.

Elizabeth leans back in reflex and the key slips from her fingers. It falls down between the center console and the seat. She sinks her butt back into the seat, engulfed by defeat.

Jay stumbles to the backdoor opposite her. He presses his face against the window, trying to eat through it.

Elizabeth hugs her knees in. *This is it.* Then her hand touches the hilt of the dagger beneath her jeans.

Jay's breath fogs up the windowpane.

Elizabeth's bound hands fumble to pull the jeans up over the goddamn boot.

The window shatters. Glass sprays across the seat. He climbs through the broken pane. Shards of glass tear at the flesh of his shoulders. His fingers dig into the seat cushion and he hurls himself toward her. The edge of his belt catches on the window frame, restraining him from reaching her.

Her fingers slide around the dagger's hilt. She hesitates. His hips breaks free and he lunges at her. She stomps his face and fumbles for the door handle behind her back. She finds it, flings open the door, and falls out to the ground, knocking the wind from her lungs.

Jay pummels her. His sweaty skin smears against hers. She clenches the dagger hilt again and jams its blade between his collarbones. Blood pours out, soaking Elizabeth's corduroy jacket. She pushes him off, rips the dagger out, and sprints up the hill for the road.

Oh my God. What have I done? Elizabeth wants to drop the dagger, but if she does, she will have no protection. She focuses on the deep tire marks carved into the soil that lead back up the hill to the road. Elizabeth follows them. The crevasses of her bootprints fill with mud as she slips on soaked leaves.

The forest is dark. A hidden moon escapes the clouds that have imprisoned it. The pit of Elizabeth's stomach knots. She glances up.

Death forms into a dark figure that stumbles down the tire track towards her.

She stops, resting her hands on bent knees, to catch her breath.

The dark silhouette walks closer.

"Oh thank goodness," Elizabeth says. "These men took me captive and I need someone to take me to the hospital. There was a car accident and ...."

The figure quickens down the hill. Moonlight ripples through the trees. His arm hangs at his side, swinging out of socket. A gust of air carries the scent of decay down from the road with him. The angle of the path is in his favor. His body plows down like a bulldozer straight into Elizabeth. Her head hits the ground. Mud smears into her deadlocked hair. The dagger slips from her fingers. She fists her hands and shoves the chain of the handcuffs across his neck to shield herself. He lunges harder, choking. Drool leaks from his lips. Elizabeth's biceps burn. His weight bears down against the metal chain and inches closer.

ABANDONED

BENJAMIN'S HEAD THROBS AGAINST THE AIRBAG—WHAT a splitting headache. He presses his palm against his forehead, but the pain won't ease. *What the hell?* He sits back. Cold air brushes his left cheek. Jay is gone and a hole in the windshield gives a good idea of what had happened.

"Are you okay?" he says, glancing into the back.

The girl is gone.

Adrenaline pounds through his veins. The driver's rear window is smashed and the door behind him is wide open. There is no telling how long he was unconscious.

Each Meadowlark vehicle has a keypad in the glovebox.

Benjamin presses the code 2-7-6 and the bright-red stereo glows: ARMED. He jumps out of the Hummer. The pressure in his head shifts, flooding his nose cavity. He takes a step and kicks something — someone.

He pushes the back door closed, revealing Jay's corpse resting at his feet. There is no time to figure out the crime scene. He sprints away from the Hummer. *She'll never make it without me. She's probably already dead.*

Up the steep tracks, the silhouette of a man is crouched in the distance, attacking the ground. Benjamin has done the job long enough to be able to spot one of the infected within three-seconds. Meadowlark had used homeless people for years to train agents. He charges the figure.

Elizabeth's petite body is pinned beneath the animal. Her handcuffs shake with the restraint of her muscles to hold the man back from her face. The stitches in her wrist burn with each beat of her heart.

Benjamin draws his gun and shoots.

The creature's body goes limp and Elizabeth's muscles give way. His blood drips onto her tongue and she can taste its salt. Her saliva thickens, diluting the cells.

His dead weight falls, pinning her to the ground.

"Let's go. We have to move." Benjamin kicks the corpse off her, grabs her hand, and pulls her up. He lets go, looking down at his hand. Moonlight glistens over the blood dripping from his skin. He draws his gun and aims it at Elizabeth's face demanding her to, "Take it off."

Cold blood drips down her hand from the jacket's cuff. Her fingers tremble as she unbuttons the heavy corduroy. It slides down her shoulders, catching on the handcuffs, stopping at her elbows.

Benjamin reaches into his front pocket for the handcuff's key. "You took it?"

"I dropped it." Thick saliva balls in Elizabeth's throat. "Just go back and get it."

He looks down the path. "That's not an option."

"Just go get it!" she screams at him.

"That's not an option," his voice raises. He takes a step back, getting ready to walk away.

"The knife," Elizabeth says, turning her cheek, guiding his eyes to the bone dagger. It has slid into the moonlight. The red lines of the etched moon and coyote glow a light blue.

Benjamin grabs it and starts to walk back to her. His shadow blocks the lunar rays from the dagger. The bone's light blue glow fades into red. He keeps walking right past her.

"Where are you going?" she yells.

He turns back. His eyes hold a million questions for her, but he looks past Elizabeth, down the hill. He slices the dagger through each of her jacket sleeves, freeing their weight and warmth from her arms. Benjamin stares down the path leading to the Humvee. There is nothing.

The thick forest hides the car accident. Even if the world hadn't gone to shit, no rescue team would have saved them. Elizabeth glances back at Benjamin, but he is gone. She sprints up the hill, slipping on his footprints. Each time she falls, soil cakes between the chains binding her wrists. She stumbles again, but this time her knee hits asphalt—the road. She has made it to the top.

Night's natural glow is so much brighter without headlights. The highway curves west around a towering mountain, leading back the way they had come. So Elizabeth continues east. *It has to be east. He has to have gone east.*

An explosion erupts behind her.

She ducks in pure reflex. That is when she sees Benjamin in the distance. The dagger in his right hand glows light blue. He keeps walking, not fazed by the vehicle's explosion, he never glances back. Adrenaline or anger builds in Elizabeth's veins. She runs after him, finding herself screaming again, "What the fuck? You're just going to leave me?"

"You're here, aren't you?" His eyebrows rise and he continues walking.

Elizabeth shuts up. He is right. She has nowhere else to go and no idea where she can get another handcuff key.

Silence accompanies them for miles. Every time a twig snaps, a leaf rustles, or a gust of wind howls, unease roils in Elizabeth's stomach. Clouds sweep over the earth's celestial body as they approach a quaint little shack. Its wood stove pumps the crisp night air with smoke that trickles to the road. A rusted, two-door 1957 Chrysler sits in the yard—nearly buried in tall grass at the house's south side, facing the street.

Benjamin crosses into the yard—trespassing.

Elizabeth stands at the grass's edge. Crossing onto private property is not something that she does.

Benjamin crouches in the tall grass beside the driver-side door, inching it open. He leaves it ajar and slides over into the passenger seat, waiting for Elizabeth to join him.

Her heart races. The dim light from the house dances on the front lawn. There is no telling how many people are inside, how many creatures could surround her—rip the skin and muscle from every bone. She focuses on the open car door and steps onto the property. *There's probably a bear trap waiting to chomp off my ankle. Just get it over with.* She sprints for the rusted car, hops inside, and slides across the Chrysler's cracked, white leather seat. It grips at her pants. Benjamin had gone to great lengths to make sure the door did not creak when opening it. So, Elizabeth feels the urge to ease it closed.

He swirls the dagger between his fingers and stows it in his duty belt.

Elizabeth's heartbeat slows. The car shelters them from the wind. She is so tired.

He unbuttons his shirt. Hours spent at the gym have chiseled his chest and stomach muscles into an eight-pack. She can't stop her eyes from following the narrowing of his waist. He holds open his unbuttoned shirt. "Come here and warm up."

Her heart races. The cold air pushes her up against his skin. His warmth is the only thing keeping her from death. Nausea pits in her stomach.

He wraps his arm around Elizabeth's shoulder, allowing sleep to engulf her.

A bloodcurdling scream rips her from slumber. The sky is still black. Benjamin's hand is cupped over her lips. His warm cheek presses against her ear, shushing her.

The residence's porch light flicks on. A woman sprints from the house, heading for the car they are in.

Benjamin pushes Elizabeth's head down onto the driver's seat, pinning his temple against hers. The woman tugs on his passenger door, trying to get in. It does not budge. Her palm whacks the glass. She screams right outside the window. Elizabeth is breathing too heavy, surely giving them away.

Whack—the second noise sounds like bone snapping. Elizabeth twitches with each crack. She tries to look up, but Benjamin forces her head back down.

The woman's screams shrilly.

"Shut up! Some of us are trying to sleep in here," a man's voice comes from behind Benjamin and Elizabeth from the back seat.

Benjamin sits up, allowing Elizabeth to follow.

A wrinkled old man is in the back seat of the rusted 1957 Chrysler. A flannel blanket that had concealed him is bunched at his waist. The odor of vodka spews with each breath.

The lawn turns silent.

Elizabeth can't breathe, can't move.

Outside on the lawn, a husband stands over his wife. Her blood drips from his mouth and her body convulses against the ground.

"Go," says Benjamin.

It is all Elizabeth needs to hear. She casts the driver's side door open and returns to the cold night.

"Dude, what the hell?" The drunken man's raspy voice fades behind her.

There are no booby-traps leading back to the road—and if there are, it doesn't matter. Elizabeth runs. The house lights fade behind her. She refuses to glance back, not even to see if Benjamin has followed. All that matters is getting as far away from there as possible.

The old man's screams cry out behind her, echoing through the forest.

A vehicle's headlights round the bend, approaching far up ahead in the distance, from the East.

Elizabeth stops. It could be anybody.

Benjamin plows into her back, knocking her to the ground.

What the hell? Her palms slide across the pavement and her knee scrapes along the road's edge, tearing her jeans.

Benjamin throws the drunk man's blanket over Elizabeth, rolls, and crouches beside her on the side of the road, drawing a gun. The vehicle is halfway to them. He whispers to her, "Go into the road and get them to stop."

This is a bad idea. She pulls the blanket over her shoulders and stands up.

"Go," he says.

The headlights are closing in fast. It is now or never. Elizabeth steps into the middle of the road. The vehicle shows no signs of slowing. The headlights become brighter. She shields her eyes with her arms. There are worse ways to die. The tires screech and the horn blares. She clenches her eyes, her jaw, and every muscle in her body.

The front of her thighs feel warm all of a sudden.

She opens her eyes.

Steam dissipates off the vehicle headlights four feet in front of her. A tall, skinny man gets out of a 1987 Bronco painted light blue with the bottom half dipped in white. The man is in his late thirties with an authentic Oregon beard and crewcut.

Elizabeth covers her face with the blanket, avoiding the blaring headlights.

Benjamin sneaks up behind the man.

The smile on the man's face fades and he puts up his hands. "Don't hurt me," he says. "My name is Wyatt Brown. I have a wife and three small children. You can take the car, money, whatever you want."

Benjamin holsters his weapon.

A branch snaps a few yards away in the woods. The Bronco's headlights have drowned out the moonlight and the forest has seeped into a pitch black background.

Benjamin looks at Elizabeth. "Get in."

Another branch cracks.

She pushes past Wyatt and sprints for the open driver's side door.

A third branch snaps at the forest's edge.

Benjamin slides in the vehicle behind Elizabeth, nudging her into the passenger seat.

CONVENIENT STOPS

THE MOUNTAIN CLIFFS ISOLATING THE OREGON COAST flatten into a rural valley. Elizabeth hugs the right side of the Bronco in the front seat. The stranger, Wyatt, mirrors her in the back. Portland is twenty-six miles west of the edge of a town called Dundee. It is a small town placed in the middle of nowhere. Its only purpose is to cater to the farmers spread out in every direction around it. Modernization has started to seep from the city, building up its eastern edge.

Agent Benjamin pulls into a gas station, whose owners have spared no expense to light every inch of the property. He cuts the steering wheel right and the car bounces over the curb.

Rubber burns into the cement as the Bronco skids to a stop under the gas station awning.

Elizabeth sits straight up, pulling the blanket tight around her shoulders. The convenience store shines with light behind a propped-open door. Her stomach growls and Wyatt's stomach echoes it. Maybe the remote town has yet to become infected.

Benjamin gets out.

"You know, you can't pump your own gas in Oregon," Wyatt yells from the back seat. "It's against the law."

Elizabeth faces him. "So where are your wife and kids?"

"What?" he says, staring at the convenience store.

"Your family," she says. "Where are they?"

"Oh," Wyatt laughs, "I don't have a wife ... or kids. I read that type of thing helps in hostage situations. Empathy and all." He climbs over the seat and slides out the driver's side door.

"Where do you think you're going?" Benjamin blocks his path. "You're not using the bathroom, it's too risky. If you gotta piss"—he points to a small grass area beside the convenience store—"piss over there."

"Chill. I'm just going to get us some food. I'm starving." He looks back at Elizabeth in the front seat and wheezes past Benjamin. "Do you want anything?"

"Hurry up. If you're not back in five minutes, we leave without you ..." Benjamin yells louder as Wyatt scurries into the small store.

Out of eyesight, Wyatt stacks the counter with junk food. *The driver must be military. And the girl handcuffed and beaten—*

probably marked as a terrorist, regardless of her real crime. It is not Wyatt's problem, but he had just bought that damn car, and spent an entire year's worth of savings on its deposit. He was not going to just abandon it now.

The midnight atmosphere lingers with an eerie stillness.

"Hello?" He looks around for the store clerk. The place is empty. The bathrooms sit at the back of the store. Only two minutes has passed. Three more minutes is plenty of time to take a piss. He glances out the window.

The Bronco is still guzzling down gasoline. He has time.

He sprints to the bathroom, shoving its door open. It is dark. His sneakers slide across the tile floor. His arms fling out to stabilize his balance. The door pulls closed behind him, engulfing him in pitch-black darkness. He reaches out, brushing the wall, searching for the light switch. Each breath echoes. His fingers find it.

The lights flick on, blinding him.

A teenage boy stands facing the back corner.

What the hell? Why's he standing in the dark? Wyatt steps backward. His heel hits the closed door.

The boy begins to turn.

Wyatt fumbles to pull the door back open. The boy moves too fast. He knocks Wyatt into the air. Wyatt's body goes skidding across the floor into the lobby. Teeth clamp down onto his left butt-cheek harder and harder. Wyatt clenches his fists and spins, punching the boy's sweaty temple. The boy falls to the floor.

The Bronco's engine starts.

Wyatt sprints for the front door, grabbing a single bag of chips on display. The Bronco has already begun to pull onto the highway by the time he has cleared the building. If they see that kid following him, they won't bother to stop. He dashes like he is headed for home base. Benjamin throws the car into park. The brake lights glow red and Wyatt's chest whacks into the back bumper.

Elizabeth climbs into the backseat as Wyatt opens the door. Benjamin could have taken off, but he waits. Wyatt chucks the bag of chips back to Elizabeth and slouches against the window. She pops open the bag and grabs a handful of greasy fried potato chips, greedily shoving them into her mouth. She manages to control herself and leans forward, offering the bag to the other two.

"No thanks," Benjamin says, firm behind the wheel.

Wyatt holds up his hand in decline, never looking back at her.

The pavement speeds by. Interstate 405 leads them into the heart of Portland. The streets are empty. Elizabeth has never seen so many dark windows, especially at night in the city.

Fear encourages her to hide like an ostrich with its head sticking in the ground. *There are so many dark windows.* She had not escaped death; it covers the empty sidewalks.

Parked cars line each side of the streets. Small fires burn in random buildings, in dumpsters, and beside playgrounds.

Benjamin parks the Bronco in the middle of the street outside of an office building. An orange *FOR SALE* sign sits in its window. He flings open his door, instructing them to, "Get out."

He has positioned them in the center of the most populous city in Oregon. Elizabeth sits on the edge of her seat, waiting for Wyatt to let her out of the back. Night's shadows won't hide them for long.

Wyatt gets out and slides the passenger seat forward, giving Elizabeth the room to hop out. They aren't going to make it anywhere without being seen. Wyatt whispers as she climbs out, "Come with me."

Benjamin walks up behind him.

Wyatt's eyes widen with the sound of handcuffs ratcheting around his wrists.

"Let's go." Benjamin pushes Wyatt toward the sidewalk. His eyes search the cityscape as he leads them to the building for sale. He pulls on the door handle like it will open, and it does. A faint Meadowlark logo decorates the door's glass. Elizabeth follows the men inside. The door locks behind them. Inside, there are cubicle walls, but nothing else. It is completely empty. Shadows line the corners and a dark hallway leads them deeper into the building. Cold air creeps up Elizabeth's spine.

"You have some explaining to do," Benjamin says to her, withdrawing the bone dagger as he walks past her, farther down the hallway.

She keeps a three-step distance back from him, just in case she needs to pivot and run.

Wyatt slows, drifting behind her.

Now, the spacing won't give her enough time if she turns to run and Wyatt blocks her way. So she slows another step behind.

Wyatt steps on the back of her heels a dozen times. His hot breath pushes up against the back of her neck.

The hallway takes them left, turn after turn. They come to a metal door with a glowing keypad mounted in its middle. Benjamin types in a code and the latch clicks. Its frame decompresses and the four-inch metal door swings outward. He pushes Elizabeth forward. "Keep going."

The hallway continues on the other side, this time bending to the right. Elizabeth's heart pounds as the door behind them begins to close. There is no getting out once Elizabeth goes in. She is grateful that her hands are bound in front of her, as opposed to behind, in case something awaits them on the other side. She brushes her fingers along the wall as she descends down the dark hallway. Her goddamn heart is beating too loud. Its rhythm fills the dark corridor.

A red glow appears in the distance. It is a replica of the previous door, but this one is guarded by a glass pad, no keypad.

Elizabeth turns around, looking for Benjamin. Wyatt is a few steps behind her. Darkness follows minute after minute. Benjamin could have left them in the corridor, two stories beneath the building—trapped with no way out. The air begins to smother Elizabeth's next breath.

He steps out of the darkness behind them, into the red glow's illumination, and places his hand on the glass pad. A bright red laser scans his fingerprints. The door releases. Bright white lights line a cement-brick hallway. It tunnels left, even deeper beneath the building. Benjamin steps past Wyatt and Elizabeth, disappearing down the corridor.

Elizabeth can't breathe. They are too deep, so deep under the earth. There is no way out. She doesn't want to die beneath the ground.

Wyatt pushes past her into the next corridor.

The door starts to close.

Elizabeth's heart throbs and the veins in her wrist pound against their tight stitches. She steps through the threshold, then sprints down the spiraling decline.

The men have just reached a third door up ahead. It is stamped with an orange biohazard symbol on its front. Benjamin lines his eye up to its center and a blue laser scans his retina.

The door decompresses.

A woman stands on the other side with her hands on each hip. She is in her early twenties, solid, and fit. An ID badge clipped to her black scrubs introduces her as: Willow. A faint Meadowlark logo partially covers the photograph. She looks past the group, searching the hallway for stragglers. "He didn't make it?"

Benjamin sighs, says nothing, and holds out the bone dagger.

"Where did you find this?" Her eyes frantically search his.

He glances back at Elizabeth and walks into the bunker buried three levels beneath the building. "Run their labs."

RUINED

WILLOW WATCHES AGENT BENJAMIN WALK DOWN THE hallway toward a glass door marked: Laboratory. Just before reaching it, he steps into a room to the right. Willow looks back to Elizabeth, down at her handcuffs, and then leads her and Wyatt deeper into the tomb. "Follow me."

Both sides of the hallway are lined with three doors, all closed. The first one on the left has a glass window. As they pass it, Elizabeth catches a glimpse of a black leather armrest.

Willow stops at the second door on the left and unlocks Wyatt's handcuffs, instructing him to, "Take the next room on the left and get cleaned up. Then I'll do blood-work."

Wyatt does as he is told, taking the third door on the left.

Willow slides the key into Elizabeth's handcuffs. "I'll find you something to wear."

The metal falls from Elizabeth's wrists. Her heart sinks to the floor. The indented skin burns, but she is free. The whole world feels lighter. Her room is a small exam room. The table looks like it has been pulled directly out of her gynecologist's office, stirrups and all. A towel sits folded atop crinkly tissue paper covering the exam table. The bottom drawer is a step-stool, meaning that the next one up contains the cold metal speculums used for pap smears. If they are in there, Elizabeth has nowhere to hide to avoid being sprawled out between the stirrups and having the thing wrench open her vagina. She grabs the towel and heads for the bathroom in the back of the room.

Its tiled wall and floor wrap into a four-foot square. There is no toilet, no door, and one shower curtain. Privacy would be nothing more than a commodity. Elizabeth turns on the shower, waiting for the lines of water to steam before stepping in. The warmth of the water beads over her frozen skin. Dried particles of blood wash away into the drain. Water rains down her back and drips through her dreadlocks. Her eyes rest, closed to the ceiling as water pounds her face. She has lost everyone, everything, and now her freedom.

"Dry off," says Willow, standing a foot behind her, holding out a towel.

Elizabeth wraps her arms around her chest, grabbing it.

"There are clothes on the exam table." Willow's eyes loosely follow the curves of Elizabeth's skin. A smile creeps across her lips and she walks out.

Elizabeth turns off the shower. The water rushes to a drip. She takes the towel, patting the bruise on her face, torn shoulder, and scraped knees. Elizabeth secures the towel in a wrap around her and steps out into the exam room.

Agent Willow sits at a small counter opposite the exam table, labeling several glass vials for blood. She waits until Elizabeth is one step away from the clothes before saying anything. "Okay, put your arms out and spread your legs. Just like airport security."

"What?" Elizabeth says, stopping in front of the exam table, facing her.

Willow stands up, walks over, and rips the towel off Elizabeth's body, throwing it to the floor. Elizabeth holds her breath. Cold air scrapes at her gooseflesh. She is freezing and naked. Willow slaps on a pair of latex gloves and clenches a small flashlight between her teeth. She begins the exam at Elizabeth's most obvious wound—the gash in her shoulder. Willow presses her thumbs on each side of it, pulling it open. "What is this from?"

Pain shoots through Elizabeth's arm, down to her spine. "A guy attacked me."

"You can put your arms down." Willow walks back to the tiny counter, fills a medical tray with the vials, and returns, placing it on the exam table behind Elizabeth. She yanks Elizabeth's left wrist, pulling it closer. Her fingers slide over the stitches, igniting her curiosity. She flips over Elizabeth's wrist. "And amuse me, explain this."

"I don't care to." Elizabeth yanks her arm away.

A dubious look fills Willow's face and she steps closer. The black threads of her scrubs press against Elizabeth's bare chest, pinning her up against the exam table. Her latex gloves brush the side of Elizabeth's face as she pushes the dreadlocks from the gash in her shoulder. Willow's breath passes Elizabeth's cheek as she leans for the tray. She takes her time bandaging the wound, placing the last pieces of tape to the gauze, and glides her fingertips down Elizabeth's arm.

Elizabeth's skin ripples with gooseflesh.

"You have such beautiful skin," Willow whispers. Her fingers flow down over the curve of Elizabeth's hip.

There is a knock at the door.

A trim-cut man enters. His black hair has been shaved clear to his scalp and his muscles press against the fabric of his sleeves. "Are you finished? I need to discuss some things with you."

"I still need to run labs." Willow withdraws her hand, clears her throat, and storms out into the hallway. "What is it that can't wait?"

"Benjamin needs you to check the authenticity of the dagger. Why don't you do that other guy's labs while she gets dressed?" He glances over at Elizabeth.

Willow attempts to re-enter the room, but he blocks her. She gives up and heads to the lab.

By the time he steps into the room, Elizabeth has finished fastening a pair of black scrubs around her waist, and pulled the first of two black tank tops on. Despite layering them, it is obvious she has no bra.

He is respectful enough to keep his eyes focused on hers. "Why don't you follow me to the lounge? Willow can find you there when it's time to draw your blood," he holds open the door, "and you can get something to eat."

"And then can I go?" Elizabeth asks, crossing her arms and stepping past him into the hallway.

He extends his hand out. "I'm Yen. What was your name?"

Crap. What had I told Benjamin? It started with a C. Carrie, Candice, Carol... "Carla."

"Follow me," he says, leading her to the door with the window.

The black leather armrest that Elizabeth had seen through the window flows into a full-sized couch as Yen pushes open the door. The room resembles a break room.

A woman with dark hair sits in the middle of the couch, staring at a phone in her hand.

Elizabeth steps into the room and the door closes behind her.

"Hey, do you have a cell phone? I'm trying to get a hold of —" The phone slides from her fingers and crashes to the floor as she looks up. "Elizabeth?"

Elizabeth's stomach tightens. She holds a breath, too afraid to let it go. Tears fill her eyes and blur the figure in front of her. *It can't be.* She clenches her eyes, forcing the salty water from view. *Hazel.* "Hazel?"

Hazel rushes into Elizabeth's arms.

Each breath tightens within Elizabeth's chest. She is too afraid to exhale. If she lets anything out, lets anything go, Hazel might disappear.

"I thought you were dead," Elizabeth says lost in breath. She clenches her eyes shut, tears rain down her cheeks into her Hazel's hair. She hugs her tighter, until it hurts. "I love you. I love you. I love you."

Hazel is holding her tight.

Elizabeth is afraid to open her eyes to find only the remnants of memories.

Found Things

MINUTES ARE WASTED AS BENJAMIN SHOWERS. THERE
is no time to stand in the warm water, but it could very well be
his last shower, so he lets several minutes drip by.

A black, pressed uniform awaits him in the otherwise empty
room. Two cots line the converted exam room. He puts on the
uniform. The clean fabric soothes his skin. It is time to get back
to work, so he heads down the hallway for Elizabeth's exam
room.

It is empty. She is gone.

"Ben!" Willow yells, popping her head out of the laboratory, holding the dagger. She walks over to him. "It's getting worse out there. We need to leave at dawn or we'll never get out of the city alive."

"Did you run labs?" he asks.

"It's the real thing." She hands him the dagger.

"And the girl?" he says.

"She's waiting in the lounge."

"No, who is she?" he asks.

"She says her name is..."

Carol, Benjamin remembers.

"Carla," says Willow. "I haven't had time to run either of their labs. I dropped everything to run this."

"Run the girl's first." Benjamin looks down the hallway at the lounge door while opening the door behind him. "I want to know who she is."

It is dark inside the second room on the right. The lights are turned off, but several surveillance monitors cast a grey glow into its dark corners. A weapon case takes up the entirety of the far wall. Clean-cut Agent Yen sits before it with his feet propped up on the desk below the security monitors. He leans back, balancing the chair on its back legs.

Benjamin counts the moving objects on the street outside. There are five zombies. The parking garage behind the building has too many shadows to confirm anything. He sits down.

The monitor reveals the woman he had brought with him. She sits on the couch in the lounge with her arms wrapped around another woman, hugging her.

Jay and Benjamin had followed every lead looking for Elizabeth. They had searched all of her frequent hangout spots: the coffee shop, school, Alex's beach house. He says to Yen, "We never found her …" He looks at him and back at the monitor. "She's probably dead by now. That zone went under two days ago."

"So who's the girl you brought with you?" Yen watches the lounge monitor.

"I don't know. We found her at a rest stop not far from Zone Two."

Agent Willow steps into the lounge, and therefore onto the screen's monitor. The young woman kisses the stranger's cheek and is escorted by Willow into the hallway, changing surveillance screens.

Benjamin feels her ice-blue eyes weighing on him as she walks past the open door. He keeps his eyes forward, saying to Yen, "But she had this." He places the dagger on the desk. "Something feels … off about her."

The laboratory monitor captures Willow and the woman sitting at a large conference table in the front of its room.

Back in the lounge, the woman picks up her phone off the floor and begins to pace.

"So do you want to try interrogating the survivor of that flight?" Yen stands up making his way toward the hallway.

What? Benjamin wonders.

"Oh, you haven't been briefed yet? One of the pilots from Flight 1801 survived, and a young woman. It appears that an *Event* occurred. They were coming from Albuquerque."

"And why weren't they terminated onsite?" Benjamin leans back, waiting for a good answer.

"The pilot was. But the woman had locked herself in the First Class bathroom. She was holding a handkerchief in her hand."

Benjamin looks back at the monitors. His heart falls. *A handkerchief?*

"It was one of ours," says Yen.

It can't be. Benjamin stands up, knocking the chair to the floor.

"We are running tests and doing all the typical documentation before we terminate her," Yen continues.

Benjamin dashes for the door, hurrying for the employee lounge. *It can't be.*

Yen sprints up behind him, cutting him off, blocking the lounge door. "What's going on with you?"

"I'll explain in a minute, just move out of my way." Benjamin's heart pounds as he reaches for the doorknob.

Yen scoots aside.

Benjamin opens the door.

The woman stops pacing, clenches the phone in her hand, and whispers across the room, "It's you."

Benjamin freezes. The room melts away. *It's Elizabeth's sister.* Dark circles hang under her eyes and her nose looks broken, but it is her. He spins around, sprinting from the room, nearly knocking Yen over. The short distance to the laboratory feels like a treadmill track creeping beneath his feet.

Willow sits inside, facing the door. The woman, who looked so familiar, sits with her back to him.

He flings open the door. It slams against the bullet-proof windowpane.

"Ouch," the woman says through clenched teeth, yanking her arm back from Willow.

Willow grabs her wrist harder, pinning it in place, and shoves a needle back into her vein. The vial fills with a deep, plum-red liquid.

"Are you finished in here?" Benjamin enters, clearing his throat to gather himself. He trades spots with Willow, sitting across from the woman.

Yen closes the door, standing guard against it.

Willow moves to the back of the laboratory to run the blood sample.

Benjamin folds his hands, staring at her irises. Photographs never captured their perfect shade of a clear blue sky.

She shifts, no doubt uncomfortable.

"You've changed your hair," he says. Her eyes rush away from his and he knows he has caught her. He yells back to Willow, "Run her fingerprints."

Willow returns to the table with a thin tablet. She places it in front of him. Elizabeth does not move. He scoops her hand up and holds her fingers down, letting the computer scan every fold of skin along their tips.

WET

HAZEL PEEKS HER HEAD OUT INTO THE CORRIDOR. SHE can hear Elizabeth's voice through the glass door at the end of the hallway.

"What do you want with me?" Elizabeth asks.

Hazel approaches the laboratory to get a better listen. Agent Yen looks back over his shoulder into the hallway. Hazel darts into an empty, dark exam room to the left.

The laboratory door opens.

She steps farther back into the room, hiding in the shadows. Her heel bumps against something, halting her before she hits the wall. She holds her breath. The surface behind her back is soft and cold.

Cool air blows against the back of her neck. A cold, wet liquid drips down between her shoulder blades. A hand grabs the back of her head, shoving it down against the exam table. She attempts to stand, but her head is slammed back down again. Fingernails dig into the back of her neck.

She screams.

Yen charges the man behind her, tackling him. Hazel falls to the floor. The hallway light trickles over the naked and sweaty Wyatt. He shoves the agent from him, returning his hollow eyes to Hazel, and attacks. She forces out her hands to keep him away, but his weight pins her and his hands wrap around her neck. She pushes his face—his teeth—away from hers, but his hands do not free from her neck. The room blurs. Gasps for air become useless. The shadows on the ceiling deepen.

All of a sudden, Wyatt's grip loosens. Hazel's lungs grab for oxygen. His blood pours into her throat. She chokes on it, swallowing the liquid.

"Go get in the shower." Yen demands, stowing his samurai sword. He pulls her off the floor. "Now!"

She sprints to the back bathroom and strips. The water runs red, swirling down the shower drain.

The Gift

"GO SEE WHAT HE'S DOING." BENJAMIN ORDERS
Willow to follow Yen, and returns his glance back to Elizabeth.
He reaches for her left hand, pulling it toward him. She yanks
back and his grip tightens around her wrist, flooding her with
pain. His fingers catch the edge of the fresh gauze Willow had
taped down.

The door flies open.

"Ben, we have an *Event*. You need to wrap this up *now*."
Willow disappears as fast as she had arrived.

Benjamin's grip releases from Elizabeth and he hurries after Willow. The door closes and the automatic lock clicks.

Elizabeth picks at the taped gauze. *Shit.* Elizabeth glances behind her into the hallway—there is no one—nothing. *Shit.* She scans the laboratory for anything that might help free her from the situation.

The door unlocks behind her.

She rips a piece of gauze loose with the noise, turning to find Benjamin and Willow behind her. The nurse hangs her head, returning to the laboratory's far side.

"What do you want with me?" Elizabeth asks.

"Stand up and turn around." Benjamin grabs the bottom of Elizabeth's tank tops, yanking her up, forcing her to face him, pulling her shirts up. The cold of the room crawls up her back as the cotton lifts to her shoulder blades. His warm fingers press against her lower spine.

Pain shoots through Elizabeth's vertebrae. It feels like Benjamin cracked a wooden bat against her back. Tears flood her eyes.

The fingerprint machine verifies her identity with a *bing.*

Benjamin whispers her name, "Elizabeth Hutchings."

"I don't understand. You gave her the vaccine." Willow's face is blank as she approaches, reading the blood test results. "We need to head out now. Just in case it has failed." She hands Benjamin the results. "She's infected."

"What do you mean I'm infected?" Elizabeth says.

Willow races out of the room.

Elizabeth pulls down shirt. The fabric brushes her spine where Benjamin's hand had been. *It hurts.* She faces him. "What did you do to me?"

"I've spent two years searching for you. Two days ago, you provided us with the perfect opportunity to take you into custody. We could say you died and no one would ever question it." Benjamin places at her back. "I administered a vaccine to you, but you escaped with the help of that stupid nurse."

What are you saying? Elizabeth sits frozen, overwhelmed with nausea. The room goes numb—no sound—all perception of the physical world is lost to her, until cold hands wrap around her shoulders from behind. Warm, soft lips press against her cheek. The same eyes that Elizabeth has looked into nearly every day of her life meet her. It is Hazel.

Willow drops Hazel's purse onto the table and walks out.

Benjamin clears his throat, prompting her to sit down. "I suppose you both deserve to hear this, and in a few hours it won't make any difference anyway … We believe that your attacker"—he looks at Hazel—"was infected with the Yosemite Z virus. This is what modern society would refer to as the zombie virus, if they knew it existed. The strain is transmitted through body fluids. It manifests as the common flu, and has a fatality rate of ninety-nine percent."

Elizabeth follows his eyes to her sister. Hazel's hair is wet and out of place. Her eyes have lost something: a light is missing from them. *No.* Tears drain down Elizabeth's cheeks. She looks back at Benjamin. "But you said there is a vaccine!"

Hazel grabs Elizabeth's hand, calming the anger, trying to calm her—to comfort her.

"Vaccines don't work like that, and they aren't a guarantee." He looks down at their clasped hands.

"But you got a vaccine, too?" Elizabeth looks at Hazel for an answer. Surely if she received one, then her sister would have too.

Hazel's eyes draw down for a second.

In that moment Elizabeth glances back at Benjamin. "Right?"

"No," he says.

"How long?" Hazel coughs into her shoulder.

"A few hours to a few days, the time frame is different for each person." Benjamin stands, looking down at them. "This may be the last chance you both get together before your systems are overloaded with the virus."

Elizabeth pulls Hazel into her arms. She could sit there forever, holding her, smelling her hair, taking in the moment of pure contentment wrapped in her presence.

Benjamin leaves, closing the door behind him.

Hazel's grip loosens and she pulls away, giving a small, forced smile as if everything will be right in the world. She reaches for the purse on the table, taking out a small box wrapped in silver paper, and smiles. "Open it. It's your birthday present."

Elizabeth leans back in her seat, shaking her head no. *I don't want it.* Salt water leaks from her eyes and burns into her cheeks. *Not without you.*

"I'm going to miss it this year," she says, pushing the box closer toward Elizabeth.

Elizabeth's fingers shake as she opens it. Inside is a necklace: a turquoise-stone fox hangs in a U-shape from a twisted string of hemp.

"You have always been the sun in my life." Hazel gently places her hand on Elizabeth's, flipping the stone over. An X is carved in its middle, its tips curve counter-clockwise to create a spiral effect, a reversed swastika. "Sometimes there are clouds that hide the sun, darkening the skies. But its rays eventually push through, reminding the world of its brightness."

The door opens behind Elizabeth. Her weight shifts. Hazel sits perfectly still. The two male agents stand guard at the only exit, behind them.

Yen steps closer. "We have to move out at dawn or we will never get out of the city alive."

Hazel grabs hold of Elizabeth, hugging her, whispering, "I want you to know I love you. I have loved you since the day you were born, and I will love you till the second I die. I can't guide you through this darkness, but I will always be with you." She places her hand against Elizabeth's chest. "Let go. And live for me."

She pulls Elizabeth in tight again, takes a deep breath, and kisses her cheek. She glances down at Elizabeth's mended wrist, then takes Elizabeth's hands, squeezing them. "We were lucky, you know. I was lucky. Perhaps this is the price to pay for allowing me another day with you. Another moment to touch you, smell you, talk to you, and love you. Cry, laugh, and hold you. I get to say goodbye this time."

She kisses Elizabeth's cheek and pulls her sleeve up. A two-inch tattoo is raw and puffy against her left wrist, where Elizabeth's own now contains stitches. It is an identical turtle to the one on Elizabeth's back shoulder. "Get out of here and fight for me." Her fists tighten at her side. She stands up and walks around to the opposite side of the table.

"Fight to live." She looks past Elizabeth, then at the agents, nods, grabs the dagger off the table, and shoves the blade through the turtle on her wrist.

No. No. "No!" Elizabeth's heart sinks to the ground. She propels forward, across the table toward her.

Benjamin grabs her, pulling her into his arms, and carries her into the hallway. The lab door locks behind them. He sets Elizabeth's feet down onto the floor.

Her body sinks to the ground—shutting out as much of the world as possible. She can hear her own sobs, but she can't feel anything. There is nothing.

The door opens behind them.

A thick needle jams into Elizabeth's shoulder. It is real. Its sharp tip slices through her cells, but it is nothing compared to the emptiness filling her every being. A warm rush of sedative courses through her veins.

SURFACE

ELIZABETH AWAKES TO AN EMPTY EXAM ROOM. THE fluorescent bulbs flicker as she slides off the table. The hallway is silent.

Willow is at the back of the dim-lit laboratory staring at a petri dish. Yen and Benjamin are sleeping in a room to the right, on some cots.

A male voice comes from behind Elizabeth. "Hey, do you know why I'm here?"

I know that voice. Elizabeth's stomach knots. She turns and there *he* is. Her hands clench into fists.

"Elizabeth?" The guy who tore out her heart and stomped it into the ground stands mere inches from her.

Dominic's eyes widen with surprise. They follow the twisted strands of Elizabeth's dreadlocks. He reaches for her hand. "I've been —"

"Don't touch me!" She pulls back from him.

Benjamin jumps between the two. "Get him out of here."

Yen yanks Dominic's arm and forces him down the hallway.

Benjamin pulls Elizabeth into the sleeping quarters.

"What is *he* doing here?" she yells.

"We were trying to find you." Benjamin closes the door. "Listen, we leave in a few hours. If you don't want him to come with us ... we can leave him. He's no use to us now."

Elizabeth sits down on a cot.

"This is your decision." Benjamin sits down beside her. The warmth from his body brushes her arm. He turns to her, gently sliding his fingers along the curve of her face. His thumb wipes a falling tear and guides her chin toward his. "Find your strength and courage."

He reaches into his pocket, retrieving the turquoise fox necklace. It twirls in the air before falling into the palm of Elizabeth's hand.

It is all she has left of her sister.

"You're going to need it." He gets up and walks out the door.

Elizabeth lays back, the cot sags beneath her. Carbon dioxide heaves from her lungs. The increased production of white blood cells within her body drains any extra energy she has. She picks at the tape sealing the gauze against her wrist and rips the bandage off. The swollen wound is tightening against its stitches. She rolls onto her side and begins to count them. The weight of her eyelids clears the tears from her eyes. The necklace slides from her fingers to the floor. She leans over to grab it, but hears a faint conversation next door.

"It's getting worse out there," says Yen, stepping into the security room.

Benjamin sits at the desk, motionless in front of the monitors.

"What are you doing with the boyfriend?"

"I left it up to her." Benjamin spins in the chair, facing Yen.

"You can't get attached." Yen sits on the desk blocking the monitors. "We have a job to do. You can't save her."

Benjamin stands, facing the weapons closet. He chooses a samurai sword and fastens it to his side, attempting to ignore Yen shadowing him.

"You know you'll have to tell her." Yen glances over at the surveillance monitors. "Shit, you should tell her."

"Tell me what?" Elizabeth steps into the room. It is half the size of the others. The wall of monitors fade into the background as she notices the weapon closet across the room. The bone dagger sits mounted in its middle.

Yen raises his eyebrows at Benjamin, then leaves the room.

Elizabeth joins Benjamin at the closet and reaches for a 19-inch sword mounted on the wall. His hand rests atop hers, stopping it. He then nods towards the two chairs in front of the monitors. She turns a seat away from the wall of screens to face him and sits down.

"Do you remember the story of Coyote and Meadowlark?" He pulls up the other chair, sitting beside her, facing the monitors. "Do you remember that Coyote promised Meadowlark the dead would not return to the earth after death?"

Elizabeth nods, sinking in her seat.

"Well, Coyote-man joined his favorite people and lived among them. He indulged in their mortal women, but never desired any as much as Awanata—a woman unlike any he had ever laid eyes on. Hair identical to the sun, eyes mirroring the sky, and skin as milky as the clouds.

"Of course, the Chief had also noticed her beauty and promised her to his son, a mortal man. On her wedding day, Coyote-man approached Awanata and offered himself to her. She declined. Soon after, an illness fell over the tribe. By night, her newlywed husband lay dying. When she went to fetch him water from the falls, Coyote-man once again approached her. He told her that if she willingly gave herself to him, her people would be saved. Again, she refused. But on the walk back to the village, the dead began to rise. The people grew empty and wild.

"She kissed her husband's cheek, knowing it would be the last time she would feel his skin against hers. Coyote-man was waiting beside the waterfall when she returned. Awanata demanded proof that he would keep his promise. That night, he created the moon—for her."

Benjamin leaves his chair, walking back to the weapons closet. "The Ahwahnee Indians say, in that moment, she killed herself, with this…" He hands Elizabeth the dagger. "Legends tell that the handle glows in the moonlight." He pauses, glancing down at it. "Coyote's howl accompanied the moon that night. He freed the people from illness and allowed them to bury their dead. As for her husband, bearing the pain of the loss of Awanata was more punishment than death could have ever brought. The Coyote-man left the moon in the sky as a constant reminder to him — and her tribe — of the decision she had made, of her sacrifice for them."

"But what does that have to do with me? That's only a legend." Elizabeth hands the dagger back.

"This legend ceased to carry on after 1864. You see it was not because of the Ahwahnee tribe's extinction. They still existed at that time. In that same year, a white child was born on their land. It is no coincidence President Lincoln signed the Wilderness Act and created Meadowlark the year after your great-grandmother was born. Nor the fact that the park was protected, guaranteeing that you would one day be able to return to the land. You are her sole heir. It must be your blood to save the world." He rests a hand on Elizabeth's shoulder. "Haven't you always known or felt that your life had more purpose?"

Elizabeth sits up in her seat, laughing so hard she nearly falls out of the chair. Benjamin stays completely silent. His eyes search the room for the humor as she catches her breath. She brushes the tears from her cheeks and slowly stands.

Clearing her throat masks the heaviness of her steps toward the weapons closet. If she chooses the biggest freakin' weapon on the wall, she can kill all of them—every last zombie—and be free of this madness. A small knife grants her attention. *It would be easy to cut open my wrist. Then Benjamin can worry about saving this fucking world.* Elizabeth's fingers touch the knife before she can finish the thought.

"Are you thinking of killing yourself?" Benjamin stops her. There is no anger in his voice, but he realizes the impact of the comment itself.

Elizabeth again reaches for that 19-inch sword.

"There is no way you can handle that," he says.

He is as sexist as his partner had been.

"That's not what I meant." He raises his hands in the air in defense. "That one's just too big for your frame. Having the wrong tool can be worse than having nothing at all."

He studies Elizabeth's body. His eyes meet hers. He doesn't smile, only pauses a moment to look for the sorrow within her. His pity floods her and she looks away.

He scans each weapon quickly and chooses a set of 19-inch samurai swords, complete with a back holster. Then he helps Elizabeth slip the straps up her arms and over her shoulders. "You don't have to forget her. She will always be with you. At least she got to see you as *you*. You had a chance to say goodbye, which is more than most of them will ever get."

Elizabeth shoves him away. "Don't act like you know me."

He doesn't move.

She grabs the set of swords, clenching their hilts. She takes a long breath and holds it—letting the wall of weapons distract her from his words. The small knife's blade shimmers in the lamplight. She reaches for it. Benjamin doesn't try to stop her. She slides it down the inside of her boot. Its presence is weak compared to that of the dagger. She reaches for a grenade next. Benjamin slams his hand down on top of hers.

"I think I'll handle these," he says, releasing his hand, pulling her face toward his. "You need to understand a few things before we leave." He lets go and paces around the room. "We move exactly at dawn. Hopefully we will have an advantage."

Benjamin fills his pockets with weaponry. "You may start feeling the effects of the virus. Some symptoms mimic the flu at first. You're going to have to convince your immune system to fight, even when you can't go on any longer." He stops, giving her his full attention. "First, initial infection occurs, like any typical flu. You feel like complete crap."

"Shit. You mean she'll feel like shit." Yen leans in the doorway and glances at the monitors. "Are you ready to go? It's almost light." Yen disappears down the hallway.

Benjamin follows and Elizabeth takes the only path available to her, behind him.

Willow squeezes by, tapping Elizabeth's ass. "Keep your eyes open, babe. It's going to be a *long* trip."

Benjamin stops outside the lounge door, looking through the window. Elizabeth continues past him. He grabs her arm, pulling her back toward him. She holds her breath. He hands her a machete and digs into his pocket. "You need to decide now"— he grabs her other hand, placing the bracelet of freshwater pearls into her palm. It is the bracelet Dominic had intended for his slut, taken from the suitcase at the beach house. "Do you want to bring him?"

Elizabeth's eyes follow Benjamin's to the door's window. Dominic paces in front of the couch. She grabs onto the doorknob and looks back at Benjamin. Her fingers slide from the brass and she begins to walk away from the door. Dominic had broken her heart, but she can't stop loving him. If she leaves him, he will be trapped down there, eventually leading him to his death. She turns back, bumping into Benjamin at her heels.

"Make it quick," he says, nodding, before joining the other agents down the hallway.

Elizabeth opens the door and steps into the lounge. Dominic turns around to face her. Anger of his infidelity floods over Elizabeth and she charges him, pressing the machete blade to his throat. *Why is he left standing in Hazel's spot and she isn't here?*

His eyes widen and he pleads, "I love you."

"Shut up," barely makes it out of her lips. She pulls the blade back and tosses the machete to him. "Don't make me change my mind."

He doesn't shove the blade through her heart, ripping every last piece out, but each following footstep feels that way. She steps into the corridor and her equilibrium wavers, pushing her into a dizzy spell. She falls against the wall, leaning for a moment to gain balance. Dominic grabs her arm and she has no choice but to let him carry half her weight until they catch up to the others.

"You protect her with your life," says Benjamin, poking Dominic in the chest, stepping closer. "Or it will cost you yours. This isn't a game. It's life or death out there"—his voice raises —"and you must be willing to give your life for her, or"—he presses a pistol to Dominic's head—"I will kill you. Either way, you will die if something happens to her."

Willow scans her retina at the door. It decompresses and begins to open. The group follows her through two of the three doors that ascend back into reality—into a dying world. The last corridor is dark. She stops halfway to the top. Her fingers brush the flat wall and a panel decompresses, opening.

Light fades in from a covered parking lot deck.

A Meadowlark Hummer sits twenty feet away. Cars litter the parking spaces. The stairwell to the right is as pitch black as the shadows. They are halfway there when two adult-sized silhouettes appear at the far end of the parking deck.

"Get down," Benjamin hoarsely whispers.

Elizabeth kneels in the middle of the parking deck, ten feet from the Hummer. Perspiration drips from her pores. She is so cold. The dawning sunlight trickles through the deck's open windows, but Elizabeth's weakness—not the light—knocks her onto her butt.

"Three o'clock," whispers Benjamin.

A third dark figure emerges from the stairwell on the right. It moans. Elizabeth's heart pounds, but her body won't move. The figure steps into the light. Remnants of a man hang in a torn business suit. His nose lifts toward the air like a hungry animal smelling for prey. His groans turn angry and loud.

A car door to their left creaks open. Two secretary-type women dying of infection stumble out of it.

Dominic steals the gun holstered at Willow's side, aims at the zombie women, and pulls the trigger. Nothing happens. Willow rips the gun from his fingers and smacks him in the face.

She clicks the unlock-button for the Hummer. It beeps and the headlights flash.

The figures closing in around them quicken.

A grenade rolls out in front of them, stopping at Yen's feet.

"Shit..." says Dominic.

"What the fuck did you just do?" Willow screams at him.

Benjamin grabs Elizabeth's arm, draws his samurai sword, and swings at the businessman by the stairwell. The man's head falls to the floor, bounces, and rolls to a stop between Elizabeth's feet. Death begins to look much different than it once had.

Benjamin hoists Elizabeth up alongside him and throws her down the stairwell. She hits the bottom cement slab. His body falls on top of her, crushing her lungs. He wraps his arms over her head and smothers her face against his chest.

The grenade explodes. The parking deck's foundation shakes. Dust fills the air.

"Keep moving." His weight releases. "Now!"

Elizabeth tries to cough in the bend of her arm, but he yanks it away, pulling her down to the lowest level of the parking garage. It is even darker than before. Cement particles condense in the air as dust. Elizabeth attempts to grab the swords holstered on her back, but exhaustion forces her arms back down. Benjamin guides her through the sub-parking deck. Darkness and dust blind any path.

Elizabeth's shoulder hits something—*someone else's shoulder*. Adrenaline floods her system so fast it hurts. She squeezes Benjamin's hand.

He pulls her into his chest, swings his sword in a circle, and slices through the particles. The blade hits something, sticking for a second before he yanks the sword back from the darkness.

The red light from an *EXIT* sign faintly flickers nearby. The door beneath it leads them outside, into blinding sunlight.

Benjamin barricades the door with his body once it closes behind them.

An obese man and an average woman stand in the street. They gaze up into the sun, soaking it in.

Elizabeth leans against the building, restraining any breath— any noise. Benjamin releases her hand and steps in front of her as protection.

The woman moves quicker than expected and charges Benjamin. With a single swing of his sword, her bowels spill out into the street. The man attacks next. He plows into Benjamin.

Willow bursts through the *EXIT* door and stabs the fucker in his chest, over and over again. Dominic appears behind Willow, bracing Yen up against his shoulder. Benjamin leads the group toward the front of the building—hugging its side—back to where the Bronco is parked.

An infected couple stand beside a minivan parked at the curb along the path. Their clothes are wrinkled and saturated with more than one type of body fluid. The woman has one arm left and the man beside her chews on it. A young child emerges between their legs from behind. The man stops chewing, looks down at the child, and follows its gaze to the approaching group.

Elizabeth can feel their hungry eyes tearing through her flesh as Willow pulls her toward the Bronco. Elizabeth longs for the cover night had provided just hours before. The Bronco blurs as her eyes burn with fever. Willow lets go of her hand. Elizabeth won't make it alone. She closes her eyes, takes a breath, and reopens them.

An old man steps out of a store across the street. The sun warms his wrinkled skin and his walk quickens. Elizabeth closes her eyes, letting the hot tears soothe them. She glances back at the man. He is right there, right in front of her when she opens her eyes. He pitches her onto the asphalt.

"Help her!" Willow screams as she elbows the mother to the ground.

"No!" Dominic shouts at the old man as he kicks him off of Elizabeth. The old man scrambles back to get to her. Dominic thrusts the machete down through the man's spine, twisting the blade. He reaches down to help Elizabeth up. "Are you okay?"

The old man rolls over, lunging for Dominic.

Benjamin grabs his silver hair, yanks his head up, and severs it. Blood runs into the cracks of asphalt. He steps around Dominic, grabbing Elizabeth's hand. "Watch your back."

"Liz!" Dominic calls out.

The zombie child sprints toward Elizabeth. She reaches for the sword over her left shoulder. Her fingers touch it. *I can't do this*. Her hand falls to the side as the once-innocent child rushes closer.

Strong arms wrap around Elizabeth's waist from behind. Somehow she ends up in the Bronco. Dominic pushes in beside her.

The child's tiny body is left lifeless in the street—broken.

INFECTION

ELIZABETH WEAVES IN AND OUT OF CONSCIOUSNESS. Benjamin has taken the driver's seat and heads west, out of the city of Portland. Yen sits beside him, focused on the road as the black pavement flows beneath the car. Benjamin angles the rearview mirror at Willow, who sits behind him, tilting it down to capture only her hands that rub the sweat-soaked hair from Elizabeth's face. The girl's body shivers with fever. She easily slides closer to Dominic as the Bronco swerves through abandoned cars on the road.

A woman stands beside the road in the distance. Benjamin speeds up. She steps into the highway. There is no time to brake, even if Benjamin wanted to. He plows into her. The metal hood and roof clanks like a tin can as her infected body goes flying over the vehicle, whacking the pavement behind them.

Cement walls transform into squished rows of small residential houses. The plots of land increase between residences as they creep closer toward the coast. A long stretch of tree farms rise out of the land, until the earth starts to flatten out again. The pounding of the ocean plays into the silence as they hit Lincoln City and head south. The mist has begun to settle on Highway 101.

There is a break in the clouds around the tiny town of Yachats. Benjamin must slow down to take the curves along the ocean's cliff. He accelerates—speeding—shooting the vehicle over a small bridge and up into the winding cliff that creates Cape Perpetua.

"Don't move for them." Yen's voice ricochets off the front window. A pair of men decked out in athletic gear jump into the southbound lane the Bronco is headed in.

"Shit." Benjamin jerks the wheel left to counteract the impact.

The right headlight clips the closest of the two men. He bounces off the hood, cracking the windshield, and falls over the cliff of the mountain into the sea.

Benjamin repositions his grip on the steering wheel and slows his speed. Once the road begins to straighten out, he glances into the rearview mirror, repositioning it to the road behind them. A car appears in its reflection. The vehicle swerves in the distance behind them, gaining on the Bronco. Benjamin slows to let them pass, but the car careens into the back of them. The Bronco shoots forward into the wall of the mountain. Darkness fills the momentum of impact and his neck whiplashes. The world goes dark in one blink, blinding every sense. The airbag bursts against his cheek, reassuring him of life. It hurts like hell, but he deeply takes another breath. His hand shakes as he releases the seatbelt, letting out a huge sigh. "Everyone okay?"

Yen nods. He is okay.

"Willow?" Benjamin's shoulder pops as he turns to look behind him.

"Fine." She pushes Elizabeth's head up off her lap.

"We need to move." Yen looks at the ocean as he climbs out. A line of grey clouds appear over the horizon.

Dominic hops out of the backseat and starts to head south along the highway. Yen steps in front of him, nodding him back to the car. Willow slides out of the vehicle, pulling Elizabeth's limp body from the back seat.

"Help her," says Yen to Dominic.

"Dude, just leave her." Dominic glances back at the women. "She's slowing us down."

Benjamin grabs the back of Dominic's shirt and throws him to the ground. He draws the samurai sword from his holster, pointing it at the car. "Now."

Dominic scrambles to his feet and follows its direction.

"Take the rear." Benjamin pats Yen's shoulder. A wall of rain pushes across the open ocean. It pours on them, soaking the asphalt, creating rivers down the mountain. His rubber soles barely grip its surface.

There is a dirt driveway on the right that leads to the Heceta Head Bed and Breakfast—the historic lighthouse keeper's old house. A white picket fence gates its antique frame. Dim porch lights accentuate the century-old body wrapped in white paint.

The house's back door squeaks open as he approaches. A dark silhouette fills its doorway, hidden by a thin screen door.

Benjamin clenches the sword's hilt, ready for anything.

"I'm sorry ..." an old woman's voice carries through the mesh screen.

Benjamin's grip eases and he continues to the steps. The scent of a blown-out candle drifts into the night.

Moonlight reveals the woman's white hair and deep wrinkles. Her hands tremble as she tries to steady a candle in her grip. "We're closed."

"Is anyone here sick?" Benjamin asks, ascending the few steps to the door.

"Sir, there's no one here." She begins to pull the door closed. "I don't want any trouble."

"I mean you no harm." He catches the door's edge, restraining its closure. "We only wish to get out of the rain. Then we'll be on our way."

She looks up at the sky and then at his drenched clothes.

Yen joins him with his Homeland Security badge already out. Obediently, the old lady steps aside and allows them in. The men secure the two story house as Willow and Dominic carry Elizabeth inside.

The woman gasps when she sees Elizabeth's limp body. She relights the candle and leads them into the living room.

They collapse onto the couch, unloading Elizabeth's body.

Benjamin blows out the candles flickering on a nearby hutch. Ocean air pushes against the rickety walls searching for a way in as he crosses the room. Its cold air howls against the thin windowpanes. Within a single puff, he blows out the old woman's candle and drops into a chair beside the front window. At the moment, it faces the fog and nothing else. Exhaustion will have to wait until the second shift.

Yen leaves the room, taking post at the back door they entered through.

"Towels?" Willow asks, pulling Elizabeth's soaked clothing off; they slosh to the floor. She wrings out each dreadlock. Water trickles into the cushions.

Benjamin forces his eyes toward the blanket of fog outside. *If she had been any other woman …* It is not a thought he can afford to have.

The old woman scuffles out of the room and back in with an armful of thick, fluffy towels.

Willow peels her shirt off. A black sports bra squeezes her breasts, until it doesn't. She strips within a single minute, fastens a towel around her chest, and begins to wipe the rain water from Elizabeth's naked body. "She's burning up."

The old woman disappears and returns with a damp hand towel that she presses against the Elizabeth's's forehead. Roberta has worked at the bed and breakfast since the time her skin was smooth and young. Now, her wrinkled hands shake as she dabs the towel against Elizabeth's hairline. She glances at Willow, "Go ahead, dear. Get dry."

Willow pulls a handgun from the pile of wet clothes and switches places with Benjamin. They have been trained that self-preservation comes last, and Willow follows it by the book.

Benjamin scoops Elizabeth off the couch, asking Roberta for, "A bedroom?"

The old woman leads him to the second floor.

He lays Elizabeth's limp body on top of a floral quilt, in a quaint Victorian room. The sound of crashing waves draws up from the fog below.

Roberta unties a knitted shawl from her shoulders and places it over Elizabeth's pallid body, then leaves the room.

Elizabeth can't move. Her head throbs and fever chills her. She shivers under the warmth of the shawl. The safety of the house doesn't ease the pain coursing through her veins, but it allows her to completely relax.

The bedroom door slowly creeps open, but there is no use forcing words to find out who intrudes. Her eyes burn. If she moves them at all, the eyelids protecting them will surely shrivel with heat.

A man's hand slides up Elizabeth's leg. Its warmth scorches her skin. Dominic's voice digs through the air, "Oh, I've missed the feel of you."

His breath smells like shit. Her stomach knots. She can't sink any farther into the mattress away from him. His fingers creep up to her knee, pushing the shawl from her thigh. The room spins as his fingers inch higher. Bile sloshes up Elizabeth's esophagus and she forces herself to swallow it.

"Get out." Benjamin's voice barges into the room, the sound of the door ricocheting off the wall. Everything is so loud.

The mattress shifts as Dominic stands. Elizabeth cracks her eyelids, seeing the old woman scoot into the room, in between the two men. Elizabeth relaxes in her presence. Minutes blend into an eternity, accompanied by the scent of her talcum powder. Pieces of *Twinkle, twinkle, little star* break into Elizabeth's consciousness. Death kisses at her skin, grasping for her life.

By morning, Elizabeth's immune system is exhausted, but when the sun rises, she opens her eyes. Roberta is asleep in a chair nestled in the room's corner, at the foot of the bed. Elizabeth sits up. The ocean pounds at the bottom of a cliff, onto a small beach cove. Stale sweat coats her skin. Rays of sunlight brush over the small bedroom, warming the air.

She scoots out from beneath a quilt and gets out of the bed, rocking its frame. The wooden headboard knocks against the wall, awakening the old woman. For she too had slept with death tempting to lure her from this life.

She smiles and Elizabeth is filled with ease. Roberta stands and the floorboards creak. She moves around the bed, places a brown tee-shirt from the gift shop beside Elizabeth on the bed, and heads downstairs, suggesting, "How about I make some breakfast?"

Agent Willow enters the room, passing Roberta on her way out. "So you made it through the night I see. How are you feeling?"

Elizabeth pulls the quilt to her neck.

Willow sits down next to her, brushing a dreadlock behind Elizabeth's ear.

"Where are we?" Elizabeth pulls her knees into her chest. The quilt draws up from the bed's edge.

Willow looks down at the shirt beside Elizabeth. "It's an amazing thing—what you're doing."

Elizabeth's cheeks are still feverish. It burns to move her libs. "I only have a few hours?"

Willow shrugs, clenching her lips together.

Elizabeth pulls the shirt on, grateful it is long enough to reach her fingertips. She stands and vertigo rushes up the stairwell, spinning her into a dizzy spell that pulls her down the steps, zig-zagging between the stairwell walls.

"Come in here, dear." Roberta's voice lures Elizabeth into a small kitchen. She places a single plate at a table meant for four.

One chair is moved to guard the back door. Benjamin sits in it. His eyes rush straight to the bottom of Elizabeth's gift-shop tee-shirt. She tugs it down enough for modesty, but her cheeks blaze with embarrassment.

Roberta smiles at them, saying, "Oh, young love."

"Ma'am?" Benjamin pulls his eyes away from Elizabeth, staring into the backyard.

"It's been quite a long time since I've felt that." She dumps two flat eggs and a pile of bacon onto the plate.

Elizabeth's stomach growls despite the eggs' nauseating smell. She picks up the fork, staring down at the plate. "Thank you."

Roberta sits down across from her. The old woman's voice, for only a moment, reminds Elizabeth of her mother's. "Eat up before it gets cold."

Elizabeth rests her hand on top of Roberta's, waiting for the old, worn-out eyes to find hers. "Thank you."

She withdraws her hand and pats Elizabeth's.

Yen walks into the room like normal, but to Elizabeth it sounds like a herd of elephants. He places her clothes—neatly folded and dried—on the table.

She devours the food, easing the hunger that churns through her stomach. She grabs the clothes and hurries into the bathroom. The tank tops are still warm from the dryer. She slides into them, absorbing all their warmth. Next, she slides into a pair of scrub-pants, and the gift-shop tee-shirt, then begins to pull on her soaked knee-high boots. Every time she touches them, she thinks of Jan—her best friend. She sees her laughing in Alex's dad's closet.

There is a soft knock at the bathroom door. Elizabeth falls over, landing on the toilet. The first boot slips on.

Roberta enters, holding out a pair of purple flip-flops. "Those are probably drenched. Why don't you take these? You better hurry. They're all waiting for you."

Elizabeth takes off the boot, ties both boot laces together, and throws the pair over her shoulder.

Roberta walks with her to the back door, opening it.

A mid-1990s Buick Roadmaster station wagon idles in the small dirt parking lot, just beyond the picket fence.

She grabs Roberta's hand and turns back to look at her. "Come with us. It's not safe here."

Her stance firms. She pulls Elizabeth into her arms, wrapping her tightly within a single hug. "I've lived my life. Go live yours."

Elizabeth is exhausted, beaten, and completely empty. She will never feel the embrace of her mom, dad, or sister again. There is nothing left to live for.

Roberta lets go, cups Elizabeth's face, and kisses her forehead.

Elizabeth closes her eyes and steps from that porch. It is what she is supposed to do.

Dominic's irritating face looks at her from behind the empty front passenger seat. She shoves the boots to the floor and climbs in. Every particle of dust lining the station wagon dances in the morning's stale air. They head south, taking a tunnel that man has carved through the mountain.

WRONG STOP

EVEN A FULL TANK OF GAS WOULDN'T HAVE GOTTEN THE station wagon to Yosemite by nightfall. They have left the Oregon Coast in the past and now rural California begins to fade behind them. A single driveway is the only thing visible for miles up ahead and the fuel gauge dips toward empty.

Benjamin cuts the wheel, turning down a long gravel road. It leads to a run-down trailer. The closer they get, the more it looks like a piece of crap.

"Where are we going?" Elizabeth hunches against the window in the passenger seat.

Benjamin parks twenty feet from the residence and hops out.

"Stay in the car," says Yen, pushing Dominic out of the backseat, dragging him along.

Elizabeth can't help but find it amusing. Dominic looks so stupid crouched alongside the agents as they inch up to an old beat-up truck parked out front of the trailer. Benjamin disappears around back. Dominic siphons gasoline from the rusted vehicle and Yen stands guard beside him.

The curtains move in the window directly behind the two.

Elizabeth glances back at Willow to see if she noticed. She has, already sitting up on the edge of the back seat.

A shotgun blasts from the trailer window.

"Get down!" She jumps into the driver's seat and floors the station wagon into reverse. Halfway down the driveway, the trailer disappears from sight. She spins the vehicle around and stops when the front tires hit the gravel's edge.

The door behind Elizabeth squeaks open and slams shut. It is Dominic.

"Shush," instructs Willow. She glances back at Dominic, who now cowers in the back seat. "Lock the doors and stay down."

Elizabeth sinks to the floor, slouched against the door, and tries to get comfortable. The window-crank digs into her arm, but adrenaline eases its pressure.

Willow gets out, shutting Dominic and Elizabeth in.

Elizabeth sits up to see where Willow heads. The long driveway is empty behind them to the trailer. Dominic blocks the rearview window with his big head and climbs into the driver seat.

"Are you really going to die for these people?" He reaches his hand down around her feet, as if searching for something, then grabs her left foot, pulling it into his lap. The flip-flop falls to the floor. He rubs her foot between his hands, warming it. "Your feet are freezing."

She pulls her leg away from him, but his nails dig into her ankle, holding her foot in place. She searches the surrounding perimeter. There is no sign of hope or a distraction.

"So, what do you say?" Dominic squeezes her ankle tighter, running his other hand up her thigh. "How about you let me fuck you before you die a virgin?"

She scoots closer to him and grabs the collar of his shirt. An inch from being able to feel his lips press against hers, she whispers, "Go fuck yourself."

She lets go and yanks her foot away, staring out the window. She can't feel his reaction and doesn't care. Anger and adrenaline restrain any tears. The thick forest framing the driveway darkens with the evening's sun. Elizabeth slouches down into the seat, ignoring Dominic's befuddled stare.

He slides across the bench seat, pinning her against the door, grabbing her knee. "Technically we're still going out."

She stares harder out the window, hoping he will disappear.

His hand slides up her thigh and his fingers dig harder into the cotton scrubs. "I'm sorry, babe."

Every muscle in her body tightens. The trees blur as tears build within her eyes. *Fucking asshole.*

"What was I supposed to do? You left me that morning. No guy is going to turn down a girl. It wasn't my fault." He releases his grip and pushes a dreadlock from her cheek. His touch is almost gentle. "Let's forget this weekend ever happened."

If only this weekend never happened. Elizabeth looks at her reflection caught in the sideview mirror, and leans her head against the window. She looks at the girl staring back at her: the brown twisted dreadlocks. She has never looked so much like her sister Hazel. Elizabeth can see her smile in her thoughts. She can feel Zach's fingers twisting each dreadlock. And for a moment, she can almost smell the scent of the campfire. Her reflection looks back. "It will never be the same."

The door behind Dominic flies open.

The vehicle rocks as Willow pushes Benjamin into the back seat. She chucks the Bronco's keys at Dominic. "Drive!"

Her hands press against Benjamin's left bicep. She yells at Elizabeth to, "Get his belt!"

Elizabeth teeters over the front seat and fumbles with his belt buckle. He lifts his pelvis, releasing the belt from behind him. Blood gushes from his arm.

Dominic throws the station wagon into drive and takes off. The vehicle shoots forward and all of Elizabeth's weight shifts, almost toppling her onto the agents.

The dotted yellow lines of the road bleed into a solid stream. The fuel gauge *pings*, near empty. It is empty.

Dominic slows the station wagon at first and then begins to speed, making the most of what fuel they have left. The hypnotizing, blurred lines brake as the road curves.

"Hold on!" Dominic yells, slamming on the brakes.

A two-pump gas station appears up ahead.

A gas station! Elizabeth breathes a sigh of relief. They are sure to have basic medical supplies.

"You hold this." Willow grabs Elizabeth's arm, pulling me into the back seat, and forcing her over Benjamin's gunshot wound. His blood oozes between her fingers.

"You …," Willow kicks the back of the driver's seat, "fill up the car." She gets out and heads for the convenience store.

By the time she reaches the entrance, warm blood has started to drip down Elizabeth's hand.

Benjamin begins to nod off.

"Hey, so where did you run off to?" she says to him.

"Kill the son of a bitch who shot Yen." He turns away, trying to hold back tears.

Elizabeth knows that feeling. If Benjamin doesn't push back the thoughts: how many moments of laughter are now lost, all the things he will never be able to say, the immense regrets—his will to live will perish. She presses harder against his arm. "Hey, you stay with me."

His eyes stay on the window.

"I won't do it without you," Elizabeth says.

He looks at her.

She presses harder against his arm. "Okay, tell me something ridiculous about yourself."

The back door swings open. Willow slides in beside her, sandwiching Elizabeth in. "Don't move. I'll work around you."

Dominic gets back in the car and takes off down the road.

Willow nudges Elizabeth's hands away, cracks open a bottle of vodka, and pours it over them. She takes a swig, does both her hands, dumps it over Benjamin's wound, and gives him the bottle. He chugs a few swigs as she pulls out a travel-size sewing kit. Night falls around them as she stitches Benjamin.

The car creeps through the city of Santa Rosa, California. The streets are silent. Dominic stops at a red light. Willow jumps out of the car, tears the driver side door open, and shoves Dominic into the passenger seat. She whacks him upside the back of his head. "What the hell are you doing?"

He restrains his anger.

She takes off, speeding toward a highway on-ramp. The city lights flicker. There is still life hiding in buildings, starving in closets, and dying with every second. Moonlight brightens as they leave the city behind them.

The station wagon headlights drift off the road, onto grass as they approach an overgrown driveway. Willow slows the car, turns off the main headlights, and allows the brake lights to guide her into the brush. She takes the keys from the ignition and glances back at Elizabeth. "Grab your weapons and come with me."

Benjamin has passed out.

Elizabeth steps into the night air, allows her eyes to adjust to the moonlight, and withdraws the swords from her back holster.

Willow pulls her pants down, squatting directly behind the vehicle. "Can you watch the woods?"

Blush warms Elizabeth's cheeks despite the biting cold air. She doesn't know why she is embarrassed; Willow sure isn't.

A stick cracks somewhere out there in the darkness.

Elizabeth's grip tightens around the swords. She watches each leaf rustle in the breeze.

"You should go," Willow says walking up behind her, handing her a torn handkerchief. "We're sticking it out here tonight."

Elizabeth takes the piece of cotton, and takes her turn behind the vehicle.

The passenger door opens. The interior light blinds the moon's natural glow as Elizabeth stands up.

"What are we doing here?" Dominic's voice pierces the peacefulness.

"Shush." Willow pulls him away from the station wagon and gently closes the vehicle door. She searches the perimeter for movement.

The bickering ceases. Elizabeth is grateful for the night's concealment. Dominic slides back into the front seat.

Willow opens the back door.

Elizabeth steps in front of her, blocking the seat beside Benjamin. "I'll take the first watch."

Willow glances at Dominic and follows him into the front seat. There is no protest or argument.

Elizabeth crawls into the backseat.

The car falls silent quickly. Its passengers take to slumber as Elizabeth awaits the howl of the coyote.

BLOCKED PATH

By morning Coyote has not come and they have hit the road again. A *Yosemite National Park* sign appears in the distance, growing in size upon approach. Elizabeth slows the station wagon as they pass by it. Just beyond are three small tollbooths barricading the entrance to the valley. Blood-splattered handprints cover their exterior. Elizabeth clenches the steering wheel, looking at Willow for guidance.

"Go slow," she says, sitting up on the edge of her seat.

The tires hum over asphalt, and crunch over broken glass and torn body parts. Elizabeth presses harder on the gas pedal. The tollbooths pass outside the windows. They begin to shrink in the view of the rearview mirror.

A tollbooth door pitches open. A girl sprints after them. It appears to be a normal sprint, so Elizabeth slams on the brakes.

"What are you doing?" Willow yells, bracing her hand against the glovebox. "Go!"

Elizabeth disobeys, jumping out of the vehicle. The girl running after them looks about her age. She hopes to hell the stranger isn't infected. She yells to her, "Are you hurt?"

The girl's deep brown eyes are wide, exhausted, and filled with fear. Breathless, she stops before Elizabeth, resting her hands on bent knees, shaking her head in decline.

"Get in," Elizabeth says.

The girl squeezes into the middle of the Bronco's front seat.

Elizabeth turns to get back into the car, but something moves in the corner of her eyes. She freezes in place, grabs onto the door, and looks back down the road.

Two men appear in the distance, close to the tollbooths. The dirt and blood covering them is as obvious as their awkward stance. One approaches, dragging his foot behind him. He wears a national park uniform. Its badge dangles from his sleeve by a thread. The other man is dressed in spandex that hugs the bulging muscles of his legs. In life, he had likely completed several marathons.

Fuck this. Elizabeth jumps back into the vehicle, shifts the station wagon into drive, and takes off.

"Stop!" Willow yells.

Elizabeth slams on the brake.

The wagon screeches to a halt.

Willow extends her arm out, restraining the new girl's body from slamming into the dashboard or through the front windshield. She then flings the door open and gets out. "We've got a jogger."

The spandex man snarls and charges her. The tip of her blade cuts through his torso and jams between his ribs. She starts to pull it back out, but he steps closer, letting the blade dig deeper through him. Her fingers curl into fists as she lets go of the weapon and punches him to the ground. An animalistic hunger intensifies within his eyes as he grapples for her feet. She steps toward his crippled body, rips the sword from its place, and jams it back down into his throat, forcing all her weight onto its handle. He stops moving.

She stands up straight and turns her focus to the infected park ranger only a few feet away.

Elizabeth's heart throbs. She can watch or she can help. She grabs Willow's gun from the dashboard, pushes the driver's door open, and falls out onto the ground, trying to hurry to her aid. Elizabeth wraps both hands around the gun and takes a shot— three feet from the son of a bitch. A ringing noise deafens another sound.

Willow yells, but it is all muffled.

Elizabeth missed. *Shit.*

The ranger redirects his assault at her. Elizabeth turns to run, but her feet slide within her flip-flops and she falls. The zombie springs for her, but she kicks him away before he can pin her to the ground.

Willow reaches him, thrusting the sword down between the back of his ribs, clear through to the ground beneath him. Blood pools around his body and flows toward Elizabeth's feet. She sits up, scooting away from it. Willow grabs the gun from Elizabeth, speaking through clenched teeth, "Get in the car."

Willow takes over driving and Elizabeth settles into the passenger seat. They pass through two open gates before a third blocks the road. Any further travel will have to be on foot.

Willow gets out. "Let's go."

Benjamin grunts as he slides out from the back. Dominic tails the agents, leaving no space. Elizabeth kicks off her flip-flops, pulls on the knee-high boots, and stows the Meadowlark knife, wishing it was the bone dagger.

The girl beside her sits stiff in the front seat. Her filthy hands are folded in her lap. Her khakis and dark green STAFF shirt are wrinkled.

Elizabeth pats the girl's knee, slides out off the station wagon, and pulls both swords from her back holster.

"Who are you?" she asks.

Tears gather in the corners of Elizabeth's eyes. The question had always been easy. Her eyes search Elizabeth's for a mere introduction, but all she can do is shrug. "I don't know."

She nods with acceptance, understanding, and restraint from crying. Jennifer had been stuck in that booth, all alone, for days. There is no telling what damage it had done.

Elizabeth offers her a sword, glances at the group standing on the other side of the gate, then back at her. "You ready?"

"On foot? In there? Do you know how many people come to this park ... in a single day?" She crosses her arms. "I'm staying here."

Elizabeth begins to holster a sword, but Jennifer needs something. Elizabeth cannot leave her with nothing. She offers it out again. "Good luck."

Jennifer's jaw drops as she takes the weapon.

Elizabeth jogs to join the group.

Jennifer's light footsteps follow. She cuts in front of Elizabeth, swinging the sword carelessly. "Wait up."

"Watch what you're doing with that thing." Elizabeth eases the sword down.

The road splits up ahead, creating a one-way loop around the entire valley floor. The right side leads deeper into the park, circles the valley, and exits on the left.

Willow heads right, obeying the laws of the road.

Elizabeth begins to follow.

"Where are you going?" Jennifer stays put, crossing her arms in protest.

"To the falls," Willow says.

"Why?" the girl asks.

Willow ignores her and continues walking.

"Because if you go this way"—Jennifer points to the exiting road—"it's faster and ..." She waits for the group's attention.

The forest rustles.

"…Less campsites," her voice trails off.

"Run!" Benjamin crosses over to the left side, following the path Jennifer suggested.

Elizabeth sprints after him. She does not wait to see what they are running from. Her heart pounds harder. Several dark brown buildings appear nestled between the trees. She stops running, but her heart continues drumming within her chest. She rests her hands on bent knees, gasping to catch a breath.

Willow joins them, pointing to the only building with a large awning attached. White letters designate it to be: *Yosemite Lodge at the Falls*. Its doors are framed by glass windows. The last thing Elizabeth wants to do is walk into another dark building, but it will be safer than being out in the open.

Willow tugs on its front door. It is locked.

Elizabeth searches the forest for movement. *They'll be coming soon.* Her heart pounds.

A branch creaks in the wind.

Elizabeth turns to check on Jennifer. She is gone. Elizabeth spins around, searching for any evidence, any spot she could have got lost in.

A breeze rustles fallen leaves, scattering them toward them.

"Are you going to just stand there?" Jennifer's voice comes from behind Elizabeth—from behind the glass door. She unlocks and opens it.

Willow, Benjamin, Dominic, and Elizabeth rush in as fast as

they can. The lobby forms a rectangle with a large counter spanning most of the opposite wall, and a closed door behind it. A tiny waiting area is cluttered with lounge chairs to the left.

Benjamin sweeps the building, leaving the door behind the counter for last. If someone is inside, they will be in there. Willow locks the door behind them as though it will keep out the zombies. Jennifer presses her back to the wall, trying to disappear from sight. Dominic finds a lounge chair and props his feet on a nearby coffee table.

Willow marches over to him, slaps the back of his head, and yells through clenched teeth for him to, "Go."

Elizabeth smiles at her reaction. *Was Dominic always such a dick?*

Willow joins Benjamin at the office door, preparing to open it. Elizabeth can hear each of them inhale as she does. Benjamin turns the knob. The door swings open, banging against the wall inside. Nothing. There is nothing but a small office. They can all relax for a moment.

Elizabeth sits down behind the lobby counter's wall, hiding behind it. Benjamin steps back into the main room. Jennifer's tired body follows Elizabeth, sinking to the floor behind the counter.

"Are you ready?" Willow asks, standing over Elizabeth.

"I'll take her at sunset," says Benjamin.

THE EMPTY WATERFALL

Elizabeth stares at the worn forest path that ascends the mountain. Jennifer has sketched a map of the Lower Yosemite Falls trail for them. Benjamin, Dominic, and Elizabeth leave the Lodge, cutting onto a path across the road from the Lodge. Benjamin moves quickly up the trail. Elizabeth struggles to keep up. Cold air that silenced the insects months earlier, brushes her cheeks. Tranquility fills the valley floor.

A rock slips beneath Elizabeth's foot. Her heart jolts. A wind drifts around the canyon wall, pushing her farther up the path. Dominic shuffles his feet, one step behind her. He could thrust his machete through to her heart at any moment. A chill creeps up her spine. *Is there anything along the path that can distract me from the thought—the pain that I'm supposed to sacrifice myself for people like him?*

Yosemite's history has been beaten through the land and forgotten beneath hordes of footsteps. Their footprints carry a replenishment of its people—its protectors. The mountain cliff lines a sky full of stars and curves into an empty waterfall. Moonlight creeps over the ancient forest. Clouds drift into the valley, trickling water over the land and their heads.

Benjamin stops at the top of the path, at a clearing in the forest around the bottom of the waterfall. Elizabeth looks up at the distant balls of gas and dust. The stars have never looked so bright, burning out in the universe. She stands in the shadow of the forest, unable to step from its edge, taking in the expanse of humanity's existence.

"So do you guys want to tell me what we're doing in Yosemite and why the fuck we're climbing a mountain in the dark, during a *zombie apocalypse?*" Dominic says, bumping Elizabeth's shoulder as he squeezes past her into the clearing.

Benjamin looks back at Elizabeth. She is his answer.

She crosses her arms, not wanting to believe it.

Benjamin reaches for her hand. "Only one person can save us —can stop all of this—and prevent the death of billions of people. You can return things back to the way they're supposed to be."

She takes his hand with regret, wanting to pull back—to run away—but the warmth of his touch keeps her there. He leads her to the empty river bank. Only in the spring will the glaciers give water to its stream. He turns over her hand, brushing over the stitches of her wrist with his thumb. He pulls out the bone dagger from his pant leg, lets go of Elizabeth's hand, and holds it out flat as an offering. "You have to be willing"—his eyes meet hers—"to be with him."

She searches his eyes for any evidence that they could be wrong. "It's quiet. There is no Coyote's howl."

He grabs her wrist, pulls her closer, and places the dagger in her palm. "He already knows you've returned."

"What if it's just a legend? What if I die for nothing?"

He looks down at the dagger. The etched handle fills with moonlight as he moves his hand from it. "I wish it were."

Lunar rays fill the bone's design: the coyote howling beneath a full moon. It glows.

Elizabeth falls to the ground. Her mouth goes dry. Her grip tightens around the dagger's hilt. *It isn't fair.*

Empty winds push against her skin. She sits on the cold, wet ground staring at the mended wrist in front of her. *What had I put Hazel through?* Elizabeth hadn't thought about how her suicide would affect her sister, she just wanted the moment with Dominic to end—for her heart to stop hurting. But now, all it does is hurt. *Now she's gone.* Elizabeth had been so stupid. She wipes the tears streaming down her lips and presses the dagger's blade to the edge of the first suture, closing her eyes.

Air rushes past her.

She opens her eyes, following the movement.

Dominic sprints for the trees, taking the opposite trail that leads deeper down into the valley's floor.

Benjamin grabs Elizabeth's left arm, yanking her to a stand. The dagger slices through the first stitch. It stings, until her attention shifts to the large shadow emerging from the tree line before them. Benjamin guards her, standing firm with his sword drawn. He whispers, "Run. Run."

The shadow forms into a large black bear. It charges. Elizabeth fists the dagger in her hand.

"Run!" he yells.

Without thinking, Elizabeth follows Dominic's path. The trailhead spits her out into Yosemite Village, at the very center of the valley. The familiar cobblestone Visitor's Center sits before her. Its interior lights blare into the night through its glass doors. She can see Dominic inside. She sprints into the building, loudly whispering at him, "Turn off the lights, you dipshit."

Her eyes jet around the room for the light switch. It is to the left. She flicks it off and braces the wall to catch a breath. Her eyes begin adjusting to the darkened room.

Dominic's fingers slide between the dreadlocks on the back of Elizabeth's head. He yanks her head back, forcing her to face him. He presses his lips against hers and pushes her up against the wall. The dagger slips from her fingers, slides across the floor, and stops beside a wooden bench. Dominic's weight pins her harder against the wall.

"You should thank me," he whispers into her ear as he brings the machete to her throat. His breath presses against her neck as he rips at the drawstring of her pants.

"For what?" *For cheating on me, making me feel like shit? For making me love you and crushing my fucking heart?*

"For cheating on you," he says, watching for a reaction.

Asshole. Elizabeth pulls back her tears. She won't let him hurt her again—make her feel inferior, pathetic, and undesirable. She does not want to feel like that—*like this.*

"I overheard the agents talking. If it wasn't for that day, you would never have been vaccinated."

"You're a fucking asshole." She shoves her palms against his chest, throwing all the love she ever had for him away. She does not want to love him. She begins to walk away, rounding the wooden bench in the middle of the room.

He grabs a handful of dreadlocks and throws her against the bench. Her spine pulses with pain and nausea floods her system. He lays all his weight on top of her. His cold fingertips slide under the three layers of shirts. His warm breath creeps into her ear, shushing her. The chill of his fingers sends a wave of goosebumps through Elizabeth. His tight jeans push against her thin cotton scrubs. She searches the window for any sign of Benjamin, but Dominic grabs her face, forcing her eyes to his.

"Don't take the other day personally." He slides the machete blade down the seam of her pants, cutting the fabric from her skin. His top teeth bite into his lower lip.

Elizabeth turns away, closing her eyes, pretending she is not there. *I don't want to be here.*

He presses the machete blade harder against her neck as he undoes his belt. His grip around its handle tightens and he grabs Elizabeth's thigh, digging his fingers into her skin. He leans back enough that his pants drop to the floor. "Besides, I saved your life, so you owe me."

She reaches for the dagger.

He crushes her with his heft, pressing the blade harder against her skin. The dagger is too far out of reach. His nails dig into her hip as he pulls her to the bench's edge, forcing her thighs apart. The outside edge of her boot rubs against the hidden knife. *The knife!* She reaches for it. The tips of her fingers brush its hilt. With her free hand, she pulls her shirt up, arching her back, and presses her breasts closer to Dominic's lips as a distraction. If she gives in a little, maybe he will drop his guard.

The blade of the machete eases from Elizabeth's skin. He lifts his weight, searching her eyes for approval before pressing his mouth against her breast. The change in position is enough to wrap her fingers around the knife in her boot. She straightens her back, easing her body back from his mouth, and pulls out the knife, jamming it into his chest. His eyes grow wide.

Elizabeth twists the blade and blood drains down her fingers. She knocks the machete out of his hand and forces all of her weight against the knife. He can't hurt her anymore. Blood drips down her elbow, splattering between her breasts.

His hand goes limp. His breaths shorten to a gasp and his body slides from hers onto the floor.

She stands and all of his blood flows down her stomach. He gasps for air on the floor. She kneels beside him, ripping the knife out of his chest. There are so many things sheI wants to say, but instead she breathes in the moment, stowing the knife back into her boot. She grabs the dagger off the floor and heads for the exit, but stops. She picks up her torn scrub-pants off the floor, and digs into their pocket, taking out the bracelet Benjamin gave her—the bracelet Dominic bought for his slut. Its smooth and imperfect freshwater pearls slide between her fingertips. Each one is a different shape, but they are all beautiful. She chucks it at his dying body. If this is her hell, it is going to be what she wants.

She steps outside. The rain clouds burst. She tears off her shirts, wipes the blood from her torso, and throws them into the mud. Cold rain washes his scent from her body. Her knees buckle and she drops to the ground.

A silhouette emerges from the trail before her.

She has killed the love of her life.

The dagger falls from her fingers. Its blue glow casts upon the mud.

DISLODGE

WILLOW LOCKS THE FRONT DOOR OF THE LODGE, hurries back around the counter and into the small office, then locks that door too.

Jennifer sits beneath the only window ornamenting the far wall. On the right is a metal desk and a rolling chair.

Willow grabs a stack of paper and begins to tape it to the windowpane, hiding them from view.

Jennifer sits still, biting the skin around her fingernails. Once she accumulates enough, she spits the pieces of flesh onto the floor.

A pink and grey canvas sky disappears behind the last sheet of paper. Willow sits down beside the girl, slapping her hand away from her mouth. "Stop it."

Silence recaptures the room.

Willow rests her head back against the wall.

Something pounds against the main lobby's front door.

Jennifer returns to biting her fingernails.

Willow shushes her from making any noise.

The last light of dusk shines through the paper, casting a square on the opposite wall. As the outside world darkens, the square morphs into a synthetic yellow glow from the streetlights. A masculine silhouette steps into its frame.

Willow gasps, pinning her hand over Jennifer's mouth. She flattens her back up against the wall, watching the shadow, and releases her hand from the girl's mouth slowly.

Jennifer bites her nails again, this time harder. Willow slaps her hand down. Jennifer inhales with pain, looking down at her nail. It has torn too low and ripped her skin. Blood fills the crease surrounding the nail.

Rain begins to drum against the roof and exhaustion soon wins. The man outside the window stands unmoving. The weight of Willow's eyelids grow heavy against the shadow, nodding her to sleep.

Glass shatters.

Willow jolts awake. There is no time to restrain Jennifer's reaction. She shoots to a standing position. The man outside the window tilts his head and presses his face against the glass taped with paper. Willow yanks Jennifer back down to a sitting position. The girl's foot hits the computer chair, which rolls into the metal desk with a *clank*.

Faint moonlight seeping beneath the office door disappears to shadow. A stale moan presses against its panel from the other side. Something pounds against the office door in slow knocks, over and over again.

Jennifer grabs Willow's hand.

Another piece of glass shatters from somewhere inside the lobby. There are at least two of the infected out there now.

Willow gets up, noticing a glass paperweight shimmering on the desk. She tears the paper off the window.

A man snarls at her.

Why the hell has all this bullshit not ended yet? Where is Benjamin?

The man's bloated and loose skin sticks to the window as he presses his face against it. Condensation sprays against the glass with each grunt.

Willow grabs the paperweight. The zombie bangs its head against the window. She hurls the paperweight at his face. The window shatters. She draws a samurai sword and jams it straight through his eye socket. His dirty nails reach through the window, clawing at her arm. She twists the blade, forcing his death.

Several figures emerge from the forest's edge behind him.

Shit. She rips the sword back, through the window. "We better go the other way."

A scratching noise penetrates the office door.

"Are you fucking kidding me?" says Jennifer.

"It's literally now or never." Willow grabs Jennifer's arm and pulls her to stand.

The clawing grows louder, quicker.

Willow signals to Jennifer. The plan is that Willow will open the door, Jennifer will kill the first man and continue into the lobby—

Moans deepen outside.

Willow bends her knees, tightening her fists. *Now or never.* She unlocks the door—no doubt the zombie beyond has noticed. She kicks the door open and steps back, allowing Jennifer to attack him. The girl swings. The blade chops into the doorframe. The man's belt falls to the floor as half of him follows.

A female zombie stands behind his fallen corpse. Her hunched shoulders straighten and she leaps at Jennifer, who screams, dropping the sword to shield her face with her arms.

Willow swings. The zombie's head falls to the floor, while her body is left standing. Willow kicks the rest of her down.

Jennifer reclaims her sword from the ground.

The lobby windows fill with a horde of visitors whose decaying shells fight to get through the broken doors.

Jennifer sprints for the back exit.

Willow holsters her own sword and draws a handgun. She aims it toward Jennifer and takes a shot.

The back door shatters and glass explodes toward the girl.

Willow sprints after her, grabs her shirt, and pulls her

through the back door. Night's cold air blankets them. She pulls a grenade from her pocket and throws it into the building. Then she falls to the ground, pushing Jennifer with her.

The Lodge explodes. The tower of windows framing the adjacent Mountain Room Restaurant crumble. Nothing moves at the forest's edge.

Willow stands, helping the girl up, and hurries for the back side of the restaurant. She rounds the corner, bumping into a large object, and falls backwards to the ground.

The dark feature of a man blends with the night's shadows. His ankles are twisted inward, but his steps aren't hindered.

Jennifer stabs the 19-inch blade into his chest. He doesn't stop his attack. She forces the blade deeper until the hilt's edge catches on his skin. Blood oozes over her fingers. She rips out the blade and slits his throat.

Willow doesn't move until his body hits the ground. She acknowledges Jennifer's triumph with a single nod.

LINGERING FOOTPRINTS

BENJAMIN CARRIES ELIZABETH IN HIS ARMS. SHE WATCHES THE STARS bounce in the sky with each step. Then he stops. A figure steps into the road in the distance. Benjamin hides behind a nearby tree, letting go of Elizabeth's legs so she can stand, leaning her body against his. He peeks around the tree trunk, looks back at her, and wraps his arms tighter around her waist. Rain drips from the branches overhead and splashes against her bare skin.

Who have I become? She grabs onto his shirt collar, looking down at her hands. She scrunches the fabric, pressing her face against his shirt. She inhales. On exhale, tears pour out.

He hushes her.

A grenade explodes in the distance.

Instinctively he pushes Elizabeth to the ground, shielding her. A layer of fallen leaves sticks to her back.

A grunt echoes from down the road.

Elizabeth turns her cheek to the ground. *Everything is broken. I'm broken. I should've let go, should've killed myself.*

Benjamin pushes her cheek back so that she faces him. Tears pool in the corners of his eyes and mix with the earth's raindrops, pelting the ground around her. He whispers, "You don't have to do this."

She turns away from him.

He sits up, unbuttoning his shirt and drapes it over her naked body. He lays down beside her, grabbing her hip, rolling her toward him. His lips barely touch hers as he whispers, "If you're going to give up … at least save the world."

She opens her eyes to the deep blue of his irises.

"But I need you to know …" He presses his lips against hers. Her heart skips and he pulls away. He whispers, "I think I'm in love with you."

She turns away from him, looking at something else, anything else but him. She sits up and peels his shirt off her body, wringing it out. He doesn't say anything. She works her arms into the drenched shirt and buttons it. Moonlight captures the tree branch shadows dancing across the road. She stands, walking down the dance floor of fallen leaves, toward the Lodge at the falls.

Benjamin joins her, but stays a step behind until they arrive at the building. It has exploded from the inside out. Pieces of the Lodge litter the clearing. The shadows move between the surrounding cabins. Zombie campers circle the rubble. Benjamin jerks Elizabeth behind a nearby tree and pins her back against its bark, again. His cheek brushes against hers as he whispers, "Wait here."

She sinks down to the ground, letting the tree bark scratch her back the entire way. Mud smears between her thighs. Raindrops pelt her eyelashes. She leans her forehead against bent knees and rests.

Her heart jumps. She looks up, and there *he* is.

The old man from the café stands at the edge of the Lower Fall's trailhead. His deep, earth-toned wrinkles contrast his authentic leather outfit. Eagle feathers fill a full headdress, hiding his long grey hair. A passing breeze caresses its feathers just before he disappears into the tree line.

Elizabeth sprints after him, to the top of the trail, and freezes.

He stands over a small bear carcass, ripping a spear from its body. The moon peeks from behind the rain cloud, drawing his attention to the clearing sky.

Elizabeth joins him beside the waterfall's empty water bank.

The old Native stands as a perfect picture: a man admiring the beauty of the forest framing the valley walls, waiting for the glaciers to melt, waiting to hear the roar of pure water rushing down the mountain.

He places his hand against her cheek. "This land has been waiting a long time for you, Awanata."

He looks back to the sky. The rain clouds have moved, revealing a half moon. He studies her eyes. "Feel the Earth breathe."

He turns away and heads deeper into the woods. Elizabeth follows. Smoke rises into a vast sky from the mountain, surrounded by an endless forest. The old man's pace never slows as Elizabeth loses breath. He never waits or turns back to see if she is following. She is lost, dependent solely on this stranger.

A warm cabin appears in the distance. Wool curtains blackout the fireplace's glow from within. The smell of burning wood swirls around a small cleared yard.

The man steps into the cabin and Elizabeth follows. Rainwater drips from her skin to the floor. Three pairs of eyes fall upon her from the couch. The old man shows Elizabeth to a small bedroom to the right, closing the door as he leaves.

A single candle illuminates a towel neatly folded on the bed's bear-skin blanket. Elderberry branches hang over a hand-carved headboard. The room grows cold. Elizabeth peels Benjamin's shirt from her body.

A gentle knock precedes the old man's return. Warmth engulfs Elizabeth as the fireplace's heat drifts back in. She tucks the towel under her arms and sits on the bedside, kicking the boots from her soaked toes. He hands her a wooden bowl. Steam rises from its liquid. He nudges it closer and nods. Radiant heat fills her palms as she cups it to her lips. Its contents warm her entire body and she falls backwards onto the mattress.

The bowl falls to the floor.

A dreamcatcher swings from the branches above. *It drifts into a dragonfly mosaic, pieced together by broken mirrors.*

UNFOCUSED

NEMO RESIDEO MEANS NO ONE LEFT BEHIND. BENJAMIN has stood by that phrase long before joining Meadowlark. He runs up behind the Mountain Room Restaurant to rescue Willow and Jennifer. *They have to be in there.* It is the only building he would have chosen to take shelter in.

Infected campers shuffle through the debris of the exploded Lodge. More will be on their way.

He opens the door to the still-standing restaurant building and slowly slides in, hugging the wall. Wind gusts from the dining room. The three-story wall of windows in the restaurant were blown out from the nearby Lodge explosion. Cold air whistles through its broken pieces of glass.

Giggles come from behind the bar counter. Playful shushing follows.

Benjamin darts to the counter, jumping over it.

Willow and Jennifer sit huddled together on the floor with a bottle of wine. Willow's reaction time is off and she barely lifts the sword beside her. Jennifer laughs hysterically at this.

Benjamin slams his hand over her mouth, pressing her head back against the wall, hushing her. He tightens his grip before removing his hand, making damn sure she won't do it again.

The snarling and moans outside have ceased. It is quiet.

Benjamin rips the bottle away from Willow and pulls her off the floor. "We've *got* to go."

Jennifer laughs. He slaps her and pours the wine over her head to wake her the hell up. Her eyes brighten as she gasps. He grabs her hand, dragging her back out the way he entered. She stumbles to follow him.

Moans return outside, but this time they grow louder in the direction of the exit.

Jennifer squeezes Benjamin's hand and stops. He steps back from the door that leads outside and pivots down the hallway. They enter into a large kitchen. She lets go of Benjamin's hand.

Willow fumbles in from behind and secures the door. Benjamin searches for another way out. He finds a back door and goes for it. Just before opening it, a bright light reflects off the door's glass window, coming from behind him.

Jennifer stands in front of an open refrigerator.

"What are you doing?" He charges her and calmly closes its door. One more noise will allow the zombies to pinpoint their exact location. He heads back to the exit and unlocks its door.

Willow joins him, leaning against his shoulder. "Oh my, that was some strong stuff ..."

"Elizabeth's out there and I need to get back to her." He nudges her hand off. "Get the lightweight over here and follow me."

Jennifer pops open a bag of potato chips she has found.

Benjamin waits for Willow to grab the girl. Once she has, and the coast is clear, he darts from the building to the large tree just a few feet away where he had left Elizabeth. She is gone—Elizabeth is gone. He falls to his knees.

Willow rounds the tree. "What are you doing?"

"She's gone." He pushes his sword into the ground, trying to stand back up.

Jennifer joins them.

"Wasn't that the point?" Willow shoves her hand into Jennifer's chip bag.

"No, I left her here." His heart pounds. "To save you."

Willow laughs, covers her mouth, and looks around. She walks past him, up the path toward the Lower Falls. "Perhaps she is with Nantai."

Jennifer bumps into Benjamin's shoulder as she follows.

Benjamin searches the perimeter, hoping they are taking the right path, then follows.

Willow finally stops once they reach the clearing of the waterfall. She approaches the bear carcass.

Benjamin catches up with them there. "Who is Nantai?"

Willow points up the mountain. A faint line of chimney smoke rises deep within the forest. She grabs another handful of potato chips and heads along a hidden path. "He is an old friend."

The path stretches for miles until the outline of a wooden cabin emerges. Willow runs for it. She scoots inside and warm light from the fireplace escapes into the cold. Jennifer enters after her. Benjamin holds his breath as he steps inside.

Willow has her arms wrapped around an old Native American man—Nantai. The rumors an old Chief still exists are true. His wrinkled fingers comb through her wine-soaked hair. He lets go, directing her to the only bedroom, then crosses the room to Benjamin.

"Yosemite." Nantai taps Benjamin's shoulder and walks out into the night. The old man is the last of the Ahwahnee. His children left for the cities long ago, but one grandchild returned to the land. Though she doesn't believe in the old ways.

Benjamin leaves with him.

Agent Willow steps into the bedroom. Elizabeth's body is wrapped in a loose towel, limp on the mattress. Willow closes the door, barricading the cabin's warmth from them. She strips, takes the towel off Elizabeth's back, pats her own skin dry, then sits on the far edge of the bed. She wrings the wine out of her hair. It splashes onto her feet. The box spring creaks behind her.

She turns around and Elizabeth's soft lips press against hers. She pulls away. "I can't. You're ... well, you're *her*."

"Please. I don't want to feel him. I don't want to feel like this ..." Elizabeth rests her hand against Willow's cheek, pulling her closer. She leans back against the headboard, sinking down into the mattress. Tears drain down her cheeks. She lets out a breath of defeat. "I don't want to be *her*."

Willow wraps the towel under her arms and heads for the bedroom door, pausing before opening it.

The orange and yellow light of the fireplace dance into the room, bringing warmth with it. The living room is empty.

Voices carry from the porch.

She tiptoes to the fireplace, wrings out her clothes again and hangs them over the fire. It sizzles with each drip. She warms her hands, looks back over her shoulder, then returns to the bedroom.

Elizabeth lays stoic against the mattress.

Willow enters, shutting the door behind her, and locks it. The towel slides off her body. She climbs into bed, warming herself against Elizabeth.

Forest Shadows

Outside the cabin, Jennifer sits down on the porch steps. The uncomfortable feeling she usually gets from being with strangers, disappears. The toll booth to get into Yosemite had imprisoned her for days. The night sky, twinkling up above it, was the only thing to give her comfort.

There are three new strangers. One is a girl about the same age as Jennifer. Kimberly is a perfectly skinny girl, with perfectly placed black curls and manicured fingernails. It is obvious she has never worked a hard day in her life. She sits down beside Jennifer.

The alcohol pumping through Jennifer's veins numbs the envy and pity she has for the girl.

Kimberly's boyfriend, Dylan, smokes a cigarette a few feet away, planting his butt on the ground beside an extinguished campfire pit. Moonlight creeps through the small clearing above. The treetops rustle in the wind. Dylan's worn shoes and faded jeans give away his lower class, but he is cute enough to get Ms. Perfect. He stands, stretching to tiptoe, holding his cell phone to the sky gods.

"What's he doing?" Jennifer asks.

"Trying to update his status." Kimberly pulls a piece of gum from her mouth and sticks it beneath the porch boards.

"Aren't they down?" Jennifer says. Her phone's battery died three days ago. Three long days ago. It still cripples her not to need a cell phone any longer. Within one day, she had been cut off from everything and everyone else. In one day it was all gone.

Dylan sinks back to the ground.

"Apparently they don't work." Ms. Perfect shrugs.

The cabin door creaks open behind them.

Its noise churns the liquid in Jennifer's stomach. The forest drifts in and out of focus. She presses her fingers against her lips. The contraction of her stomach muscles push its contents up through her throat. She leans over the side of the stairs and spews.

"She's infected!" Kimberly screams. She jumps off the cabin steps and darts toward Dylan.

The cabin door bursts open, and slams shut. Heavy footsteps stop behind Jennifer.

"I think I had too much to drink." She wipes her mouth with her sleeve.

Sven's broad shoulders brush hers as he sits down beside her on the porch step. He is the third stranger.

She waves off the couple cowering at the fire pit. "Relax."

Sven loads a hunting rifle in his lap while staring at her. Sweat beads on her forehead. She is about to tell him her body *just doesn't respond well to alcohol*, when something dark moves at the forest's edge. Both Jennifer and Sven shift their attention to the shadow forming in the distance. The forest barricades the moonlight from identifying it. Sven steadies the rifle, eye level.

"Shush ...," Jennifer whispers, batting the gun down toward the ground. "Ya gotta be shush." She places her finger to her lips, picks up the sword Elizabeth gave her, and hands it to Sven to use.

He smiles, no doubt finding her intoxication amusing, and takes the weapon. The weight change nearly knocks her over. Her stomach bubbles and a deep groan releases, easing the pressure.

Sven stands to defend them. Moonlight glistens bright against his blonde hair. The darkness of his eyes mirror the forest before them.

It is coming. A head forms out of the dark shadow. It molds into the outline of claws and—as moonlight touches them—they transform to feathers. It is the old man.

Sven lowers the sword. The wind dies down. Peace sweeps through the group in the old man's presence.

A second figure emerges behind him, dragging something. It draws closer, grunting.

Sven broadens his shoulders, blocking Jennifer's view. His grip tightens around the sword in his hand.

The moon waits for the second shadow.

"Hey, can one of you give me a hand?" The dark figure has Benjamin's voice. He gives himself away before the moon does.

Neither Sven or Jennifer move.

Benjamin steps out into the moonlight, dragging the bear carcass from the bottom of the waterfall.

Sven hands the sword back to Jennifer and hurries to help. Her stomach churns as the men drop the carcass at the foot of the cabin.

"Do you know how to clean it?" Benjamin asks.

Jennifer sure as hell doesn't.

Silence presents itself, beckoning Benjamin's eyes toward the large man. Sven stands with his arms crossed, as if not having heard a word.

"Food?" Benjamin nudges him, pulls out the bone dagger, and points at the bear.

"Da," says Sven in a thick Russian accent. He nods and pulls out a skinning knife from his belt. Benjamin steps back. Sven kneels, cutting into the skin of the bear.

Jennifer cups her mouth and runs into the cabin for the bathroom.

Nantai stares at the dagger with wide eyes. His hands extend, almost touching the blade with his fingers. "May I see that?"

"You speak English?" Benjamin asks.

"I never said I didn't." Nantai smiles.

Benjamin offers out the dagger and looks down at the large Russian. "What about you? Do you speak English, too?"

Sven doesn't look up.

"I have only heard legends of this blade. My grandfather used to dream of it. But that was in a time when stories were still left to be told." Nantai's wrinkled fingers shake as he takes the dagger into his grasp. He walks toward the cleared fire pit where Kimberly and Dylan sit.

Benjamin follows.

Moonlight captures the seven-inch blade made of white bone. Nantai sits on the ground across from the teenage couple, holding the dagger out into the moonlight. The red tribal bands carved into the bone glow into a pale blue color. His fingers circle the full moon, tracing it to the coyote howling beneath, ending over the word *Pyhij*, and into the last tribal band wrapping its hilt.

Kimberly kisses Dylan on the cheek and hurries off inside. Dylan fumbles for a cigarette-lighter that has become stuck in his pocket. Once in grasp, he pulls out another cigarette. The tobacco stick hangs between his lips. "What is that?"

Nantai pulls a calumet from behind his back. It is a long,

ancient smoke-pipe that reaches to the ground. Feathers hang from it, displaying a semicircle. He pulls a stick from a side pouch and holds it out to Dylan, who in return lights its end. A small flame burns at its tip. Nantai slides his fingers back into the pouch for a pinch of herbs. He packs the bowl and presses the flame to the leaves. Smoke trails into the dark, crisp sky. He inhales and passes the pipe to the boy.

Dylan inhales the thick smoke in a long and slow puff, then hands it back to Nantai. The old man stares at the moon, passing the calumet to Benjamin, never taking his eyes off the sky.

It is no time for Benjamin to let down his guard, but there is no bigger honor than to share the moon with a Chieftain on ancient land. He is the last storyteller. Benjamin fills his lungs with the smoke, releasing it into the autumn air.

"It is a story not yet finished." Nantai takes the calumet, pressing his wrinkled lips upon it.

Bad Habits

The Native hadn't said much more to Dylan except, *"You are already part of this forest."* Whatever the hell that is supposed to mean.

Inside the cabin, Jennifer had passed out on the couch. Kimberly has taken the middle sleeping bag on the floor. Dylan takes the spot between Kimberly and the couch, sandwiched on both sides—shielded from any zombie attacks.

As he hunkers down into his safe spot, the remainder of night eases into the next morning.

He is awoken by a warm breath against his neck. A female body sits on his lap, hunched over so that her lips barely touch the skin of his neck. With his eyes closed, he can imagine anything he wants. *Bet the new girl looks hot as fuck naked.* He clenches his eyes, restraining the need to see his fantasies drip into reality. Another warm breath blows against his neck, deep, heavy. Her weight shifts against him, but not in an intimate or sexual way, more limp and hungover. He doesn't care. He grabs her ass. "Damn, girl."

His girlfriend, Kimberly, screams in his ear, "What the fuck, Dylan?"

His eyes jolt open. Kimberly is lying on the floor next to him. Her eyes are glued to the limp girl on top of his body.

"Oh, my god," Kimberly shrieks. She gets up and gets as far away from him as possible.

"Kim, wait, it's not what you think!" Dylan throws Jennifer off of him—onto the couch.

Kimberly sprints for the door, for the only exit.

Dylan trips, stumbling after her, and falls to the floor. He rolls, but it is too late. Jennifer passes him, lunging for Kimberly's neck, tearing her teeth into it. Blood squirts from Kimberly's artery. His girlfriend screams. He turns away, unable to look. Her cries die and the cabin shrinks down on him as he collapses to the floor.

SURRENDER

THE DREAMCATCHER INSIDE THE BEDROOM GENTLY swings from the elderberry branches above Elizabeth. Sunlight flows through its strings. The natural light of morning beams into the bedroom. She rolls onto her right side. The warmth confined by the covers, fades from her bare skin. The comforter is tucked tightly behind her back, as if barricaded by someone. Fingertips brush the turtle tattoo of her left shoulder. Goosebumps crawl along her skin. The last memory of the night is of a wooden bowl touching her lips—its warm liquid taking all the thoughts from her mind—all with the swinging of the dreamcatcher above her.

Elizabeth rolls over and the fingers move away. A teenage boy lays beside her. She had seen him before. Last night he sat beside a girl his age on the couch. Now, he lays fully clothed, staring atElizabeth, past her. Tears well in his eyes.

Elizabeth brushes a dreadlock from her cheek, finding her fingers shaking. The white of her nails has turned yellow from the soot compacted beneath them. The stitches on her wrist create a staircase to the deep blue branches of her vein. Sunlight dances across her arm, its warmth longing to deepen her pale skin.

The boy grabs her wrist, jerking it toward him.

"You're hurting me." She tugs back, but his fingernails dig into her skin.

He pulls out the bone dagger, pins his hand against Elizabeth's wrist on the mattress, and jams the dagger's tip beneath the second stitch.

She relaxes, looking up at the ceiling, ready for death.

The blade shakes as he severs the suture.

The dreamcatcher sways. Wind gusts outside, pressing against the cabin windows in protest.

"You can't do it," says Benjamin. He stands just outside the doorway. "And it won't bring her back."

The boy's hands shake harder. The blade stops before the third suture.

Benjamin's footsteps move toward the bed. He extends his hand out for the dagger. "If you do it, we're all dead."

Elizabeth looks back at the boy who holds her fate. His face drowns in tears. His fingers loosen from her wrist. Elizabeth lets out an exaggerated sigh of relief.

Sunlight caresses the white bone blade as Dylan hands over the dagger to Agent Benjamin.

Benjamin stands guard at the foot of the bed until the boy has left the room. Then sits down beside Elizabeth. "There are some clothes in the closet, and food in the kitchen. We're leaving in a few minutes."

Where is there to go? Death creeps from every corner of the earth. There is no place to go.

He grabs her hand, pulls it into his chest, pinches the severed stitch, and pulls it out. His thumb presses against the seam, dulling the sting.

As much as Elizabeth wants to stay, she slides from the bed and wraps a towel around her body, looking back at Benjamin before stepping into the closet to dress.

The closet is silent with the door closed. Modern-day jeans hang beside beaded and embroidered collared-shirts. A single dress catches her eye. It is all the way smushed up against the far wall, behind the same blue plaid shirt Nantai had worn in the cafe. She pulls out the dress. It is made of soft, earth-tone suede, with a v-shaped neckline, framed by turquoise beads.

Its color instantly reminds Elizabeth of the turquoise fox necklace Hazel had given her. Her fingers reach for it around her neck, but it isn't there. She lost it. It must have slipped from her fingers in the city ...

No, no, no.

The dress falls out of her hands, to the floor. Elizabeth could easily take its place. Instead, she picks it up and slides into its fur-lined, long-sleeved suede. It warms her perfectly. She steps out of the closet.

Benjamin is gone, replaced by her knee-high boots.

She scoops them up, carrying them to the bed where her swords make a pair. *Jennifer didn't make it.* She pushes them aside and sits down. No matter how bright the sun shines, each dawn will carry death.

"Awanata," the old man says as he enters the room. Elizabeth does not acknowledge that he is there until he sits down beside her. "I've always wondered what she would look like."

Elizabeth wonders, *She?*

The old man rests his hand upon her cheek. He searches her eyes for answers. "What *you* would look like ...." He presents the dagger. "I can see why Coyote chose you."

Elizabeth turns away from him. *No.* She shakes her head. *No.* She stands, pacing in front of the bed with her fingers pressed against her lips. There has to be a mistake. *This isn't real.*

Benjamin leans in the doorway.

Elizabeth freezes her pace.

"Are you ready?" His eyes focus on hers.

She sits back down beside Nantai on the bed.

Benjamin comes closer, looking at the old man. "What about you?"

"This is not my path." Nantai pats Elizabeth's knee, gets up, and walks past Benjamin. Upon exit, he stops and looks back at her. "Is it yours?"

She lets herself fall back onto the mattress. He walks out and she stares at the ceiling, trying to avoid all of it.

The dreamcatcher rocks as Benjamin lays down beside her.

"You don't have to do this." His deep-blue eyes gaze down upon her. His hand cups her cheek, giving her its warmth. He bites his bottom lip, restraining what he really wants to say.

Elizabeth turns away to the empty part of the room. Tears drip down her eyelashes, blurring the world. *I do have to do this.* She has to give up herself to save the world, to save them. But she refuses to feel it. She won't feel, won't let it overtake her and push her down into the ground until there is nothing left. Before her thoughts suffocate her, she leans over, placing her cheek against Benjamin's. The grease of his skin slides against hers as she leans against his.

He presses his lips against hers. All the loss, pain, and existence of the dying world disappear. She forces every ounce of herself in reciprocating his kiss. His fingers slide up the outside of her thigh, pushing up the edge of her suede dress. The tips of his fingers follow the curve of her butt, squeezing really hard. Then he pushes her off of him. He leans over to kiss her cheek. "I can't."

The smell of cooking meat wafts from the living room,

bringing a set of footsteps with it. They charge for the bed. Before Elizabeth has a chance to sit up, Dylan is holding a gun to her face screaming, "This is all because of you!" He presses the gun harder into her cheek. It digs into her bone with each enunciation, "Kimberly is dead because of you!"

If Elizabeth focuses on the dreamcatcher hard enough, it will rip this nightmare from her.

The gun fires.

SWARM

THE DREAMCATCHER FLYS FROM THE ELDERBERRY branch as Benjamin knocks Dylan to the floor.

The gunfire creates a deafening ringing in Elizabeth's ears.

Agent Willow sprints into the room. The boy's screams of pain pierce through the static as Benjamin pulverizes him to the ground. Willow ratchets a pair of handcuffs behind Dylan's back and jerks him off the floor. Benjamin scrambles to his feet.

Elizabeth slides off the mattress, picks up the gun, and approaches the boy. She presses the barrel of the weapon to the sweet spot between his eyebrows. "I didn't ask for this."

Fear doesn't replace his sadness.

She breathes, exhaling my anger. She holds the next breath with pursed lips, contemplating the room. *They didn't ask for this either.* She lowers the gun, allowing shame to render her eyes to the ground.

The dreamcatcher lies broken beside Dylan's foot.

Elizabeth jams the gun back to the indented circle of his forehead. "If you're going to do it—do it right."

"Elizabeth." Benjamin's voice is a whisper behind her neck. His hand slowly reaches under her arm. Calmness sweeps through her. He rests his hand on top of hers, pushing her hand and the gun down.

She elbows Benjamin away and points the gun at him. He puts his hands up in defense. She points the gun to the floor, hands it to him, and walks away. Her heart pounds. She grabs the set of swords off the mattress, holsters them to her back, and storms out the cabin.

The world disappears into a blurred tunnel as Elizabeth runs away, making it halfway down the mountain.

Two zombie-hikers pop out of nowhere on the faint trail ahead. They perk up once noticing her.

Anger floods Elizabeth's veins so quickly and carries her so fast down the path, she almost missed noticing them. Heavy hiking backpacks have arched their spines back. Their eyes are filled with hunger and their heads tilt to one side. Then they move for her.

She withdraws both swords and charges. The right blade slices into the first hiker, but the second zombie moves out of reach and Elizabeth loses her balance, tumbling down the path. Branches scrape at her face and leaves stick to the wax of her dreadlocks. Dirt skids beneath the stitches of her wrist. She finally stops rolling and stands before a six-foot boulder, three inches from her face. *That was close*.

The remaining hiker has followed her down on foot. His speed increases with the mountain slope.

Elizabeth waits. Her heart pounds so hard it could crack a rib. Once the zombie is a step away, she slides right, grabs the back of his head, and smashes it into the boulder.

A rotten smell leaks from his mouth with a moan. He climbs back to his feet and stumbles closer. Blood oozes from his skull. His expression is empty.

Elizabeth thrusts the sword between his ribs. The blade reaches for his cold heart. His fingers tear at her. She kicks him to the ground and keeps kicking. Blood splatters the edge of her dress. Her heartbeat drowns out the world as she fights for the will to live.

A set of hands grab her from behind. Black sleeves wrap around her arms, forcing her swords to the ground. Benjamin shushes her.

A breeze presses against Elizabeth's dress, ruffling the fur lining above her knee. Her chest presses against the boulder as he shields her from the wind. Goosebumps ripple over her body. She squirms, attempting to nudge him away, but his arms only tighten. The warmth of him ultimately draws her closer.

"I want you," he whispers.

The wind whistles as it passes by.

His breath warms the side of Elizabeth's neck, sending chills rippling down her spine. He loosens his arms, allowing her to face him, pulling her waist closer, kissing her.

She holds her breath and lingers in the softness of his lips against hers.

"But I can't," he says, half-heartedly pulling away, shrugging. "You belong to *him*."

A tree branch snaps just behind the boulder.

He picks up the swords, pushes Elizabeth flat against the granite, and forces one of the weapons into her hand.

A black boot emerges from behind the rock. Green pant-legs draw up to a worn-out park ranger uniform. It is the woman, Nevaeh, from the campfire at Camp Curry—the one with the story. She pulls a gun on them. Her eyes stick to Elizabeth and her jaw drops—gaping—as she stares. With her free hand, she digs into her front pocket and takes out a folded piece of paper. She unfolds it, glances at Elizabeth once and returns it to her pocket. "Are you Elizabeth?" she says. "I've been looking everywhere for you."

Drops of rain trickle from the clouds.

"Come with me." She grabs Elizabeth's wrist, pulling her away from the boulder, leading down the mountain. She stops at the bottom of the trail. An old, beat-up crew cab truck with a vintage park logo is parked, silent, beside the road.

A storm begins to blow in, carrying with it slow-moving shadows.

Elizabeth jumps into the passenger seat of the truck. Benjamin nudges her into the center seat.

Willow throws Dylan—still handcuffed—into the back and hops in beside him, sword out.

Nevaeh takes the driver seat, forcing the truck into drive.

Death is close. The campgrounds awaken with movement as they drive by. Infected campers begin to flood the road, reaching for the windows, fighting to get at them. Nevaeh slows for a turn and they overtake the back bed of the truck. One smashes through the rearview window. Dylan screams. A zombie rips him out. The truck levels out and the mob of zombies fall out of the back with Dylan. They tear his limbs and shred his body. His cries cease.

Elizabeth tries to force herself to look ahead, instead of back, but forward is no better.

A large section of primitive camping sites appear in the distance. There are several fabric tents nestled between trees on the right, but most have been knocked down.

Nevaeh grips the steering wheel, preparing for impact. Elizabeth can see the blood smeared upon the broken tents. Mangled bodies stir and their crusted eyes follow the truck. Nevaeh cuts the wheel, taking them up a driveway—somewhere much too close.

Rusted Cabin

THE WINDING ROAD ASCENDS DEEPER UP THE mountain, wrapped in forest. A small cabin identical to Nantai's stands in an unfamiliar pattern of trees. There is no fire pit and no porch. Neglect has allowed the moss to grow and vines to flourish. An ax is stuck in a large stump before the cabin's rotting steps.

Benjamin studies Nevaeh as she hops out of the vehicle to unlock the cabin's rustic door. Upon doing so, she fills her hands with firewood, nodding the group in to follow. Benjamin blocks Elizabeth from getting out from the middle seat. "Why don't you wait here with Agent Willow?"

She sinks back into the seat, forcing herself not to focus on the fact that Dylan had been right beside Willow moments ago. Now he is dead. She doesn't want that same fate. She scoots to the passenger side door, waiting to run.

Benjamin gets out, withdrawing his sword. He shuts the door behind him, demanding Elizabeth stay put. He follows Nevaeh, yanks the ax from the stump, and enters the cabin. His boots clunk, announcing his presence. He slams the door shut behind him.

The sound requires Nevaeh's attention and she gives it to him from a fireplace. He charges her, pressing the ax against her throat. "Who sent you?"

"What are you talking about?" Her words catch on parched lips.

"Who sent you to find her?" He presses the blade harder.

"A guy from the park." She squeezes her eyes shut. "There's a reward."

Benjamin lowers the ax.

She pulls a wad of $100 bills from her front pocket. A folded piece of paper falls to the floor. "I'll even split it with you."

Benjamin picks up the paper.

The word *Liwa* is scribbled on its backside.

"The deal is, you help me deliver her ..." Nevaeh continues to ramble.

He unfolds the paper.

Nevaeh paces. "Do you know what I could do with that money?"

The paper is a printed photograph: a zoomed-in shot of Elizabeth sitting in the small café across from Dominic, smiling. It had been taken at 9:56 in the morning. Elizabeth's blonde curls had bounced on her shoulders as she sat talking to her boyfriend. Benjamin knew all those minor details, because he was the one who had taken the photograph. He asks, "Where did you get this?"

Nevaeh stops pacing.

"Where?" He grabs the wad of money from her fingers, crumpling it.

"Are you crazy?" Nevaeh says.

"Where?" He throws the money into the fireplace and grabs onto her shirt collar.

"From a guy at the hotel." She flinches. "I don't know anything else."

"And the word?" He releases her, moving away toward a stack of wood beside the fireplace. He grabs a large box of matches sitting on the floor. "What does it mean?"

She shrugs, not knowing.

He lights a match and throws it onto the crumbled currency. A small line of fire eats at it.

A cell phone rings outside, from the truck.

CLOSE CALL

DYLAN'S PHONE PIERCES THE SILENCE THAT WILLOW and Elizabeth have tried so hard to keep. Willow frantically searches the truck's bed, needing to silence its ring. Elizabeth hops out of the truck and leans over the side of the back to help look for it—help stop the noise.

A tree branch snaps in the woods behind her.

The phone's screen lights up with a picture of a brunette named Matilda. She looks a lot like Dylan.

Another branch snaps.

The night sky is returning behind the clouds. Darkness molds into outlines of once-human figures. The small clearing circling the cabin gives little warning of the approaching crowd.

"Hello?" has already escaped Elizabeth's lips as she answers the phone.

Two male zombie-hikers step out of the tree line, into view.

"Where's my brother?" asks the girl on the other end of the phone.

Elizabeth doesn't say anything.

The first hiker is so bogged down with infection that he walks with a hunch. A fanny pack hangs at his waist. The hiker behind him walks with a limp, dragging a torn and twisted foot.

"Where's Dylan?" the girl asks.

"Listen, I don't have time for this shit. Where are you?"

"The Chapel," she says.

Elizabeth hangs up. The fanny-pack hiker lunges for her. Elizabeth climbs into the truck's bed. He starts to climb in after. She puts her right foot on the edge to jump out, but slips on broken glass, falling over the truck's side and landing on her back. Pain floods through her.

The second hiker rounds the back of the vehicle, heading for her. He moves faster than she can to get up.

Benjamin comes from behind Elizabeth, draws his sword, and slices the zombie's mangled leg clear off above the knee.

Elizabeth stands, brushing the dirt off her ass, and faces him.

He swings the blade at her neck. A single dreadlock falls onto her shoulder—then to the ground. The blade stops just before her skin. Fanny-pack zombie boy's head hits the side of Elizabeth's boot. That was close.

A shot fires on the other side of the truck.

Elizabeth ducks in reflex.

A second shot fires.

Her heart skips and adrenaline floods her system like the ringing in her ears.

Willow's loud grunt precedes the sound of a hard punch on the other side of the truck. Then a third shot is fired. She stands up, making herself visible from the other side of the vehicle, over three dead bodies. She holsters her gun and climbs into the passenger seat. "Let's go!"

They jump in.

Nevaeh speeds down the mountain. The engine rumbles against the night's return to silence. A river of zombies barricade the driveway. Infection seeps from their gashes, crusted eyes, and soiled clothing. Nevaeh slams her foot against the gas pedal. Limbs hit the windshield as the truck bounces through the crowd, leaving their shadows struggling to follow.

"Do you know where the chapel is?" Elizabeth yells over the rumble of the dirt road.

"Yeah," says Nevaeh.

"We need to get there." Elizabeth feels for Dylan's phone in her pocket.

"No way. I'll take you straight to the safe house." Nevaeh stops the truck at the end of the driveway, looking back at Benjamin for approval.

Elizabeth pushes open her door and jumps out. "Go without me."

"God damn it." Nevaeh turns off the truck and follows Elizabeth, taking the lead through an open field.

Elizabeth can hear Willow and Benjamin's footsteps behind her as they cross a wooden bridge. Once she has cleared it, she stops. Nevaeh continues toward the cliff in front of them. There is no path to follow. Elizabeth sprints after her, hugging the bottom of the mountain's cliff, lost between trees, blindly trusting another stranger, leaving the others behind.

Nevaeh and Elizabeth disappear into the tree-line. Benjamin has made it to the end of the bridge before a female zombie steps into his path, knocking him to the ground. She falls beside him and quickly recovers to all fours. A piece of flesh hangs from her cheek, exposing the silver fillings of her molars. Her blouse hangs open, revealing saggy breasts flopping as she scrambles for him.

A gun fires.

The zombie falls, lifeless.

Willow holsters her firearm, wipes the splattered blood from her cheek, and helps Benjamin up.

He draws his gun, points it at Willow's stomach, and pulls the trigger. "I'm sorry. I can't let her die. Not now."

COLONIAL CHAPEL

Elizabeth's heart jumps with the sound of the second gunshot.

Nevaeh keeps moving quickly through the trees, to the backside of a red building. She hugs its south side, crouching toward the front.

Elizabeth follows, mimicking Nevaeh's stance, though it will not prevent her from being seen.

The front of the building faces a huge clearing in the valley. Shadows line the trees. There is no movement, for now.

Nevaeh and Elizabeth step out onto the lawn—exposed—as they quietly climb each step of the hundred-year-old chapel. Nevaeh reaches the last step. It creaks. Elizabeth freezes. The recent gunshots have stirred the undead. Any noise could draw the entire valley to them.

The wind ruffles a pile of leaves across the lawn. Elizabeth waits for the tree's shadows to flood them to death, but they never move.

A window frames each side of the chapel's double doors like a pair of eyes watching them. Silhouettes move inside. The right door cracks open.

Elizabeth has a bad feeling, but in a world saturated with zombies, it is a feeling she will have to get used to.

"Who is it?" The girl from Dylan's phone peeks out the door.

Nevaeh and Elizabeth come as the bearers of bad news: her brother is dead. Elizabeth doesn't have the strength to move her lips. The more she tries to tell Dylan's sister anything, the harder they press together.

"*Usted idiota,* zombies don't knock." Jasmine bumps Dylans's sister, Matilda, out of the doorway. Jasmine is a bit older and darker. Her tight black curls tangle in large gold-hoop earrings.

The chill of death rushes up Elizabeth's spine, pushing her into the chapel. The room is fifty feet deep and lined with empty pews. An older man in his sixties huddles in the left corner, clutching a Bible. The tips of his fingers are white from clinging to it for dear life.

"You must be Elizabeth," Matilda says, grabbing her hand, pulling her into a hug. "Thank you for saving us."

Elizabeth stares at the door, waiting for them—for Benjamin—to open it.

"I still expect to see him walking through that door," says Matilda, letting go. She hangs her head and sits down beside the Bible-man, pulling the last water bottle from a now-empty case. She tosses it to Elizabeth. "We've been stuck in here for days."

"Yeah, I've yet to grow balls..." says Jasmine, pointing at the Bible-man, "and apparently his don't work."

The door bursts open.

Benjamin storms in, slams the door shut, and leans against it. His chest heaves to catch a full breath. Blood drips from his sword's blade. He charges Willow and Elizabeth. "Are you trying to get us killed?"

Elizabeth holds her breath. *What did I do now?*

"The only way we could survive was on foot," Nevaeh says, shielding her face with both forearms.

He stomps towards Nevaeh, grabs her wrist, and pulls her tightly to him.

"Oh," Jasmine says, biting her bottom lip, enjoying the moment too much. "Me next."

Nevaeh clenches her eyes shut, not wanting to watch what he is going to do to her.

"She's more precious than money," Benjamin whispers, placing the bone dagger in Nevaeh's hand.

Jasmine's eyes scan Elizabeth up and down, wondering what is so special about her.

Nevaeh's eyes widen. She steps toward the chapel window — into the lunar rays streaking in. Her tears drip onto the blade as it glows blue.

Elizabeth can't breathe. No matter how much she wants to deny it — wants it to be untrue...to believe that she is not....

Nevaeh looks at her. "Awanata?"

The weight of the room thickens. They all stare at Elizabeth. Their eyes weigh against her, pulling her down.

"Meadowlark." Nevaeh glances at Benjamin's uniform as if knowing exactly what it means. She approaches Elizabeth almost with caution and shoves the dagger into her possession. Willow slides her hand across Elizabeth's cheek. Her eyes search Elizabeth's for something. Then she moves around Benjamin, sprinting for the doors. She flings them open, and runs out into the darkness that blankets the cleared lawn.

"Dear Father —" Bible-man begins.

"You!" Benjamin points at him. "Do you know how to get to the hotel from here?"

He nods that he does, but pulls his knees into a fetal position and rocks.

"He's not going to be any help." Jasmine crosses her arms, sick and tired of waiting for her hero to come and rescue her. "My pops works here, so"—her voice shakes—"I'll show you the way."

"Wait! I'm not leaving. Those things are out there." Matilda jumps up, pointing at the doors.

"Zom-bees," says Jasmine while walking over to her. "Come on. Commercial media has been preparing you for years for this shit."

Matilda crosses her arms, unamused.

Jasmine grabs a candle holder from a donations table to the left of the door. "Besides, you can get revenge, or you can sit in here and starve to death."

Matilda uncrosses her arms and slowly stands. "So, what's at the hotel?"

"She said there's a safe house." Benjamin watches Nevaeh disappear into the park. He looks at Elizabeth. "I honestly don't know what awaits us there."

"Over the bridge, through a parking lot, and across a field to the trees' edge." Jasmine gives directions and steps out onto the chapel porch. Night's wind rushes into the cabin. Staying still will get them killed. There is no time to waste. Jasmine grabs Matilda's hand and runs down the porch steps.

Elizabeth follows.

Water pours from the sky. Mud encrusts the bottoms of Elizabeth's boots as they trek to a cobblestone bridge. Elizabeth stops. The East calls to her. She turns and sees it: the white silhouette stained into Half Dome's granite cliff.

Her heart presses against her lungs. The outline still looks like a middle-aged man with a severed nose, or even a witch. Nothing resembles Elizabeth. There is nothing female or beautiful about the hideous face—a shrine for the pioneer assholes who have taken the land.

Elizabeth falls to her knees. *They could all be wrong.* If she is all alone—if they leave her—it could be so easy to let one of those creatures tear the rest of her apart. Raindrops pull the tears from her eyes and dilute the stinging of her cheeks.

Bible-man sprints by, clenching his book.

Mud splashes across Elizabeth's face. She looks back up at the mountain, and there it is: beneath the broken nose, within the witch's chin—is a young woman's face. Awanata's true identity, displayed for all to see—and the world has never even noticed.

She looks like … me. Elizabeth stands and leans against the bridge. The dagger's glow rests while the moon hides behind the downpour. She looks down at the stitches of her wrist. *They'd be so easy to open.* Dominic had poisoned their love. All Elizabeth had wanted was to free it from her veins. She had given him herself, all her worth. *No man should have that power.* She wipes the rain from her brow and stares at the reflection in the mountain. Half Dome stands, reaching into the clouds, and Elizabeth can almost feel the mist across her cheek.

Benjamin grabs her right arm, pulling her after the group. As they near the North side of the parking lot, a large garage nestled between the trees comes into view. Bible-man lays on the ground, pinned beneath a large maintenance worker. The man bites into his face. Jasmine tries to pull him off, but he doesn't budge. Bible-man kicks to scoot away and whacks his attacker with the book, but it has no effect. The worker sinks his teeth into his neck.

Matilda stands, frozen beside them, with wide eyes.

Elizabeth charges, yanking Matilda to follow her, and heads for the field that frames the hotel.

Benjamin goes for Jasmine.

"No! He's my Dad," her voice fades behind Matilda and Elizabeth as they clear the field's edge.

Two dark shadows rush them from the right. Everything fades into complete darkness.

THE AHWAHNEE

THE NOVEMBER AIR SENDS A CHILL THROUGH BENJAMIN
as he crosses onto the field. Elizabeth's body lays face down and
motionless on the ground, beside Matilda. Her fingernails have
disappeared deep into the mud of a puddle.

Jasmine lets go of Benjamin's hand and falls to the ground
sobbing, assuming they're dead.

A pistol presses into his spine. Handcuffs slap onto his wrists
and he is kicked to his knees.

A familiar female voice yells above the pounding rain, "So, rookie, did you find her?"

"I have." Benjamin straightens his shoulders, taking attention, staring forward like a good soldier.

Agent Jane steps in front of him. They only met once. She had shaken his hand and given him the badge he carries in his pocket. Jane Penelope Albright had worked for the Canadian Security Intelligence Service for eight years before becoming Meadowlark's commanding officer. She takes orders directly from the Chief—someone you don't get to meet with only eighteen months in.

"She is, however, lying about her identity," says Benjamin.

Jane nods at an adjacent man. Agent Eddie Menendez had gone through basic training with Benjamin. The prick had kissed a lot of ass to get on Agent Jane's team. He approaches Elizabeth and Matilda's limp bodies, awaiting further instruction.

Benjamin has waited for this moment his whole career. He tries to sit straighter and taller on his knees. He would be stupid to give up his career—his dreams—for Elizabeth. He stands, walking over to her unconscious body. Out of the corner of his eyes he can see that they are surrounded by agents. He has no choice. He points down at Matilda.

"Take her to the Library Suite," says Agent Jane as she approaches Benjamin. "You know what to do with the rest."

Menendez scoops the girl off and another agent grabs Elizabeth.

"No!" cries Jasmine. Her protests quickly cease with a piece of duct tape to her mouth. Several agents help assist her into the building.

The Ahwahnee Hotel looks like a Native American castle constructed with piled stone, wood, and turquoise awnings, but its very foundation covers the remnants of the Native village that had once lived in the Valley. It stands as a shrine to America's colonization, built for the rich.

"Good work ..." Agent Jane extends her hand to Benjamin. In doing so, the tip of her boot slides through the dirty water and hits something. She looks down at the mud puddle, abandoning the congratulations to swish her fingers through the muck, pulling out the bone dagger. Her eyes light up. She clasps it, looking up into the night sky, waiting for the moonlight. "Why don't you get cleaned up? Dinner will be soon."

The handcuffs fall from Benjamin's wrists and he hurries into the hotel. It is just as elegant inside. Luxury is an understatement. It was built to separate the wealthy from the poor and middle-class and had succeeded until now—now it headquarters Meadowlark. Agents walk, oblivious, over the large tribal designs tiled into the floor. They don't seem to notice how the desert-colored columns lining the lobby match the tile.

The rustic red elevator doors are framed with a black tribal pattern. When the doors open, Agent Benjamin steps in, followed by another agent who looks like he has just graduated middle school.

"What's your name?" Benjamin asks.

"George," the kid says, drumming his fingers on his sword's holster.

"I'm Be—"

"I know who you are." George stops drumming. "We went through training together."

You're shitting me. The elevator jerks and settles at the second floor. "Listen, kid, I need to find one of those girls that were just brought in."

The doors slide shut.

"Please?" says Benjamin.

George smirks, nods, and hits the third-floor button. They are transported one level higher. "Check the rooms at the end of the hall."

Benjamin steps out and gives the kid a nod of thanks before the elevator disappears. He walks into a sprint down the hallway. There are two doors at its end. *Left first.* He shoves the door open. It bangs, hitting the wall.

Elizabeth's naked body lays on the bed, still unconscious. Her knee-high boots rest at its foot. A female agent stands over her, folding the earth-toned dress.

He steps into the room. "Leave."

The woman flinches, takes the dress, and obeys.

He walks to the edge of the bed and picks up a towel. Elizabeth's skin is covered in gooseflesh. He dries her rain-soaked body as she lays unconscious. Blood rushes through his veins as he blots her breasts dry. He wipes the mud from her thighs as his cheeks burn. He slides the towel down to her toes, his lips brushing her belly button. The tranquilizers Meadowlark uses prove to last for hours.

He brushes a dreadlock from her cheek. Mud covers his fingers. He climbs into bed, pulling the comforter up over the smooth curves of her skin, spooning in beside her. Just the warmth of her body against his is enough, maybe even too much.

TEMPTATION

IT IS MORNING BEFORE ELIZABETH'S SEDATIVE WEARS off. She finds herself once again naked in a strange bed. The bathroom door across from her is cracked and dark. She feels the warmth of a body beside her. There is no way she is looking back, not after the last time with Dylan. It can't matter who it is anyway—not in this world.

She leaves the bed for the bathroom, finding its light switch, closing its door, and turning the shower's heat up as high as it will go. Steam begins to swirl in the room. The air grows heavy. She knows it will be the last warm shower she will ever feel. She steps in, letting the water scald her skin. She grabs the soap, rubbing it between her hands.

There is a knock at the bathroom door and it opens. The shower curtain hides Elizabeth from view, but they know she is here. She breathes deep and slow to extinguish the pounding of her heart.

"Hey," says Benjamin. He pulls back the curtain, letting in cold air and taking away all modesty. He is naked. His muscles aren't huge, but they're ripped. The stitches in his bicep tighten as his arm flexes. He steps in, pulling the curtain back behind him.

Elizabeth bites her lip to restrain the smile pressing to get out. She turns and foams the soap more, then smears it over her face. "So from the looks of it, we made it to the hotel. What the hell happened?"

Benjamin steps up behind her. She turns to kiss him, but before she can, he grabs her hands and pins them to the wall. His chest presses against her back. He kisses her neck and continues to the tattoo on her shoulder. His right hand releases hers, but she stays still, holding her breath.

"Yes," slips out of her lips.

He pulls away. His hand brushes the turtle tattoo on her shoulder.

There is a knock at the bedroom door.

"I better get that." He kisses her, pulls away, and steps out of the shower. "I'll meet you downstairs."

The blood pumping through her body has no place to go, no release.

DEMANDS

THE SECOND KNOCK IS MORE OF A POUNDING.

"Coming!" says Benjamin, pulling on a clean and pressed uniform. He opens the bedroom door and his heart sinks.

Agent Jane stands in the hallway with her arms crossed, blocking the doorway. "Agent Ben, the Chief is requesting that you meet with him after breakfast."

The sound of the shower running overtakes the room like an airport runway.

She steps through the threshold. "Which one is it?"

"What do you mean?" says Benjamin.

"Which one are you fucking, Agent?"

"That's none of your goddamn business." He puffs out his chest, blocking her from further entry, and takes a step forward, pushing her into the hallway. He pulls the interior lock before shutting the door closed behind him. He moves for the elevator. Jane's sword blocks him.

"You'll do well to remember your place, Agent." She brings the blade closer to his neck. "The Chief wants to see you in the Library Suite after breakfast."

Agent Jane returns the sword to her side. Benjamin continues to the elevator. He has worked for Meadowlark nearly two years, and has yet to meet its Chief. Inside the elevator, he can drop his guard for the first time in eleven days. His shoulders drop down, which is almost painful.

The doors slide open to a busy hallway, and his shoulders inch back up. Meadowlark agents fill the lobby, but none speak. Benjamin's boots squeak as he enters the dining area.

Thirty-four-foot pillars hold up the room. An elegant green ceiling fills the space between rafters. Chandeliers hang by long chains. The left side of the room is filled with windows that stretch to the ceiling. The opposite side is lined with serving tables. Round tables sporadically fill the floor in between, covered in white cloth. The illusion that everything is right in the world still holds its place in the hotel.

Black-uniformed agents fill every table except one. Jasmine sits there, waving frantically at Benjamin. She wears a hotel robe that is a blinding white. He heads for the table. She jumps up from her seat and throws her arms around his neck. Her wet hair sticks to his cheek.

"Thank you for saving us," she says. Her hug weakens and she pulls back, staring over his shoulder.

Elizabeth walks into the room wearing an identical hotel robe. She heads for Jasmine and Benjamin across the room, knotting the robe's belt. The blue of her eyes is obvious even from so far away. If anyone else knew who she was, she wouldn't make it another step. They would cage her, and break her until she begs for death.

Benjamin freezes, scanning the room for suspecting eyes.

Matilda walks up behind Elizabeth wearing a Meadowlark uniform. She charges past—for Benjamin. Background conversation dulls as she yells at him, "Who the fuck is Elizabeth?"

Any remaining conversations cease. All eyes are on them.

Elizabeth places her hand on Matilda's shoulder.

Matilda spins around. Anger quickly fades from her cheeks. She pulls Elizabeth into her arms, giving her all the remaining love she has.

Elizabeth feels guilty her brother isn't here, but embraces the hug. Matilda deserves to know who Elizabeth really is. Elizabeth's fingers press against Matilda's hair as she kisses her cheek, whispering, "I am Elizabeth."

Benjamin pulls out a seat at the table for her.

"Why didn't I get one of those outfits?" Jasmine says to Benjamin.

He looks at Matilda for an answer.

"I don't know," Matilda says. "They gave it to me after that blood test." She shoves her sleeve up, exposing a cotton ball stuck beneath a band-aid.

The kitchen opens and the tables empty as agents form a line at its serving tables.

"Grab her," Benjamin says to Elizabeth.

Elizabeth grabs Matilda's hand right before Benjamin grabs hers, leading them through the dining room, toward the elevators. They flow like a chain passing through the lobby.

The elevator. Elizabeth lets go of Benjamin's hand and stops.

Matilda runs straight into the back of her.

"What are you doing?" Benjamin asks. He hits the elevator button and reaches back for her.

The red elevator doors are framed by a black and red Native American design. The mere look of it chills Elizabeth, as if all the wrong in the world will come pouring out of its doors.

"Oh my God, it's that movie." Matilda takes her hand away from Elizabeth's, cupping her mouth.

The Shining.

The elevator doors open.

No river of blood pours out, but Elizabeth's heart knows no different. She refuses to step inside. Benjamin yanks her in and Matilda follows before the doors close.

"I'm starving. Where are we going?" Matilda waits for an answer. None is given. She faces Elizabeth. "What do they want with you?"

The elevator doors open.

Benjamin leads them back to Elizabeth's room. He shuts the door, locks it, and presses his back against it. "Take off your clothes."

"You're a freak. Let me the fuck out of here." Matilda attempts to shove him away from the door.

"A few days ago I was just like you," Elizabeth begins.

Matilda stops.

"Just trying to keep my head above water. Now ... now I'm expected to be some fucking savior."

Matilda turns to face her.

Elizabeth can't hide her eyes from Matilda's. Her chest rises slowly with a long inhale—it is all she can do to keep from crying.

Matilda unbuttons her blouse.

A knock pounds against the door. A man's voice follows, "Sir, the Chief is ready for you now."

"Give me a second." Benjamin walks over, sweeping Elizabeth into his arms, untying the robe. It falls open, allowing her body to freely press against his shirt. He kisses her, lingering as he stands her back up. Then he lets go and heads for the door. "Get changed. I'll be right back."

Matilda slides into Elizabeth's robe and plops down on the bed. Elizabeth is still buttoning the Meadowlark shirt when another knock pounds against the door. Out of reflex, she reaches over her shoulder for a sword, but there is none. *Crap.* There has to be something around the room she can use. *The hotel phone.* She yanks it from the wall.

Another knock comes.

If it were Benjamin, surely he would at least whisper to them. Elizabeth opens the door and smashes the phone into a man's face.

He falls to the floor.

She steps over him and starts for the elevator.

"Elizabeth," he calls.

She freezes, not yet three steps away from him.

"Elizabeth," his voice is familiar.

Her heart falls to the bottom of her chest. Tears drip down her cheeks. *I know that voice.* She turns back to face the man as Matilda runs past.

He stands, cupping his jaw, leaning against a walking cane. His warm eyes meet hers with a smile.

Zach? She reaches out to touch him, to feel that he is real. "You're alive?"

He steps closer, allowing her fingers to rest against his cheek. The cane falls to the floor as he wraps his arm around her waist, pulling her into his arms, pressing his lips against hers.

"Is it really you?" She clenches her eyes, not wanting to open them. Not wanting to lose another person. Salty tears drip onto her lower lip.

"Yes," he says. He kisses her, allowing the tears to soak into his lips.

She forces herself back from him. "Have you been bitten?"

"Howard attacked me." He wobbles, bending down for the fallen walking-cane.

"Shouldn't you be dead?" She crosses her arms in defense and steps back.

He pulls her back to him, kissing her. "I've been looking everywhere for you."

Her lips clench, avoiding his affection. He will die just like everyone else.

"Relax, babe. I'm fine. Aren't you immune anyway?" He takes another step that pins her against the wall, kissing her harder. Her lips melt to his. The smell of campfire trickles through her neurons. Each dreadlock tingles in memory of his touch twisting their strands of hair.

"Hey! Let's go!" Matilda waits at the elevator. Its doors *ping* open.

Elizabeth braces Zach's shoulder, walking him down the hall.

Matilda pops her head out of the elevator with a smile. "Do you think you could share one?"

They stumble in.

"What does she mean?" Zach leans against the elevator wall.

"It's a long story." Elizabeth releases his hand and nervously picks at her nails.

The doors open at the ground floor. Benjamin paces outside of them. His eyes shoot straight to Zach. Meadowlark had tracked Elizabeth, but was her entire past in one of their files? All the way back to when she was eight—to her first kiss? Nausea pummels her with the thought that there is a whole entire file on her.

Benjamin takes to Zach's side, bracing him, tossing a set of car keys at Jasmine. She had been sitting off to the side reading a magazine. Elizabeth leans against the wall, forcing the bile of her stomach back down, then follows the group through the lobby. The entrance doors spit them out onto a long breezeway with a red carpet rolled out to meet the road. A park ranger cruiser is parked oddly at its end.

"I'm driving!" yells Jasmine, sprinting down the red carpet.

Matilda hurries after her and slides into the backseat, leaving the door open. Elizabeth follows, taking the middle backseat, allowing Zach to take the window.

Benjamin hops in the front passenger seat. "Go."

Jasmine peels out, speeding down the road. The hotel fades behind them. The forest to the right is littered with boulders that have fallen from the valley's wall. The sun captures a slab of raw granite the size of a house ahead. It makes the car-size boulder, hugging the road, look miniscule. Masoned stone around its edge forms a guardhouse. A black circular sign sticks out of its top. It would have gone unnoticed if not for the gold paint displaying the Ahwahnee Hotel's logo. The post on the opposite side of the street hints at a once gated road. Something is draped across the path.

They hit it. The cruiser's tires pop, deflating. The rims scrape into the road. The cruiser makes it around the next bend before grinding to a stop. A Meadowlark Hummer awaits them.

Agent Jane steps into the road.

"I'll handle this." Zach flings the rear passenger door open, shoves his cane to the ground, and pushes all his weight from the cruiser. "Ma'am, if I can explain—"

"Sir, I need you to get back into the vehicle." She nods at Agent Menendez, standing ready behind her.

He steps in front of her as a shield. Zach punches him to the ground. He extends the cane out in front of him, pointing its tip at Agent Jane's chest. A gunshot blasts from its end.

Her body falls to the ground.

Zach leans back on the cane, walks to their Hummer, climbs into the backseat, and leans his head back against the headrest.

They trade the cruiser for the Hummer.

"Go!" Zach yells at Jasmine. "What are you waiting for?"

Jasmine throws the Hummer into drive, speeding out of the park. They travel an hour before reverence is broken.

Zach scoots to the edge of the back seat. "Where are we headed?"

Benjamin turns around. "Where'd you get that gun?"

Zach leans back into the seat, crossing his arms, refusing an answer. The town of Mariposa, California surrounds them. Silhouettes show in the frames of store windows. Jasmine slows the Hummer as they approach the main street. Eyes creep from the darkest shadows into the midday sun. The tires roll into a school zone. Townspeople flood the vehicle. Children flow from a nearby playground to join the crowd. Their yellow, swollen eyes are caked with mud. Loose skin hangs from their eye sockets, arms, and cheeks.

"Floor it!" says Benjamin.

What did he just say? Elizabeth's neck nearly snaps at the words, turning to verify that he really suggested they run over children. It is a river of children, for fuck's sake. You can't do that. Jasmine gives him an identical look of impossibility.

He holds his hands up in defense, sitting back as the infected mob swarms the vehicle. The Hummer inches through the crowd, bumping their little bodies out of the way. Weak hands pound against the vehicle doors. The sea of children grows more reluctant to move. Older kids begin to tug at the locked door handles.

The double doors of the nearby elementary school swing open. Two male custodians and a lunch lady charge out.

"Now!" says Benjamin.

The employees push the fragile little bodies from their path, gaining on the Hummer.

Jasmine steps on the gas. In the moment before the Hummer shoots forward, Benjamin's window shatters. An eighth-grader grabs onto his collar. Benjamin elbows the kid in the face, shoving him away. Small pieces of glass scrap into Benjamin's cheek. The cold outdoor air pushes into the vehicle. The last small child, clinging to the vehicle, falls away and is crushed beneath the wheels.

"My lake house," says Zach.

"No, bad idea." Benjamin glances back at Elizabeth. "It has to be someplace completely unrelated to any of you. Some place not in your file."

"I agree with him," Matilda perks up.

"Okay," says Zach, slouching back down in his seat, forming a grin. "You guys pick."

The wind whistles through the broken window.

A Safe Place

Benjamin knows of a gun shop not far from where they are—situated in the middle of nowhere—down a long driveway framed with trees. The asphalt molds into a dirt road with a building at its end. The windows are fastened with bars, but an ax sits beside the front door among a pile of wood. Unease fills Benjamin's stomach. "You guys should stay out here for a minute. Hank is a little quick on the trigger, even under normal circumstances."

Benjamin gets out of the vehicle. His boots slide into the muddy driveway. The front door has a small window with its blind drawn. The sections part and someone peeks out.

"Hey, it's Ben. I'm in a situation and I could really use your help." His hand braces the door and his voice lowers. He turns his eyes to the ground. "I lost Yen."

The door opens.

He falls through the threshold, crashing to the floor. The front room of the shop still looks the same as it had eighteen months ago, even from the ground. The glass countertop displaying handguns and knives is still intact. Wooden panels above, display nine types of rifles on the wall. The Ruger 10/22 rifle is missing. It is unlikely Hank sold it since he had priced it way too high. Benjamin turns to search the other displays when the rifle's barrel is pressed against his cheek. A twenty-something-year-old man gazes down its barrel. His elbows are too straight to handle its kickback if he fires. In one motion, Benjamin grabs the barrel, rips the rifle from his fingers, and turns it on the man, aiming it at the center of his chest.

Luke has a feminine quality about him, making Benjamin guess that he doesn't even know how to use the damn weapon. The guy throws his hands up. "How'd you do that?"

"Where's Hank?" Benjamin lowers the rifle and rolls to his feet. The store is still stocked and there is no sign of a struggle. The only thing out of place is the boy.

Luke's finger shakes as he points toward the back room.

Without hesitation Benjamin climbs over the counter and passes an occupied bathroom to his left. The smell of urine reeks from its seam. The velvet green couch he and Agent Yen broke as tweens still sits against the back wall—empty. The back closet creaks open. An old lady walks backwards out of it, rhythmically mopping the floor.

The bathroom door flies open.

"Ben?" Hank's overweight body looks more worn than usual. His grey beard has lightened since the last time Benjamin saw him.

The past year and a half in the Meadowlark program had kept him away for far too long. After getting assigned to Elizabeth's case, he was considered to have no other life, at least not until she was dead.

Hank takes Benjamin into his arms, just like the day when he and Yen were placed into his foster care. He had never been hugged before.

Benjamin made his way into Child Protective Services at the age of twelve. Yen was two years in when they first met. There weren't many foster parents willing to take on boys of that age, or at least not ones that weren't child molesters.

Benjamin smiles, pats Hank on the shoulder with a quick but deep embrace, lets go, and heads back to the front room. He pushes the door open, waving the carload in.

Jasmine sprints inside, immediately noticing Luke, and gives him a nod. "What's up?"

Elizabeth follows, shaking Hank's hand in greeting and appreciation for his hospitality.

Dylan's sister, Matilda, steps inside, spoiling the introductions with a, "This place is a dump."

The door begins to close behind her. Bloody fingertips reach around its edge, yanking it back open.

Matilda screams as its nails dig into her shoulder. The fluorescent orange ball cap of a middle-aged man precedes his torn camouflage outfit and flesh, streaked with mud. His purple and bloated skin is peeling. Saliva drips from his mouth. He grabs a chunk of Matilda's hair, yanking her backwards.

Benjamin charges them, trips, and plows his shoulder into the man's cheekbone. The ball cap flys through the air as all three fall to the floor.

Blood curdling screams push into the small room as the creature's teeth tear into Matilda's stomach.

The ax. Benjamin climbs to his feet and reaches out of the door for it. Adrenaline lifts its weight and he swings the blade down between the man's shoulders.

Matilda's eyes fill with tears.

There is no saving her. Benjamin swings the ax back over his head. Infected blood soaks into her exposed and torn intestines. He closes his eyes and swings the ax down with an, "I'm sorry."

Elizabeth stares at Matilda's frightened eyes as the life spills out of them. The sound of rubber sliding across a wet floor takes her attention to the backroom. An old woman stands a foot behind her. Elizabeth's heart spikes and she shoves the woman back from her.

The woman's body is hurled backwards, down to the floor. The back of her head smashes against the concrete tile. Hank's cries replace Matilda's as blood pools under the woman's head. The old man makes an attempt to run to her, but Benjamin tackles him. The old woman's frail body convulses on the floor.

Elizabeth steps back. Her stomach knots. *It was an accident.* The bathroom doorknob is within reach. She pulls open its door and locks herself into seclusion. She lowers her head into the piss-stained toilet. The bile of her empty stomach splatters onto the rim. She pulls her face away, gasping for a clean breath of air. She attempts to stand, but her knees buckle. She closes the lid of the toilet seat, sliding the tips of her fingers into tacky urine.

A light knock at the door is followed by Jasmine's voice, "Yo! We're heading out. There's a storm rolling in, so you better get your shit together."

Elizabeth grabs onto the sink, stands up, and wipes the stomach acid from her lips. The reflection in the mirror resembles anyone but her. She tugs at a dreadlock framing her cheek. *Breathe in, breathe out.* She forces herself to open the door.

Jasmine guards the doorway. Her gold hoop earrings swing beside her thick black curls. "So is he still worth it?"

Elizabeth pushes past her.

"All of this death, for a single person," she says.

"What makes my life less valuable than yours, or theirs?" Elizabeth shoves her nose an inch from Jasmine's.

"You could save everyone," she gestures around the room, "the entire world."

"You tell me, what is worth saving?" Elizabeth turns away from her. "My sister didn't die for nothing."

Elizabeth said the words out loud. Her sister is dead. She storms out of the gun shop to the Hummer and slides into the backseat behind Zach. He sits with his feet propped up on the dashboard, resting his head back. The darkening clouds overhead have weighed his eyelids down. Cool air rushes through the broken window.

"Do you remember our first kiss?" He turns around, placing his arm over the headrest. "God, I love your eyes."

Elizabeth should have smiled, but she couldn't.

"We were eight. The day was fading beneath the lake in spring, and we'd spent the entire day trying to catch baby turtles. Just as dusk approached, you looked down on the water's edge and there, trapped between twigs, was a red-ear slider turtle." He rests his chin on his arm. "I wanted to keep it, but you insisted it should be free, given a second chance."

Tears pool against her bottom eyelashes. She looks away. *How foolish an eight-year-old can be.*

The shop's front door bursts open and the group heads toward them.

Zach looks at Elizabeth. "You gave him a chance to find his soulmate."

The stitches along her wrist throb beneath her sleeve. Warm tears stream down her cheeks. She looks back up at him. "I killed Dominic."

He faces forward.

Benjamin watches Zach abandon his conversation with Elizabeth. Nothing in her file suggested Zach was anything but a good guy, but there is something Benjamin doesn't like about him.

Zach had been right; they should've gone to his lake house. According to the case file, he is rich and prepared enough to survive an apocalypse.

Benjamin climbs into the driver's seat and Luke slides in beside Elizabeth. He isn't much competition—a city boy in tight jeans. His petite frame fits perfectly in the middle of the backseat, until Jasmine and Hank squeeze in.

Benjamin speeds the Hummer down the dirt road. It will take thirty minutes to get to the lake and ten more to reach the house.

Something moves at the tree line. It forms into the silhouette of a man. He jumps onto the driveway. The vehicle plows into him. His body thumps beneath the tires. The Hummer screeches to a halt.

"No!" Hank jumps out of the back. "Gary!"

Shit! Benjamin throws the car into park, grabs the Ruger 10/22 rifle, and gets out.

Hank leans over the man's broken body. Car exhaust fumes spew into his face. His fingers brush the man's eyelids closed. He rests his forehead against his friend's.

The man's bloodshot eyes open up. He sits up straight, forcing Hank off of him. Perspiration drips from his pores. His teeth catch Hank's arm and he bites down.

Benjamin draws the rifle to the man's crusty, swollen eyes and pulls the trigger. A shot brakes through the air. Gary's dentures, dripping with saliva, fall out of his mouth.

Benjamin offers out a hand and pulls Hank's heavy frame off the ground. "You okay?"

The only man who had ever been a father to him, nods. "What was I thinking? You aren't hurt, are you?"

Benjamin shakes his head no.

Hank cups his hand around his arm. If he had been bitten, he knew better than to admit it. "It's just a surface scratch. He didn't break any skin." Hank pats Benjamin's shoulder with the other hand. "Let's go before any of my other friends try to kill me. Gary always was kind of an asshole."

They take their seats. Benjamin puts the car back into drive, looking at the old man in the rearview mirror.

Hank doesn't turn to watch the corpse of his friend disappear behind them.

Benjamin's eyes drift toward Luke's reflection in the rearview mirror. He has nuzzled closer to Elizabeth. She is too busy staring out the window—trying to pretend this all is not happening—to notice him.

THE LAKE HOUSE

RAIN TAPERS OFF AND CLEARS THE EVENING SKY. Elizabeth thought she would never return to the lake. Her family's house had burned down right after the kissing incident with Zach. Gossip unleashed through her new third-grade classroom—that she had kissed a boy. What a sucky year that turned out to be.

Forest hugs the lake's edge. The neighborhood appears just the same as when they had left it. The Bennetts' brick mansion remains three stories on the right. It is old money, and there is no sign that it is running out anytime soon. Next is an empty lot

371

framed by a few trees—the place Elizabeth's family cottage once stood. The lake hugs the back of the property.

She turns away from the window and closes her eyes. It is all gone. *They're all gone.* All she has left are memories.

The brakes squeak to a halt. Elizabeth's seat belt tightens with the slight jerk of the car. Zach's two-story cabin stands at the end of the road. Every detail of the lake house screams bed-and-breakfast. Inside, the plants, knickknacks, and furniture sit exactly as they had eight years ago.

Zach kicks off his shoes in the foyer. To the left, a bear carcass sprawls the length of the living room floor, head and all. The kitchen is to the right. It has the cutest breakfast nook Elizabeth has ever seen. The stairwell is directly in front of them, hiding the basement beneath it. Zach heads to the second floor and Elizabeth follows. The first door leads to the master bedroom. Windows fill the far wall, capturing the full width of the lake. Gusts of wind pick at the last of the deciduous leaves, dropping them to the water's edge.

"Do you know the story of Coyote?" Zach leans on his walking cane and lights a candle beside the bed.

Elizabeth freezes, her heart jumps into a race. Every muscle tightens as Zach hobbles back to her.

"Coyote and the stars?" His fingers pull her chin toward his.

She restrains his pull, staring out the window. The abyss of space frames the twinkling white dots in the sky.

"No? Well, Silver Fox spent half the night painting the sky. She placed each star in a specific location. Not only would her designs comfort the humans in night's darkness, but they would also remind them that there is always another stargazer out there, lying beneath it."

"All I see is chaos." Elizabeth walks to the window, press ing her forehead against the cold glass.

"Just as Silver Fox turned her back—only for a second— Coyote spilled the remaining stars into the sky. And here they stand, to this very day. Most see chaos …, but there are some that can decipher her painting."

The lake is a perfect mirror to the constellation's mess.

"What an asshole," Elizabeth says.

Zach stands silent. A grin fills his face.

"So, what happened to Silver Fox?" she asks.

"One story claims she hid on the moon, another said she hid amongst the Ahwahnee people. Coyote searched all over earth— in every stream and under each rock." Zach steps closer, pressing his chest against Elizabeth's.

"Did he find her?" Her lips are only a breath from his.

"No," says Benjamin from the bedroom's doorway.

"No one knows." Zach steps away from Elizabeth, looking out the windows, staring up at the clear night sky. "But they say *the answer is in Tissaack.*"

Benjamin straightens up. "What does it mean?"

Zach comes back to Elizabeth, brushing her cheek with his fingers. "Half Dome."

She holds her breath as he pulls her toward him. Her body screams for his, wanting to push the rest of the world away.

Benjamin clears his throat.

"I can wait a little longer." Zach kisses her forehead. His lips linger and then all at once he walks away.

Benjamin unblocks the doorway.

"I can show you to your room," says Zach.

"That won't be necessary." Benjamin crosses his arms and steps into the bedroom.

Zach takes his time walking out the door.

Benjamin slams it shut behind him.

"What is wrong with you?" she says.

"I don't trust that guy." Benjamin sits down on the edge of the bed, loosening his bootstraps. "I've read your entire case file. Don't you think it's weird that your third grade boyfriend just happens to attend the same high school as you, *after* all those years of being gone from your life?"

"I think it's weird that a whole division of the United States government was created to track me down, capture me, and force me to sacrifice myself based on an old legend." She storms into the attached bathroom and locks its door.

Marble flows from a garden-style bathtub into every inch of the room.

An outdoor generator kicks on outside and the room floods with light. Elizabeth hurries to turn on the hot water. It spills out in a roar, echoing off the walls and drumming through the pipes. Steam rises to the ceiling. She peels the clothes from her body and sinks into its hot liquid. Exhaustion and hunger seep from her. It would be so easy to collapse into the water's warmth and drown out the world.

The lights go out.

SHOTS FIRED

Downstairs, Zach pulls the generator plug and returns inside, closing the back door behind him, shutting out the cold. Luke managed to find the generator and switch it on. With his help they will all be dead by morning. The noise had carried across the lake, but with luck, the sound echoed against its vastness.

Zach doesn't have to wait for his eyes to adjust to the night. He heads straight for the kitchen counter and grabs a handful of long candles from the cupboard.

Luke sits across from Jasmine at the breakfast nook. Its wooden bench hugs the window overlooking the lake. Beside the water's edge is forest as far as one can see.

Jasmine had found a jar of almonds and sits stuffing her face.

Luke scrunches his nose and draws up his lip, watching her guzzle down the nuts.

"Anyone else hungry?" Zach sets the candles up around the room and heads out the back door to a brick patio.

"Do you need some help?" Luke follows him.

"Grab some wood." Zach nods at the boy and grabs a stack just outside the house. "So what's your story?"

Luke loads his arms and heads back for the house.

Zach blocks the backdoor. "How did someone like you get stuck at a gun shop amid all this?"

"I was in there shopping for a gun. You know those small ones that fit in your hand?" Luke's arms wobble, bearing the weight of their load.

"Like a Beretta Nano?" Zach walks into the house, making no attempt to hold the door for Luke.

An autumn breeze swirls the stale air inside.

"I guess," says Luke as he follows.

"Do you mind if I ask why?" Zach kindles a brick oven nestled in the kitchen wall. The only modern appliance is a stainless steel refrigerator.

"Protection." Luke clears his throat. Silence persists until the last piece of wood is lifted from his arms. He had gone looking for a gun before the zombies, so it had been for something else.

"Oh, what the hell …" Zach suspected Luke was gay, but it would be rude to ask. With no laws to protect him now, the guy would surely be more vulnerable to life-threatening situations. Zach yanks open the third kitchen drawer from the refrigerator and pulls out a Glock 45.

Hank walks into the room, releasing a loud fart. Jasmine breaks up laughing. Hank sits down across from her, resting his head in his hands.

"Let's go practice, shall we?" Zach smiles, hands Luke the gun, and makes his way to the back door, holding it open.

Luke steps past him into the bitter night.

Zach sets up, facing the lake. If anyone is going to have a gun around him, they better know how the hell to use it. He steps up behind Luke, wraps his arms around him, and brushes his fingers along Luke's hand, pushing him to hold the gun up—straight—out in front. The boy shivers. Zach whispers, "The bird house by the edge of the lake."

"Dude!" Jasmine comes bursting out of the house behind them.

The gun fires, echoing through the still forest.

The silent night rings with white noise as Jasmine yells, "I'm next!"

Zach yanks the weapon away from Luke, pointing it to the ground. "You never place your finger on the trigger unless you're one-hundred-and-ten percent ready."

Jasmine wastes no time taking Luke's place. She nuzzles her shoulder back into Zach, gets into position, and fires. Her first shot disappears between the trees in the distance.

"I'm guessing you're a lefty?" he asks.

"How the hell do you know that?" she yells over the ringing in their ears.

He smiles and repositions her hands—left hand on top of right.

She fires. The second shot blasts through the tiny wooden house in the distance. She jumps with excitement.

The gun discharges again.

A window in the master bedroom shatters.

"You both need to be careful. These aren't toys." Zach glances up at the broken glass and heads back inside.

Jasmine bumps into the back of him as Luke pushes them faster through the door, afraid of the night. Zach steps to the side, letting them pass.

The darkness behind him knots his stomach. Outside, death waits in the bareness of autumn. The cabin is the only sanctuary. Without it, the cold of winter could kill them. And it is coming.

November's air gusts across the back of his neck. He turns, yet there is nothing but stillness. He takes a step backwards, loading his arms with firewood. It will be cold tonight. He steps inside and heads for the living room.

Luke sits at the breakfast nook, nervously rubbing his hands.

Jasmine follows Zach to the living room. She slows as they approach the bear carcass lying in the middle of the floor. It is one of Zach's favorite pieces. Its teeth have been bleached, which makes the open mouth look twice as large. The walls of the room stretch to its second-story rafters. A large fireplace spans the opposite wall, extending to the ceiling's arch. His prize piece is a full-grown black bear, stuffed in a standing position beside the fireplace.

"So, I take it you like bears." Jasmine kicks off her shoes, sliding her white socks across the fur rug, and sinks down into a brown leather couch.

"To the contrary." He starts the fire.

Its glow climbs up the walls of the room. Its kindling pops and crackles as warmth radiates to the ceiling. Without death, there would be no life.

A gentle knock comes from the front door.

"Are you expecting someone?" Jasmine jumps up.

Zach draws the Glock from his pants, clenching it to his side.

The knocking gets louder.

STOLEN

WHEN THE FIRST GUNSHOT WENT OFF, BENJAMIN pushed Elizabeth to the floor. Glass rained down on him and a bullet hole now ruins the perfect view of the lake outback.

"You okay?" he asks. His weight shifts.

She can breathe.

Cold air rushes through the broken glass, chilling her skin. She reaches for the edge of the towel, still wrapped around her, and tightens it at her chest.

Benjamin brushes a wet dreadlock from her cheek. His lips stop before reaching hers, and he whispers, "If you trust him, that's all I need."

His body feels so warm. His fingertips follow the curve of her shoulder until finding the edge of the towel. Elizabeth inhales, pushing her body harder against his, restraining the towel and all urges.

He leans back, reaching into his front pocket, and pulls out a necklace. A turquoise fox dangles from a string of hemp.

The necklace! Elizabeth can't believe it. Her entire body tightens. Her breath chokes.

He leans over top of her, shifting his weight to one side and kisses her. Elizabeth shuts out the world. The turquoise stone rests upon her chest, fueling her adrenaline and lust. She pulls her lips from his, turning her head away. There is no taking it back.

An owl's hoot ripples through the broken window.

Benjamin kisses her again.

A second hoot fills the air.

She gets up and runs to the bathroom, closing the door behind her. Watermarks on the mirror reflect the stains of her self-image. *Shit. What are you doing? Shit.* She tightens the towel around herself and reaches for the door. She does not want a relationship. She does not want another guy to dig their fingers into her heart, scraping it's pieces out onto the floor. She does not want another man to trick her into loving him.

Elizabeth opens the bathroom door, dashes for a dresser opposite the bed, and searches for something to wear. Top drawers are for junk, socks, or underwear, so she tries the second one.

A vintage green tee-shirt lays neatly folded in an otherwise empty drawer.

She grabs it, speechless. The towel slides from her fingers and falls to the floor. *It can't be.* The shirt unrolls, revealing a simple screen-print: a circle that forms a tree at its end in the center. There is a very faint purple stain on the left shoulder.

Dominic and I had been eating blackberries at a belly dancing show during the Oregon Country Fair. The sun was bright, and when he went to kiss me, I fell over. Damn blackberry popped beneath my shoulder and stained my new shirt. I almost gave him my virginity that night.

"Is something wrong?" Benjamin asks from across the room, beside the large bed.

Light conversation carries up from downstairs.

Elizabeth turns her attention to the bedroom door. *Why had Zach stolen my shirt?* She shakes any guilt or long contemplation from her head and slides the shirt on, climbing into bed beside Benjamin. The night's end approaches. She squints at the gallery of windows.

The owl's outline hugs a tree branch. Its eyes reflect the lunar rays, watching her drift into slumber.

Benjamin pulls Elizabeth close, spooning her. His warmth counters the night. Surely the owl's omen is coming, but there is nothing Elizabeth can do to stop it.

REPAYMENT

ZACH OPENS THE FRONT DOOR DOWNSTAIRS. ITS doorknob slams into the wall.

A female park ranger stands on the front porch. Nevaeh wastes no time, and pushes past him, to the living room's fireplace.

He slides the gun back into his pants and locks the front door behind her.

She stands in the living room, warming her fingers at the flames.

He passes her, opening a black door almost hidden at the back of the room. The office space is twice the size of the living room. A grand wooden desk stands in front of a stained-glass window. A dusty typewriter sits at the far end of a bookcase. On the opposite wall is an oil painting of the lake. Zach takes down the painting, revealing a safe mounted in the wall behind it.

Jasmine's voice carries into the office from the living room, "Where the hell did you go?"

Nevaeh shushes her as she approaches the office door.

Zach grabs a wad of hundred dollar bills and returns to the living room just as Nevaeh enters its threshold. He shoves the wad of cash into Nevaeh's arms and pulls the office door shut behind him.

That makes both the girls shut up.

"I went to see Nantai." Nevaeh's eyes narrow at Zach. She throws the worthless paper into the fire and pulls a knife to his throat. It cuts into the first layer of his skin.

A smirk replaces the fear she expects to fill his face. He grabs her hand that holds the blade to his throat, crushing it. She falls to her knees. He rips the knife from her fingers and pushes her to the floor.

"What do you want with her?" Tears swell in Nevaeh's eyes.

Luke steps into the room. "Dinner's rea—"

"She's just an old friend who means a lot to me." Zach extends a hand down to Nevaeh, offering to help her up.

Reluctant, she slides her fingers into his.

He pulls her to stand and hands over the knife. "Here."

Luke slinks back out to the foyer. Zach follows. The aroma of brick-oven pizza drifts from the kitchen to the bottom of the stairwell. Zach stops, staring up at the closed bedroom door, waiting for Nevaeh to catch up—waiting for Elizabeth to come running down those stairs and leaping into his arms.

"Seeming how I still owe you"—Zach pulls another wad of hundreds from his back pocket, jamming it into Nevaeh's front pocket—"here."

Her jaw drops.

He smiles and walks into the kitchen. Money can have such a hold on people.

Old man Hank is propped up at the breakfast nook in the corner. His love handles hang out from the bottom of his shirt, touching the bench. Jasmine has followed into the kitchen and sits down beside him. He doesn't turn or look at her. His head stays hung low, staring at the pizza served out before them.

"Why did you ruin the pizza with all these vegetables? I can't eat this," says Jasmine.

The men don't utter a word. She will eat if she is hungry enough. Half a minute later Jasmine is wolfing down a piece. On her last bite, she reaches for a second slice. Luke slaps her hand. Her face turns bright red. He nods toward the foyer. "What about the other two?"

"Eat up." Zach stands up from the table, making his way to the back door for more wood. "We can make another."

"Shouldn't we spare as much food as possible?" Luke presses.

"That's the nice thing about having a greenhouse." Zach laughs. He steps outside, closing the door behind him. The others will not survive if things never go back to normal.

Luke comes out with a candle, assuming its light will show him more than the moon could.

Zach blows it out and tosses a piece of firewood at him.

"You like her, don't you?" says Luke.

Zach chucks another log at him.

"It's the way you look at her. Like she could fill the last piece of your soul ... or something like that." Luke stares past Zach to the forest, somewhere else in his head, reliving a memory.

"Hey," says Zach, nudging Luke's shoulder. "You sound like you could use some rest."

Night presses deeper toward midnight. They walk inside. Hank moans—a long, satisfied moan over the empty pizza pan.

Jasmine jumps to her feet. "So is there somewhere I can crash?"

"Anyone else?" Zach examines the old man, who doesn't look so good.

Luke chimes in with a "Ditto."

Zach leads the two up to the second floor. The stairs creak as they continue down the hallway to their rooms. He stops outside the master bedroom, resting his fingers on the doorknob. He takes his time, slowly turning it. It is locked. He knocks.

There is no answer.

His heart races. He knocks again.

Benjamin cracks the door open to find Zach standing there. The agent straightens up a little, smug in his tight boxers.

"Hey." Zach walks down the hallway. "It's your watch."

Benjamin closes the door, glancing at the petite figure still wrapped between the bed sheets. *If I refuse to stand guard—*

There is no time to waste contemplating it. He stumbles into his pants and kisses Elizabeth's cheek. Walking away from that bed and closing the door behind him, quickly disappears into the past.

The hallway is empty.

Benjamin reaches around to the inside of the bedroom door and locks it. Elizabeth will be safe until the morning. His boots clunk down the stairs and into the kitchen. Hank is sitting face down in an empty pizza tray filled with vomit. The smell burns Benjamin's nostrils. He runs to him. "No, no, no …."

He slides his hands into the vomit, scooping Hank's face up and leans the old man's head back against the wall. It rolls forward. Limp. Un-alive.

Benjamin slams his elbows against the table and buries his head into his hands. The first man to show him love is gone. His father is gone. Tears drain from his eyes, diluting the fumes of bile soaked into his sleeve.

Hank moans.

Benjamin's heart stops. He doesn't want to look up, to see him like that—an empty, savage creature—but he does. Hank still sits motionless beside him. There is only one thing to do. He reaches for the sword holstered at his side, but it is not there. He left it lying on the bedroom floor. His heart sinks. He doesn't want to have to fight Hank hand-to-hand.

He sprints to the kitchen cabinets and pulls open several drawers. The first is filled with old menus and a phone book. The second rattles as he pulls it out. Inside is silverware and *a meat cleaver*. He grabs it, but doesn't move—can't move. After tonight, he will have no one. He has lost Yen, and now he is going to lose Hank. He stares at the floor, bracing himself against the counter.

Hank moans. His chest rises, falls, and then stops—nothing.

Benjamin's palms sweat as he steps toward Hank, making it hard to hold the cleaver. He grips it tighter, lifts it over his head, and forces it down. *No!*

He thrusts all his weight backwards, stopping the blade three inches from Hank's neck. *I can't.* He takes a breath, clenches the hilt and walks outside, pacing in the darkness. The night air fills his emptiness. It is cold. He longs for warmth.

He notices a pile of wood resting to the right of the back door. He bends over, taking a stack of it.

Something presses against the back of his pants. He attempts to stand, but a sweaty palm grabs the back of his neck. Hank's love handles press against the curve of his back. The wood falls out of his arms. His fingers tighten around a large log which he swings as hard as he can. It smashes against Hank's cheek bone. The momentum of Benjamin's swing carries him halfway around before he can stop.

Hank is on the ground. Chunks of snot fill the blood, pouring out of his broken nose. His chubby body rolls in an attempt to stand up.

"I want you to know I loved you," Benjamin whispers. He lifts the cleaver above his head and swings it down.

Hank falls to the ground moaning.

Benjamin drops the cleaver, wiping drops of sweat from his brow, not being able to swing again. His body cries, but he stays focused. A few more minutes and it will be over. He smears a falling tear with the back of his hand and reaches for a shovel beside the back door.

Hank musters everything he has left and stands up from the ground. The primitive part of him knows what is coming.

"You were the closest thing to a father for me." Benjamin swings the flat end of the shovel at Hank, smashing his face, sending him backwards to the ground. Benjamin swings it back over his head—as far as he can—and thrusts it through Hank's neck, all the way through to his spinal cord.

Hank chokes on the metal.

Adrenaline blurs the moment: Benjamin jumps on the shovel's head and forces its tip through to the ground.

Rain drips from the sky. Clouds cover the moon and darkness wraps itself around him.

Hank's blood soaks into the soil.

The Return of Coyote

The bedroom door creaks open. A male silhouette steps into the room, closing the door behind him. He spoons into bed, allowing his warmth to blanket Elizabeth. Soft lips gently kiss her neck as his fingers brush the curve of her hip. She turns to kiss his lips, but his arm tightens, restraining her. She hugs the pillow beneath her, watching the stars twinkle in the night between fast-moving clouds. They drift her to sleep and, as if instantly, they fade into dawn.

Morning has come.

The warm body is still lying beside her. Sun rays dance across the sheets as she rolls to spoon him. Contentment fills each breath. She closes her eyes, guiding her fingers over the front of his chest. She open her eyes. *Sandy-blonde hair!* It is not Benjamin.

Elizabeth's heart pounds. She pulls back, brushing his bare ass with her knee.

The sheets roll as he turns to face her. Blush burns into her cheeks. It is Zach. His warmth caresses the goosebumps rippling over her skin. Before she can fathom words, he kisses her, pushing her body deeper into the mattress. She melts against his soft lips, allowing them to smother her as he nudges her hips down to his.

"I can't," she exhales. Elizabeth turns her cheek toward the windows, waiting for the grey sky to numb her. But the sky is blue, and the clouds are still pink with a waking sun.

"Whatever you want," he whispers, kissing her neck, "I'll give you."

She melts.

He leans in and kisses her again, then searches her eyes and returns his lips to hers. He pauses, waiting for any disapproval.

She holds her breath, not sure, too desperate to stop.

He grabs a handful of her dreadlocks and kisses her neck.

The sun dances across his tattoo-painted back. The image of a moon is inked between his shoulder blades. Every muscle in Elizabeth's body tightens. She pushes him off and sits up against the headboard.

"What's wrong?" He sits up, placing a hand upon her knee.

She pulls her legs into her chest and tugs at the bottom of her shirt. She nods at him. "Your tattoo?"

A warm smile fills his face and he stands up, turning so that she can see the entire design. The moon sits high above a howling coyote covering the center of his back.

Fuck. Elizabeth curls her toes and scoots back from him, pinning her spine to the headboard.

He sits down, resting his hand on her foot with a sigh. "I've been looking for you for a long time. I found you once, a few lifetimes ago, hidden with the people of Yosemite. They called you Awanata, which was quite fitting for your love of turtles."

My tattoo. In reflex, Elizabeth cups her shoulder.

"But you had forgotten who you were … who I was. Your mortal body had come with a price. The day you sacrificed yourself to save your people, I once again lost you. So, I waited for your return. Imagine my excitement when lifetimes later a pale baby is born on the same land from whence you first hid."

Florence Hutchings.

"But she wasn't you. Decades passed and I watched each woman of your family tree die." He stands up, walking into the bathroom. "When you were born, I was ready."

"For what?" she asks.

Silence stretches to every corner of the room.

Elizabeth runs into the bathroom after him for answers, landing straight into his arms. The hairs on her body quiver to stand.

"For you. So I could join your second attempt at mortality."
He twists a dreadlock that rests against her cheek. "You see, I
was afraid of losing my memory as you had, so I left myself
clues. And I did forget. But your words that day beside the lake
reminded me."

I will always be beside you.

"I will always be beside you," he whispers.

No, no. Elizabeth shakes her head in protest. *No!* She pulls
away from him, storms out of the bathroom, and scoops her
pants off the floor. She cannot get them on fast enough. Her toes
manage to find every possible snag of cotton. Then they catch
on her butt. She buttons them on, hurrying to the door, fumbling
with the knee high boots, not bothering to tie them.

"Elizabeth!" Zach yells.

She stops in the threshold and looks back at him.

"Awanata, you are my Silver Fox."

She can't breathe. The room feels like it is caving in on her.
Her heart's being strangled. Tears soak her lips and drip off their
edge as she stands still.

"Stay with me," he says.

"You're fucking crazy." She steps out into the hallway and
descends the stairs.

"He killed your parents," Zach says.

Secrets

Dawn brakes as Benjamin stands over the sink, wringing out his shirt. Despite the mandatory vaccine for all Meadowlark staff, constant exposure to infection is draining his immune system. The last bits of night grieve with him.

He walks into the living room. The fireplace—no matter how hot—cannot warm him. Shadows flicker over the mantle and reach across a black wall. *A door.* He glances back at the foyer for signs of Zach. The coast is clear. He slowly opens it.

Beyond is an elaborate office. A large oil painting of a lake frames the wall. Brush strokes capture two children sitting at its shore. At closer glance, he notices the girl holds a turtle. A tiny metal plaque fixated to its frame is etched with the word *Liaw*. It is the same word that was scribbled on Nevaeh's picture of Elizabeth.

The floor boards creak behind him.

Park Ranger Nevaeh steps into the room and sits down behind the desk. "It means lake."

He faces her. "So, did you receive your reward?"

"You were right. I now know my path. But what is yours?" Nevaeh squints at him. "Where do *you* fit in?"

"I don't know." Benjamin swipes the grease of his forehead into his hairline. "So it was Zach who offered the reward?"

"Yes," says Nevaeh, looking around the room. Native American artifacts fill the shelves and otherwise empty spaces. "I saved him a week ago. There was an attack at the park before all of this happened."

"He was bitten?" Benjamin's shoulders broaden in alarm.

A door upstairs slams.

He runs out of the office, through the living room, and stops at the bottom of the stairwell. Elizabeth charges full steam at him. Her hands are fisted and her face has melted with sadness. He has been in enough fights to know when one is coming for him. She swings and he catches it.

"You killed my parents!" She sinks to the floor.

How could you know that? He bends down beside her.

"Get away from me." She pushes the words between clenched teeth, and stands up.

He reaches for her.

She tears her arm away and runs out the back door.

Cold air rips it back open before it can latch shut. The cabin's temperature drops within seconds.

Benjamin begins to follow, but Nevaeh tugs him back.

"I'll go." Her eyes squint at him. She knows something does not sit right.

He nods, allowing it. A girl would be able to fix things more than he ever could.

The floorboards upstairs creak.

Benjamin turns his attention to the top of the stairs. His heart pounds as he climbs the steps. He shoves the door open. It slams against the wall, ricocheting back.

Zach stands naked in front of him, as if he had been waiting.

Benjamin freezes in the doorway. Last night he had stood in the same room, in the same spot, smug in his boxers. Now the boy from Elizabeth's childhood replaces him—naked. *How could she?* He rolls his shoulders back, tightening his fists. *How does he know I killed her parents?* "What did you say to her?"

Zach sits down on the used bed, too calm.

The smell of sex warms the room. Or maybe it is all in Benjamin's head.

Zach leans over, picking up the sword Benjamin had left laying on the floor. "Agent Benjamin Joseph Osbourne, you've broken all the rules."

What the fuck?

Zach stands, spinning the sword in his hand, and walks closer. "You've complicated things. And we both know what I said was true. Do you think that I wouldn't have seen this coming?"

What? Benjamin's body stiffens as Zach walks closer.

"You work for me." Zach draws the sword to Benjamin's chest. "This could've all been avoided if you had made our meeting in the hotel."

Benjamin steps closer, allowing the blade to press against the sweet spot between his collarbones.

Zach lowers the weapon.

He is the Chief of Meadowlark? Benjamin cannot believe it.

"I am Coyote." Zach raises his arms to the sky, brings the sword back to Benjamin's throat, and steps closer. "Now bow to me."

Benjamin stares at him, wondering if this is some sick training exercise, then kneels to the floor slowly.

Zach leans down and whispers, "Did you really think she would choose you over me?"

Blood boils in Benjamin's veins and pulsates through his fisted hands. He punches Zach in the face.

Zach falls to the floor, clenches his jaw, and wipes the fresh blood from his mouth. He grins, standing back up. Then he swings the sword.

Benjamin rolls. The sound of car tires speeding down the gravel driveway outside automatically steal his attention. Zach clocks him. Benjamin falls, and darkness engulfs his consciousness.

SUBMIT

ELIZABETH RUNS INTO THE WOODS TOWARD THE LAKE. Thoughts of how, *Zach is fucking crazy,* flood through her head. Autumn leaves crunch beneath each step. *Benjamin killed my parents?* The trees blur around her as the sun sparkles off her tears. The tips of her boot catch on a tree root and she trips, falling to the ground. The air is knocked from her lungs. Dirt skids across her face. Blood rushes to her head. *No.* Everything is so messed up. He is supposed to love her—not be some crazy stalker.

Fingers slide over her arm. It doesn't matter anymore who it is—what it is. Elizabeth throws her head down into the dead leaves. She is ready.

"You're not alone." Nevaeh's fingertips brush her hair.

Elizabeth looks up. "You left us. What are you doing here?"

"I'm sure you can understand." Nevaeh slouches against the trunk of a nearby tree. "I was told many legends as a child. One was of a woman I had grown up admiring. Nantai always told me I would one day meet her. When I was little, I believed him. Over the years I lost interest in fairytales." She grabs a handful of crispy leaves. "And then there you were." She looks up. "I never pictured you my age." She crumbles the leaves into tiny pieces and throws them to the wind. "But I had already promised to return you to a man. He offered me a reward—more money than I could ever want—to return you to him."

Zach. A passing breeze pushes against Elizabeth's body. She searches Nevaeh's eyes for truth. Can she trust her? The park ranger abandoned them when they needed her the most.

The next wind brings the sound of the car with it. It speeds down the driveway.

Elizabeth lays her head flat to the ground, resting it on her arm. Nevaeh flattens down beside her.

A black Hummer pulls up beside the one already parked in the driveway. This one's Meadowlark biohazard symbol is much larger, taking up both side doors. A woman and three male agents exit, storming the cabin.

Nevaeh presses her head to the ground and whispers, "What do you want to do? I'm not leaving your side again. But I can't tell you what to do. Your heart is your own."

"I don't know." Elizabeth searches Nevaeh's eyes for guidance, but gets none. A breeze gusts by, masking any noise leaving the cabin—concealing anything that is happening inside.

"Then we'll stay here until you do," she says, "but we're running out of time."

Leaves rustle.

A gunshot blasts inside the cabin.

Elizabeth looks up.

Jasmine races out from the back door, sprinting for the vehicles.

A male agent closes in on her from behind and draws a gun.

"No!" Elizabeth screams, grabs a nearby stick and stands up, charging him.

He looks at her and shifts the gun's barrel straight to her heart. A shot fires.

Elizabeth falls to the ground.

"Get up!" Jasmine runs to her aide, tugging her arm.

Elizabeth's head throbs, but there is no other pain. Her hands rush to the hole in her chest, but there is none. He missed.

Nevaeh grabs Elizabeth's other arm and pulls her from the ground. Each step burns with the pounding in Elizabeth's head. The girls carry her to the newer Hummer, throw open the back door, and shove her in. Jasmine pushes her across the leather seat as she climbs in behind.

The cabin's front door pitches open.

Agent Jane steps out, eyes growing with fury. She is supposed to be dead. Elizabeth saw Zach kill her. Jasmine had too. She aims a gun at them.

"Go, go, go!" says Jasmine.

Nevaeh hops into the driver's seat, forcing the vehicle in reverse.

Zach steps beside Agent Jane, easing her aim to the ground.

The vehicle quickly fades into the distance

"Let them go." Zach takes his hand off the weapon. After all this time, he found her—this time it would be easy.

Agent Jane lets out a grunt of frustration.

"I see the bulletproof vest worked," he says.

She smiles.

He returns to the house and she follows. He grabs his cane beside the door and continues down into the basement beneath the stairs. Dust coats his fingers as they slide down the railing.

Benjamin is handcuffed to a chair in the center of a circle of candles. The light flickers off his still unconscious, slumped body.

"The way I see it is this—you have one option. Do what I say, or I kill you." Zach has no time for games. He paces in the shadows. "I get that you love her, but she is not yours to love."

Benjamin's head rolls, limp on his neck. Moans trickle down his chin with drool—pathetic.

Zach clenches the cane and whacks Benjamin's calf.

Benjamin groans with agony, shaking his head in an attempt to focus on the pair in front of him. His words are dry and broken, "You can't do this. Who the hell do you think you are, God?"

Zach grins, steps closer, and leans in. "But I am."

Benjamin holds his breath and tongue.

Zach squeezes Benjamin's cheeks. *I was so close to getting her, and she has slipped away. If not for this asshole, all this shit would already be over.*

Footsteps creak down the stairs. A second agent enters, dragging Luke behind him, throwing him to the floor.

A gunshot blasts out from upstairs.

Agent Jane sprints up the steps. She is halfway up when a second shot goes off.

Zach pulls Benjamin's confiscated sword from his belt and steps up behind him, dropping it on the cement floor, un-cuffing Benjamin. He stands up tall, leaning against his cane. "I need you to help me find her."

"Chief!" Jane screams down the basement stairwell.

Zach sprints up the steps.

The men follow. Sunlight blinds their dilated-pupils as they emerge from the basement.

"A little help would've been nice." Agent Jane is covered in blood. Two bodies lay on the floor in a crimson puddle before her.

White hair frames the face of the first body. Death had swept over Mr. Bennett many years ago and the zombie outbreak had easily taken the rest of him. His dentures slide from his gums and follow the pooling blood into the puddle. Mrs. Bennett's neck is sliced just above her pearl necklace. The cabin is contaminated. They will have to move fast.

Zach tosses the group some empty fabric bags and heads for the greenhouse. "Load up, we're leaving."

Outside, beside the lake, a twelve-year-old girl slowly walks into the yard. Zach tosses his gun to Luke, who catches it, offering it back just as fast. Zach steps up behind him, shoves the gun tight in his hands, and wraps his fingers around Luke's, just like the night before. He steadies the Glock in Luke's hand.

The girl's head rolls to the side, giving no doubt that she is infected.

Luke pulls the trigger before Zach can force it. The bullet strips a nearby tree of its bark, missing.

The grotesque little girl continues, unflinching, toward them.

"Again." Zach nudges his shoulder into Luke's.

Luke pulls the trigger.

The shot explodes and the petite zombie falls to the ground.

Benjamin erupts with applause, out of habit.

The girl's head lifts off the soil of the earth. She pulls her body through the leaves in a wounded army-crawl.

Excitement drains from Luke's face.

"Finish it," says Jane, joining them, grabbing the gun from

Luke's hand to replace it with a sword. "Or you're not coming with us."

Zach walks away with Jane to the car.

"You're going to have to do this sooner or later." Benjamin places his hand on Luke's shoulder. "Just do it fast."

Luke takes a breath and, with it, Benjamin has gone to join the others. Luke swallows hard, approaching the zombie girl.

She drags herself with one arm, while the other hangs loose and limp at her side. Her shirt is soaked with blood that oozes from the bullet hole in her shoulder. She had probably gotten straight A's in some expensive private school before all this. Her long, brown ponytail sways, tattered, past her shoulders.

Leaves gather around Luke's feet, crunching as he steps closer.

The bronze of her skin has faded with illness. Several scabs cover her arms. Her gums bleed. Yellow crust clogs her tear ducts. Dirt is lodged beneath her fingernails. Blood gushes from the bullet hole each time she pulls forward.

Luke kicks her over onto her back. She sits up, growling. If he doesn't kill her, he will be left alone out there to fend for himself. He stabs her. Her nails hook his arm. He thrusts the blade back down, again and again, until her nails loosen.

The engine revs in the driveway.

Luke clasps the sword and tears it out. She is much too young. What joy is left in this world?

The car horn blares.

Luke sprints for the vehicle. He hopes that when he jumps

into the Hummer, he can leave what he has done behind—forget he has killed a child.

Zach speeds the vehicle down the driveway. Dust flies into the air behind the Hummer.

The car slams to a stop beside a mailbox marked with the name *BENNETT* that sits on a stone pillar. Its brick mansion looks like a Tuscan villa, sitting vulnerable with open gates.

Zach glances back at Luke through the rearview mirror and smiles. He jerks left, down the driveway, and stops in front of the grand entrance—whose front doors have been left wide open. He gets out, and the rest follow without asking questions. Inside, the foyer stretches three stories with a grand staircase.

"Benjamin, food. Jane, check for ammo. Mr. Bennett was a hunting enthusiast. Luke, loot the bathrooms for medical supplies," Zach instructs.

Luke holds tight to his sword and ascends the stairs. The rest of the group disappears throughout the house. The steps are easy. There are no walls to block his view, no closed doors required to open. The second floor consists of a long hallway. Bedroom doors line each side. The bathroom is likely to be at the end of the corridor. The first door is closed. He keeps walking. The next door, to the right, is cracked open. Sun rays sneak into the hallway from its windows. Pink walls glitter in its brightness. Teen-boy posters line the room. Two twin beds sit adjacent to one another against the left wall. The name *Amy* is painted in big purple letters above the first headboard. *Erin* is painted in green above the other.

The closet door rattles.

The hairs on the back of Luke's neck stand up. His fingers grip tightly around the sword. He should not have stopped to look in the bedroom. Sweat builds in his palm. He inches toward the closet. His free hand rests on the doorknob. He hopes for a pile of stuffed animals. The door bends a quarter of the way, then jams. Something prevents it from opening—or someone. His heart pounds. Any noise or breathing is blocked out. With both hands, he tugs the doorknob toward him.

The door pops off the track and flies open.

A twelve-year-old girl screams.

Luke falls to the floor. He had left her lifeless body among the leaves, yet here she is, cowering before him. Her skin is pale in contrast to her sister's, and her hair is cut right beneath her chin. He had killed her twin. Her face stares at him, alive— unaffected.

She jumps over him, darting for the hallway.

"Wait!" he yells, stumbling to stand and hurry after her.

She makes it to the bottom of the stairwell by the time he has taken the first step. She is getting away. He tries to go faster but he falls, tumbling down a few steps, and twists his ankle, screaming in agony.

She stops. The healthy cells of her skin wipe the image of her dying sister from his memory. She stares at the sword in his hand.

He drops it, holding up his hands.

Agent Jane steps into the foyer with a handful of hunting rifles. She sees the girl and freezes mid-stride.

Benjamin enters from the kitchen hauling several trash bags of food. He sees the girl and drops a bag of food. A metal beer-can falls out, busting open. Liquid sprays all over the floor.

An engine revs outside.

Benjamin, Agent Jane, Luke, and the young girl turn their attention to the door.

Zach steps out of a black Dodge Challenger. "Let's go."

Little Erin relaxes and sprints out of the house to him, wrapping her arms around him, nearly knocking him backwards.

Zach refuses the hug at first and then embraces every inch of it. "You've gotten so big."

She smiles, not hesitating to climb into the back seat of the sports car.

Agent Jane follows the girl.

Benjamin supports Luke, saying to Zach upon his approach, "Hey, maybe he can use your cane since you're getting around pretty good."

Zach lifts the gun and fires.

Luke feels the momentum of the bullet tear through him. He falls onto Benjamin and they slide down the steps.

Moonlit Trail

Without a plan or destination, Nevaeh, Jasmine, and Elizabeth follow the road. Nevaeh stares at Elizabeth the entire ride. She gives it a rest once they stop at a bridal shop. It is guaranteed to be empty and have a bathroom. It would be the last place Meadowlark would look for them. There is no food, but the manager hid a bottle of whisky in her desk. It is enough to curb their hunger for a few more hours.

Jasmine grabs a handful of dresses, piling them in the middle of the room. She tears off her robe and stands naked in a circle of mirrors.

"Wouldn't you feel more comfortable using a dressing room?" Nevaeh tries to look anywhere but at Jasmine. Blush deepens in her cheeks.

"Hell, no. I'm not risking my life so that a couple of chicas don't see my ta-tas," Jasmine says.

Elizabeth locks the front door. Rows of white satin dresses of which she once longed for, now make her sick. She browses the second row from the front windows and door. A few hundred dollars will buy you a white sheet with a line of sequins around the neck or bottom. Now, in this life, Elizabeth can have any she wants. She stops at the one with no detail, no beads, no pearls, and no lace.

Jasmine twirls in a $1,000 dress in the center of mirrors, deeper toward the back. Dusk's light bathes her through the large front windows. Just enough sun escapes the sky, hitting the circle of mirrors, before it descends into night. Each imperfection of her body goes unacknowledged and she looks stunning.

Nevaeh lays on a nearby bench, staring at the ceiling.

They are safe and warm.

"So, where were you two during the Last Day?" Jasmine ceases spinning and flops down on the pile of dresses.

"What's the Last Day?" Nevaeh gets up and sits down behind Jasmine, fastening the pearl buttons running down the back of her dress.

"You know, the day before the zombies," says Jasmine. "The last day you had with family and friends. I was skipping school to hit up this crazy Halloween party in the park."

Nevaeh's finger slides away from the last pearl button.

"Me and this guy, Julio, were getting freaky and *bam!* This guy comes out from nowhere, jumping and attacking our tent." Jasmine swallows, staring past their reflections in the mirror.

"And then what?" Nevaeh lightly nudges her.

"Now I'm here." Jasmine shrugs. "What else is there to say?"

"I spent the day with my grandfather. All morning we talked about our people, things he wanted me to know before he left with the Great Spirit." Nevaeh glances at Elizabeth. "But what I remember most is the owl sitting beside his porch. I had never seen such a large bird. It sat so still, sure of itself, determined to display its presence."

The plain dress slides from Elizabeth's fingers, brushing the stitches of her wrist. She looks down at the mutilated skin, but the shadows conceal the line of stitches. *My Last Day was Thursday morning in the café*. The weight of their stare falls on her from across the room.

The glass entrance explodes, shattering.

"Find them!" Zach's voice carries from the explosion, cutting through the ringing in Elizabeth's ears.

She falls to the floor so fast that her cheek whacks the hard tile. She rolls under the first row of fluffy gowns, easily concealed. Once her throbbing cheek is plastered to the floor, about an inch of view remains.

"I can understand you're a little freaked out right now. And I'm sorry it took until now for you to know who I really am," Zach says from inside the building. "We belong together."

Elizabeth watches his shoes move toward Jasmine's empty pile of dresses toward the back.

Footsteps stop behind Elizabeth. Her chest pounds against the floor. Blood pushes a deafening sound to her eardrums.

"I will love you like no mortal ever could," Zach says.

A hand grabs her shirt, ripping her off the floor. Agent Jane twists the cotton in her fist, so the shirt strangles Elizabeth.

She can't breathe.

Agent Jane pushes Elizabeth toward Zach. "Chief."

"I've loved you since before you were born," he says, nodding at Jane, who then releases her, flinging her toward him. He catches Elizabeth's fall and presses his lips lightly against hers.

Elizabeth tries to resist the flood of adrenaline. Her heart is sure to burst. She refuses to feel anything.

"What about the others?" Jane clears her throat.

He eases his lips from hers. Elizabeth looks away. He grabs her arm, tightening his grip, and leads her outside. "Burn it!"

"No, you can't ... please!" Elizabeth tries to free herself.

His nails dig deeper.

Agent Jane exits through the broken door.

A fire ignites inside.

"Please save them for me." Elizabeth tears her arm from his grip and makes for the building. He catches her arm as fire engulfs the rows of dresses. She sinks to her knees—to the ground.

The Challenger's engine starts behind her.

With all her strength, Elizabeth gets up and dashes for it. Its door is locked so she bangs against the driver's tinted window.

Zach and Jane run after her.

"Please let me in!" The palm of Elizabeth's hand slides down its glass. She can see a twelve-year-old girl clutching the steering wheel in the driver's seat. "Please."

The door unlocks.

"I wouldn't do that if I were you." Jane points a gun at Elizabeth. Zach steps closer.

Elizabeth yanks open the door, pushes the girl to the passenger seat, and takes off out of the parking lot and down the road. She refuses to be forced into anything.

Flames engulf the building as she speeds away, down the highway. Darkness blankets the car and the strip mall fades in the rearview.

Jane takes a shot.

The car's wheel pulls left and a glowing triangle with an exclamation point in its center pops up on the dashboard. *What the hell does that mean?*

Erin hugs her seatbelt and squishes herself to the door.

Elizabeth pulls over, resting her forehead on the wheel. "See if you can find a manual."

"Up there, there's a four-way," the girl says. She knows exactly where they are.

Elizabeth pulls back onto the road.

A stop sign approaches in the headlights.

"Left," she says.

Elizabeth floors it, cutting the wheel to the right. Rubber burns into the asphalt as the car fishtails. She eases the car into a glide and coasts to a stop, avoiding any more marks. She turns the car around, following their tracks to the intersection then blows through it in the opposite direction. With any luck, they will at least lose the agents for a few hours.

Erin slumps lower as Elizabeth presses the gas pedal to the floor. The car shoots through the darkness. The headlights capture three feet of asphalt before them at a time.

A small illuminated building appears in the distance. Elizabeth slows and coasts to it. Neon lights spell out *Gene's Used Cars* above a shack. They are in the middle of nowhere. The land is paved with empty farmland as far as the moon can reach. Elizabeth squeezes the car between two minivans in the very back and parks. With some luck, the night will bore them.

"What are we doing?" Erin slouches down into the seat—any deeper and she will disappear.

Their breath begins to fog the glass.

"Waiting." Elizabeth cracks down her window, allowing the condensation free. In the distance comes the faint sound of tires screeching. A passing breeze rips through the crack, whistling into the car. She grabs the keys from the ignition. "See if there's a manual."

Erin pops open the glove box and withdraws a book.

Elizabeth grabs it from her hands, thumbing through the pages. *Come on.* There it is: the triangle with an exclamation point inside—tire pressure. *Shit. She shot my tire.* Elizabeth throws the book to the back seat. Her heart pounds. She can't hear anything else. They won't make it if they continue driving. What the hell are they going to do? The parking lot is filled with cars. They can hide under one.

Erin shivers beside Elizabeth.

The sound of a car racing down the road seeps into the window. Elizabeth's heart jumps and, with it, she hops out of the vehicle.

Headlights appear far in the distance. Sure enough they will stop. After all, she had.

"What are we going to do?" Erin hugs her knees.

Elizabeth searches the car lot for ideas.

Something pounds from inside the trunk.

HIDDEN

A RICKETY PORCH FRAMES THE FRONT OF THE CAR dealership. Decades of neglected paint peel from it. Elizabeth crawls onto her elbows, dragging her body beneath the porch's crawlspace. They won't have much cover with the lattice fencing, but the piles of junk crammed beneath it should hide them. The damp soil wiggles with insects beneath her stomach.

The Hummer pulls into the car lot. Its headlights sweep over the lattice as the tires crunch closer toward the building.

A wolf spider drops down from the floorboard overhead.

Erin begins to scream, "Ah—"

Elizabeth shoves her hand over her mouth.

Zach gets out of the Hummer.

The wolf spider lands on Elizabeth's hand. She grits her teeth and presses her hand harder against the girl's lips, hoping to restrain them both.

A November wind chills the air and nudges the eight-eyed arachnid along its way across her skin.

Agent Jane gets out and scans the scene. She sprints toward the Challenger nestled in the back row, squeezed between two vans. "Chief!"

"Check the trunk." Zach braces his cane and follows. His shoulders drop as he approaches the car.

Jane slides into the driver's seat, but won't find the keys.

Zach reaches into his pocket and pulls something out.

The spider's legs tap across Elizabeth's arm, embracing its power over her. Goosebumps flood her skin.

The floorboards creak above them.

The spider creeps up Elizabeth's arm, scurries up her cheek, and digs down at the base of a dreadlock.

The abandoned Challenger explodes in the car lot.

Agent Jane and Zach head toward the shack Elizabeth and Erin hide beneath.

The spider nuzzles deeper against Elizabeth's scalp. Her heart pounds and adrenaline makes it hard to stay still. The little spider body wiggles and nestles between strands of hair.

The floorboards creak again and the front door squeaks open above their heads.

Zach stops ten feet from the building's porch. Elizabeth should have looked away. The white of her eyes could easily give away their location, but it is all she has to distract herself from the spider.

The steps creak. A pair of wet sneakers slosh down the porch steps. A dark liquid spills out of his shoes into the soil. The zombie is a hollow remnant of a man dressed in overalls. His feet drag on approaching Zach. His deep moan carries into the night.

Jane tosses her sword to Zach. He throws it back, lets his cane fall to the ground, and rolls up his sleeves. "Well, today is your lucky day. You get to finally meet your maker. Me."

Jane leaves them and heads for the porch steps. Elizabeth's chest drums against the ground with a racing heartbeat. Jane stops at the steps and sits down.

Zach takes a swing at the man. Drool sprays from the zombie's mouth upon impact. Jane shifts her weight to pull out a handgun. Elizabeth can hear her slow, deep breaths.

She removes her hand from Erin's mouth and motions for her to stay quiet. Careful not to make noise, Elizabeth slides her fingers into her hair for the spider. The movement stirs the dust, tickling her nose. She digs deeper in after the spider, grabbing its squishy body. It slips from her fingers and burrows deeper. All she wants to do is scream. Instead, she holds her breath and digs down, pushing the spider forward and through from behind the dreadlock. She clenches the squishy body between two fingers. Its legs push against her grip, trying to free itself. She cups it in her palm. It runs around inside her closed fist. Her jaw tightens. She leans over a pile of rusty fenders and soggy oil filter boxes, closer to the lattice. Zach is still hammering away on the zombie's face. Jane's boots are firmly placed on the bottom step. Elizabeth opens her hand, holds the spider out, and waits for it to grab hold of the side of her boot.

The zombie falls to the ground. Zach pounds all his anger and frustration against its skull.

The spider lifts from Elizabeth's hand and crawls up Jane's pant leg.

She screams, stands, and rips down her pants.

Zach looks up from his triumph. The bruised and beaten man bites into his forearm. Zach screams.

THE WAY BACK

THE HUMMER IS GONE. ELIZABETH HAD NOT MEANT FOR anyone to get killed or hurt, but it worked and there is no changing it. She climbs out from beneath the building, shaking off the creepy feeling.

Erin follows behind her and begins to run in circles. Her hands pat every inch of skin and scrape into her scalp, ruffling her hair. "Oh my god, oh my god, oh my god. Is there one on me?"

"I really don't think I could've done that," says Benjamin, rolling out from under the porch. Elizabeth wanted to forget he was there. If she had left him in the trunk of the car, he would have gotten everything he deserved. There is no smile, no happy greeting on his face. Luke's splattered blood covers his left cheek. He comes closer. "Hey, I want to talk to you."

"I have nothing to say to you." She turns away from him, heading for the road. Nevaeh and Jasmine could still be alive. There had been a back door to the bridal shop. It is not too late to go back. *Nevaeh saw the same owl that I had, but why?*

Erin stands between them like she is trying to decide which parent she wants to live with after a divorce. Elizabeth does not care who she chooses and continues on. The girl soon hurries after her, saying nothing until they reach the end of the driveway.

"Where are you going?" she asks.

"I have to know if they're dead. I have to know." Elizabeth starts into a run down the road. If I hurry, I can make it back to the bridal shop within an hour. *A long dreadful hour.*

An engine revs from the parking lot and headlights shoot up from behind them. Benjamin pulls up alongside Erin in a green minivan. Her teeth chatter and a quick glance around at the surrounding darkness is all the motivation she needs to get in the vehicle. As the girl takes a seat in the back, he waits for Elizabeth.

She crosses her arms, slips into the shadows off the road, and begins to jog. The van inches up alongside her. She runs faster and it follows.

Benjamin keeps pace with her, yelling out the window, "Would you like a ride?"

She stops. Air heaves in and out of her lungs. "What the fuck do you think?"

She sprints from him—from them. The van continues to follow. She stops and it stops. She leans over, catching her breath, and scoops up a handful of gravel throwing it at the van. "Would you leave me alone? Don't you think you've done enough? You've ruined my whole life. I've lost everything."

With that, he takes off down the road.

Clouds have hidden the moon, bringing bitter cold and darkness. Elizabeth's scalp itches where the spider had squeezed. Stillness leaves the perfect opportunity for her mind to stir, crippling her to the ground. Her kneecaps bang against the asphalt. *Only being alive can hurt this much.* She is wasting time, so she forces herself up. *You're going to risk your life for some strangers—to find out more about a stupid owl?* Elizabeth shoves the chatter of her mind down with each step. She has to know if they are alive.

The road is longer than she remembers. The chilled air numbs the tips of her fingers, ears, and nose. The darkness forms into the shadow of a vehicle parked in the middle of the four-way stop up ahead. She is too cold and tired to care whose it is, so she sprints for it.

It takes the shape of the minivan—of course it does. She pulls open the passenger door. The interior light gives away the young girl asleep across the back seat. Benjamin's hands tighten around the steering wheel as Elizabeth climbs in beside him. He keeps his eyes on the road, saying nothing as they head toward the bridal shop.

Its fire lights up the sky in the distance. Smoke chokes out the stars. Worn and wounded bodies of infected shoppers gather around the blaze. Elizabeth's heart sinks. *They have to be here.*

Benjamin parks at the edge of the shopping mall's parking lot.

Elizabeth gets out of the minivan and sprints toward the building, pushing her muscles until they burn. Benjamin's fingers slide over her shoulder and grab the collar of her shirt, yanking her backwards. Her feet fly into the air. Her head snaps back. Her spine slams into his body as he catches her fall.

He pushes her off—upright. "You're going to get us all killed."

They can't be dead. She sits, heaving her shoulders in defeat. The fire's perfect autumn colors devour the last wedding gown.

The hollow shells of zombie-shoppers turn their attention to them.

Benjamin presses his hand against Elizabeth's cheek. Its weight is the only thing she can feel. He eases her eyes to meet his, and speaks as softly as he can, "Just one more day."

She looks up at him, holding back tears. He has no right to comfort her. One more day and this can all be over. Her body has already given a light nod before she can make the decision.

He helps her stand.

A shadow moves from the blazing bridal shop building, running straight for them. The infected never move that fast at night. It gains speed.

Library Suite

Nevaeh opens her eyes.

Zach paces back and forth in front of a fireplace. A painting of the Yosemite Valley hangs on the room's wood-paneled wall. She knows in an instant where she is: the Library Suite. But why did he bring her back to the Ahwahnee Hotel?

He sits down beside her on the small couch. The warmth of her breath floods the duct tape already sealing her lips. His fingertips pick at its sticky edge. Handcuffs secure her arms behind her back, pushing her chest out. He moves his hand to the name badge pinned to her front pocket. She holds her breath. A smile crosses his lips. He rips the badge from her shirt, tearing the grey stitching. "Something tells me you're more than an ordinary park ranger."

You're an asshole.

His hand slides down the curve of her waist and between her thighs. She shifts her weight back from him. His fingers continue down her leg, stopping at the tip of a knife holstered in her boot. He pushes her pant leg up, grabs it, and slices the first two buttons of her blouse. The fire's glow dances across her white bra. "I never get tired of the female body."

Pig.

He heads over to a table nestled beneath the windows. Moonlight trickles in through the chevron-patterned glass. It dances across the table, finding the bone dagger, flowing into its design. He exchanges the knife for it. His thumb runs along the grooves of the glowing lines. His chest rises with a deep inhale. He slides the blade across his empty palm. Blood drips onto the tip of his shoe. He glances up at Nevaeh, charges her, and tears the duct-tape from her lips.

A moan is the only thing that can dull the pain as she hunches over.

He grabs her hair and throws her head back against the couch, pinning her only inches from his lips. "So you must also know ... who ... I ... am."

Her eyes say everything.

He smiles, looks at the dagger, and presses it to her throat. His free hand slides up her leg, resting an inch from her inner thigh. Her cheeks burn. He presses the blade up to her neck and digs his fingers into her leg. The blood of his hand soaks into her jeans. "Say it. Who am I?"

She looks away.

He frees her leg and jerks her hair back, forcing her to look at him.

"The Great Spirit," she whispers.

He lets go and eases back, sitting beside her in silence.

"If you really are"—she looks at him—"why don't you end all of this?"

He says nothing and glances down at the bleeding palm of his hand.

"You can still change this legend," she says.

Agent Jane enters the room.

"I think it's time to pay a visit to the old man." Zach wraps his hands around Nevaeh's throat, strangling her.

No Chance

THE MINIVAN DRIFTS BACK AND FORTH OVER THE
center line of the highway. The tires' hum pushes Elizabeth to
sleep, but she won't falter.

Benjamin begins to nod off. His eyes close for a second. The
tires bump over something. His body jerks from sleep and he
grips the steering wheel.

Elizabeth grips the door handle and straightens up in her seat,
asking, "Would you like me to drive for a while?"

"I'm sorry." He sits up, keeping his eyes on the endless
highway. "It was just a job assignment. I didn't know you, not
like I do now. Your parents' death was supposed to look like an

429

accident. Jay and I didn't ask questions. We just did our job. When it was done, we knew exactly where you'd be."

Elizabeth sinks into the seat. She doesn't want to hear it.

He clears his throat and steps harder against the gas. "I believe the man you know as Zach is the one who gave the order."

How—?

He slams on the brakes.

Erin rolls off the back seat and thumps to the floor. "Ouch!"

A huge *Yosemite National Park* sign sits to the right of the road.

"Why are we here?" Erin climbs back onto the seat, rubbing her head.

Benjamin hands Elizabeth a folded piece of paper with the word *Liaw* scribbled on it. Inside is a photograph of ... Elizabeth ... in the cafe—the woman she thought herself to be. Elizabeth kneads a dreadlock between her fingers. She barely recognizes the girl with curly blonde hair. The photograph captured the last moment life had been right. It captured her last day. If she could go back to that moment, she would savor every second, enjoy every breath, and find happiness in every exhale. In that moment, life was wonderful and she had failed to see it. The handwriting on the paper looks familiar. Her heart pounds as her brain races to trace its origin. *Zach?* She crumbles the photo. "You're as crazy as him."

Benjamin stays quiet.

"I don't understand."

"The order to kill your parents came directly from the Chief of Meadowlark. Zach controls Meadowlark. He always has." Benjamin eases Elizabeth's face toward his. "I don't think saving some park ranger is worth your life."

"Really? That's funny, since only a few days ago you thought very little of the value of my life. I was just some job assignment. What next? You were supposed to guarantee that I sacrificed myself?"

The van is quiet.

Elizabeth sits silent, trapped with her thoughts. "You know, I waited up there, beside the waterfall. I waited for you to say something—anything. To give me a reason to live."

He looks at her. He knows he has let her down, but she doesn't want to hear it now.

"If you don't want to help me—fine." She hops out of the vehicle and slams the door behind her. The world disappears and all she can do is storm off for the park gates.

Pieces of flesh are crusted to the handprints smeared across the toll booths. Blurred movement emerges in the background of the path, behind her. She stops and the world comes back into focus. Eight campers emerge from the shadows and the damaged buildings.

Elizabeth is not going to take shit from anyone anymore. She lets adrenaline fill her veins, tightening her fists. She charges the mob. It is a stupid idea.

The first zombie-camper is a thin old lady. She goes down with one punch. The second is a middle-aged man. He grabs Elizabeth's shirt. His fingernails tear into the skin of her arm. *It fucking hurts*. She knees him, knocking him to his ass. Another zombie comes from her left. Before she can react, he clothesline's her to the ground. All the air from her lungs spills out. He takes a bite at her arm, missing by a hair. She shoves her fingers into his eyes. The hard, wet balls pop beneath her fingernails.

Benjamin blares the van's horn.

Elizabeth ignores the asshole, finger deep in eye sockets.

Benjamin floors the van towards her. It hits a zombie, sending him flying into the windshield and over the van's roof, to splatter on the asphalt. Benjamin jumps out and snaps the neck of Elizabeth's attacker.

The other two attackers lay crushed beneath the van tires.

"Whatever you want." Benjamin kicks the last camper down to the ground and stomps his face, turning toward Elizabeth. "Whatever you need."

The zombie stands up behind him.

Elizabeth swings her fist toward Benjamin's face. He closes his eyes. She punches the camper to the ground.

Benjamin opens his eyes and stares at her. "I will help you. Before morning, or there is no hope for her."

Elizabeth nods and heads for the van.

Erin slides the back door open for her.

A thin female hiker rounds the back of the vehicle, lunging inside. Erin screams. The zombie bites into her flesh. The twelve-year-old's blood pours onto the floor mats.

The cargo door is thrown open and Jasmine falls out of the back where she had been sleeping. They had rescued her from the bridal shop, but they are too far away this time. A decaying park ranger stands behind her. His hat sits straight on his crooked head. Crusted blood stains the front of his uniform. Jasmine sprints around the van, climbs up the hood to the roof, and lays down like she is invisible. The fabric of her wedding dress hangs over the edge.

Erin's cries die out as the zombie feeds on her corpse. Benjamin yanks the creature out of the van, throwing it against the tollbooth. Elizabeth kicks the zombie ranger to the ground. Jasmine slides off the roof and into the driver's seat. Elizabeth takes the front passenger seat as Benjamin jumps in through the side door. His boots slide through the blood-soaked floor. Jasmine speeds the van through the tollbooths. Benjamin kicks Erin's tiny body from the vehicle.

Pieces of Elizabeth's heart fall out the back with her. She picks the photograph off the floor.

Jasmine takes them deeper into the Yosemite Valley. Elizabeth crumbles the photograph. Everything had been right until she saw *him* sitting beside the dragonfly in the café— *Nantai*.

LAST BREATH

ZACH AND HIS AGENTS SURROUND THE OLD MAN'S cabin. Reports indicate a large Russian man is also staying there. Agents kick in the door. Pieces of wood splinter into the air. A solid-built man is indeed standing beside Nantai inside. Zach charges the large man, taking him down in one sweep. The floorboards vibrate with his fall. He instructs his agents to, "Take him outside."

Jane lifts a single finger and five men accompany her to the Russian.

Nantai sits down on the floor in front of the fireplace. He withdraws the calumet pipe from his back and pulls a stick from his pouch. Zach sits down across from him. A breeze slithers through the door, teasing the fire's flames. Nantai offers the calumet. Zach bows his head, taking the pipe. Smoke swirls from his breath around the room. Another gust of wind pushes the door closed.

The old man takes the pipe and puffs slowly against it.

"I will admit I never fully believed it. Until I saw this ..." Zach takes out the dagger, setting it on the rug.

"Coyote." The pipe falls from Nantai's lips and he looks into Zach's eyes. Smoke leaks from the old man's lungs. Silence drifts with the white smoke. He offers the pipe once more to the young man.

Zach declines. "Where is she?"

"On the wind," says Nantai.

"Old man, I have no time for games," says Zach.

Nantai grins. "You have changed, then. But this is your last chance. For without her, you keep the earth in death. You will not get another lifetime."

"What are you not telling me? How do I make her mine?"

"You cannot force a flower to grow." He takes another puff. "Nor catch a turtle that does not want to be caught."

Blood rushes to Zach's head and his cheeks burn. *I don't have time for this shit.*

"You cannot force love, no matter how much you want it." Nantai reaches for Zach's bandaged hand.

Zach allows the wrinkled fingers to pull the gauze from his skin. Crusted blood opens and fresh blood drains from the zombie bite.

Nantai opens a different pouch and presses a leaf against the wound.

Zach's fingers tighten around the dagger. It is as if everyone thinks this is a game—funny—just a pathetic mortal life. He shoves the blade into the old man's lower right side.

The pipe falls to the floor.

Zach wipes the blade on his bleeding palm. "Tell her that her path is with me and I will spare you in death."

Blood seeps through the old man's fingers as he falls onto his side, pressing against the wound.

Zach stands, kicking the pipe as he opens the cabin door. Wind forces itself inside, pounding against Nantai's headdress.

The fireplace's warmth trickles out, bringing Coyote with it.

INFIRMARY

ELIZABETH HAD NOT SEEN THE SOUTH SIDE OF Yosemite   National Park since Friday's trip with Jan. *God, I miss her.* The mountain walls framing the valley reach for the moon in the sky. The beauty found within Yosemite's walls leaves no hint of the sheer amount of death it once held and now holds.

Jasmine slows the van as they approach the exploded Lodge. She parks at the foot of the Lower Falls trail. Elizabeth leads the group up to the empty waterfall. Something is different. Deep footprints track away from Nantai's cabin-trail and continue away from the fall, toward Yosemite Village. The same path that leads to Dominic's corpse.

"Well?" Benjamin steps up beside her. She keeps her eyes forward, focused on the path. He takes the trail down to the village and stops at the edge of a small creek. She stops at the deep footprints, beside him. Her boots sink two inches into the mud. No footprints carried to the other side of the creek's bank. They had taken the creek, hiding their tracks.

Jasmine groans, stuffing the wedding dress into her hands and over her head.

Elizabeth steps into the water. It soaks between the laces of her boots. They walk the creek until they come to a brown building the size of a single-wide trailer on the opposite bank. The footprints continue, straight to the building.

Elizabeth begins to climb up the bank.

Benjamin yanks her back down. "This is the Medical Clinic."

The wind picks up and blows toward the building. A yellow leaf drifts with it.

"So?" She climbs from the soggy creek, following the leaf. Her boots suction to the mud. A second tug dislodges her faster than expected and her fingers slide through the cold wet dirt, smearing between her fingers.

Benjamin climbs out of the creek behind her. "You know, we might be heading into a trap."

"Or following a fucking zombie." Jasmine climbs out of the creek's bank, shaking some mud off her fingers and wiping the brown soil from her hands onto the sides of her dress.

The leaf Elizabeth followed, drifts to the infirmary building's front corner, falling. She follows. The cold air nips at her damp skin. Just as she is almost there, Benjamin grabs her shoulder, pulling her back to the side of the building, pinning her there with his arm.

The leaf disappears, sweeping to its inevitable decay in the valley.

Elizabeth pushes his arm off and peeks around the corner. The coast is clear outside of the building, but anything could be hunting them in the open. Anything could be waiting inside.

A fresh footprint is in the mud outside the closed door. The wind pushes Elizabeth's body back against the wall. Benjamin steps around her, taking the lead and opening the door. Before he can turn the knob, the door bursts open. He goes flying to the ground.

"Pree-vyet!" Sven says, smiling at Elizabeth. His face has been beaten, but he is still as charming. He pulls her into his arms, rushing the women inside.

A handful of hospital beds are separated by privacy curtains. In the very back corner rests the old man. His headdress sits on a medical tray beside him. Blood pours from a gash in his side.

"No." Elizabeth runs to him, cupping her hand over his. Warm blood oozes between her fingers. "Help me!"

No one moves. They all just stand there, looking at her.

"Benjamin!"

He steps up and scoops Nantai into his arms.

Sven moves to the exit, without instruction, holding the door open. Benjamin carries the old Chief out into the night and rests his body beneath a tree.

Pain eases from his wrinkled face as moonlight caresses his cheeks. Nantai weakly points at Elizabeth, beckoning her closer. He removes the eagle feather from his hair, placing it in her hand. "Tell her, lykj-mhi."

Lykj-mhi.

Nantai rests his head against the tree trunk. Lunar rays trickle through its bare branches. The wind rests and he smiles at her. "Within the moonlight of the empty waterfall, she will find the path." He takes a breath and places his hand against Elizabeth's cheek. "Awanata."

Then he is gone. His hand falls loose to his side, and his chest rests. The light in his eyes disappears.

Sven hides behind the closest tree, clearing his throat to hide how they all feel.

Elizabeth closes her eyes and connects with her breath. A breeze passes, blowing west. She stands and follows its direction.

"Burn him," says Benjamin. "Meet us at the stables."

Elizabeth stops at the field's edge. Just beyond is the Ahwahnee Hotel.

"They'll see us a mile away." Benjamin approaches behind her, cuffing her right wrist. She turns to face him and he cuffs the other. "Are you sure you want to do this?"

Her shoulders drop. She is not sure. She looks at the eagle feather in her hand and slides it down, carefully, within her boot, then steps onto the road and walks toward the hotel. Each beat of her heart burns. They make it to the little stone guardhouse before Meadowlark agents storm them. Benjamin only has to say her name and two agents are escorting them back to those fucking elevator doors in no time.

"We'll take her from here. Why don't you get something to eat?" the younger of the two men says to Benjamin as he grabs hold of Elizabeth's arm.

Elizabeth looks to the floor—this is it.

Benjamin's fingers brush hers as he lets go of the handcuffs.

She steps into the elevator leaving him. Both agents take their place guarding the door. The seconds drag like hours to get to the sixth floor. At the top, she steps into the hallway. Her knees weaken. The corridor appears to go on forever. *What am I doing?* She leans against the wall.

One of the agents steps up behind her, urging her to keep going.

A door opens down the hallway.

"Leave us." It is *his* voice.

The agent steps back into the elevator.

Before Elizabeth can push off the wall and gain composure, Zach's body is pressed against hers. His hands cup her face. He kisses her deeper than ever before, and she lets him. He pulls away slowly. "I've waited *so long* for you."

She turns her cheek as he attempts a second kiss.

He grabs her handcuffs, leading her into the Library Suite.

Nevaeh's body is slumped, motionless on the couch.

Elizabeth jerks her hands away from his and runs to her. Elizabeth's knees slam to the floor as she bends over, resting her cheek on the couch nose-to-nose with Nevaeh. Nevaeh's eyes are closed. Elizabeth cannot tell if she is breathing. *No.* Tears fill my eyes. "No."

"She'll be fine. Well, she'll have a hell of a headache, but she'll be fine." Zach walks over, places the bone dagger on the coffee table, and sits on the floor behind Elizabeth. His chest presses against her back and he wraps his arms around her waist. His warm cheek lays against hers. He unlocks the handcuffs. "It's been so long."

She closes her eyes. *I can smell algae growing on the lake, hear the sound of baby turtles splashing from the rocks.* Elizabeth spins in his arms. *I can feel the wet, hard turtle shell in my hands.* She feels his lips before they touch hers. *Warm sunshine braised my arm as he kissed me.* It isn't real, not anymore. She pulls away. *What am I doing?*

"I can wait." He pulls her back, squeezing her into his arms. His eyes widen. Anger spews from his mouth, "When every last one of them is dead, you'll beg for me to take you."

"What happened to you?" she says. He had been so gentle when they were eight.

He glances over at the dagger and loosens his grip. "I'm sorry. I should've never messed up your stars. Silver Fox …."

Hazel's gift, the necklace. She couldn't have known about the fox, or could she?

"I made the moon for you." His hand rests on Elizabeth's cheek. "Awanata, immortality is torture without you."

The tips of her fingers touch the turquoise fox.

"Elizabeth." He leans into her, stopping an inch from her lips. "Come home with me. Stop all this. Give yourself to me."

She takes a deep breath and the necklace shifts against her skin. She looks over at Nevaeh's motionless body and back at Zach. His warm eyes feel so familiar in a world that has become so cold. She whispers, "No."

He pushes her to the floor, pinning himself on top of her. "Once your earth crumbles and its creatures lie rotting in pain, you'll beg for me. I will deny you every single time that godforsaken moon rises—every single time its soft glow brings back the eternity I've waited for your love—every time you scream at it, begging for your heart to stop hurting—I will deny you."

"You're scaring me," she says.

A tear drips down his cheek, but his face melts into a calm and normal state. He brushes his finger along her cheek. "Will you stop these games? Elizabeth, it hurts to live without you."

She turns away from his touch.

He kisses her neck and continues to the collar of her shirt. Soft kisses continue down the fabric. His finger brushes the curve of her breast. The warmth of his breath seeps through the cotton fabric.

The necklace shifts and the fox — spinning like a yoyo on a string — falls to the floor, beside Elizabeth's cheek. She reaches for the coffee table, sliding her fingertips across the wood until touching the edge of the dagger.

Nevaeh opens her eyes, looking down at Elizabeth, to the dagger, and back at her without moving. Elizabeth closes her eyes with a subtle nod. Nevaeh is asking for permission to seek her revenge. And Elizabeth approves it.

Zach's lips and warm breath move down.

A tear drips from the corner of Elizabeth's eye. She spent hot summer nights watching tadpoles in the lake beside him. She had given her permission to wipe away the distant memories of the boy she once loved. She shouldn't have.

Nevaeh sits up, grabs the dagger, and plunges it down into his back. Then tears it out and thrusts it back down on him. Elizabeth throws him off into the coffee table. It snaps. Nevaeh holds her head, fighting a dizzy spell. Elizabeth takes the dagger from her, stows it in her pants behind her back, and braces

Nevaeh with her shoulder. Adrenaline eases Nevaeh's weight from Elizabeth's frame—it is the only thing pushing her toward the hallway to the elevator doors. Nevaeh gets to them first, frantically pushing the *DOWN* button. *Tap.*

Elizabeth's heart pounds.

Tap.

The hallway lights flicker.

Tap.

Zach steps into the hallway with a gun pointed at them.

Tap, tap.

Elizabeth holds her hand out in front of her chest and walks toward him. With the other, she clasps the turquoise fox charm and closes her eyes, continuing for him. There is no way to know if she will live through the next step. She deserves death. For how can she take another's life without offering up her own? Her hand presses against Benjamin's chest. His energy feels so familiar and comforting. So perfect. Elizabeth had placed her hand against his chest that summer before they moved, just as she does now. She was falling into the lake. He caught her and pulled her close. She landed with her palm bracing her heart from pressing against his chest.

She opens her eyes and he is there—right across from her. She moves her hand to the side of his face.

He lowers the gun.

The elevator doors chime open down the hallway, behind her.

Elizabeth would give anything to be little again and make all the right choices. She presses her lips against his and reaches for the dagger behind her back. But she is no longer a child. And she refuses to cave. She shoves the blade into his stomach, kissing him harder, and pushes him away from her. As he falls backwards, the blade leaves his body. His arms fall out to the side and he hits the floor. Elizabeth stomps on his fingers, freeing the gun from his grip.

"Awanata!" says Nevaeh.

DISTRACTION

BENJAMIN ENTERS THE DINING HALL ON THE MAIN floor of the hotel. Meadowlark agents fill the tables and food line just as before. Another perfectly timed shift break. He moves to the end of the line and grabs a plate. He is preoccupied with his rescue plan and escape, when the weight of a single set of eyes crawls up the back of his neck.

The room goes completely silent.

Benjamin turns around.

Agent Jane stands at the edge of the room with her sword drawn, eyes fixated on him. The agents beside Benjamin back away. In training they had always dueled, but the chandeliers hanging from the turquoise ceiling cast an inevitability of death.

Someone sitting nearby tosses their sword to him. It is George, the agent who led him to Elizabeth's room, what feels like ages ago. Benjamin thanks him with a nod and charges Jane. She stays firm until the last second, then spins out of the way, shoving his shoulder. He falls to the floor.

Her sword returns to her with such grace, he almost forgets to shield its blow. But he does. The clink of their swords can be heard throughout the still room. He thrusts all his weight against the weapon and shoves her to the floor. He could easily have the last swing—kill her here—but he doesn't. He stands back. Her foot hooks his ankle and drops him beside her.

Roll, roll! He rolls, finds his footing, jumps onto a dining chair, kicks off, and swings the sword so hard that his body twists with its movement. Jane swings for his chest. He scoots back, bumping into the dinning table. Plates and food go flying.

She misses, but swings again, like a warrior dancer. The blade chops through George's forearm. He screams as blood spurts out. Benjamin's eyes dare not leave her, but he notices Agent Jane's right-hand man, Menendez, sitting a table away, front and center—her perfect disciple.

Jane thunders toward Benjamin. Menendez slides out his leg, tripping her. Her face whacks the floor. Blood pours from her nose as she looks at Benjamin. He doesn't want to win like this.

Within a single breath, the room inhales.

Something moves in the corner of his eye to the left. Elizabeth and Nevaeh sprint past the windows outside, back toward the field.

That isn't the plan.

Jane stands up, swaying on her feet. Benjamin uppercuts her back down, and swings the sword as fast and as hard as he can at her. Her arm falls to the floor. The sword's blade sticks out of her ribcage. She falls to her knees. Blood pools from her body.

The room holds its reverence and grief.

Benjamin yanks the sword back. *Now. Now!* He turns and runs out of the dining hall as fast he can, slowing at the front door just enough to fling it open.

An agent spills out of the elevator, yelling, "Medic!"

She did it. She has killed Coyote-man. Benjamin runs out the back door. His heart pounds. The girls head west, but the stables are east. He stops running. *What is she doing?* There is no wind blowing to guide him. *Stick to the plan.*

GRAVE

Elizabeth knew Nevaeh had to say goodbye to her grandfather Nantai, or it would haunt her like it haunts Elizabeth. You never really do get to say goodbye. It is never enough.

They returned to the fire beside the Medical Clinic, watching it dwindle. Sven has created a teepee of logs around Nantai, giving his body reserve as it turns to ash. It will not be long before the dead come for the burning flesh.

Nevaeh falls to her knees at the fire's edge. Red embers take the last of her grandfather. Tears roll down her cheeks, dripping into the ground where her people once lived. The fire engulfs the last purity of her culture. Her body slumps into a ball. She cries with no regard for its consequence.

Elizabeth rests a hand upon her shoulder and kneels, wrapping her arms around Nevaeh. Elizabeth never asked for this, but it *is* all her fault. She tells Nevaeh, "He wanted me to tell you, lykj-mhi."

"I love you too," Nevaeh tells the flames.

Elizabeth pulls Nevaeh toward her and slides the eagle feather from her boot, into Nevaeh's hand. "He wanted you to have this."

She looks at Elizabeth with tear-soaked eyes. Rain clouds warn them that they are coming. Soon the fire that frees Nantai's spirit will die.

Sven and Jasmine are waiting for them at the stables. The trees paint deep shadows on the ground with the coming clouds.

"We have to go," Elizabeth says, searching the tree line for agents or zombies.

Nevaeh looks down at the dagger clenched within Elizabeth's hand and holds out hers for it.

Elizabeth gives it to her.

"Pyhij," Nevaeh reads the word on the hilt. "It means to not know or recognize."

The wind swirls.

"Have you found yourself yet?" she asks.

Elizabeth's eyes run away from Nevaeh's, straight to the flames dancing behind her. Elizabeth hasn't found anything but death. "We better go."

"In the empty waterfall, she will remember. And when the earth breathes, she will return." Nevaeh hands the dagger back to her.

By now Meadowlark agents will have realized their beloved Chief is dead.

Nevaeh grabs Elizabeth's hand, leading them down a trail behind the Medical Clinic. She lets go at the trail's head—the Lower Fall. Its riverbed is still empty, waiting for the glaciers to melt. Elizabeth sits at the edge of the forest and looks out at the open sky. Nevaeh sits down beside her, hugging her knees in, and leans back against the tree.

They sit in silence. Elizabeth spins the dagger's point on the tip of her finger. Nevaeh twists the turquoise beads of her grandfather's eagle feather into her hair; it suits her.

The wind picks up, taking all the warmth from Elizabeth's body. The moon reaches high in the sky as midnight approaches. The clouds push out of the valley and moonlight crashes over the land. Lunar rays stretch through the tree line, filling the bone dagger. It glows blue.

They could all be wrong. Why can't they be wrong? I'm all alone, so alone. A tear escapes and Elizabeth reaches to wipe it.

Nevaeh grabs her hand, holding it tight.

Elizabeth looks at her, but something catches her eye in the trees across the way.

A Great Grey Owl sits staring at them. Its beady yellow eyes float above the tree branch.

Within the moonlight of the empty waterfall, she will find the path. Elizabeth gets up. Rainwater drips down her arm, over the stitches of her wrist, and lingers at her fingertip.

Nevaeh stands.

The owl blinks.

Elizabeth reaches for the necklace Hazel gave her and closes her eyes, holding her breath. She can almost hear her sister's voice: *Let go, and live for me.* Elizabeth's thumb digs into the dagger's letters, tracing the word *Pyhij.* The letters are warm. She opens her eyes.

The bone dagger's blue glow sharply brightens to a flash, blinding her.

She drops the dagger and it sinks into the mud.

Nevaeh picks it up. Its glow has dimmed back to a soft blue. She stares at it, speechless.

The owl screeches.

She holds it out to Elizabeth, whispering, "Awanata."

Elizabeth takes it. The curves of the word have shifted, spelling *Awanata*.

"Are you ready?" she asks.

The ancient winds are still. The valley is silent. The moon casts a steady glow across the clearing. The owl's big yellow eyes stare at them.

"Elizabeth?" says Nevaeh.

Elizabeth traces the glowing blue line over the word again and again with her thumb.

"It's time." Nevaeh places her hand over hers.

Elizabeth swallows hard, nodding in acceptance. When she looks up, Nevaeh is already walking down the path they had come on, toward the owl.

TRIBE

IT IS QUIET AT THE STABLES.

"Thank God Joe put the horses away." Nevaeh hurries past a small building to the park's brown and green stables. Elizabeth follows, peeking in around her. The smell of week-old manure spews from the doors. Half the stalls still contain horses. They are too busy gobbling fresh oats to care that Nevaeh and Elizabeth are there. The office to the right is dark. A chill rushes up Elizabeth's spine.

Nevaeh gently closes the stall door and they sprint to a small building they passed. She reaches for the doorknob, but it turns. The door opens. Jasmine jumps out, scooping Nevaeh into a hug. She pulls her inside and then moves on to Elizabeth next. The warmth of Jasmine's body comforts the emptiness she feels.

Sven is passed out in the corner. His cheeks shimmer with the sticky residue of tears. Strong bonds form when society crumbles.

Benjamin has taken the other far corner. He stares at Elizabeth, dropping his shoulders with a sigh of relief that she is not dead yet. His left sleeve is torn off and tied around a fresh wound. "You came back."

Elizabeth looks away, diverting her attention to Jasmine—to anyone but him. "So have you guys found anything to eat?"

The biggest, shittiest grin crosses Jasmine's face. She scoops something off the shelf. "Twinkies!"

Nevaeh looks at Elizabeth, as if she should know what is so funny. Benjamin smiles. Elizabeth lets out a laugh. It feels too much like a movie.

Sven opens his eyes.

Jasmine tosses the junk food at Benjamin. "So can we leave now? I don't want to get stuck in some tiny-ass building again for days."

Sven closes his eyes and nuzzles deeper into the corner.

"We'll wait an hour," says Benjamin, unable to pull his eyes off Elizabeth.

Jasmine takes a seat on the floor and taps her fingers to a song in her head. Grief catches back up with Nevaeh and she buries her face down in her knees—twisting the feather in her hair.

The man who killed Elizabeth's parents stares across the room at her. She was stupid to fall for those cold blue eyes.

PROMISE

AN OWL'S HOOT FILLS THE AIR.

Elizabeth wakes to a quiet and dark building. She clenches the dagger. Jasmine slid into Sven's corner and snuggled in his safety. Her soiled wedding dress covers them both. Tears had sent Nevaeh to sleep quietly. Benjamin's eyes are finally closed. There is no telling how much darkness is left in the night. Elizabeth stands up. *They don't deserve to have their lives risked for me.* Except Benjamin, he owes her much more than his life.

She nudges the wedding dress away from her feet and tiptoes toward the door. A floorboard creaks. She grabs hold of the doorknob, cracking the door open. Moonlight trickles over her boots.

Nevaeh grabs her ankle. Elizabeth presses a finger to her lips, instructing Nevaeh to stay quiet. Nevaeh stands. Elizabeth places her hand flat against Nevaeh's chest, shaking her head no. Elizabeth cannot be the one to make her lose more than she already has.

The warmth of Nevaeh's hand covers hers. Elizabeth nods her out, and she follows.

Every shadow shifts in the lunar light. The tree branches look like witches' fingers reaching down to scoop them up. Moon rays dance over Elizabeth's skin as they walk to the stables. Once inside, the large door clunks closed behind them. Nevaeh grabs a bucket of oats from beside the office. Its door is still cracked. Elizabeth walks past it in an attempt to look inside, but it is darker than it had been earlier. Goosebumps trickle down her back, to the bottom of her spin, radiating pain at its base.

Nevaeh has moved to the back of the stable, petting a brown horse that feasts from her bucket of oats. She says to Elizabeth, "You're not leaving without me."

Something nudges against Elizabeth's back. She jumps. The pounding of her heart spins her around. A light brown horse stares at her. He has a white streak of hair that runs down the center of his nose that looks brushed-on. He nudges Elizabeth's arm. She reaches out her hand to pet him. His wet nose nudges her hand, encouraging her. She brushes his coarse mane with her fingers.

A shovel behind them—outside of the office door—falls to the ground.

A whisper escapes Nevaeh, "No."

A park ranger in his thirties stands outside the office door. His shoulder hangs broken and he leans to his right. A week ago, girls would have thrown themselves at him. Now his skin hangs loose and drool leaks out of his drooping lips.

Nevaeh lets out a deep exhale. She is supposed to kill him.

"I'll do it." Elizabeth tightens her grip around the dagger. If she waits, the horses will panic and death will flood the place in a matter of minutes. Her heart pounds. She sprints toward him before she is too afraid to move.

"No!" Nevaeh yells. "Let me."

Elizabeth skids to a halt halfway to the soulless man. His ranger hat falls to the dirt floor and rolls to the tip of her boot. The sound of hooves to her right stomp to the back of their stall. The man moans and steps toward her. The name badge hanging from his shirt announces him as *Joe*.

Nevaeh charges past Elizabeth to crash into him. They fall to the ground and the man's skull smacks the dirt. A moan sprays from his bloody lips. Nevaeh rolls to the side, off him, and cries, "I can't."

He stares at Elizabeth as he rocks to get up and stand. Then looks down at Nevaeh.

A pitchfork slices through his back and out the front of his torso. The three prongs drip with blood and his corpse thumps to the ground. Sven stands behind him, holding the weapon and stomps on the back of the zombie's head, ripping out the pitchfork, then offers to help Nevaeh up.

"Are you going somewhere?" Benjamin steps out from behind the Russian.

Elizabeth begins, "I—"

"We were checking on Cymy. Liz was picking out a horse." Nevaeh approaches the horse with the white brushstroke down its nose. "I think we should call this one Ben. He's always stuck up your ass. What do you think, Liz?"

"Can I talk to you?" Benjamin asks Elizabeth, then steps into the dark office.

Elizabeth hesitates. *Hazel had called me Lizzy.* She enters. Moonlight trickles through the windows and into the bone dagger. Benjamin stops at an unused desk. He turns with his lips easily resting three inches from hers. His breath moves to her neck and he whispers, "Don't leave me. I'm sorry. I will go a whole lifetime to fix this. Elizabeth, I didn't know."

She breathes and kisses him. *He hadn't known it was my parents?* Her lips quiver on the edge of losing all control. *Bullshit! He knew exactly what he was doing.* She tightens her eyes and presses her lips harder against his. Her heart pounds in her chest, urging her closer to him. *Does he think I'm an idiot?* She leaves her lips against his and steps closer. She slides her hand down his back, grabbing his ass, pushing his pelvis harder against hers.

He fumbles to unbutton her pants.

She slides her hand down his butt to his back pocket and grabs the pair of handcuffs. Her finger slides against something hard. A stone? She withdraws the handcuffs and ratchets them tightly around his wrists before he realizes what she has done, then digs the object out of his pocket and steps back from him.

Mom's stone. It is Elizabeth's mother's stone. Carved in its center is a dragonfly. She had promised to one day give it to Elizabeth. She looks at him. "You knew."

He knew exactly what he had done. His big blue eyes harden the heartbreak she feels. She pushes him to the floor and walks out, never looking back. She will never look back.

He is speaking, but Elizabeth cannot hear a word.

She closes the office door and his sentences grow into yells. All she hears is silence. A numbing silence.

The darkness of the sky begins to lift to dawn.

"Lets go," spills out of her lips in a whisper.

Nevaeh hands a bucket of oats to her and pulls a saddle from the wall.

"What about him?" Jasmine looks at the closed office door.

Elizabeth wants to leave him for dead, but Sven catches her eye. His hand is already extended out to her. He accepts the burden. Elizabeth accepts that he cannot come with them. She shakes his hand, lowering her head at the thought. He has accepted another burden in such an already desperate world.

Am I doing the right thing? she wonders.

He cups her chin, pulling her eyes up to his, and nods. She grabs a saddle and walks back to the horse now named Ben.

"Hey. What about me?" Jasmine hurries up.

The horse backs away.

"You can ride with us, or you can stay with them." Nevaeh nods at the men, fastens the saddle girth on Cymy and moves on to Elizabeth's horse. Once he is properly fitted, Elizabeth climbs up, yanking on the reins. He neighs, turning his head back at her. Nevaeh hushes him, stroking his mane. She grabs Elizabeth's hand and places it against his neck, brushing him. "He is a creature, not an automobile. Understand?"

She doesn't wait for Elizabeth's reply and heads back to her horse.

"Wait!" Jasmine grabs a bucket of oats and sprints toward them, spilling half the food as she approaches.

Nevaeh remains completely silent while helping Jasmine mount a horse, then climbs on her own.

Sven throws the stable doors open and steps out of the way. Nevaeh stops beside him. Her horse makes no movement as the large Russian pets its long, dark mane. She rests her hand on top of his and whispers, "Thank you."

Jasmine makes her way beside Elizabeth. "I'm gonna call mine Ferrari."

Elizabeth smiles, but only for a moment. The Great Grey Owl rests in a tree across from them.

"Where do we go from here?" Jasmine's hair blows with the last pieces of night. The strands of her hair reach for the South.

A yellow leaf follows the same gust—like a yellow petal leaving the fingers of a little girl. It reminds Elizabeth of the past —of her childhood.

"He loves you, he loves you not, he loves you ..." Hazel is ten, picking the petals from a buttercup in a field of wild flowers. Her lips press against my cheek as she wraps her arms around me. "I love you."

Elizabeth wipes the tear that drains down her cheek, trying to wipe the memory away with it. Its saltwater trickles to her wrist, flowing over the sutures. It was a moment of weakness and passion. She thought stopping her heart would stop the pain, but all it did was solidify it.

She looks back up at the owl, unwilling to look back into the park and see the remnants of a forgotten tale. Unwilling to accept what she is about to leave behind. She promised Hazel she would live. She had not thought of her sister when cutting the flesh of her wrist open. She just wanted the pain to stop. Now, she promises to endure it. For all those who can't. She keeps this world in darkness and decay, so that the earth can heal.

"South," Elizabeth says. "I have a promise to keep."

Not just to Hazel, or herself, but to the Earth.

She pulls the dagger out, letting night leave one last kiss upon it before dawn takes away its blue magic. She rubs her fingers along the word Awanata as it returns to red. She has found herself.

ACKNOWLEDGEMENTS

To my readers, thank you. To my kids, for being awesome during writing time and just in general. I'll fight like hell to survive the zombie apocalypse with you. To Dan, for supporting me through the rollercoaster of writing my first book. To my first readers Lisa W., Mandy, and Diana, thank you in so many ways for walking through the trenches. To my first editor, Cheryl, for making my words shine. To Partners in Crime Book Service for editing the second edition and making it feel complete. To my writer friends Bill, Carla, Charlie, and James for being brutally honest and making me feel normal. To those who protect the legends, true history, and spirit of all who came before us.

To the Ahwahnee Indians, who once lived, may your legends and memory be carried on.

ABOUT THE AUTHOR

Julie Embers graduated from Stockton University with a degree in Biology. Writing ignited her journey into enlightenment. In a constantly changing world, she writes full-time. She recently traded the Pacific Northwest for the Gulf beaches of Florida with her kids and french bulldog.